SWORD AND SORCERESS XIV

EDITED BY

Marion Zimmer Bradley
with Rachel E. Holmen

DAW BOOKS, INC.
DONALD A. WOLLHEIM, FOUNDER
375 Hudson Street, New York, NY 10014
ELIZABETH R. WOLLHEIM
SHEILA E. GILBERT
PUBLISHERS

Introduction © 1997 by Marion Zimmer Bradley
The Bargain © 1997 by Laura J. Underwood
The Impression of Power © 1997 by Lee Martindale
The Naming of Names © 1997 by Adrienne Martine-Barnes
Changelings © 1997 by Diana L. Paxson
Death Hunt © 1997 by Raul S. Reyes
A Single Soul © 1997 by Deborah Wheeler
The Needle and the Sword © 1997 by Jessie D. Eaker
Small Considerations © 1997 by Judith Fielder Leggett
If You Can't Stand . . . © 1997 by P.E. Cunningham
Silver Bands © 1997 by Syne Mitchell
The Hand of a Lady © 1997 by Anne Cutrell
To Have and to Hold © 1997 by K.D. Barnes
A Knight on Tower Hill © 1997 by Kathrina Bood
The Longest Night © 1997 by Lisa S. Silverthorne
Blood Moon © 1997 by Cynthia Ward
By the Skin of Her Teeth © 1997 by Heather Rose Jones
Friends in High Places © 1997 by Christina Krueger
The Blade of Unmaking © 1997 by Elisabeth Waters
The Stone-Weaver's Tale © 1997 by Cynthia McQuillin
The Hollow Dancer © 1997 by Mary Soon Lee
La Faie Suiateih © 1997 by Lisa Deason
Vengeance © 1997 by Dorothy J. Heydt
The Moongate Troll © 1997 by Patricia Duffy Novak
Lifestone © 1997 by Mary Catelli
White Elephants © 1997 by Christopher Kempke
Traveler's Aide © 1997 by Kathi Thompson
The Last Word © 1997 by Rachel E. Holmen

First Printing, March 1997

1 2 3 4 5 6 7 8 9

DAW TRADEMARK REGISTERED
U.S. PAT. OFF. AND FOREIGN COUNTRIES
—MARCA REGISTRADA
HECHO EN U.S.A.

PRINTED IN THE U.S.A.

The Sorceress

The dark hour finally rolled around. Ginny could feel it, for it brought a thick veil of old magic alive to vibrate her mage senses. And with its coming, she felt the growing miasma of dark powers roaming the moors. Powers so dreadful she could not help but shiver from the chill of uncertainty sliding down her spine. What if she was unable to stop the Black Hunter?

Oh, Arianrhod, Lady of the Silver Wheel, she prayed. *Do not let courage fail me now.* She took a deep breath to still the flutters in her stomach, crossed the room, and pulled open the door.

Moonlight was masked by a black cloud, and a heavy mist was swarming about the path. Ginny stopped in the doorway, careful to stay just behind her protections, and crouched.

At length, a shape loomed out of the mist, a tall man wrapped in a plaid of black that was woven with thin strips of red and white—the blood and bones of its victims, some claimed. Eyes of flame were visible within the shadows of his hood. From his head rose gleaming branches of antlers. He rode upon a skeletal mare draped in ebon tatters. Her eyes flashed like embers, and she reared just beyond the threshold, shrieking in an otherworldly manner that set teeth on edge. Ginny steeled herself and did not flinch.

"I have come for the soul of Manus Mac Greeley," the Black Hunter said in a voice like thunder. "If you will not send him forth, then I and my mare shall tear down this miserable hovel and crush your bones beneath it!"

"Sorry, but I cannot oblige you," Ginny answered.

MARION ZIMMER BRADLEY
in DAW Editions

ANTHOLOGIES
SWORD AND SORCERESS I–XIV

DARKOVER NOVELS:
DARKOVER LANDFALL
STORMQUEEN!
HAWKMISTRESS!
TWO TO CONQUER
THE HEIRS OF HAMMERFELL
THE SHATTERED CHAIN
THENDARA HOUSE
CITY OF SORCERY
REDISCOVERY (with Mercedes Lackey)
THE SPELL SWORD
THE FORBIDDEN TOWER
STAR OF DANGER
THE WINDS OF DARKOVER
THE BLOODY SUN
THE HERITAGE OF HASTUR
THE PLANET SAVERS
SHARRA'S EXILE
THE WORLD WRECKERS
EXILE'S SONG
*THE SHADOW MATRIX

DARKOVER ANTHOLOGIES
DOMAINS OF DARKOVER
FOUR MOONS OF DARKOVER
FREE AMAZONS OF DARKOVER
THE KEEPER'S PRICE
LERONI OF DARKOVER
MARION ZIMMER BRADLEY'S DARKOVER
THE OTHER SIDE OF THE MIRROR
RED SUN OF DARKOVER
RENUNCIATES OF DARKOVER
SNOWS OF DARKOVER
SWORD OF CHAOS
TOWERS OF DARKOVER

*Coming soon in hardcover from DAW Books

To Rachel Holmen who did much of the
hard work so I could do the fun part,
reading and selecting the stories.
Thank you, Rachel.

CONTENTS

INTRODUCTION

It's hard to believe that I've been doing these anthologies for fourteen years now. When I started, they were an experiment; nobody was certain that "female" Sword and Sorcery would find a market. But, over the years, it certainly has—it's even made it as far as television, as well as onto the cover of *Ms. Magazine.*

Today there is Xena. And just as Xena is a spinoff from the TV show *Hercules, Sword and Sorceress* was my answer to all the sword-and-sorcery stories where the woman (there was usually only *one* woman) served just as the bad-conduct prize for a brawny hero. They were almost all male-centered, so I made the decision that in my anthology, there should be at least one strong female hero in each story, and if there were men in the story, they should not have a starring role, because stories with strong men could be published anywhere.

I told Don Wollheim that I had always wanted to do a series, and he looked at me and said, "All right, make up an anthology." I started by calling it *Swords and Sorceresses.* He said that was too many S's. He knew an awful lot about marketing. The first couple of years, it was hard to get enough good stories for *S&S;* today the problem is the opposite—I get enough to fill at least three anthologies. Although more women than men tend to write this kind of story, I've had stories by men from the very first volume. This year we have stories from three men: Raul S. Reyes (who first appeared in *S&S II*), Jessie D. Eaker *(S&S VI, VII, IX, XI)*, and Christopher Kempke (new to the series). Another story submitted to this anthology by *two* men was purchased for *Marion Zimmer Bradley's FANTASY Magazine* instead.

I still look forward to the intense few weeks each year when I read submissions for this anthology, and especially to the stories from the writers who have appeared again and again, many of whom started here and went on to publish their own novels: Deborah Wheeler, Elisabeth Waters, Mercedes Lackey, Diana L. Paxson, Dorothy J. Heydt, and many more. Misty Lackey didn't send us a story this year—she's probably too busy with her own projects—but the other four did.

There are a lot of very nice stories this year, but the only consistent theme seems to be the shapechanger. In a number of these stories, a woman disguises or transforms herself (or her intentions) in some way to accomplish a goal. In Cynthia McQuillin's story, a woman learns the magic to walk through stone; in Deborah Wheeler's, twins try to unite as one soul. In Diana Paxson's story, babies are accused of being changelings. In "Moongate Troll," there are two transformed characters. Heather Rose Jones' story is about a shapechanger and her student, and in "White Elephant," the warlord may be able to transform himself. There are more examples, but I might be giving away the stories so I'll let you find out for yourself.

Rachel Holmen is my co-editor on this project. Like me, she has a nephew named Ian, and she lives near me in Berkeley in a little house she bought two years ago. Rachel has been working with me on *Marion Zimmer Bradley's FANTASY Magazine* for five years, and she writes quite well. I enjoy reading her "Last Word" column in the magazine.

* * *

P.S.: If you want guidelines for future volumes of *Sword and Sorceress,* send a SASE (self-addressed stamped envelope) to me at PO Box 72, Berkeley CA 94701-0072.

If you want subscription information or guidelines for *Marion Zimmer Bradley's FANTASY Magazine,* send a SASE to *Marion Zimmer Bradley's FANTASY Magazine,* PO Box 249, Berkeley CA 94701-0249. (We have a Web page, too, though I've never seen it; Rachel's column in the back of this book has the details.) From overseas, send two IRC's (International Reply Coupons) instead of putting a stamp on your return envelope. If you write to me, please type, rather than writing in longhand, use a fresh, dark ribbon on your typewriter or printer, and be sure that your print is 12 point or 10 pitch (Pica). I have had eye surgery four times and wish to preserve what sight I have left.

THE BARGAIN

by Laura J. Underwood

Laura Underwood has been with us since the fifth of these volumes and we regard her as one of our own, though she has sold fiction to other markets including *Appalachian Heritage*. We have also been especially fond of her tales of the magic harp Glynannis and the harper who owns—or is owned by—it. (Underwood has a similar harp, designed and built by her father.)

This, though not one of her Glynannis stories, was inspired by her own Cairn terrier, Rowdy Lass, "who is currently sitting at the entrance to the study, trying to look cute and hoping to wangle another rawhide cheesy fry out of the alpha dog currently trying to type this bio on her computer."

The prick of the moor terrier's ears hinted as much of the visitor's presence as the touch of essence on Ginny's mage senses. She knew the visitor was friend and not foe, for Thistle, as the beast was dubbed, bounded to his stubby legs and raced to the cottage door, nearly tumbling Ginny, who had been trying to brush the burrs from his coarse coat. It was her own fault for sending him to chase the fox from the hens, but she had already lost two good laying hens to the wily beast in the last few nights. Moor terriers were tenacious when it came to the hunt, never minding where they actually ran. She was grateful that Thistle was generally well trained. He would have sought the fox from here to the Highland Ranges, had she not called him back.

Now Thistle stood at the door, wagging his short tail in eager anticipation. Mage senses told Ginny that the *friend* had not been of this world for some time. *Manus,* she thought, putting the brush aside and rising from the floor by the hearth to approach the door. What would *he* be wanting now?

She threw open the door. Moonlight flooded the trees of Tamhasg Wood, white light pouring through gnarly branches that rattled like dry bones in the gentle breeze. And there upon the path, she could see the faint mist that grew into the shape of a man. Ginny crossed her arms.

"Manus?" she called.

He became clearer at the sound of her voice. "Ginny," he responded and stepped up to the light. "You're looking well."

Thistle bolted forward, dancing on hind legs to greet his old master.

"And what brings you here this night?" she asked.

Manus knelt down, passing one hand through the moor terrier's head. Thistle didn't seem to notice that the hand was unable to pet him properly. He continued to leap and dance for his old master, giddy as a child visited by a beloved grandparent. Sadly, it was an attention that could never come.

Manus rose with a sigh. It had been two years since he'd met his untimely death at the hand of bandits, late one night on the moor road. The moon had been full, and the heather ale so sweet in his veins. Unfortunately, though mageborn were long lived, their flesh was mortal, and in his inebriated state, he was unable to fend off his attackers.

Manus had always told her that what the mageborn did in their lives would follow them into death, and Ginny suspected that was true. The spirit that stood before her swayed like a man who had indulged too deeply of his favorite brew.

He'd been a handsome man, too, taken in his prime. He stood before her now, tall, wrapped in several ells of his red, green, and gray plaid. His long, reddish brown hair tumbled about his broad shoulders. He wore his plaid kilted in the old Keltoran style, bereft of trews.

She didn't really know what had attracted her to him, other than the fact that she had been a young mageborn with no one to train her. She had fled her home one night, for in spite of her calling, her father had wanted her to wed a loathsome man just to increase his own herds with a dowry of fine fat Keltoran cattle. Manus offered Ginny shelter, though he never took advantage of her. He had allowed her to share the cottage with himself and Thistle, and had taught her the meaning of the power growing within her.

But, like some men, he had a weakness for the heather ale that she could not abide. She had sworn those spirits would be the death of him. Alas, that prediction had come true.

"So what brings you here?" she asked again. "You never visit me when the moon is full. You're usually out staggering about the moors, searching for your murderers."

Manus grinned. "Aye, lass, and that search will go on until I've had my vengeance unless . . ."

"Unless what?" she insisted. There seemed to be a hesitation to Manus' gaze. He had been secretive sometimes, never telling her just why he went out on the moors on moon-washed nights to imbibe.

"Well, lass, you see . . . I really just came by to warn you."

"Warn me of what?"

"That you might want to keep the cottage door locked and little Thistle inside tonight."

"Oh, and why is that?" she asked, casting mage

senses about in uncertainty. Tamhasg Wood was thought haunted by the locals, though the only spirit Ginny had ever found was Manus himself. Still, there were other things to be found in these woods. Bogie and unseelie alike came lurking about the cottage from time to time, forcing her to repeatedly strengthen the spells she cast to keep them at bay. Most of them were harmless, but she had learned long ago that even the gentlest of them could be dangerous when teased or provoked.

"There's a Black Hunter roaming the moors this night," Manus said.

"A Black Hunter?" she said and gave him a hard look. "What have you been up to, Manus Mac Greeley?"

He grinned. "No more than a spirit is able," he said.

"I'm serious, Manus, what have you done?"

"Oh, 'twas a long time ago, lass. Years before ye came knocking on my cottage door, looking all bedraggled and begging for shelter and not sure what to do with yourself and your powers."

"What happened?"

"I was wandering out about on the moor one night when it came upon me."

"It?" she repeated, fixing him with her sharpest glare.

"The Black Hunter," he said.

She knew what Black Hunters were. Some called them soulless men, while others swore they were the spirits of men who had done evil in life. They were the servants of Arawn, and their task was to ride out on dark nights, seeking souls to fill Arawn's Cauldron that he might have warriors to serve him in the final battle between dark and light.

"What did you do to earn a Black Hunter's wrath?" she insisted.

"Not much," he said. "It was an unseelie night, and the heather ale was especially sweet. And I was still full of the grief of one who had lost what he loved the most. . . . Could we go in by the fire, lass? This is no short tale I have to share, and the wind is bitter."

"You can't feel the wind," she said with a frown.

"No, but poor Thistle is shivering."

Ginny rolled her eyes. She wasn't sure she liked the idea of letting a spirit into the cottage, even if it had once been his own home. Once she gave Manus permission to cross the magics she had set to ward herself from harm, there would be no keeping him out. Still, there had been a time when she had sought shelter from him, and he had not denied her.

"All right," she said. "But don't make a habit of coming whenever you please."

"Would I do that?" Manus insisted, arching his brows comically as Ginny turned and led the way into the cottage.

She could feel his mage essence as he approached the threshold and paused. Turning to the door, Ginny gestured with one hand. "Enter and be welcome, Manus Mac Greeley," she said.

The spirit looked relieved as he crossed the threshold and stepped over to the fire. And there, he sank to the floor while Ginny bolted the cottage door. Thistle darted over to the hearth, leaping back and forth through his old master in a frenzied attempt to encourage petting.

"You've been neglecting him, lass," Manus said. He looked disappointed over being unable to return the moor terrier's affection.

"No more than he neglects me," she assured him as she took herself to her favorite chair. "He's a lot like you when it comes to the moors." She sat down and looked at Manus who seemed no more than mist in the brightness.

"You're fading," she said.

" 'Tis the firelight," he said.

"So, are you going to tell me what happened?" she

asked. "Or shall we continue to trade short amenities until dawn forces you to leave."

"You were never a patient lass."

"I learned that from dealing with you."

Manus scowled and stared at the fire. "Aye," he said. "I only wish I had learned a little common sense from you. It happened long ago, but I remember it well. You see, my wife had died—"

"You never told me you had a wife," Ginny interrupted, feeling absurd at the hint of jealousy she heard in her own voice.

His smile came back. "That's because you were no more than a sweet child of six the winter she died."

"Illness?" Ginny ventured.

"Old age," Manus said. "The curse of our kind, sweet Ginny, is to stay young and outlive those we love . . . but that does not matter now. My Mary was a good wife, and she crossed the veil peacefully in her sleep, so I buried her out on the moor under a full moon, wrapped in two ells of my plaidie. I even built a cairn so I could visit her from time to time."

"The Tamhasg Maiden?" Ginny said. "So that's where you would go."

"Aye," Manus said. "Ten years had passed since my Mary died, and not once did I miss the anniversary of her parting. And 'twas on such a night that I met the Black Hunter. He was riding across the moor on a bone mare draped in ebon trappings. Her hooves hardly touched the heather, yet the clatter was the thunder of a thousandfold riders."

Ginny frowned, for she could not abide a spirit that was so poetically long of wind. "And he found you at the cairn?" she said, hoping to hear the end of the tale before cock's crow when Manus *would* be forced to flee.

Manus rested his chin in his hands, elbows propped against his knees. "Yes, I was at the cairn, drowning my grief when he came looking for mortal souls to appease his master. The sight of his grim face and glowing eyes set my knees to knocking under my kilt, but the ale that soothed my grief gave more courage to my tongue than was good for me."

"But not the wits to match," Ginny said, narrowing her eyes.

"I challenged the creature," Manus said, ignoring her. "I called a ring of white mage fire and trapped him before he could flee. Alas, while I was safely outside the flames, my beloved Mary's cairn was not. Outraged at being trapped, the creature threatened to order its bone beast to tear the grave asunder before my eyes!

"I was aghast to think it would be so cruel, but then, I remembered that the heartless bogie shared a weakness that was heather ale sweet to all its kind . . ."

Ginny closed her eyes. "You didn't . . ."

Manus reared upright. "Oh, yes. I begged it to spare sweet Mary's cairn, and offered my soul in trade, for all know that the soul of a mageborn is a priceless essence. I swore that if it would but give me seven years to put my affairs in order and spare her stones, I would gladly give it my soul for the Cauldron of Annwn."

Ginny sighed. Seven years. The faery bargain was as old as most granny tales. As ancient as the Old Ones from whom all mageborn were said to have descended. "Well, you've been dead two years, and I have lived here for five. . . ."

" 'Twas two years before you came that I made my foolish bargain," he said.

"Then this is the night?"

"Oh, aye. The anniversary of Mary's death seventeen years ago—and the seventh year since I met the Black Hunter and allowed the heather ale to rule my wits."

"So when will it come for you?" Ginny asked. Thistle had given up bouncing through the mageborn's spirit and was now begging for her attention. She drew the moor terrier into her arms, where it struggled before settling down to wag its tail and pant noisily.

"The dark hour is its time," Manus said and rose from the floor. "Which means I'd best be on my way."

"What?" She lurched out of the chair, Thistle still in her arms.

"I'll not bring the danger here to you, lass," he said. "I owe you that much for the kindness of listening to my tale."

"You mean . . . you're just going to give up?"

"I can do nothing else," Manus said. "A dead mageborn has no power, remember, for it has no flesh through which to channel its spells. And a live mageborn who has not seen as many years as her master should not be so foolish as to think *she* could meet the creature and defeat it."

"And why not?" Ginny said. "I know the old tales as well as you. The Black Hunter cannot abide the light of day nor the white mage fire. When it is set to a task, it must finish before dawn or the bargain is forfeit. And like all bogie folk, it has an aversion for cold iron and steel."

"You don't have a sword."

"I have a horseshoe over the door and iron hinges and bolts on the windows. It cannot pass those."

"It will not let those stop it from claiming a mageborn soul," Manus said. "You'd be wise not to follow me from this place."

He started toward the door. Ginny stooped to put Thistle on the floor and rose, stretching forth her hands. And in the mage tongue she hissed, *"By my will, I bind you to this place!"*

Manus gave an angry cry and turned, fists raising, flames filling his eyes. "Do you realize what you have done?" he shouted.

Thistle bolted for the space under the chair, but Ginny held her ground as Manus' spirit seethed with fury and rushed at her. He could not harm her, and her will was strong enough to prevent him from entering her flesh and bending her to his will. A mageborn might not have power in death, but if a willing host could be found, the mageborn could cast spells again. She would not give him that, no matter what debt she owed.

"I have stopped you from ever leaving this place," she said and crossed her arms. "In spite of the fact that it brings me no joy, you will not leave here until I decide to set you free. Which means, if the Black Hunter wants your soul, it will have to bargain with *me* now."

"Why?" he insisted. "Why risk your life that way?"

She hesitated. It did seem foolish. "Because when I needed help, you didn't turn me away and leave me to my fate," she said hesitantly. "You took me in and gave me a home. And though there were times I thought I regretted the commitment, especially when I found out what a messy man you were when it came to keeping a decent house, I still owe you for that."

Manus lost his fury as quickly as it had come. The fire flickered and left his eyes. He turned away. "You can't possibly defeat the Black Hunter, lass," he said.

"I'll never know unless I try," she said.

"But what could you possibly offer it in place of my soul?"

"Let me worry about that," she said, glancing towards Thistle. The moor terrier had ventured out of hiding and crept up to her, tentatively wagging its tail. Ginny knelt, rubbing the beast's head to reassure it, and smiled. "And I think I know just the bargain," she said.

She spent the next few hours strengthening her protective wards with the essence of white fire and the chill of cold iron. Manus watched from the hearth, commenting now and again on how her skill had grown in the last two years. "Your old books helped," she said. "And I was able to concentrate more without you hovering like a mother hen."

He made a face when he heard that.

The dark hour finally rolled around. Ginny could feel it, for it brought a thick veil of old magic alive to vibrate her mage senses. And with its coming, she felt the growing miasma of dark powers roaming the moors. Powers so dreadful she could not help but shiver from the chill of uncertainty sliding down her spine. What if she was unable to stop the Black Hunter?

Oh, Arianrhod, Lady of the Silver Wheel, she prayed. *Do not let courage fail me now.* She took a deep breath to still the flutters in her stomach, crossed the room, and pulled open the door.

Moonlight was masked by a black cloud, and a heavy mist was swarming about the path. Ginny stopped in the doorway, careful to stay just behind her protections, and crouched.

"Thistle," she said. "Fox, Thistle! Go fetch the fox!"

The moor terrier bounded to its feet, and with a cheerful, high-pitched bay, he bolted out into the night. Ginny rose, listening to his fierce hunting growl as he disappeared in the mist.

"Horns, lass, what did you go and do that for?" Manus said. "He'll run all night searching for the beastie!"

"I'm counting on it," she said, looking out at the mist and hoping the fox was nowhere near. 'Twould be just like the beast to come back tonight for another of her hens. She trained her ears on the night. Faintly, she could hear the clatter of bony hooves on stone. "It's coming. Stay where you are, Manus, and please be silent."

He muttered something that only mage ears could detect. Ginny smiled and watched the dark.

At length, a shape loomed out of the mist, a tall man wrapped in a plaid of black that was woven with thin strips of red and white—the blood and bones of its victims, some claimed. Eyes of flame were visible within the shadows of his hood. From his head rose gleaming branches of antlers. He rode upon a skeletal mare draped in ebon tatters. Her eyes flashed like embers, and she reared just beyond the threshold, shrieking in an otherwordly manner that set teeth on edge. Ginny steeled herself and did not flinch.

"I have come for the soul of Manus Mac Greeley," the Black Hunter said in a voice like thunder. "Send him out to me."

"Sorry, but I cannot oblige you," Ginny answered.

"What?" the creature shouted, and his voice fairly rattled the dishes in the cupboard.

"By iron and by fire, you cannot cross this threshold," Ginny said. "And by my will, his spirit cannot leave this place. So you might as well take yourself back to Annwn. Arawn will have no souls for his cauldron this night."

"Foolish wench, how dare you!" the Black Hunter howled. The bone mare reared and struck at Ginny. She stepped back to avoid the dangerous hooves, startled to see the ease with which they gouged the oak frame of the door. "If you will not send him forth, then I and my mare shall tear down this miserable hovel and crush your bones beneath it!"

And he would, Ginny was willing to bet. Still, she had another bargain in mind, and could not have him know she feared his threat. "I'll just have to call white fire against you," she said, "And where would that leave us? Me without a home, and you in ashes. Still, I might be willing to bargain with you, provided you're willing to pay a price for the release of his mageborn essence."

"What price?"

"My geas is this," she said. "Fetch me home my moor terrier before cock's crow, and Manus' soul shall be yours."

"I am no dog chaser!" the Black Hunter said.

"What?" Ginny said. "I would think a creature that had followed the Wild Hunt would be quite adept at chasing one small moor terrier. Or are you afraid the geas is beyond your power?"

"There is nothing beyond my power!" the Black Hunter insisted with a snarl, and she swore she saw sparks when he gnashed his teeth. "I will bring you your filthy hound!"

"Terrier," she corrected.

"And you shall give me the mageborn's soul!"

"Only if you swear on the Cauldron of Annwn that you will bring me my dog before cock's crow," she said. "Elsewise, the bargain is forfeit and Manus' soul is free of its obligation to you. Agreed?"

"On the Cauldron, I swear, before cock's crow you shall have your filthy cur!"

Still snarling, the Black Hunter jerked his bone mare about and set her on a course through Tamhasg Wood. The hail of her hooves rattled through the dark. Ginny covered her ears until the sound faded.

"What have you done?" Manus said.

"Merely set a geas upon the Black Hunter," she said.

"But what if he captures poor Thistle?"

"He'll have to be more clever than that greedy fox to do so," she said, and crossing the room, she seated herself to wait the long night, watching the open door. Manus' spirit paced up and down as the hours passed. Now and again, Ginny heard the moor terrier's raunchy howl as it gathered a new scent, and mage hearing also detected more than one string of curses out on the moor beyond the woods.

As she leaned back in the chair, Ginny closed her eyes, falling into a peaceful doze. An urgent voice suddenly aroused her.

"Ginny, it comes!" Manus cried.

Ginny awoke with a start, looking out the door. A faint glow was visible on the eastern horizon, and marching ahead of it, she could see a tall figure in ragged plaid. The Black Hunter was indeed returning. Nor was it riding the bone mare. She was limping along behind her master, looking as worn and weary as a real mare. The Black Hunter held forth its arms as though disdaining to carry the wriggling bundle in its grasp.

Thistle! It had caught the moor terrier. Ginny rose and moved to the door, leaning against the jamb. Mage sight revealed that the terrier's coat was a mass of burrs and heather blossoms, as was the Black Hunter's plaid.

"Has the cock crowed?" she ventured, glancing toward Manus. He slowly shook his head. *Blessed Lady of the Silver Wheel, what shall I do?*

As if in answer to her prayer, a bright red coat snapped across the path leading to the cottage. The fox. The very one she'd sent Thistle after the previous evening, was making for her hen house again.

"Thistle, the fox!" Ginny cried.

There was a clacking of agitated fowl as the fox dove in among the hens' roost. Thistle gave a yelp and began wriggling madly in the Black Hunter's grasp. Though the unseelie creature tried to maintain its hold, terrier tenacity won out. With a mighty twist, Thistle was free, bolting after the wayward fox making off with one of the hens in its jaws.

The Black Hunter gave a howl, throwing himself after the moor terrier. Like a bird of prey, it flew, only to land among the nattering hens who were scurrying about in wild abandon. Still snarling, the Black Hunter scrambled to its knees.

At that moment, the old cock, irritated by all the commotion in his yard, began to crow.

"No!" the Black Hunter howled and turned.

Ginny put one hand on her hip, stepping across the threshold and calling white fire into the other. "I fear you have failed, Black Hunter," she said. "Your quest for Manus' soul is forfeit by the geas I put on you to which you agreed. I suggest you leave before the sun rises higher."

Still howling in outrage, the Black Hunter surged to its feet and charged after its mare. The skeletal creature had already turned her bony tail and was fleeing for the last shadows of night, her angry rider in pursuit.

Ginny turned toward the cottage where Manus stood just inside the door. Dawn's light would soon fade his essence as well. "I am impressed," he said. "And I am still your prisoner."

"By my will, I free you from this place, Manus Mac Greeley," she said. "Go and be well."

He smiled, stepping out of the cottage and bowing to her. "Until the next full moon, lass," he said and faded from view.

Ginny whistled. "Thistle, come!" she called. For now, she decided, though it had cost her a hen, the fox had earned its keep this night. Besides, there'd be other times for Thistle to catch it.

Within moments, the moor terrier came ambling back. Bracken and burrs were all she could see of its coat. She shook her head and knelt with a smile.

"Look at you," she said. "It'll take me a moon just to get you clean again."

The moor terrier merely snorted, shaking its head and sending a flutter of fox tail hairs drifting to the path before following Ginny into the cottage for a well-earned rest.

THE IMPRESSION OF POWER

by Lee Martindale

Lee Martindale begins by saying she is "unabashedly female, unashamedly 47, and unapologetically fat." In a society which none-too-subtly insists that women should conform to the dimensions of a Barbie doll both physically and mentally, that's a refreshing approach. She describes herself as a "size rights activist" probably because most women in this country are over size sixteen while more than half of all dresses are cut below size nine. She is also a publisher/editor, an SCA Bard and Merchant, filker, paraplegic, and access rights advocate. As in her previous bio, her husband still calls her a redheaded "Hell on Wheels," and she adds, "In addition to a fairly respectable list of non-genre credits, my fantasy credits to date consist of 'Yearbride' in the *Snows of Darkover* anthology and "Mrs. Bailey's Harp" in *Zone 9 Magazine*." She has also just made a second sale to *Marion Zimmer Bradley's FANTASY Magazine*. She still resides in Dallas with, "in order of appearance," two cats, one husband, and one writing partner. The separation of husband and writing partner makes me very curious. Married twice, I never found a writing partner. Not yet anyway.

In ages to come, it would be called the greatest gathering of power and the wielders of power ever seen upon the Blessed Isle. With bold phrases and intricate rhymes, bards and chroniclers would strive to convey the sounds and sights and splendor of the coming competition. But as a cold gray day moved into colder, grayer twilight, it could be called nothing other than chaos.

At the main gate to the High King's fort, harried guards danced a fine line between deference and authority carrying out their charged duty of granting admittance or turning away—a line that became finer as a cold rain began to fall on flaring tempers in the crowd seeking entrance to the shelter, warmth, and opportunities within.

Among the noted and notables jockeying for position and admittance, one young woman stood hunched against the icy drizzle, inching forward with the press of the crowd. Surrounded by the bright boldness of multicolored bardic cloaks and wizards' intricately patterned robes, she was almost remarkable in her plainness. It was that plainness which allowed her to slip through the gate under cover of a rather heated exchange between one guard and an ill-tempered clan chief. And it was the same that caught the corner of the detail commander's eye as he moved to defuse yet another confrontation.

"You! Girl! Hold!"

The young woman turned to see the commander motioning her back with a short, impatient gesture, even as he spoke fair to the disgruntled clan chief and bade him through the gate.

"Soldiers' camp outside the north wall, girl," he said when she was close enough. "There's none of your kind allowed within."

"Your pardon, sir," she replied in quiet tones, "but I am no camp follower. I come to take a place among tomorrow's competitors."

The commander glanced at her sideways, then turned to look at her more closely. A plain wool shift and nut-dyed cloak, bare of ornamentation beyond a carved wooden clasp, concealed the lines of her body in a way no camp follower would have the imagination to use.

No artificial colors touched the clean paleness of her face or the mouse-brown hair that hung in one long, damp braid down her back. And while a camp follower might return his gaze as boldly as she did now, the look would likely be one of teasing promise. This one's hazel eyes held nothing of that.

The commander pursed his lips, then told his man, "Carry on here," before motioning the young woman to follow him a short distance away from the noise of the gate. In the light of anther torch and under some small measure of shelter provided by a platform on the log wall, the commander stopped. Turning again to the woman, he cocked his head to one side and slowly looked her up and down. She did not grow uneasy, as he had half expected her to do under his deliberate examination, nor did she look around, as he might expect of someone newly come to the bustle of a noble's seat of power. She merely stood quietly, holding her small bundle in one hand and watching him evenly. It was a touch unsettling, and it caught his interest.

"If not to sell your company in the encampment, then what? Did you think to find a place in the bed of a noble or one of the Great Bards? Become companion to one of the wizards, perhaps?"

A faint smile touched the young woman's eyes. "As I told you, sir, I have come to take part in the contest." Her voice, the commander noticed, was low-pitched and sweet.

"I see," the commander chuckled. "And I suppose you are some great mage come across the Storm Sea and traveling in guise?"

The smile in the young woman's eyes now touched her lips. "I am as you see me, sir. And my journey, though long, has crossed only those waters that pour from the heart of Eire."

The commander shook his head, amused and puzzled all in one. "Well," he said after a time, "at least you have the good sense not to put a lie under my nose. And in return, I'll give you truth for truth. You have as much chance of joining the company of competitors as I have of seeing a son of my seed or fosterage on yonder High Throne."

The woman's smile did not waver. "Was not the King's Word sent to all, and that Word an invitation to any and all who would seek to win the office?"

"Why, so it was," agreed the commander, thinking that her voice reminded him of well-aged mead. "But the King's Word and the King's Intent are not always quite the same." He glanced around, then motioned her to come closer. Lowering his voice, he continued, "It matters not if you are the most skilled of village wise women or the most clever hedge witch in all Udd's kingdom. He seeks a man, preferably one of venerable age, who conveys by countenance alone the appearance of great wisdom and great skill. What he wants is less the power than the impression of power. If the truth is less than the appearance, well—little harm in that. I suspect, in fact," he shrugged, "so much the better."

The young woman in front of him nodded once, and the commander was again both unsettled and intrigued. "I thank you for your kindness in showing me the King's needs," she said with a smile. She bowed a farewell and turned toward the gate.

"Wait!" called the commander, before she had gone more than a few steps. "The gods alone know why, but I'll not send you back onto the road on a night like this." He fumbled with a leather thong tied to his belt, then handed it and the painted wooden disk through which it was strung to the young woman. "Go to the camp outside the north wall, and look for the tent marked by a banner matching the design on this. Should anyone challenge you or think your favors up for the taking, show them the token and tell them you are under my protection. Show it also to my aide, and he'll see you to meat, bread, and drink. Tell him I said you were to sleep in my tent tonight."

The woman's hazel gaze met his again. "And the reward you expect for this generosity?"

The commander answered in something akin to embarrassment. "Well, lass, and that's where I think the gods have addled my manhood. I expect nothing. I'll not be off-duty till dawn."

"Then may your gods and mine bless you doubly for yet another kindness." She smiled warmly and again began to turn.

"Have you a name, girl?"

"Indeed, sir. It is Myr Aelyn."

The commander's tent had not been hard to find. A soldier at the entrance to the encampment laughed and made a crude remark when she showed him the token but beyond that had offered her no more than to point the way. The commander's aide, a scarred old veteran well beyond fighting years, rose from his own bed without complaint at her approach and had gone back to it gratefully when she declined all but a mug of mulled wine. He'd shown her the commander's bed and roughly bade her sweet sleep.

Waking refreshed two hours before dawn, she wrapped her cloak around her and left the tent to find that the rain had ended. She pulled a chair to the banked fire and settled back to savor the crystal sharpness of air and sky, found only in the coldest hours of the night when false dawn can be caught only out of the corner of the eye.

Myr Aelyn reviewed the commander's words. She laid them atop other words and older messages carried in her mind, fitting one to the other and weaving her plan. With eyes fixed on the coals that glowed through a lace of ashes, she then began to weave a whispered chant.

* * *

"Your pardon, m'lord, but what are you doing in my camp?"

The old man roused from an apparent nodding sleep and looked up from his seat by the dying fire. An obviously tired young officer stood regarding him with a puzzled expression.

"Ah, commander," the old man said as he levered himself up awkwardly from the chair. "Is it dawn already? I must have dozed off, and small wonder, considering the hour when I arrived."

"Wandering around in the cold and dark like an addled old bull, I was," he continued, "and would probably have done so till sunrise or until I dropped from exhaustion. But there was a most charming young female creature sitting by your fire when I stumbled past it. Sat me down here and heated wine in her own mug, all the while telling me of the kindnesses you had done for the likes of a . . . what did she call herself . . . oh, yes . . . a 'simple hedge witch.' I tell you, young sir, it warmed my heart to hear, it most certainly did."

Despite fatigue and the momentary irritation of finding a stranger in his camp, the younger man chuckled. He invited the old man to be seated again before calling out his aide and instructing him to heat some water for washing "And wake the girl in my tent . . . gently, mind you."

"Blast an old man's memory! I was to tell you that she has already gone."

"What?"

"Gone before dawn, she was," the old man continued as he began to sit down again in the chair by the fire, "charging me with a message for you. Now . . . what was it she . . . ah, yes. Asked me to return this token to you and to say that it served her as you said it would. Said you'd done service this night passing that she would not soon forget, and which she promised would someday be repaid, although you might not recognize it when it came. A most delightful young creature. Told me her name, but I can't quite recall. . . ."

"Myr Aelyn was the name she gave me."

"That was it! Bless the memory of a young man . . . that was it indeed. Knew it was something similar to my own, but the ears and the mind play tricks at my age."

The commander's latest guest chatted on, making him and even the aide laugh as they broke their fast. Finally, the younger man asked the old man's business.

"To become the King's Enchanter, of course," he answered in so droll a fashion that the commander grinned.

"Then, by all means, my lord, avail yourself of my tent for whatever preparations you require. And then I will be pleased to escort you to the contest."

The old man cocked his head to one side and regarded the commander for a moment. Then he smiled. "Another kindness to be marked and rewarded."

The sun was above the horizon, and both soldiers' camp and king's fortress bustling with activity, when the old man came out of the tent. "Well, young sir, do I look sufficiently like a wizard to be counted among the competitors?"

The commander rose to his feet in amazement. Plain travel clothes had been exchanged for a richly-dyed robe covered in arcane designs worked in the finest embroidery, and it draped a body that somehow seemed taller. A mane of white hair flowed away from the face and down his back, and an equally white and impressive beard ending in four braids lay upon his chest. The staff in the old man's left hand, which the younger man could have sworn had been nothing more than a length of plain wood, was intricately carved and set at its top with a piece of honey-dark amber the size of a large man's fist. But for all the new display of finery, it was the old man's eyes that held the young commander. Laughing and alive with power, and a hazel shade he knew he had seen only once before in his life, although he couldn't recall where.

The younger man bowed deeply to the older. "My lord wizard, will you do me the honor of allowing me to escort you to where the competitors gather?"

The answering smile was merry. "The honor will be mine. But before we go, I would have your name."

"I am called Hector, m'lord."

"A good name that, and one I will remember."

A few moments later, as they walked toward the main gate, the old man asked, "Tell me, young Hector, have you any sons?"

"Not yet, m'lord. I've only just been pledged to a lady up near the Great Forest."

"A fine thing that. And if you'll allow me a small bit of prophecy, I see grand futures for the boys who grow up between you and your lady . . . yes, grand futures."

The commander looked amused. "The first foreseeing of the King's Enchanter, m'lord?"

"Well it may be, young Hector . . . well it may be."

THE NAMING OF NAMES

by Adrienne Martine-Barnes

Adrienne Martine-Barnes is the author of ten novels and a great number of short stories. When not writing she spends her time painting, quilting, dollmaking, and engages in a number of other time-consuming activities. At present she is learning Japanese braidmaking and bookbinding because she does not have enough things to do in a day. I met Adrienne Martine when she was a fragile teenager who promptly fainted into my arms; later we knew one another in the context of the SCA East Kingdom—the first of the subsidiary kingdoms. It's hard to realize that the SCA is now well over thirty years old; it was really splendid back in those days when we were only the second of the kingdoms, and I look back on that time as a period of special freedom and glory.

Nowadays, Adrienne lives in Portland, Oregon, with Caitlin the Wonder Cat.

"The Naming of Names" features a very powerful woman and a lesson she must learn.

The Lady Blackthorne stirred restlessly, rising unwilling from the depths of sleep. She sensed someone in the room, beyond the bed curtains, but there was no sound, no rasp of breath nor rustle of fabric. She frowned for just a second, then let her features smooth. She must not mar her famous beauty, even for a moment. It must be one of the maids. Hadn't she left orders not to be disturbed? No one would dare to risk her rage, her wrath, would they?

Slowly, reluctantly, she raised her eyelids, her thick black lashes shadowing her vision. She had beautiful lashes—everyone said so. Everything about her was beautiful, now that the child had been born and she was no longer huge and ungainly. How she had hated being pregnant, being forced to support that alien in her belly for all those months. She had been ill every day, and even as her stomach expanded, she herself had grown slimmer and slimmer. But, it was over now, the child born—a girl, which she had known it would be, from the terrible moment of conception. A girl who would take her place, her powers, if she did not prevent it. And she would prevent it. The Lady Blackthorne did not doubt that.

The midwives had given her the child, washed and wrapped in clean linen, and Lady Blackthorne had thrust it away, ignoring the tremendous impulse to press it to her breast. She had given it no more than a glance, and that had been more than enough. It had her dark hair and white skin. Small pink hands curled above the blanket, perfect, like tiny stars. But the babe had looked at her with unclouded eyes, knowing eyes, as if she sensed the rage and hostility in the arms which held her, all unwillingly. How could a newborn child know anything?

Lady Blackthorne pushed herself up onto her many pillows, remembering the toils of birthing despite her desire to forget the ugliness of it. She had been drenched with sweat, her lovely hair plastered against her skull, her nails cutting into the flesh of her palms. The room had reeked with the scent of blood and bowel, and she had screamed and screamed. How odd. Even now her throat was sore, and it had been several days. She had never made such disgusting noises in her life. No one had warned her that childbirth was such a vile occurrence. All anyone ever spoke of was the delight of children, the pleasures of having a babe at the breast, and a great deal of other nonsense.

Hannah, the ancient midwife, had taken the child when she shoved it aside, her wrinkled face full of rebuke. She should have gotten rid of the woman years ago! She had delivered the Lady Blackthorne, as well as the rest of her mother's children. She had been bringing babies into the world for almost *seventy* years—hundreds of squalling brats. But none had been so beautiful as Lady Blackthorne, nor had any others been so gifted in the arts of sorcery.

This was all *his* fault! If only he had been less comely, less charming, she might have never slipped. She wanted to rage at him, at her darling Wrolf, so badly named, for he was more like a sleek cat than any canine, but it was impossible. Every memory of him made her smile, made her weak with desire. Wrolf Stinegrim had done what no other man had managed in the thirty years of her life—he had seduced her.

Certainly she had known the risk she took when she bedded him on that particular night. She had lain with him before, many times, but never with the new moon rising, never when she was fertile. But Lady Blackthorne had been so confident that she could manage to abort, if she needed to. She had done it before, once, when she had been young and inexperienced. Her sorcery could solve anything. She had been hot with lust, and the result had been nine months of misery and spewing.

The Lady could still remember the very instant she had conceived, as if it were only a moment ago, instead of the better portion of a year. She had been lolling in the aftermath of pleasure, her limbs slack, her mind nearly empty. Wrolf had been asleep beside her, utterly spent with their mutual passion. He was a neat sleeper and never drooled or snored or did any of the things she always found so distasteful in her previous lovers. He was, in short, quite perfect, like herself.

Then she had felt a tiny prick, a stab of pain in her smooth belly, like a hot pin penetrating her flesh. It had only lasted a second, but she knew it was a child entering her body. And the Lady had known, by her arts, that this was a female child, a being who would take her beauty, her power, who would usurp her place.

It had been a startling realization, frightening, really. She could still recall the flood of rage that ran along her blood. Rage at Wrolf and rage at herself for being so stupid, so weak! She was the Lady Blackthorne, and she had never had a moment of weakness in her life!

Immediately she had bent her will to destroy the spark of life within her, bringing all her sorcerous talents, a lifetime of study, to bear against it. She would not surrender her position! She ignored the stirring of her conscience, the prick of awareness that what she was doing was utterly wrong. Let other females, weak-willed women she despised, have daughters who would destroy their beauty and assume their arts. She was the Lady Blackthorne!

It was such a simple matter, really. One only had to dislodge the tiny presence from settling in, prevent it from finding a nurturing place. It did not matter, and no one would ever be the wiser. Any half-trained hedge witch could do it, and likely did. The Lady did not have a high opinion of witches, hedge or otherwise. Amateurs! All their bleating about the sanctity of life, about the Blessings of the Mother, was such nonsense. They all said they longed for daughters, pretending they did not know that once they brought a girlchild into life, their arts would diminish and fail.

But, for once, her will was as nothing, and her own sorceries had not obeyed her. The spark did not flicker and die, as she ordered it to. Instead, it seemed to expand, to burst into a small flame, an ember in her womb. Nothing she did made the slightest difference, and her rage and fear grew. She had spewed up wine and oysters suddenly, and the taste of them, mingled with bile, remained on her tongue, no matter how she cleaned her mouth with sweetmints, remained throughout the months which followed. The vile taste of that spew was in her mouth still, and she twisted her lips with unease. Was she never to be free of it?

And soon after, the dreams had begun. When she tried to sleep, she found a face looking down at her, a small, well-formed face, with eyes that knew everything. The Lady had tried draughts of nightbloom steeped in warm wine, and oil of poppy. Nothing had brought her any relief from the stern gaze, and nothing stayed in her belly long, except milk and bland cereal.

She might have been able to dismiss the dreams, if those knowing eyes had been different. They were gray, almost silvery, the eyes of a Moonthorne, that most rare and peculiar form of the sorcerous. She had awakened time after time, shaking and soaked with loathsome sweat. She had banished her darling Wrolf from her bed, not wishing him to see her in that state, and slept alone, furious and frightened. This had not improved her temper, and the servants had sulked. She lacked the strength to beat them, even, to express her raging emotions and release them.

There had not been a Moonthorne born in seven generations, and the Lady could see no reason that one should come now. Or, if one did, let it be born to one of her brothers, Silverthorne or Sundart. She had read all the ancient, moldering volumes that filled the scriptorium of Thorne Keep, and she knew the history of the Thornes as well as she did her spells and sorceries.

There were Redthornes, violent and martial, and Bluethornes, calm and serene. Sunthornes and Silverthornes abounded, cheerful sort of folk, and quite unremarkable. But Moonthornes were different, with a strange kind of sorcery in their blood which presaged change. The Lady Blackthorne had never thought that change was a good thing, for the Thornes of various hues had ruled firmly for generations. She liked things as they were, with herself at the center of all eyes, and she was not going to have some little brat disrupting the natural order of things.

The worst part of it was that she knew it was her own folly that was to blame. The Lady had known the danger of coupling at the new moon, particularly the Moon of Mists. But she had been too proud to regard anything but her own desires, as her mother had often warned her. She was not wilfull, as old Lady Darkbarb had sometimes said. She only knew what was right and proper, better than anyone else. How could it be otherwise? Was she not the finest Blackthorne sorceress since the almost legendary Kornelya? Perhaps she was even better, for surely the tales had enlarged her deeds and skills over the centuries. It was unthinkable that a mere infant could bring all that to an end!

The Lady Blackthorne had been fascinated by the stories of Kornelya when she was a child, filled with an ambition to surpass her fabled ancestor in all things magical. She had bent her considerable energy to the task, and her reward had been acclaim and power. She had delved deeply, conquered the most esoteric branches of her art, and still been restless and unsatisfied. Indeed, it was not until Wrolf Stinegrim had appeared, his golden hair gleaming in the candle's light, his sweet smile gladdening her heart, that her restlessness had been quenched. And just look where it had gotten her!

The Lady Blackthorne pursed her lips at this thought, and looked toward the curtains surrounding her huge bed. She could still sense the presence beyond the drapes, a quiet intrusion where none should be. "Go away!"

"It is the seventh day," came a voice she did not recognize. "It is time!"

The seventh day! Had she slept so long? The heart of the Lady Blackthorne swelled with joy! She was going to preserve her place after all. The solution had been before her all along. So simple, really. If she had not

been so very clever, she would have seen it sooner.
There was no need to kill the girl—all she had to do
was refuse to name her!

Without a name from her mother, the child would
wither and die within a few hours of the end of the seventh day. All she need do was remain silent until
moonset, and the deed would be done. She would
remain beautiful and powerful, and none could gainsay
her again. The little usurper would be gone forever.

At the same time, the Lady felt a prickle of apprehension. There would be gossip—for servants always
talked about their betters, no matter how often they
were beaten. Old Hannah would know, if no one else.
It must be she who stood beyond the curtains, for the
Lady could think of no one else who would dare to
enter her chamber unbidden. Well, Hannah was old,
and the old could be silenced. It would not be the first
time she had disposed of a nuisance, nor probably the
last. Her mother had discovered this fact just before
she had perished.

Quite suddenly, the Lady felt chilled all over. It was
a mistake to think of her mother, for it made her
remember the last words she had spoken, gasping for
air, her wrinkled face a pale blue, her eyes bulging in
her shrunken skull. *"Your daughter will be . . ."*

That was all she had said before she fell back in her
chair, cold and dead. It was a curse, of course, a dying
one at that, and therefore potent. But she had not completed it. Unless the words had formed in her mind and
remained unspoken.

The Lady shivered all over, then frowned again
before she remembered that she must not mar her love-
liness. There was nothing in any book she possessed
which said anything of such occurrences. Curses must
be spoken to have effect, mustn't they? Unless, as the
witches claimed, the thought was equal to the deed.

Doubt gnawed at her for a moment. Then she dis-
missed it. The witches were fools, and what they knew

about real magic could be put in a cup and still leave room for tea. Lady Darkbarb had never finished the phrase, and there was nothing to worry about. She was not cursed—she was the Lady Blackthorne!

For once the invocation of her title brought her no reassurance. Instead she felt almost frightened, weak and powerless, as if the brat had already stolen her art. What an idiot she was. She should have taken the babe and smothered it, instead of rejecting it into the hands of wet nurses and midwives. She was so used to using her arts that she had almost forgotten there were other, simpler ways to deal with obstacles. But she discovered she shrank from that, from the use of flesh upon flesh, from touch. Too late for that, in any case.

She must decide whether to refuse to name the child, or to give it some name that would cripple it. The Lady paused, remembering how she had not been able to abort the child at its inception. What name could she give that would be strong enough to hamper a Moonthorne, even one so young?

The name must be given and it must possess some truth, so it would do her no good to call the miserable brat Ugly or Spavined—although she found that both these gave her a deep satisfaction. But a false name would be even worse than none at all, in one way, for it would rebound against her eventually. Perhaps the better course was to remain silent, and deal with the talk later. Yes, let the baby die nameless, to be tossed to the dogs from the walls of Thorne Keep. What a delightful thought!

"Mathild!"

The Lady Blackthorne froze. No one knew her name, not even her lover. Only her mother had known her true name, and she was worm food, and had been for years. To know the real name of another was to have power over them, and no one skilled in the arts would reveal it. It was only after one was dead that one's name was known, as Kornelya's had been. While she

had lived, she had been the Lady Blackthorne, and
nothing else.

Terrified, she glanced down at the tiny amulet
hanging about her neck. She clutched at it, testing the
wards on it, to see if someone had managed to penetrate them while she labored to bring forth that brat, or
while she slept. No, it was intact, secure. Her name was
written there, in cyphers only readable to those who
had studied the arts. She must be dreaming!

Yes, that was it! No one could know her name, and
therefore no one had spoken it. Of course. There was
no one on the other side of the curtains—-not even
Hannah. It was just a vivid dream, the result of her
exertions in childbed. Her mind was playing tricks on
her. She gave a little sigh of relief, and felt better
instantly. All she had to do was wake up and it would
all be done with.

"Mathild—it is time!"

The Lady's sense of well-being fled at the voice. Her
momentary reassurance drained away, leaving her
trembling and shaken. "Go away!" She listened, and
when she heard nothing, she put her hand out to open
the curtains. Part of her wanted to pull the covers over
her head, as she had done when she was very young.
She hated herself for this childish weakness, for feeling
fear. She ground her teeth and brushed a lank strand of
dark hair off her face. Her breath was ragged, almost
panting, and she did not move until she had regained a
small measure of calm. It took more energy than she
expected, more strength, strength she no longer seemed
to have easy command of. She knew this was not a
dream, and that she had to know what thing waited
beyond the hangings, even though her heart pounded
with terror. But she was still the Lady Blackthorne, and
she could look at anything!

She put a trembling hand to the curtains, parting
them a finger's width, and peered through the opening.
A figure stood in the middle of the room, a woman

dressed in garments no living person had worn in centuries. The dress was dark red, cut narrow across the breasts, and very full below, so it looked as if she were standing in a pool of freshly spilled blood. There was a wide band of black thorns embroidered around the hanging sleeves and along the hem of the gown. The hair was concealed beneath a smooth cap, and crowned with a band of barbs.

The Lady took this in, then noticed that she could actually see through the woman, that she could glimpse the unlit fireplace on the other side of the room. Her skin was lucent and transparent. And, in spite of this, she carried in her arms a wriggling bundle that could be nothing but the child that Lady Blackthorne did not want.

For a moment she just stared at the apparition, biting her lower lip. She had never seen this woman before, this ghost, and she did not pause to wonder how such an insubstantial thing could support the squirming infant. The Lady Blackthorne summoned a banishing, let it coalesce in her trembling hand, then cast it toward the thing.

There was a slight popping sound in the stillness of the room, and then the Lady felt the banishing rebound against her like a bucket of icy water against her skin. She gasped for air as her body shuddered with the shock, and her ears rang. She felt dizzy for a moment and clutched the thick fabric of the hangings with a shaking hand.

The ghost gave a grave smile. "Now, that was rather stupid, Mathild. I expected better of you."

"How dare you speak my name!" Wrath warmed her flesh, and she shoved her legs over the edge of the bed, fury bringing back her energy enough to stir her to movement, to dispel some of the terror which gripped her.

"The finest thing about being dead is that you can say anything you like," the woman answered calmly.

Her bare feet struck the carpet, and her legs carried her across the room. The Lady flew at the figure, snatching at the bundle in the transparent arms. She tried to tear the infant away, to dash it to the floor and spatter its brains on the hearthstone, but her hands slipped and she could not get a grip. It was as if the babe were covered with grease or oil. She screamed with frustration, then heard the sound of footfalls in the corridor beyond. A moment later there was a rattling of the knob, and frantic pounding, but the door remained firmly shut.

"Now, Mathild—give a true name, now!"

"I will not! Let her die—the filthy little monster. I will not give up my powers to this . . . thing!" She shuddered with rage and disgust.

"Would you have me name her, then?" The ghost's voice was serene, and the words had no threat in them, but the Lady felt terrified. She took a step backward and rubbed her damp palms against the fine linen of her sleeping gown.

"Only her mother can give that boon, and I refuse!"

"With an ordinary babe, that is so. But this child is no ordinary being—as you well know!"

The words cut into Lady Blackthorne like a whip, and she looked down at her arms, surprised to find her flesh intact instead of bleeding. "What do you mean? Who are you?" Her skull was pounding and she could barely think.

"I am she whom you conjured, all unwilling."

"What?" Lady Blackthorne tried to marshal her thoughts, quelling her anger and her fear as much as she was able. Her mouth was dry, and she could feel sweat trickling down beneath her arms. "Conjured? I made no—Kornelya?"

"I knew you were clever!" The ghost looked quite pleased, as if the Lady Blackthorne was a rather stupid student who had finally perceived the obvious. The banging on the door became more frantic, and she could hear the voices of servants shouting in the corridor.

She ignored the racket, bringing her attention back to the transparent woman and the wriggling bundle. "But, but . . . I did not! And I have your name, so I have power upon you and. . . ."

Kornelya smiled and shook her head. "The lifenames of the dead have no potency. Even you should remember that, with all your plots and delvings. Now, it is time. Either you gift the child with her true name, which is concealed in your cold breast, or I shall do it, and the consequences will not be happy ones for you! Choose, and quickly."

"Either way, I will lose." The taste of defeat lay on her tongue like the flavor of ashes. At the same time, she tried to think of some means to cheat fate, to avoid this monstrosity. It was not fair! She had everything, and she remained determined not to lose it to her child.

The ghost, Kornelya, Lady Blackthorne of old, gave a sigh, as if the entire matter wearied her, and she wished to be done with it. "That is true! All you can choose is which losing, for there is no winning in this. You lost that chance when you tried to unseat the girl at the moment of becoming. Now you must pay the price."

She was the Lady Blackthorne, and she knew all the secrets of sorcery. She knew that what the ghost said was true, that she had brought this upon herself by trying to abort the girl. She felt no regret or sorrow in this realization, but only rage that she had not succeeded. "This thing will destroy me—take all my powers and kill me."

Kornelya looked rather sad. "On the contrary—she will not do anything to you, no matter what. You will do all that needs to be done."

"I can't . . . I just can't!" She took a step closer, her feet dragging, her voice thin in her aching throat. It was as if she could not stop her body, as if the ghost was compelling her. Impossible—the dead could not force the living, or there would be no peace in the world at all. So, how was she standing no more than a handspan away?

She closed her eyes and breathed deeply, trying once more to regain her control. She felt her neck extend, as if drawn from her body, and she tried to resist. But as the Lady Blackthorne bent her head, a smell came into her nostrils, a clean warm smell, of milk and warm skin. Then her eyes opened, against her will, and looked down at the infant.

"Consider the consequences if I am the namer, proud Lady. They will be terrible."

She hardly heard the words, for she was looking at the bundle in the arms of the ghost now, looking into a small face, with silvery eyes and a rosebud mouth that seemed to smile. A tiny hand escaped the swaddlings, reaching toward her, fingers grasping, and the Lady drew back. "She sees so much," she gasped, hardly aware that she spoke. "I cannot bear it!"

There was a stillness in the room, and the only sound was the frightened banging of servants outside in the hall. Then the ghost spoke softly. "It is not the name I might have guessed, but it will do. It will do very well!"

"Name! I gave no name!"

"Ah, but you have. She will be Fithania, she who sees much."

Then the vision vanished, ghost and baby gone completely. The doorknob turned, and the door swung open. Wrolf Stinegrim led a gaggle of anxious servants, and the room was suddenly full of people. She hardly gave them a glance, even Wrolf Stinegrim. She had been tricked, beaten, defeated by a wee babe and a dead woman, and nothing would ever be the same again. Nothing would be right in the world as she had known it.

Tears filled her eyes, and she blinked them away,

furious and exhausted. If only she could die now, unde-
feated and strong. But she knew that even that surcease
was beyond her grasp. That mewling brat would not
allow her to die, but would make her remain alive, to
witness the outcome of her folly. Neither her sorcery
nor her will would avail her now.

The foul taste of oysters and wine rose in her throat,
flooded her mouth, bringing back the memory of ardor,
the pleasure of Wrolf's body against her own, and the
moment when Fithania had manifested in her flesh. It
was so bitter a flavor, and so undeserved! For just an
instant, the tears threatened to overflow, to course
down her chilly cheeks. She charmed them away,
though the effort cost her greatly. Already she could
sense her powers were fading, diminishing, though it
would be some years before she had none left.

She straightened her shoulders, brushed her hair
back over them, and turned to the clacking servants
around her, dry-eyed and calm. There were questions
she did not answer, but ignored as if no one had
spoken. She was not about to satisfy the curiosity of
the ignorant.

Instead, she blinked a few times, to remove the last
remnants of her sorrow. Then she glared at her lover,
the source of her defeat, and the servants, grim and
silent, until they quieted and scurried away, afraid to
risk her wrath.

The taste of her loss was in her mouth, closing her
throat with the pain. She felt the anger and the loss
remotely, as if was something far away. Tears rose
again and again, and each time she held them back,
fiercely clinging to this one thing she could command.
The emptiness in her battled with her will, that great
will that had made her what she was, the greatest sorceress of her age.

At last only Wrolf remained, looking at her with his
gentle eyes, concerned and caring. How had she ever
loved such a man? She must have been mad! She

wanted to send him away, but her voice was too weary, too weak.

Nothing would ever fill her now, neither love nor power. The taste of her defeat would never leave her, and she must learn to savor it somehow. The sense of devastation swept away any other emotion, as Wrolf watched her, concerned and adoring. It had the taste of bitterness in it, and regret for all that she had lost. New tears brimmed, and she turned away quickly. She was the Lady Blackthorne, and no one had ever seen her weep, nor ever would.

THE CHANGELINGS

by Diana L. Paxson

Diana Paxson is my sister-in-law and almost my closest friend; she is the first of us to become a grandmother, and wants to dedicate her story to two of her grandchildren (second and third children of her son Ian). So here it is: to Michael and Ariel Grey, born April 5, 1996. I hope to become a grandmother myself in the next year or so. I am looking forward to meeting my grandchildren. They're the only future any of us has.

Diana is one of the very few writers who has appeared in all my anthologies, from the very first. She may have missed one when I was racing for a deadline, but my impression is that she's never missed one of my anthologies though she often waits till the last moment to turn a story in; so we call her, laughingly, I hope, "the late Miss Paxson." When I began editing anthologies, I made a promise to her that I'd buy a story I liked even when other editors stupidly kept rejecting it. I still like her work although now she has many fine novels in print, including one on the unlikely subject of King Lear *(A Serpent's Tooth*, Morrow 1991), which is not nearly as depressing as the subject sounds.

Here is a story of jealousy warring with duty, and how a woman battles to save twin babies whom she helped bring into the world.

After the harvest, it was the custom of the seeress Groa to travel with Bera Steinbjornsdottir, her apprentice, to some place where they might spend the

winter. The year Eric Blood-Ax was driven from
Jorvik they turned toward Raumsdale. The steading
belonged to Halvor Skjalgson, a man of Jarl Sigurd's
following. The farm was on good soil, with many stout
buildings of fitted logs for men and animals, and for
the health of the land, the Alf's ancient mound where
they made the offerings to the ancestral spirits at
sowing and harvest time.

Bera eyed it with interest as they turned up the road
toward the cluster of farm buildings beyond the
meadow. Such mounds were doorways to the world of
the Invisible, where the spirits of the dead and other
beings, less friendly, made their home. This one was
larger than most, a smooth hump of green turf higher
than a tall man, with the ends of the stones that roofed
the inner chamber poking through the soil.

Then the cart lurched into the farmyard, and Halvor's wife came out to greet them, and with her a
fair-haired child with Groa's eyes.

"Yes, she is mine—" the Vœlva answered the question in Bera's eyes. "Her father is Jarl Sigurd, and he
arranged for her to be fostered here."

Silenced, Bera nodded. She had not known her
teacher had any children. The Vœlva must have made
Bera her apprentice the year after Gerdis' birth. She
wondered now if it were for her own merits that Groa
had taken her or as a substitute for this child.

That night Bera watched them from her own place
farther down the board, trying to decide whether what
she felt was envy for the mother, or for the child. She
had been not quite as old as Gerdis when her own
mother died.

If I had a child, she thought fiercely, *I would not
give it away!* Other girls her age had two or three children by now. For the first time Bera ached for the
life she had given up when she chose to follow the
Vœlva's path.

She forced herself to look away, her gaze passing

from the frowning face of Halvor's wife Borglind, who ruled the steading while her husband was away with the jarl, to the other men and women of the farmstead and the thralls who were serving them. One of them, a pale girl with red hair, was so heavily pregnant she could hardly carry her platter. As she came into the circle of firelight Bera stared, for her skin was so white it was almost luminous, a coloring found only in some of the folk of Ireland. No doubt the girl had been taken on a raid, as her own mother had been. But Bera's mother had been one of the little dark breed of Irish, and she took after her.

Bera wondered if the child was Halvor's. As she watched, one of the other servants thrust roughly past the Irish girl, who fell hard against one of the pillars. Bera saw her face contort in pain, but she made no sound. What was Borglind about to let her servants treat the girl so? But the bonder's wife was watching with a grimace of satisfaction. Almost certainly, then, Halvor was the father, and his wife was jealous.

In the years Bera had traveled with Groa she had learned it was not always so—folk said that King Harald Hairfair had married a wife in every kingdom he laid under his rule—but it was hard for two women to share both a man and a hall, especially when one of them was well-born and old, and the other young, and fair, and a thrall. Borglind had borne sons to her husband; two of them were dead and the other with his father. She might well fear that Halvor would favor the thrall-woman's offspring.

Bera watched as the Irish girl, holding her belly, crept from the hall. Did Halvor know how the girl was treated in his absence? No doubt the people of the steading feared Borglind's wrath if they told him, and indeed they might resent the girl themselves. *But he would believe Groa,* she thought then. When they retired for the night, she would ask the Vœlva to help.

But the women were still sitting talking around the

fire when one of the servingwomen came and whispered in Borglind's ear.

"Is there a difficulty?" asked Groa. "You do not need to stay here for me."

Borglind shook her head, frowning. "It is only one of the thrallwomen. The little bitch is having a hard labor, and these silly fools are afraid."

"The Irish girl?" asked Bera. The woman looked at her in surprise, as if one of the benches had spoken, and Bera judged she was one of those for whom folk of lesser standing were scarcely visible.

"The Irish slave—" Borglind replied. "Halvor should have sold her with the rest."

"I have some knowledge of birthings. Perhaps I can be of assistance."

Groa, recognizing the tension in Bera's tone, raised one eyebrow, but she made no objection as Bera followed the servant, who was called Halla, out of the hall.

They had spread straw for the birthing in one of the barns. The Irish girl lay moaning, her shift strained over the great mound of her belly and the wadmal blanket thrown aside.

"How long has she been in labor?" Bera turned to Halla.

"Since this afternoon, I think, but she was afraid to say. Her waters broke during the feasting, and since then her pains have come hard and strong. The mistress will not grieve if she dies of this birthing, but it will go hard with us if the talebearers report any lack of care to the master when he comes home." The woman's voice held neither sympathy nor rancor. Halla was not unkind, Bera judged, but she could not afford to take risks for an outlander.

"You were right to speak up," said Bera. "Wyrd can wind a knotted thread, and it is not unknown for the son of a thrallwoman to end as master in his father's hall."

Halla looked thoughtful, and Bera knew her shot had

gone home. She hoped so, for she would need the woman's cooperation. She knelt beside the Irish girl and smoothed her hair.

"Don't fret, my dear, we will bring you through this—" she began, then took the girl's hands as her body tensed in another pain. The intensity of the grip told Bera how hard it had been, though the girl made no sound. "There, there, *mo chride*," a fragment of the speech with which her own mother had comforted her surfaced from the depths of memory.

As the girl's body relaxed, she clutched at Bera's sleeve and burst into speech in the Irish tongue.

Bera shook her head. "I am sorry. My mother was a woman of Ireland—just such a one as you, but that is all of her tongue I know. What are you called?"

"Devorgilla—" The girl's gaze went inward as her belly tensed again.

"Well then, Devor . . . gilla," Bera struggled to get her tongue around the name, "try to lie easy while I see how open you are—"

The blue eyes closed, but Devorgilla bit her lip as Bera probed, and was visibly relieved when she sat up again, smiling.

"You're doing very well, my dear. It hurts because it's going so quickly. Don't lose courage and very soon you will hold your babe in your arms."

The girl bit back a whimper and tried to smile. Bera drew the rune of the aurochs upon her belly, putting most of the energy into the down stroke to bring the energy of the womb into manifestation in the outer world. She drew a lake rune point downward, flowing from its opening, to ease the way, and the birch rune, with a prayer to Frigga and the Mothers, over all. But though the labor went more swiftly than most, midnight passed, and then the out-tide, and it was nearly dawn before Devorgilla's moans changed to grunts of effort as she began to bear down.

Bera knelt between her knees as the baby crowned,

and in another few moments received it, bloody and squalling, into the world.

"A manchild!" exclaimed Halla. "Halvor will be pleased! But he is ugly as a troll; he surely does not take after the Raumsdale kin."

The woman spoke truly, thought Bera, laying the child on a linen cloth. Even for a newborn his features were crumpled, his skull elongated and deformed beneath the abundant dark hair. But she had seen uglier infants grow fine and fair.

She let the cord drain, then tied and cut it, and handed the baby to the servingwoman to clean and swaddle while she waited for the afterbirth to come. Devorgilla lay panting, her belly still hard, though its mound was not so great as it had been. Bera watched her, frowning; then she pressed down on the taut skin of the belly, struck by a sudden surmise.

"There's another child here." She met Devorgilla's eyes, smiling. "You have twins."

The girl's eyes widened, and Halla made a sign against evil. Twins were not unknown, but they were uncommon, and uncanny, whether for good or for ill.

"Is it lying crosswise?" asked Halla, peering as Bera probed again. "You'll never get it out living—" she stopped as Bera glared.

"I've helped with the birthing of twin calves and lambs. This will be much the same. You must try to relax—" she looked back at Devorgilla, "while I turn the child." She drew the rune of the hailstone above the womb to alter the energy.

But this babe, perhaps enjoying having room enough at last in its mother's belly, was in no hurry to leave it. A gentle pressure had no result, and finally Bera greased her hand, grateful that she was small, and worked it up into the birth canal, gasping as a contraction gripped her arm. After an agonizing moment she touched first one tiny foot and then the other, and muttering another prayer to Frigga, gently tugged.

Devorgilla cried out, and with a rush the second infant slid free.

It was a girl, pale and limp, so that for the first agonizing moment Bera thought she had been too late. Swiftly she wiped the mouth and nose and lifted her by the heels, and was rewarded by a thin mewling as the baby began to breathe. This child was as fair and smooth as the other had been distorted, and as Bera finished cleaning her, she saw that the baby had delicately pointed ears. *She is as fair as one of the huldre-folk,* she thought, smiling. But the babe's back was firm and smooth, with neither hollow nor tail to be seen.

She finished swaddling the child and set her at her mother's other breast, poking the nipple into the tiny mouth until, like her brother, she began to suck and the plaintive mewling ceased.

"The protection of the holy gods be upon you," Bera whispered, drawing the victory rune upon each tiny brow. "Be you welcome to the world!"

"Both alive, and likely to stay so if she has the milk for them," said Halla. "Indeed you have been well-trained."

"The Vœlva is a woman of great wisdom, and gives the jarl good counsel. Halvor will listen to her as well when she speaks of her visit here," said Bera evenly. "So I think it would be wise to get mother and children tucked up warm in bed, don't you, so that all three will be here to greet him when he comes home."

Halla took her meaning, and by the time the sun showed above the hills, Devorgilla and her twins were tucked up in a boxbed in the servants' house, with a bit of iron bar hung from one of the posts to keep the huldre-folk away, for until the children had been named by their father and sprinkled with water to welcome them into the kin, they would not belong entirely to the human world.

The other servants went out to their work, leaving Bera to watch by the new mother, who was sleeping with her children by her side. And as the place grew silent, Bera, exhausted by the night's work, felt her eyes grow heavy and slept as well.

Bera lifted the boychild from the basket which was serving as cradle and settled him against her shoulder, patting him until his querulous crying turned to hiccoughs. He weighed no more than a cat, and the feel of his silky hair against her neck was a delight. He turned his head, nuzzling hopefully, and she laughed.

"See how he seeks his food! Surely he will be a warrior."

"Hungry?" asked Devorgilla. "But I just fed him—"

Three days after the birth her belly still sagged like an empty sack, but there was a color in her cheeks that had not been there before. Her milk had come in and she was gaining more strength every day. The babies had a good hold on life as well, though they seemed to have spent most of the past day crying.

"Some babies are like that," said Halla, who had borne six. "Always fussing, while the Norns gift others with happiness. But even those who fuss can grow well if they have enough to eat."

The girl had fallen asleep. Bera laid the little boy at his mother's breast and he began to suckle greedily.

"You must rest, and feed the babies when they cry. Has Borglind tried to make you work again?"

Devorgilla shook her head. "She has been kind. She sent good broth for me."

Bera blinked in surprise, but perhaps the woman might fear what her husband would say if she let the babies die. Bera gazed down at the two heads, fair and dark, and her eyes blurred. If she herself was fated to have neither man nor child, at least she could help these little ones grow.

It had been easy to tell Devorgilla to feed the infants when they cried, thought Bera as she finished changing the girlchild's clout and laid her back in the cradle. But for the last three days, it seemed, the twins had done nothing *but* cry. They drank Devorgilla's breasts dry at each feeding and screamed for more. But there was no other nursing woman in the steading. The babies were hungry, and their thin mewling filled the thrall-women's house and carried to the hall.

Some of the folk were beginning to mutter darkly that it was not natural for a human woman to bear in litters, like a beast. When twins were born, it was rare for both to survive. If the Irish girl could not feed them both, it would be best to choose the strongest and expose the other on the mound. Until they were named they were not fully human, and to let one die would be no crime. It was not done often, but in time of famine or great poverty, or if the child was deformed, folk accepted the necessity. Only Borglind said nothing, but continued to send the new mother bowls of broth and stew, until Bera began to wonder if she had mistaken the woman's earlier hostility.

Bera did what she could to quell the whispers, but the constant crying got on her nerves as well, and when she caught herself thinking that perhaps it would be better of one of the babies *did* die, she began to be afraid.

"Are you upset because it was you who delivered the children?" asked Groa. "I have helped bring many to birth, and some lived and some did not. It does not reflect on you."

"But these are both healthy babes! There is no reason that both should not survive. Yet if even I, who want them to live, find their crying hard to bear, am I not right to wonder if one of the folk of the steading, perhaps hoping to gain favor with the mistress, might do them some harm?"

Groa set down the kerchief she had been embroidering and considered her thoughtfully. "I have Gerdis here to help me. You are a grown woman, Bera, and you have learned most of what I can teach you. If you wish to tend the thrallwoman, you have my leave."

Bera stammered her thanks, but in truth, the Vœlva's faith in her skills only increased her anxiety. Groa would not have released her from her usual duties if she, too, had not felt there was reason to fear. If only Halvor would come home!

But the master of the steading did not return. It was Borglind, her brow furrowed in a convincing frown of concern, who came on the ninth day to the thrall's house to speak with Devorgilla, who lay propped up in the boxbed, her hair spread across the coarse linen like flame.

"It had been brought to my attention—" her glance flickered toward the cradled infants and Bera stiffened, "that your children do not thrive. They fret constantly, and are weak and thin."

As if to prove her point, the boychild's dark features creased and he began to wail. Bera picked him up and laid him against her shoulder. But the baby girl lay still, her pale skin almost translucent, watching them with unreadable gray eyes.

"It is common for babes to lose flesh after the birthing, but they will pick up when my milk flows more strongly!" Devorgilla's protest was silenced by her mistress' glare.

"Indeed, as you say, they were fine and lusty babes at birth," said Borglind. "I mean no harm to your children—if they *are* your children. . . ."

There was a silence as they all stared. Bera had been prepared for a claim that these were not Halvor's children, but what was the woman at now?

"I delivered them myself," she spoke up, "and will take oath on Thor's ring that they are hers."

"You delivered her babes," said Borglind, "but are these the same? The whisper that goes round the steading now is that they are changelings."

"Impossible!" retorted Bera. "We hung iron over the bed, and she has never been alone."

"Perhaps you did, but I do not see it there now." Borglind pointed, and indeed, though the thong still dangled from the post, the bit of iron bar was gone. "And after the birth did you not sleep, both of you, when all the other servants went to their work and left you alone?"

It was certainly true, but Bera was not about to admit it. "Woman, do you question *me?*" she challenged in as good an imitation of Groa's manner as she could manage. "I have walked between the worlds and faced the folk of the Invisible on their own ground. I warded this place before the birth; if anything uncanny had entered it, even while I slept, I would have known." She believed that was true—she hoped it was, and that she was not herself being deceived by pride.

"It may be so, but there can be no profit in rearing a changeling, and I would fail in my duty to my husband if I allowed him to raise a child of the Invisible as his own!"

"If they are changelings, then the huldre-folk must be made to give them back!" Halla exclaimed. "My mother's cousin had a baby taken by the folk of the hill, and they got it back safe and sound."

"But how did they know? What did they do?" Now everyone was babbling.

"You put the child on the floor and sweep around it for three nights running, is it not so?" said Bera, attempting to gain control of the situation once more. "On the third night, take both baby and sweepings out to the refuse heap. The huldre-mother will come with your own child, complaining that she never treated it so badly as you have dealt with hers, and you can make the exchange."

"Yes!" Halla nodded vigorously. "That is exactly what I heard!"

Bera met Borglind's gaze with a bland smile. The

babies would come to no harm by being set on the floor. There were other ways of testing a changeling, involving fire or water, that were less benign. Devorgilla, holding the other child to her breast, looked from one woman to the other fearfully, but Bera's smile reassured her, and she held her peace.

"Shall we do that, then?" Bera's grin broadened as she saw Borglind's mouth open and close again as she failed to find any reason to refuse. "Halla, bring me a broom!"

By the next morning, Bera realized that she had only postponed, not removed, the danger. By agreeing to test Devorgilla's twins, she had tacitly admitted that Borglind's accusation might be valid, and that was enough to set tongues wagging for miles around.

"Half of them are already convinced the babies are changelings, and they will hold that opinion whether a troll-wife appears to claim them or not," she said to Groa that night when the second sweeping had been done. The Vœlva sat on a bench by the long hearth with Bera at her feet. The coals made a welcome warmth, for autumn was advancing and the nights were chill.

"Are you so sure the babies are human?" asked the Vœlva.

"I washed and swaddled them when they first came from the womb. I know every hair on their heads. My flesh knows them, Groa, as if they were my own!"

"But they are not your own. You must remember that, however things fall out here."

Bera nodded. "I'll remember." Her own gaze slid away from that of the Vœlva and fixed on the figured hangings on the walls. Was it the flickering light, she wondered, or the draft behind them that made the figures seem to move? She told herself that her own feelings did not matter so long as the twins survived.

"One good thing has come out of this," she said then. "When Borglind was being so kind, I had no reason to suspect her, but now that she has shown her hostility I cannot help but wonder what was in those soups she so carefully prepared for Devorgilla. Certainly it was not the huldre-folk who removed the bit of iron I hung over the bed. I've arranged with Halla that the girl shall eat nothing but what we prepare for her, and we are giving the babies a little goat's milk until her own improves. They are sleeping better already."

"Perhaps that will satisfy the doubters," said Groa, but she did not sound as if she believed it.

"If it does not, will you use your powers to help us?" asked Bera, gazing up at her teacher's face once more.

"My powers?" Groa raised one eyebrow. In the shifting light her face showed alternately serenely beautiful and ancient as the crags. "You have been with me for five years; have you learned nothing, girl? My gifts are worth little if folk will not believe. And here, I am not the Vœlva who walks with the Invisible, but Gerdis' mother. For her sake I must remain neutral if I can."

If you can? Bera clung to her knees, and after a few moments Groa sighed.

"If you are endangered, I must aid you. You are my daughter, too. . . ."

Then those twins are your grandchildren, thought Bera fiercely, *for I love them as if they were my own.* But she did not say so aloud.

On the third night, the twins were laid for the last time on the rough planks of the floor. Devorgilla swept carefully around them, as if to delay the moment when the children would be taken out into the cold. Bera watched her with mingled sympathy and exasperation. Was the girl afraid the babies *were* changelings? One way or another, they would be better off the sooner this was done.

The folk of the steading watched with barely suppressed excitement. This tale would be all over the district before a moon had passed, and an eyewitness account ought to be good for a drink or two at the next fair. But Bera managed to get most of them to stay back, peering through the doors and windows, when the babies, swaddled warmly, and the sweepings were put into a basket together and Devorgilla carried them outside. Only Borglind and Bera followed to bear witness.

At least, thought Bera as the Irish girl lifted the babies from the basket and emptied the sweepings around them, the natural heat of the dung-heap would keep them warm, and they were too little to put anything in their mouths. But predictably, as soon as Devorgilla moved away, they began to cry. The mother was weeping as well, but silently, hiding her face in her shawl. Now, according to the stories, was when the huldre-wife should appear to upbraid her and return the human babes. But nothing stirred.

Presently the infants fell silent. The buildings were darker shapes against the dim line of forest beyond the fields. All shapes looked strange by starlight, even Borglind, a cloaked shadow waiting in the angle of the barn. An owl called once, and then again, and from somewhere farther off came the cry of a fox, answered by a chorus of barking from the steading's dogs. Then the silence crept back, invisible as the beings for which they waited, as Bera had expected, in vain.

She cleared her throat and stepped forward. "Devorgilla has done what you asked of her. Let us take these children back inside where they belong."

"The troll-wife did not come," said Borglind in a tight voice. She, too, came forward, and Devorgilla, who had been crouching a few paces from the dung-heap, got to her feet.

"No," Bera repeated patiently. "These children are not hers."

"Then they are something worse! Something so evil

that even the huldre-folk will not have them," Borglind cried, "evil as that red-haired witch who lured my husband to her bed! I must protect him from the evil, protect all of you! The troll-spawn must go to the mound!"

Her venom was open now, but to the folk who listened it made no difference. In her husband's absence, Borglind was master here. Bera heard the avid, growling undertone beneath their murmured commentary and shivered. She had heard it the summer before, when men watched a murderer die. They had been prepared for wonders, but tragedy would make as tasty a dish to serve up over a winter's fire. Devorgilla screamed as Borglind thrust the squalling infants back into the basket, and Halla held her. With an effort Bera kept herself from making a grab for them, knowing that if she tried to take the babies by force, she would be prevented, or worse.

"One night!" She pitched her voice to carry over the clamor. "Leave them to the Old Ones for one night, and if nothing uncanny claims them, or kills them, we will know they are blessed by the gods!"

"Listen to the Wisewoman!" called someone. "One night—" others took up the cry. "That's fair enough. We'll know the babes are human if they live till dawn!"

So near to winter's beginning the wind blew cold, but Bera dared not go back for a warmer cloak. Slipping on the stubble of the harvested field, she forced her shorter legs to keep up with Borglind's long stride. The mound bulked pale against the darker shadow of the forest. Where the stones protruded through the skin of soil there was a shadow, the entrance to the mound. For a moment light seemed to flicker above it. Bera blinked, and saw it again—the *hauga-eldrinn,* the ghostly flame that burned where treasure lay hid. But such fires gave no warmth.

At least, prayed Bera, who feared the supernatural

less than the cold, *let Borglind place the babies in the shelter of the stone,* and sighed in relief when the older woman bent and shoved the basket into the opening. From inside it came a thin wailing that carried clearly in the night air. *Freyr and Freyja, twin-born and blessed, watch over them!*

Borglind straightened and turned away, then stopped as she saw Bera waiting there.

"Go back. You have no right to interfere."

"I welcomed those babies into the world. You may drive me from your doors tomorrow, but this night I will stay by you, to hold you to your word."

"You dare—" she began, but Bera interrupted.

"For your own honor, let me bear witness. There will be many eager to carry the tale of this night's work when your husband comes home." As she had expected, that gave Borglind pause, and Bera went on, "The fate of those children will be decided by the holy gods."

"Very well," Borglind capitulated abruptly. "There is a shed at the edge of the field. We can wait there."

Bera had hoped that the long vigil might give her a chance to persuade the other woman to be merciful, but Borglind's harsh profile discouraged any attempt at communication. To her relief, it was not nearly so cold once they were out of the wind. What Borglind thought about she did not know, but none of Bera's own promises prevented her from spending the time in silent supplication. She had always honored the gods, but her dealings with them had been primarily in the course of her work with the Vœlva. It had been a long time since she had wanted anything enough to appeal to them on her own. And it was not the gods only that she should be addressing, she realized presently, but the alfs of the mound, and the disir who protected Halvor's family line.

From time to time Bera strained to see the mound,

but the only movement was that of the stars, that showed her the passing hours. Gradually her prayers became less desperate, and with the coming of calm, her mind opened sufficiently to receive, if not an answer, a measure of peace. Too great a peace, perhaps, because in the gray hour before dawn she passed from vigil into sleep.

It was not sound, but the lack of it that awakened her from a dream in which white-robed women danced in a circle around the mound. The regular rasp of her companion's breathing had ceased. Borglind had gone, but the ground where she had been sitting was not yet cold. Bera rubbed her eyes and glimpsed a ghostly figure moving through the mists that clung to the field. Cursing under her breath, she got to her feet and stumbled after.

Borglind stooped at the entrance to the mound, and Bera heard a sudden thin wail. The older woman was fumbling with the folds of her shawl—to cover the babies? No, she was trying to smother them!

Bera shouted, and like a small, furious, she-bear launched herself forward. But before she reached her, Borglind lurched away. Bera grabbed her arm and her momentum brought them both to the ground. The girl got to her knees, ready to fight, but Borglind lay where she had fallen, odd, choked sounds coming from her throat as she pointed toward the mound.

It was the mist, said Bera's ordinary self, that clung so thickly. But the priestess in her spoke otherwise. This patch of mist had a shape to it, that grew more tangible with every moment until she perceived a warrior, armed and helmed in the fashion of ancient days, sitting behind the basket that held the babies with his sword laid across his knees.

For a long moment she simply stared. The spirit stared back at her, in all ways like a living man, except that there was no color to him, and a strangeness—not emptiness, but something almost too alive for containment—in his eyes. Bera swallowed. Whatever he was, he seemed prepared to wait forever without a word.

"Bera I hight, the daughter of Steinbjorn," she whispered, remembering her training. "I walk between the worlds; I have wrestled with mighty powers. Say then, spirit, by what name shall I call thee, who hover by holy howe."

That uncanny gaze fixed on her for the first time fully, and she shivered, but she held her ground.

"Halfdan am I, son of Ulfgrim, kin to Halvor by many fathers. Long have I watched over well-loved land . . ." His eyes held hers, and she felt the whole long tale of years pouring into her memory. "Why," he said at last, "dost thou question me?"

"For the sake of these children, whom I would keep safe—"

His gaze moved to Borglind, who whimpered and hid her eyes.

"Not well hast thou warded them, but I have kept watch while the world moved toward dawn."

Bera flushed, but an idea had come to her.

"When Sunna rises, I will return them to their mother's side, but though they grow healthy, they are yet unhallowed. Say to me, spirit, who the Otherworld hast seen, if they are indeed of human kin."

Though Halfdan's figure still seemed solid, a wind was beginning to lift the mist from the field. A bird tried out the first notes of its song.

"Of my kin these babes have truly come," he said, smiling, "though father be far from home. As clanfather, I claim them; to them these names I fasten—" He bent over the girlchild and made a sign on her brow. "Alfhild she is, for to defend her the alf gives battle. And this one shall be Alfhelm, for he is crowned with my protection—" he blessed the boy.

And in that moment the sun rose over the trees.

The sudden light set myriad droplets of water ablaze. When Bera could see again, the alf was gone. For a confused instant she wondered if she had dreamed this. But the tally of Halvor's lineage sang in her memory, and the babies, their basket, and the cloths that wrapped them were quite dry, except for the drops of dew that glistened on each small brow.

"Alfhild and Alfhelm! Welcome to the world!" she whispered, scooping the infants out of the basket and tying her shawl to hold them. They did not cry, but as soon as they felt her warmth they began to rootle hungrily at her breast. "Best get you back to your mother, little ones!"

Borghild still lay where she had fallen. When the woman recovered, she might question Bera's tale, but the knowledge the alf had provided should be proof enough that the children were Halvor's kin. And yet, as Bera carried the babies back across the field, it occurred to her that there was a sense in which all children were changelings, bright spirits returned from wherever it was people dwelt between lifetimes to inhabit an infant's fragile body in an unfriendly world.

She would be sorry to leave the twins behind when she and Groa moved on. But they would not need her, for they had found their kindred. She understood now that her road lay elsewhere.

I was a changeling, she thought, *born among strangers, with gifts they did not understand. It was Groa who gave me a family. . . .*

DEATH-HUNT

by Raul S. Reyes

Raul S. Reyes has appeared before in these anthologies; his first story was in *S&S II*. *Sword and Sorceress* was a definite counter-effort to write in the sword & sorcery market, one of whose traditions I was trying to break—women in that field being regarded only as bad-conduct prizes for the standard Hulking Heroes.

The reason I began this series of anthologies was to give the heroines a chance at adventures of their own, and at first, understandably, most of my writers were female. Now, however, there is a long and honorable list of men who have become "token males" among our writers: Jessie Eaker, Lawrence Schimel, Rick Cook, and Raul.

Myself, I never met an editor who gave a tinker's curse whether I was a man, a woman, or one of Aldous Huxley's fifty million monkeys who given eternity and typewriters would (Huxley said) eventually write all of Shakespeare's sonnets. (Personally I have my doubts.)

This story reminds me of something Randall Garrett would have written. Except that while Randall was humorous, Raul is deadly serious. As in the story which preceded it, this is a tale of honor toward those in your care.

Istepped out of the mess tent to survey our camp. It was located on a hillside clearing near a path leading down to the stream's edge. The tents were strange in the dawn light, festive in their stripes and tassels and vivid colors. Not what I was used to for safari, but then, wizards didn't normally do the outfitting. The Otherworld wasn't what I normally led hunts into either.

I abandoned that line of thought. The fact was that I hadn't normally led many hunts, period. The opening up of the Otherworld to hunting parties had been a boon to the few women in the Guild of Guides and Hunters. I usually was the "assistant" to the main guide, usually a man, despite my talents and experience. But for some reason we women were the ones with the best success rate in this strange new hunting ground, and our bookings had suddenly grown like tarran weeds in spring. I was booked through the rest of my career. I'm MaCallan Arish, Professional Guide and Hunter. I was the Senior Guide on this safari.

This was only my sixth safari in the Otherworld, and I was glad it seemed normal, for a change. Whatever "normal" means in that place. It looked like a savannah, with short dark trees vaguely like parasols and wispy grass the color of straw. We were under a sky that had a vague pinkish tint at midday and more purple at night that my eyes were used to. From our hillside vantage point we could scan the grassland for quite a way. The wildlife looked familiar. On the horizon a herd of something that looked like wild cattle grazed near a stand of trees that would provide shade from the midday sun. The span of horn on the cows was good, easily as wide as I was tall, although that's not saying much. The bulls, which were not in evidence and might be solitary at this time of year, would go even better.

The only difference between what I could see in the distance and the wild cattle on the plains back home was the color. These were black. Not the black of my cat back home, named Shadow for obvious reasons. These were really black, so black they seemed to drink in light. So black that detail was hard to make out. Black the color of death. Which is what they were.

Don't ask me for the theoretical details. As part of my training for my new career I'd sat through a series of lectures on the theory of Otherworld ecology, geology, meteorology, and assorted other -ologies at the Academy of the Arcana at Dienni. Death lived, in physical, you-can-touch-it, it-can-touch-you form in this strange new ground. Along with a lot of other things, all of them seemingly hostile or hungry.

Most of the lectures had gone in one ear and out the other. But it seems that every death in "our" world has a physical form in the Otherworld. That doesn't mean a one-to-one match. It seems that death, like everything else in our world or in the Otherworld, breeds. So if we kill a few Deathbeasts, it won't slow down the death rate in our world. Death is a certainty. Naturally the Crown was quick to see the revenue enhancement possibilities and immediately opened up Otherworld lands to hunting, with the requisite fees and taxes. Those are the other certainty.

Breakfast was breaking up. Tanil Alana came up to join me. "Communing with nature?" she asked. I looked around before answering.

"Find me 'nature,' " I replied. She laughed at that. Tanil is my tracker, a Registered Witch, fully licensed and bonded, with a degree in Practical Thaumaturgy. She finds the game. I lead the client to the kill, and maybe do the kill myself if he loses his nerve. That's happened, now and then.

I hefted my custom crossbow. Behind us two saberhorn pelts and skulls were drying on the makeshift racks. The Wizard team that came with us included specialists who "fixed" the hides and heads of the trophies so they could be taken back in their Otherworld form to our world. Otherwise there'd be no trophies. One saberhorn had almost taken his own trophy in the form of one of our clients before he'd sent a crossbow bolt into the saberhorn's brisket. The saberhorn still had a lot of fight in him and I'd had to send my own bolt into him as a stopper. The box quiver at my belt held a dozen bolts, each spelled by Tanil. She had also spelled the short sword on the other hip. Killing Death requires special weapons.

We had four clients on this outing, and assorted hangers-on. One client came up to join us. I put on a neutral face. "Good morning," he greeted us jovially. I nodded in reply. Karran Taillan had made his money in wine, then invested in horses and built up the best stables on the banks of the Dienni River. With wealth had come a new wife, an honorary commission in the Dienni Royal Guard, and a large estate and manor on the banks of the Dienni RIver. He was busy stocking it with trophies of his hunts. I wondered whom he'd bribed to get to the head of this year's lottery for Otherworld hunting permits.

"Good morning to you, Ser Karran," I replied formally. I didn't like him. Call it instinct. Add in his wine-sop looks to a personality that had been found under a damp stone, and I found the fees he paid to be the best part of him. Tanil nodded in a friendly way. Karran looked at the horizon, eyeing the herd of Deathbeasts.

"Maybe some good bulls paying court to the ladies of the grassland?" he speculated. I smiled slightly at the weak witticism. Tanil pointed to some birds circling over the herd.

"Sorrowbirds," she noted. "For some reason they don't appear in mating season. But I smelled Deathcat scent over that way while we scouted it out yesterday. He's taking his meals from that herd. But the Deathcat is old, ready to cross over and match a death in our world. He'll have a head and mane on him worth the taking."

Karran nodded, licking his lips for a moment. He looked vulgar. I looked away at the herd. The females were arranged in a loose defensive formation. The calves were too small to see at this distance, but they would be in the center. Like all young ones they'd be frisky and anxious to bolt from mommy's protection and out into the wide world. Where Death waited. I made my decision.

"We can make the herd by noon," I said. "That'll give us time to scout the lay of the land and plan our approach at about the same time as the Deathcat starts his evening hunt." I looked at Karran. "If that meets with your approval, Ser Karran" He waited just long enough to make it appear as if it was his decision, then nodded in agreement. Deathcat trophies are quite spectacular.

The others were either heading back to the tents for whatever reason or joining us at the hitching line to saddle up and mount. Cheila MacLeish was the Junior Guide, only a couple of years younger than I. She was dark where I was light, raven-haired and slender where I was stocky and red-haired. Smart and tough. She'd be heading up her own safari in a year or two. A trio of apprentice guides rounded out our party. They were Cheila's responsibility.

Two other clients were joining us. One was another horse breeder from the Dienni banks, Arslan Ashailli. A spice and tabac merchant, he was old money, and had had the best stables on the river banks until Karran's runners had started winning most of the prestigious races. Arslan was lean and graying whereas Karran was heavy and red. Red of hair, red of nose, and red of eye. They were pretending to amiability, two sportsmen relaxing on a hunt together. Right, and if you believe that, I have some land on the Delta you may want to buy. To add to the brew, Arslan was Karran's de facto father-in-law. Karran's new bride, Salia, was Arslan's niece. Since her father had died a few years before, Arslan had been her guardian, and had given her away at the wedding. She was back at the tents. She was what you expected in a second wife of a wealthy man—all hair, curves, and pheromones.

The third hunter was named Ronelli Amandor and was a graduate of the Legal Academy who had practiced trade and bond law for ten years in Dienni. The other two were clients of his. He was a good-looking sort with what my aunt used to call "good prospects." But he was still unmarried, so I wondered. Still, he had an eye for the ladies. He'd given Tanil and Cheila an appreciative look, and Salia as well for that matter. Armand Do'Sateno was the fourth hunter in the party. He'd killed a saberhorn the day before and was still sleeping off the victory dinner. He was minor nobility and a retired Officer of the Royal Guard at Dienni. Not all that bad a sort, compared to the rest.

The mounts were good, the pick of both stables. Before we mounted, Salia and some servants came out with the hunters' gear. For safety's sake the arms were kept in a separate tent, with only short swords allowed in camp. The crossbows and box quivers were all custom-made by Purdum of Dienni. The short swords were chased in silver. Quite a stash of plunder. Salia made a production out of sending Karran off on the hunt, kiss and all, but I noticed the look she gave Ronnelli before heading back to the tents.

The nine of us mounted and headed off. Mercifully there was little talk along the way. The grassland was made for horses and we made a brisk pace through the warm morning air. The day would be hot by noon. We circled downwind for our approach on the herd, and the Deathcat that was preying on them. Stands of trees screened us as we neared the beasts. By noon we were close enough to scent the sweaty herd. I motioned for the group to stop and we dismounted.

Cheila made some hand signs, and one of the apprentices took the mounts away to some trees where there was shade and grass. With the other apprentices and Cheila to watch our rear, I led my little band to the largest stand of trees in the area. Tanil touched the side of her nose, a sign that she scented the Deathcat nearby. For all I knew he might be waiting under the trees. The approach was slow and stealthy. It was late afternoon by the time we made the shade of the trees.

I settled us under the largest tree, set the two apprentices to guard, and then took stock. Karran alarmed me. Years of wine and a sedentary life had taken their toll, and he was exhausted. Heat, the long ride, and the tension of a stalking approach had made his face red as a winter scarf. I unstopped a large gourd of water and poured him a hefty draught. When he had swallowed that and gotten some strength back, I gave him another.

"Feel better?" I asked. He nodded and grinned. I looked up at Tanil.

"What do you think?" I asked in a low voice.

"Let me work on him a bit," she replied. I slid aside on the cool ground to let her work and looked around while she settled in. Licensed Witches can do some practical healing, which qualifies them as Emergency Healers, although there are specialists for that in the big cities. She set her hands on his chest and closed her eyes. Slowly his breath and his color began to return to normal.

My own instincts were of more concern to me at the moment. Tanil was occupied with Karran, and so wouldn't scent a Deathcat unless it was right on top of us. That possibility suddenly seemed all too good. I didn't need to be a Licensed Witch to tell me that Death was nearby. Years of hunting deadly game had honed my own instincts. I checked my quiver by touch. The next bolt was ready and in the exit clamp. A slight pull would free it for use. I brought my crossbow to the ready and was pleased to see the others following my lead. My little team moved into a rough defensive line around the tree we were under. I slowly stood to get a better look around.

The shade that had seemed so inviting a short while

before now was threatening. Every shadow was a potential warning of an attack. The tension was something you could feel. The vegetation was sparse under the shade of the trees, but that only made the shadows more stark. The heavy foliage overhead made things worse. I heard crunching sounds behind me as Karran came to his feet and stepped to my side. I spared him a sideways look. Tanil had done fantastic work. He looked almost healthy.

"He's here," Karran breathed. I nodded. Slowly he pulled a bolt from his own quiver and loaded his crossbow. A soft rattle told me he was cocking it. I motioned to a spot in the line and he stepped into it, an apprentice and Arslan moving aside to give him room. He took up position in a good "ready" stance. At least he could do that right. Tanil came to my side and touched the side of her nose, then motioned toward the interior of the grove. I nodded, and waved her to the rear.

With hand signs I marshaled my tiny force into a fighting line. A Deathcat can weigh as much as three or four men, and it moves as smooth as silk and as fast as lightning. Suddenly the odds didn't seem so much in our favor. We started to move forward.

Midway into the grove the hair on the back of my neck stood on end. That was it. I shouldered my crossbow and looked over the sights at my stretch of the line. On the edge of my vision I saw the others follow suit.

Suddenly it happened. A shadow detached itself from the ground and came for us, angling to my left, toward Arslan and Karran. I heard the snap and whir of crossbows being fired and my own bolt shot into the side of the beast. There was a blue flash as the spell released its charge too far back to do much good.

The Deathcat snarled with a force that shook me to my soul. His dark bulk completely covered the body under him, and I saw his long black fangs slash downward. A body slammed into mine from behind and I went down, my crossbow under me.

Time is odd in that sort of situation. It seemed to flow like honey in winter, but he had barely raised his head for another slash before I had a second bolt in my crossbow and had cocked it. I fired without aiming, on my side on the ground, one-handed, and at point blank range. Not very elegant, but it worked. The bolt went in just behind the rib cage, angling upward.

I hit the spine, or whatever it had for one. He arched his back in the death spasm. His jaws opened wide and a rasping snarl escaped. Dimly I heard the sound of other bolts hitting, and the smell of spell charges unraveling on the impact. It's an odd smell, rather like the one that follows a lightning blast.

Cheila was pulling me to my feet. I remember yelling to everyone to pull the Deathcat off the body underneath. It took a while, but eventually it was off and we saw Karran's ravaged corpse. I didn't even think of asking Tanil to look at him. He was gone.

"Bring the mounts," I told one of the apprentices. She took off at a run. I looked at the other two. "Get to work cutting branches for a travois. Cheila," she looked up at me at the sound of her name. "You take charge of the clients. Get them back to camp." She nodded grimly and motioned Arslan and Ronelli to follow her, which they did. I noticed they didn't seem too upset. Somehow I wasn't surprised.

It took a while to load both Karran and the Deathcat on the two travois we made. Tanil did a preliminary "fix" on both, so they'd keep on the journey back to camp. Don't get me wrong. At that point I didn't care about any trophy. But Dienni Law and Guild regulations both required an investigation and report from me, as the Senior Guide. As a licensed and bonded Guide, I am an Officer of both the State and the Royal Guard, as a sort of unorganized Reserve, and both Civil and Military law gave me legal powers and authority in hunting lands while leading a hunt

I made Tanil ride a mount back to camp, with an apprentice as a guard. The rest of us walked alongside our mounts, who had enough to do pulling their loads. It was a long walk back, and it was dark by the time we reached camp.

Cheila took charge of the mounts and their loads, and I went to see Tanil. She was in her tent writing a preliminary report. She looked up from the parchment as I entered. I stopped at the look on her face.

"You brought back the Deathcat?" she asked. I nodded. "When I was 'fixing' it," she went on, "I noticed that a bolt had entered the mouth and lodged in the back of the throat. I left it in place. The fletching is Karran's."

"A good shot," I acknowledged. "But even the best shots don't always give a quick kill."

"True," she agreed. "But I was curious. Something seemed wrong. So Cheila and I went to the armory tent and checked the gear there." She reached to the ground next to her and pulled up a box quiver. It was fully loaded.

"All the spelled bolts were in the quivers set aside for hunting," she said. "These are the bolts they were using for practice. Watch." She pulled the top bolt out of the exit clamp. There was a soft snap as the bolts under were pushed up by the spring and the top one was gripped by the clamp. She set the bolt on the table top and held her hand just over it, her lips muttering just under my hearing. After a moment it glowed with a dim bluish light. It was spelled.

I cursed softly under my breath. "A switch?" I asked. She nodded. My mind raced. It was no longer a simple hunting fatality. I thought for a moment. "An accident?" I asked. She shook her head,

"I scent evil intent," she replied. She nodded down to the parchment. "I have so noted in my report." I felt relieved at that. A Witch Statement, either oral or written, has legal force in any Court.

I sat down on the other camp stool. The gate back to Dienni Prime would open in three days; there was no way to send a message back asking for an early retrieval. The Dienni authorities would take over then and do their own investigation. My own investigation would be perfunctory at best, since under law they could not be questioned without their consent without legal counsel present. And legal counsel was three days away.

"Any idea as to who did the switch?" I asked.

"No, it's too jumbled. Everyone had access to the armory and the practice bolts." I nodded.

"Motives?" I asked. She looked at me, cool brown eyes level.

"I doubt if anyone really liked him," she replied. "Arslan hated his guts, his wife married for money, so the gossip goes, and more gossip says she really would prefer Ronelli Amandor. He seems to return the interest. A nice, happy bunch."

"I'm surprised Arslan allowed his niece to marry him," I said, "if they were on such bad terms." She made a wry face.

"I'm a regular gossip tonight," she noted. "I hear she was 'hot stuff' among the fast young blades in Dienni society. A potential scandal if she wasn't married off soon. She was also socially connected, and good looking. A good catch for a social climber like Karran. Arslan may have thought they deserved each other. His idea of a good joke." I took a deep breath as I digested what I'd heard.

"By the time we get back to Dienni, the trail will be stale and cold, and it'll be only good luck if the Board of Inquiry finds it more than just a hunting fatality."

"Whoever did the switch was clever," Tanil agreed.

"Let's look at the Deathcat," I suggested. "I still

have to write my report, and I want your views." She nodded and followed me out into the starlit night.

We had company. Armand Do'Sateno was viewing the Deathcat as we approached. He greeted us with a nod and a grunt. He was an elderly sort, still in good shape, and a good shot. Guides wish for more clients like him.

"Evening," he said as we approached. He nodded down at the 'cat. "Ugly brute, eh?" I had to agree. Deathcats can have an elegant, if deadly, grace, but this one was ugly. The jaws were propped open, and I took a torch and played the light into the dark cavity. I could just see the tattered fletching of the crossbow bolt. The head and shaft were deeply embedded in the back of the throat.

"Good shot," I commented.

"Hum, yes, yes," the old soldier agreed. "Good man, he was. And a good shot, even after all this time." I looked up in puzzlement. He saw my face and went on. "Yes, back before your time young girl, in the Guards. We served together in the campaigns against the Upriver bandit kings. Good man. Too bad he left the Guards to take up trade."

"So that was it," I breathed. He gave me a questioning look. "He handled his weapon well," I said, "as if he'd been trained. And he took his place in the line like a trooper." A small smile appeared under the graying mustache. He grunted and nodded in agreement and approval.

I motioned to Tanil. She came up next to me to peer into the fetid maw. After a moment she reached in and held her hand over the fletching inside and muttered something. Nothing happened.

"A practice bolt," she said. "That clinches it. There was a switch."

"A switch?" Do'Sateno asked.

"This is a practice bolt," I told him. "Someone appears to have replaced one of Karran's spelled bolts with an unspelled bolt." Surprise was rapidly replaced by anger on the old soldier's face, to be followed by a grim look.

"Any suspects?" he asked. Tanil gave him a quick rundown on the situation, including the legal complications. He had his own opinion of those, using a soldier's phrase I won't bother repeating.

"Not like in the old days," he said. "Military Tribunals gave us a way to rid the land of the bandit kings." I grunted something noncommittal, and Tanil and I stood. I looked down at the Deathcat, recalling tales I'd heard years before. One of my instructors at the Guild House had lost an arm in those campaigns, scouting for the Guard. Those had been hard campaigns, and he had mentioned the Tribunals with which the Guard had meted out swift and certain justice. Hard justice for hard times. So there had been more to the wine seller than I'd thought. I revised my opinion of him, too late to do him any good.

Don't ask me when the idea came to me. It may have been while Do'Sateno was talking about the old days, or maybe while I was wallowing in guilt over my rash judgment of Karran. But I looked up at my two companions.

"Ser Armand Do'Sateno, Sera Tanil Alana," I said. They looked at me, Tanil startled by my formality. I went on. "We are out of communication with the Dienni authorities. We are in foreign ground." They both nodded. No doubt about that, the Otherworld was as foreign as you could get. "As such we are governed by Military Law." That was a sophistry. The Guild used Military Codes as a guide for Otherworld safaris for want of anything better. It was all too new.

"Why, yes, we are," Do'Sateno replied, his face lighting up. Tanil looked a bit more dubious.

"I'll want to consult my Lawbook," she said.

"Please do," I went on. "Ser Karran Taillan was an Officer in the Guard, was he not?" I glossed over the fact that it may have been honorary. "So his death was an offense against the Guard." Do'Sateno nodded slowly, his face grim. "So, unless Talin's research says differently, we can convene a Military Tribunal, and call all likely suspects to Oathspell, even without their consent." They both looked at me, Do'Sateno elated, Tanil somewhat dubious.

"I don't know," she said slowly. "Let me look at my Lawbook." I nodded and she left us to go to her tent. Do'Sateno and I went to get a cup of wine and we talked, mainly about the old days and campaigns, while we waited. It was just for something to do. After a short while Tanil rejoined us.

"I think we may be able to get away with it," she said.

"Excellent," Do'Sateno said. I was more subdued. My initial enthusiasm had subsided a bit. But it was too late to backtrack. We spent the rest of the evening planning, after I'd had a few words with Cheila.

Dawn came up with a clear sky and a spectacular sunrise in the hills behind our camp. Those hills were still casting long shadows across the plain when I called the camp to assembly after breakfast.

"Under Guild Codes, Military Codes, and Dienni Statutes governing expeditions in foreign lands," I began, "I convene today a Military Tribunal to investigate the death of Ser Karran Taillan, Citizen of Dienni and Officer of the Dienni Royal Guard." I looked around. Both Cheila and I were armed with short swords, with our crossbows slung to shoulder. Ser Do'Sateno wore his short sword, not a dress sword such as a gentleman might wear, but an old and worn Guard issue sword. The three apprentice Guides were armed as Cheila and I were. In addition two of Do'Sateno's servants also were armed, sword and crossbow, with the latter at port arms. They had the look of old soldiers, and probably were.

"Under the codes and statutes just mentioned," I

went on, "I, MaCallan Arish, Senior Guide of the Guild of Hunters and Guides, Convene this Tribunal. Sera Tanil Alana, a Registered, Licensed, and Bonded Witch, will represent the Academy of the Arcana and the Witches Guild. Ser Armand Do'Sateno, Officer of the Royal Guard, will represent the military." Camp stools and a table were set up in the lower clearing. We moved to our makeshift Court and began.

It was pretty much cut and dried. We took statements under oath from everyone. I, Tanil, and Do'Sateno made our statements under Oath. It turned out that everyone had access to the tent used as the armory, and the switch, which we were careful to present as a possible accident, could have been done by anyone. By noon we had done the basic groundwork and we recessed for lunch.

Over broiled saberhorn, which is good, Armand, Tanil, and I plotted strategy.

"Getting the three to agree to Oathspell may be difficult," Tanil commented.

"We can so order it," Do'Sateno said.

"We can," I agreed. "But let's try a bit of subtlety first." I outlined my plan, and got agreeable smiles in response.

The Tribunal reconvened after lunch. Cheila had charge of the Court Guard scratched together from the three apprentices and Do'Sateno's two servants, and she had them posted strategically on either side of the assembled camp. We started.

"Ser Arslan Ashailli, Sera Salia Taillan, and Ser Ronelli Amandor," I called out. "Please come forward." They had front row seats, and stood to stand before us.

"There is a remote possibility that Ser Karran Taillan may have inadvertently, or perhaps deliberately, replaced the spelled bolt with a standard bolt." A very remote possibility, but I was being honest about it. I went on. "The tribunal wished to question you three, as close associates of the deceased, regarding his possible state of mind, and perhaps any personal or business matters that may have affected his judgment or actions." I stopped for a moment to gauge the effect on them. So far none. I went on.

"Because of the possible sensitive nature of your testimony, it will be taken in private with the Licensed Witch-Juror of the Tribunal, under Oathspell. She will report to the Tribunal only that testimony relevant to the case at hand, if any."

I stopped, and it was easy to see what was going on in the minds of the three before us. Anyone of them would be glad to dish out dirt on Ser Karran, especially under Oathspell, and if it was found relevant and made part of the Tribunal record, so much the better. And if there was a guilty one among them, he, or she, would not want to call attention by refusing to testify. And I had not said that Tanil would ask about the possible switch. But then, I hadn't said she wouldn't. After some hesitation Ronelli Amandor nodded and said he'd go first. Salia and Arslan followed, with Arslan showing some reluctance, but evidently deciding to go along with the procedure. Cheila secured Tanil's tent, where the testimony would be taken, and Amandor was led in.

It took a while. Oathspells are not easy, and legal interrogation under them requires care in the procedure if it is to hold up on appeal. But finally it was done, with Salia being the last to leave the tent. I recessed the Tribunal for tea and met with my two Co-Jurists.

"Do you feel well?" I asked. Tanil was pale, but otherwise seemed in good spirits.

"I'm fine, but you won't believe what I have to say."

"We'll see about that," I replied. By law she could not reveal testimony under Oathspell except under Court Process, so we would have to wait until I reconvened the Tribunal. But I could wait. We finished our tea and returned to work.

"This Tribunal is reconvened," I said. "And Sera Tanil Alana will report on testimony made under

Oathspell by Ser Arslan Ashailli, Sera Salia Taillan, and Ser Ronelli Amandor, that is relevant to the case under consideration. Sera Tanil Alana, please report." She stood and faced the assembled camp.

"I, Tanil Alana, Registered Witch, Licensed and Bonded by the Academy of the Arcana at Dienni, have this day questioned under Oathspell the three Citizens identified already by Sera MaCallan Arish.

"I have determined that all three had animosity or perceived cause against Ser Karran Taillan. These ranged from perception of unfair business practice to neglect and abuse and alienation of affection with the lure of great wealth and prestige." It was nice of her not to assign grievances to individuals.

"I have also found that all three did willfully and with evil intent attempt to substitute an unspelled, standard crossbow bolt for the first bolt in Ser Karran Taillan's quiver, replacing the practice bolt in the racks with the bolt removed from Ser Karran Taillan's quiver.

"I was unable to determine the exact order in which each acted, alone, and unknowingly to, and of the other two. But it appears, from my questioning, that the first one to act removed the first spelled bolt from Ser Karran Taillan's quiver, and replaced it with an unspelled one. The second one reversed, unknowingly, that action by replacing the unspelled bolt in Ser Karran Taillan's quiver with the spelled bolt taken from the quiver holding the practice bolts. The third, in turn, reversed the action of the second one to act, by removing the spelled bolt from Ser Karran Taillan's quiver and replacing it with an unspelled bolt. That was the bolt that failed Ser Karran Taillan in his confrontation with the Deathcat yesterday.

"While only two actually replaced a spelled bolt with an unspelled bolt, we are unable to determine who they were, and I note that actions with intent to commit felonies are themselves felonies, regardless of the success or failure of the acts. So I pronounce Ser Arslan Ashailli, Sera Salia Taillan, and Ser Ronelli Amandor are all guilty of attempted murder, by their own testimony, given under Oathspell, this date."

She sat, to a stunned audience. I looked at the three responsibles. They looked back, stunned. I didn't blame them. Armand recovered his wits first.

"Cheila MacLeish," he ordered in a tone many Cadets would have been familiar with, "take charge of the prisoners, and keep them secure and separate until they can be turned over to Dienni Court Authority." Cheila actually snapped to attention before giving the necessary orders. I recovered my presence of mind in time to properly dismiss the Tribunal. Then we went to the mess tent for a cup of wine. We all needed one.

It was late, and the cooks put together a scratch meal for the camp. It was good and informal. The day's events were all the talk of the tables, and we rehashed the outcome. But I noticed Tanil was being quiet and sober. I put it down to the work she'd done that day. Oathspells are hard to do.

After the meal had broken up, she came to Armand and me and asked us to accompany her. She led us to the Deathcat that had killed Karran and pointed down at the head. "Notice something?" she asked. Armand and I took a hard look and shook our heads. "Let me help," she said. She placed her hands on our heads.

The sensation was odd, a curious combination of languor and sharpness of sense. Tanil was sharing, extending actually, her Witch Sight, letting us see what she saw. I looked down at the Deathcat body, seeing nothing at first. Then it hit me.

"It's Karran!" I exclaimed.

"By gods profane and defiled!" was Armand's reaction, rather poetically I thought.

"Yes," Tanil said. "It's really Karran's death. Both

were old, and the Deathcat was ready to cross over to meet Karran at his life's end."

Tanil let go and the vision faded from my sight. But not the memory.

"Karran Taillan was fated to meet his death here," Armand breathed, almost in disbelief.

"I don't know if fate is the proper word," Tanil replied. "There may be forces of nature or the Arcana that are at work here in ways we are not aware of. Or it could simply be the most bizarre happenstance. But that was Karran's own death he was hunting, and it found him." We stood there for a long time, each with our own thoughts, before breaking up and going back to our tents.

It's the winter season here in Dienni as I write this final report. A Dienni Court found all three guilty of attempted murder while on safari in the Otherworld, and severe fines were levied. Arslan Ashailli still has his estate, but was fined most of his fortune. Ronelli Amandor was stripped of his right to practice law and fined heavily. He married Salia and they went to live with her Uncle. She lost her right to inherit from her dead husband's estate, which was divided up among his relatives.

I have the fangs from the Deathcat on my wall over the fireplace. Armand and I wrote a book (with help from a professional writer) about the events of that safari, and made a nice sum from it. The proceeds from the book bought me a nice house on the better side of town. I still lead safaris, but I wonder, if somewhere, there is a Deathcat waiting for me. Tanil says that is possible, but death finds us all, wherever we may be. I'll see. . . .

A SINGLE SOUL

by Deborah Wheeler

Deborah Wheeler is another member of our "extended family" who has written various stories for most, if not all, of my anthologies. By now, she has appeared in many anthologies and even has two novels in print (*Jaydium* and *Northlight* from DAW Books).

She has two daughters—it would not be correct to call them little girls any more. Sarah is now looking at colleges, and Rose, a baby when I first saw her, plays the piano remarkably well. In fact, they both do. Although, quite properly, they don't really care to be shown off to visiting adults.

Who knows, one or both may even grow up to be writers.

Deborah's story, like Diana Paxson's, is about twins, and the preparations and the strange journey which frees them.

On the night of the summer solstice, a breeze rippled through the plainsgrass and whispered to the Azkhantian nomads as they lay dreaming in their tents. To the east, mountains rose stark and silent, only the highest peaks still touched with snow. Below them, on a solitary hill, a bonfire set within a circlet of ancient stones sent billows of smoke to the heavens.

An aged *enaree*, his robes stitched with mystical symbols in threads of gold and blood-saffron from faroff Meklavar, labored to the top of the hill.

Two girls barely into womanhood waited for him, so

alike they seemed like a doubled image. The flickering orange light burnished their brown skin to bronze. They wore sleeveless jackets of camel-wool stitched with their tribal emblem, the lioness, and both carried short, curved bows.

Seylana, the younger by ten minutes, stepped forward. "We have prepared everything, even as you asked." With a tilt of her head, she indicated the fire, the pots of nightskull and orienna root, the young man poised over his drums.

"It is you, my daughters, who have asked," the *enaree* replied in his quavering, singsong voice. He raised his hands, accompanying his words with intricate gestures. "Not asked to be born as you were, one soul split between two bodies, but asked to be reunited, to be made one. The risk of such a Change is great, the risk of death, the risk of madness. The risk of the shadows which lurk in the dark of the eclipse."

Meriadess shivered at her sister's side. "Qr . . ." She whispered the single syllable.

"That's just an old legend." Seylana bit her lip. "It must be. What clan would follow the totem of a scorpion?"

The *enaree* shook his head. "At the solstice, in the time of the eclipse, the walls between the worlds grow thin. Power flows freely. Power to bring you through the Change. Power to give flesh to your fears. Think again if you truly wish to do this thing."

"We are Azkhant." Seylana tossed back her bronze-gilded hair. "We fear nothing." She had always been the bolder of the two, the first to tame a pony to her hand or ride out to hunt the savage plains boar.

Her sister said nothing, only gazed into the brilliance of the fire.

The *enaree* took a handful of orienna and one of nightskull and threw them into the fire. As the flames shot up, filling the air with pungent smoke, the boy began drumming. Seylana listened for a moment before laying aside her bow and unfastening her jacket. She knew all the rhythms of war and dance, but this was different, like an echo of her own heartbeat.

The *enaree* drew his cloak tighter around his bony shoulders despite the mildness of the summer night and the heat of the fire. Eyes grown far-sighted with age searched the heavens.

Naked, Seylana faced her sister before the fire. The drums were louder now, the sound filling her head and resonating through her bones. She raised her hands, palms outward, pressed against an invisible barrier that separated her from her sister.

Seylana closed her eyes and hummed in their secret language. Meriadess merged her voice with her sister's into a single pure note. Music, like spirit, strained against the boundaries of flesh. Vision blurred as the two glimpsed the world from each other's eyes.

Their heartbeats pounded close and closer to the rhythm of the drums. They began moving as one, dancing to a single rhythm.

Darkness crept across the rim of the moon.

One fire-gilded woman reached for the other, a mirrored gesture in the honey-dense light. Twin bodies glistened like yellow marble, eyes locked on one another, arms reaching, fingertips spread and touching.

Touching.

The web glowed between their hands like a veil of molten gold. Their bodies bent and swayed, supple young willows tossed by a single wind. Linked by the glowing web, flesh churned out incandescent heat. The Change spread over their arms and legs, flaring brighter than the sun, dwarfing the bonfire in brilliance. Minds and bodies burned as one. Separate thoughts melted in that inferno, dissolving.

Abruptly, the drumming stopped.

Seylana's eyes jerked open. Breath seared her lungs. In the flickering shadows, a shape began to gather. Out

of the corner of her vision, she caught the flash of
silver in the amber light.

During those few moments, the radiant web had
thickened into a sticky membrane. Shadows flowed
beyond the ring of stones, gaining substance. The night
air crackled with unspent lightning.

Dark shapes seeped between the standing stones to
fuss into solid form. One figure loomed larger than the
rest, the scorpion badge of Qr glimmering on its brow.
A curved blade lifted into strike position.

Seylana glimpsed the sword. Despair lanced through
her, because she saw it not with the double vision of
accelerating Change but from a single viewpoint.

Too late—

The *enaree* rose from the darkness, his face laced
with blood. With an inarticulate cry, he threw himself
upon the shadowed Qr. The figure whirled, blade
slashing in a sweeping horizontal cut.

Seylana screamed as the blade touched her twin.
Shock chilled her to the core. The web flared and died,
falling away as powdery ash. She threw all her strength
into one last chance for wholeness, grasping through
exploding chasms of darkness for her twin, her soul,
her self. . . .

Brightness seared her eyes like a molten brand. A
breeze fluttered over her bare skin. Her fingers tightened around stalks of tallgrass which felt limp and
oddly sticky. Her back burned as if she had lain in the
sun all day. As she stirred, a dozen cuts on her back
and thighs broke open, stinging. But worst of all was
the feeling of loss beyond words, of utter emptiness.

I have lost half my soul.

She lifted her head, immediately dizzy. Even focus-
ing on the ancient sacred stones brought little comfort.
Squinting, she made out other shapes, the remains of
the fire, contorted lumps that might have been bodies,

tatters of colored cloth. She lowered her head and slept again.

Voices, murmuring, woke her a second time. She did not know them, although she knew she ought to. She could hear the sorrow in their words. Hands lifted her, wrapped her in a blanket that prickled her skin. She felt herself being carried, rocked like a baby. As if in a dream, she saw the familiar stitched felt of a tent overhead, the stylized lioness she knew like the beating of her own heart.

For days, they told her afterward, she lay in a fever. She ate the food that was placed in her mouth, she rose and walked at the healer-woman's command.

The camp moved on as the summer faded. At first, she was carried in a travois behind a sedate old camel. Later, she walked, drawing strength from the endless sky above and the smell of the plainsgrass sweet in her lungs.

The healer-woman had to explain the simplest things to her—her name, how to dress and eat and wash, how to draw a bow and sit a pony.

Why do I feel so alone? she would ask, sitting over her bowl of camel's curd-cheese.

You have lost your sister, said the woman who was her father's mother. And we have all lost our *enaree*. There is no one to guide you, my poor lost calf.

What was her name? Tell me again.

Meri, she would repeat as she lay awake in the milky hours of the night, holding herself as if she could enclose the emptiness there. *Meriadess*. With each repeating of the name, pain would rush up inside her, a wound beyond healing.

Summer burned the tallgrass into tinder. Storm clouds swept across the endless skies, bringing lightning and downpours. Nights turned chill. The Azkhanti turned their fattened herds of camels south, toward the winter pastures. Here the tribes gathered and traders from Gelon and far Meklavar brought their wares—salt and silver, amber, myrrh, and dried fruits—from the Spice Lands. Here the young men and women entered into contests of strength and bow-skill, danced and drank *k'th* into the long nights, played their harps, and found warmth in each other's tents.

Here Seylana heard once more the whispered name of *Qr*.

Along Gelon's northern forest border, the Meklavan trader said, bending over his knife blades, arrow heads, and sewing needles. Once or twice last summer, and then again at the autumn Turning.

No, his partner said, the Geloni didn't admit to the existence of such things. They built temples of stone, didn't they? and studied the stars with map and compass.

But they were good customers when it came to sword steel, the first insisted. Then a youth, a chieftain's son from the eagle tribe, paused to examine a set of bridle buckles, and there was no more talk of Qr.

Gelon, Seylana turned the name over in her mind. Gelon invaded Azkhantian territory when her mother was a child and had been thrown back at great loss of life on both sides. Such hurts were not soon forgotten. They might kill her outright, or think her a spy like the legendary Aimellina.

I am dead already, she thought, and went to pack her few possessions: some clothing, a small brazier of finely worked bronze that had been her mother's, her pony. She left her bow behind and went into the land of her enemies.

Seylana bartered her pony and one of her three knives for Geloni clothing, an onager trained for riding, and a handful of coins. The inn host took her money with a suspicious glance, but once she had left the border behind, everyone assumed she was Pithic. Azkhanti had never been known to travel peaceably through Geloni lands.

When her purse grew thin, she got a job as a live-stock handler for a caravan heading east, into the heart of Gelon. Traders picked up all sorts of useful information, anything having to do with the safety of the roads. Many rumors came to her ears: that the Ar-King was recruiting for a campaign against Meklava, that the border to Azkhant was open, that it was closed, that the wells at Borriventh were poisoned, that the scorpion emblem had been sighted in some isolated place. Late at night, with the onagers fed and tethered, she pored over the master's maps.

Here and then here . . . a pattern?

Emptiness throbbed, a constant companion.

She had to know more, to be able to move without suspicion about this land. Traders weren't the answer. Their motto was to keep as far away from trouble as possible. She wanted trouble to come to her.

The next morning, she headed for the nearest large town. She had to smash her way past two local bullies to enlist in the Ar-King's army.

The Meklavan campaign soon ended in another stalemate, and Seylana inched up in rank. Soon her sword and onager felt as familiar to her as her bow and pony once had. She drank, but not too much, and dreamed, but not enough.

Sometimes she would awaken in her barracks bunk, sweating and trembling, her fingers closed around the hilt of her sword. Her eyes would dart from one shadowed corner to the other, searching for something she had forgotten. Not even the taste of wine or the warmth of a lover's arms could fill the inner emptiness.

And every so often, she would hear the whispered name of *Qr*, and something inside of her would tremble like a bowstring.

From her place near the door, her back to the wall, Seylana could see both the public room of the inn and a slice of the dusty street outside. This late in the day, off-duty soldiers rubbed elbows with cattle drovers, traders, and crafters in iron and leather. She took a sip from her tankard, swirled it over her tongue. Geloni wine still tasted too sweet after the raw pungency of *k'th*. A low murmur flowed around her, from which her ears picked out an occasional word or phrase.

A thin, tall shape dimmed the slanting afternoon light. Her muscles knotted. Her knife slipped into her hand. She held it hidden and ready.

"We stand before you in peace," the man said, his voice soft. "There is no need for fear."

Seylana let out her breath. She had seen Geloni priests from a distance, but had never spoken to one before. Now it surprised her how much this one was like the *enaree* of her youth.

"How may I serve you?" she said politely.

He sat at her invitation, taking a backless stool from a nearby table. "The question is how we may serve you." Like all Geloni priests, he spoke of himself as a multitude. They believed all souls were one limitless sharing. They did not even have individual names. "You seek word of the forces of Qr."

Dry-throated, she nodded.

"Of such, we have gathered knowledge across the centuries," he said. "The true danger lies in ignorance. You have been asking questions."

"Will you answer them?"

"The path of knowledge is open to all who truly seek, and through that knowledge, the ultimate freedom, release from the tyranny of desires. We battle for good when we must, but we do not make a home for hatred, no matter how righteous, in our hearts."

She brushed away the suggestion that she could set aside all memory of what she had lost, of who she was and what she might have been, without the unspeakable evil of Qr.

"Most of what we once knew of Qr was legend," he said, "stories told to frighten disobedient children."

"More than frighten." *They have stolen half my soul.*

The priest met her eyes with a steady gaze, as if measuring her courage. "Of late, we have witnessed bodies found disfigured, wells poisoned, animals wandering witless."

Things glimpsed in shadows ... She shuddered against her will.

The priest pressed his seamed lips together. "When we clear our minds, we can sense how the fabric of the All has been torn."

Seylana had heard this before, spoken by herbal women at the Mherivar markets. Some said the rent grew wider with every passing moon.

"Through the ages, we have preserved our ancient writings," the priest said, "and in them, knowledge of the worlds beyond our own, of the nature of death and the soul. Do you thirst for such? Will you come to us and drink?"

She shook her head, Azkhantian style. "I am promised to a term in the Ar-King's army. And I cannot read."

Slowly he smiled. "We require no breaking of old vows or pledging of new. Come to us as you can and we will teach you."

I'm dreaming, she thought, even as tendrils of ice squeezed her heart. Any moment now, the shadows would begin to drift together, to take on arcane substance. And then would come the deadly glint of razor-honed silver. . . .

In the next instant, Seylana sat upon her war onager in the middle of a crossroads. She blinked to clear her vision. Her companion, a priest she knew only slightly, knelt on the dusty road, absorbed in his prayers. Fields too poor and pocked with rain-eaten boulders for farming stretched along the dusty ribbon road. A few short-legged mutton picked at the slivers of yellow grass.

Stationed at Mherivar, she had acquired a lover and a reputation for looking into strange happenings. From the priests, she had learned to read and even write a little. So when a priest asked for an armed escort to Foresthold, she volunteered. Despite the inducements of bonus pay, few had offered, even the most hardened veterans. The captain would not send any of his people unwilling to such a place, out there on the border of myth and madness, not with the growing rumors of a nightmare, insectile shape glimpsed in shadows or dreamsmoke.

Now Seylana waited for the priest to mount up. She noticed the creases in his age-worn face, deeper than before.

"Whatever it is," she promised, touching her sword, "it will have to pass my steel to reach you." She said nothing of the pull which grew stronger within her every hour.

The priest looked doubtful. "We at Foresthold will protect us."

They continued down the little-traveled trail; the natural pacing gait of the onagers covered the leagues. Late in the afternoon, a line of ancient trees loomed on the horizon. They passed the first solitary trees, whose straight trunks bore no kinship with the tangled, knotted giants ahead. The sun dipped below the horizon, leaving an eerie green dusk-light below the canopy of leaves. Shadows took on the texture of clotted ink.

In the gloom, Seylana's vision lost its focus. Misshapen figures seemed to move beneath the tree trunks. Her palms itched inside her leather gloves, a warrior's certain omen of fighting ahead.

Sometimes, in the chill hours of the morning, lying alone in her barracks bed or beside snoring Tomas, she wondered if it had not all been a dream, that night on the Knoll. Sometimes she could not remember the name of her sister or her voice or the touch of her hand on the harp.

And sometimes it seemed like yesterday, that loss hot and raw and bleeding. Wounds of the body healed; as a soldier, she knew this well. But there were other wounds which did not.

The onager shifted sideways, tossing its head. A tremor rippled through its body. Seylana took the reins in her left hand and drew her sword. The blade whispered as it left the scabbard.

"Stay back," she whispered to the priest. She could smell the sorcery in the air as she urged her mount forward, the familiar pungent smell of leaf mold overlaying something else. . . .

They rounded a bend, past a cluster of ashleaf trunks, all growing from the same massive bole. Filtered moonlight shone on the smooth bark.

Foresthold stood before them, a block of stone. The flames of its lights glittered unnatural blue against the night. Keeping control of her prancing onager, Seylana approached obliquely, circling through the night and curling shadows.

She completed a circuit of the hold and swung in for a closer look at the portal. It was closed tight, but the barred windows to either side were unshuttered. Seylana pulled the onager to a halt and peered inside. Within the hall, blue-green phosphorescence clashed with normal flames from an ordinary wood fire in the floor hearth. Five white-robed priests stood in a ring around it. Something about them, their erect stillness, reminded Seylana of the circle of stones on the Knoll.

A siege, raced through Seylana's thoughts, but she could see no invader, no enemy, no threat except the unnatural stillness of the place.

Seylana wheeled the onager for a better look at the door. From the corner of one eye, she caught a movement in the center of the ring. A robe flickered white as one of the acolytes dashed toward the portal.

The heavy wooden door swung open, wide enough for a mounted warrior to pass. Seylana glimpsed the panic-blind face of the acolyte, little more than a child, eyes and hands lifted in appeal. The acolyte rushed past her, into the arms of the Priest.

Seylana dug her heels into the onager's sides and the animal leaped forward. Its shod hooves clattered loudly on the glazed tile floor. The nearest priest looked up, his face etched with despair.

Seylana's war cry died in her throat. The shadows drew her eyes, caught her like a hapless bewebbed insect. They encircled—no, *strangled*—the hall. Slowly they began to take on solid form.

As they had before, so many years ago. As they had in her nightmares.

The natural orange fire of the hearth died in a billow of lung-searing smoke. Metal gleamed in the darkness. The nearest priest screamed once, horribly. Seylana whirled the onager to face it and slashed diagonally upward. Her sword pierced the swirling mist, a mist which immediately healed and condensed.

The onager coughed, a soft pathetic sound. It swayed, then toppled to the floor. Seylana jumped free and landed on her feet.

Seylana drew back into ready position, her heart hammering in her ears. She felt as if she had been training all her life for this moment, for what lay beyond that darkness.

The shadows deepened soundlessly. Suddenly, a curved sword appeared at chest level in the depths of the darkness, a blade held by a hand with seven taloned fingers.

Seylana parried the lethal sweep of the blade. She

danced away from its instant riposte. Her body responded as a second sword appeared, then a third. In the flickering ember-light, she glimpsed the outline of a head and shoulders. On the brow of the head was an emblem with armored pincers and a curving, stinger-tipped tail.

Cold fire sizzled through Seylana's veins. She wheeled and slashed, sweeping one blade away and stabbing past another. Death cries shivered the air. Summoning all her skill, she fought her way toward the tallest of the scorpion-badged figures. It drew back from a fallen priest, the last, and turned toward her. The hall fell silent, not even the slither of a leather sandal over tile.

Only the steady beating of her heart as she stood alone against the shadows.

Without thinking, she had taken up a two-handed grip, sword raised in a posture of power, her legs bent and body centered, one shoulder toward her opponent.

Meri, she thought.

The figure came at her.

She waited, staying on balance. The scorpion shape seemed to glow, to burn itself into her mind. Another shape, deeply buried, echoed it. This was the very creature which had haunted her nightmares. Still it came, shambling now as its form grew more and more solid.

Closer . . . closer . . .

It bent its arm, bringing its nightmare blade into position. Seylana sensed the opening before it appeared, felt the creature commit to the attack—and lunged.

A war cry splintered the air, hardly recognizable as her own. Power surged through her body, drawn through the point of her sword. The tip slid through flesh as if it were gauze.

She twisted, using both hands to guide the blade down and sideways for a killing stroke. Inky smoke poured from the wound, charring whatever it touched. Tears flooded her eyes. Her legs trembled. Breath caught and stuttered in her lungs. Vision wavering, she clung to the sword hilt and jerked with all her strength.

Suddenly her blade was free, slipping through empty air. She staggered, caught her balance, blinked her eyes clear.

Tatters of colorless fog melted. The hold was gone, the firepit, the bodies of the onager and the fallen priests. Even the surrounding forest, all gone as if they had never existed. She stood in a shallow depression of smooth-grained stones set so close that not a blade of grass could pass between. A dense silence pressed down on her. Her clothing had disappeared along with everything else. Instead, she wore a garment of some filmy stuff which clung to her body and yet did not hamper her movements. A braided strand of light, winking with a hundred points of liquid brilliance, ran from the center of her body into the distance.

Only the sword in her hand remained the same, familiar, battered, serviceable. Deadly.

Real. Perhaps the only thing in this eldritch place that was.

Slowly she turned to survey her surroundings. Gray stone stretched in every direction, forming a low horizon. But there were two twisted ropes of light, one stretching ahead of her, the other from her back, from the direction she had come.

With her free hand, Seylana brushed a fingertip against the light. Instead of heat, or perhaps a crackle of dry lightning as from silk rubbed over amber, her hand met only a pleasant coolness. She curled her fingers around it, testing its thickness and elasticity. A step forward was as easy as gliding over ice. Sideways, though, brought pain lancing through her body, so hard and fast her muscles locked and her breath froze.

She tightened her grasp on her sword and took a step forward, then another. The stone beneath her bare feet felt neither cool nor warm, neither rough nor smooth. The horizon grew no closer, nor did it recede. She glided along the rope of light in unbroken silence.

Gradually, she became aware of a thickening in the air, as if shadows gathered there. These shadows, however, were composed of light instead of darkness. At first, they hovered at the corners of her vision, disappearing whenever she turned to face them. When she called out, her voice came as a tinny whisper. She went on, watching as the diaphanous shapes grew thicker and took on a semblance of form, even as the Qr shadows had.

Abruptly, she reached the end of the stone depression. Before her, a hundred paces away, stood half a dozen figures, not these ghostly shadows but flesh like her own. She could not call them men, not with their narrow shoulders and too-many-fingered hands. Some kind of dark gauze wrapped their rounded heads, obscuring their features. But on each brow, a white band shone with the scorpion badge of Qr. No, she saw now it was not a true scorpion but a symbol of some sort, like the Meklavans used instead of ordinary writing. It was only human imagination that had given it the form of a deadly insect.

The ribbon of light ran straight into their midst.

Seylana raised her sword, felt the answering surge of power. Battle-fever pulsed through her veins. Her heart leaped eagerly, hungrily.

The figures waited, giving no sign of fear.

An instant before she was to begin her charge, they drew back, parting around her rope of light. Her sword lowered, and it was only by long hard training that she did not drop it entirely. She rushed forward, half afraid that the image would vanish as she neared.

A mirror it was, and yet not, that figure unscarred by the years, clad in the same filmy garment.

Meriadess.

Seylana's twin stood as if blind, her face giving no sign of either recognition or despair, joy or pain. She simply waited.

Seylana had thought to avenge her sister, not to free her. Heedless of the waiting Qr, she rushed forward. "Meri! Meri, come with me!"

She reached out her free hand . . . and met only air. Her fingers passed through the solid-looking form. Was this an illusion, a vision born of smoke and light?

No, she could feel the tie between them, the pull which linked the empty place in her heart with this mirror of her sister.

Seylana brought her sword once more to ready position. She turned to the nearest Qr. "Free her or die!"

"We cannot," a hollow voice rang in her mind. ". . . Cannot, cannot, will not . . ."

"Why? What have you done to her?"

The creature lifted its shoulders and shivered.

"Cowards and liars! You owe me kin-blood! You struck down my sister, along with the boy and the *enaree* of my tribe! I say again, free her now!"

"She is held by bonds we cannot sever." Again came that voice with its chilling echo. ". . . Sever, sever, never . . ."

Seylana took a gliding step toward the nearest Qr. "Then we will see what *I* can sever."

". . . Leave, leave, bereave . . ."

One of the figures stepped forward. A sword, no more than condensing cloud, appeared in its hands. Seylana slashed diagonally, starting at the join of neck and shoulder. The razored sword cut cleanly.

Solid-looking flesh healed itself.

Seylana parried its returning thrust. She lashed out, low and straight through the creature's belly. Again there was no wound.

She drew back, breathing hard. If she was not here to kill, what then?

She glanced down at the braided light joining her on one end to her sister, on the other to—what? She had thought it was to her own death in the blood-spattered Fortress. Now the thought crept into her mind that she was tied to life.

And life itself linked through her to her twin-bonded sister.

And through Meri, evil now had a gate into the world.

Qr had burst through the walls between the worlds, doubly thinned by solstice and eclipse, on that night on the Knoll. In the natural order, the priests taught her, such a thing could last but an hour. But now they had a door which could not be closed as long as she and Meriadess were still linked.

It would be a simple thing, to cut the cord to the world of the living to stay here with Meriadess. Perhaps she would spend all eternity battling the Qr. As long as they were together . . .

Meri?

Seylana gazed into the eyes which were so like her own. There was no response, not even a flicker. Sadness swept through her like a wave. The old wound throbbed, subsided. She could never take her sister into her arms, hear her voice, share the breath from her lungs. Whatever happened now, Meriadess was lost to her forever.

To save the living world, Gelon and Azkhant and all the wide lands beyond, she would have to release Meriadess. To let go of the emptiness she had hoarded like a precious treasure over the years.

Seylana looked down at the sword in her hand, at the bonds of light. With a single movement, she brought the sword down and slashed through the tie between herself and her sister.

The image of Meriadess winked into nothingness.

Seylana's sword shrieked, as if in human agony. Light exploded around her. The air splintered with sound. Stone shattered, bursting into flame. The dangling cord shriveled. She felt herself moving backward through space at breathtaking speed. Her mouth opened in a soundless scream. Qr receded in the distance, swept up in the maelstrom.

Wind howled in Seylana's ears. She tried to cover them, but her hands would not obey her. Her body twisted and bucked, yet still she went faster. A shivery weakness seeped along her veins. Her head lolled, her heart faltered.

She landed in a graceless clump on a hard cold floor. The sharp-edged stones bit into her palms. She blinked, shook her head. She was in the middle of the hold, morning light sifting through the eastern windows. Her sword, its blade blackened and warped, lay beside her. With a snort, the onager scrambled to its feet. Moans came from across the room. The priests held out their arms to one another, their cries like the cooing of doves. Seylana's priest and the child acolyte rushed in through the portal.

Seylana watched them, apart. When the onager ambled up to her and thrust its whiskery nose at her shoulder, she patted it absently.

The eldest priest, a man with skin like leather and eyes bright as garnets, held out his hands. His fingers, strong and warm, encircled hers.

"We have closed the gate." He did not mean the priests had done it, but that they now included her in their midst.

Seylana saw then how she had moved through her own life like a Qr shadow, defined only by what she had lost. By her own choice, she could never go back.

Outside the hold, a bird burst into song. The first rays of dawn sifted through the unshuttered windows. One by one, the priests sank to their knees and held up their hands to the golden light.

Something inside Seylana rose to meet the new day, whole and strong. She no longer felt empty, but over-flowing with grief and joy, anger and contentment, all jumbled with the sudden discovery that her half-sized soul had somehow grown to fill the entire world.

THE NEEDLE AND THE SWORD

by Jessie D. Eaker

Jessie Eaker says that despite the traditionally female spelling of his name, he is male; Jessie, with an ie, is the Eaker family's traditional spelling. He adds that his family name, Eaker, is pronounced more like "acre" in his native country in Richmond, Virginia. He admits that this causes both gender and phonetic confusion, but he is proud nevertheless to bear a name so rich in the South's history. So far, he has sold four other stories to *Sword and Sorceress;* it seems to me that other editors are missing something good.

He says he works as an "information consultant" (whatever that is) for a Fortune 100 company based in Richmond. He adds that he and his wife Becki "are kept constantly busy with all of our exceptionally bright and talented children." I'm not sure whether that is a sentiment seemly for a father, or an objective reality, but whatever it is, more power to him.

Jessie says his story was inspired by his wife's needlework supplies, which share the walk-in closet he uses for an office.

At the sudden commotion coming from the courtyard, Ora looked up from her sewing—a sudden sense of dread clenched her stomach. There could be no mistaking the clopping of horse's hooves, the hails of the guards, or the orders to call Mistress Trista. *It couldn't be time. Not yet. Not again.* She stared down at the growing pattern of black stitches on the red gown. She had just finished a single lonely petal of what would become a simple flower. After all these years, despite her fading eyes and the slight tremble in her hands, she could still add beauty to the plain. But she doubted if she would be allowed to complete the pattern anytime soon.

New victims had arrived.

She tried to ignore the sound drifting up to the tower window, tried to make her needle go back into the fabric. But her hand stayed frozen and her fingers stiff and unmoving. Fighting the impulse, but unable to resist, her gaze slowly drifted across the cold stone of the wall to the slit of a window which provided the light for her work. From her stool, all she could see was the calm blue sky and a few lazy clouds—belying the clamor she heard below.

It was better not to look, she told herself. Better not to see them at all. She turned back to the robe and managed to get her fingers started on another careful stitch . . . when she heard a change in the situation below. An exclamation of pain. And the wail of a child.

"Mother!" came the haunting cry of a young girl.

Instantly, Ora found herself standing at the window, her heart pounding in her chest. She still clutched the gown and her needle.

Below, two struggled against their captors. The closest was a young woman, her dark hair loosely captured in a long braid and wearing a torn blouse and dirty leather pants. One of her sleeves was torn, allowing a view of the hardened muscles beneath, which along with her stance, indicated one accustomed to battle. With hands tied behind her back, she struggled with the two guards restraining her. "LEAVE HER ALONE!" she yelled.

Showing amazing strength, the woman jerked one shoulder free, and hinging on the remaining guard, jammed her knee into his groin. He crumpled as the other one reached to grab her from behind. She immediately squatted, his bear hug barely missing her head and throwing him off balance. Then bouncing on her haunches, she drove the crown of her head into his chin. Ora heard his teeth click together even from where she stood. He fell back stunned.

Go! Flee! Ora shouted in her mind. *The gate is still open. Save yourself.* But instead the woman ran to where another guard held a struggling girl of about eight or nine seasons. Ora was instantly mesmerized by the sight: the child had a beautiful delicate face and hair so blonde it was almost silver. It was as though her own Elita had been reborn. Tears sprang to Ora's eyes. *Elita had been such a beautiful child. And I failed her so badly. So completely.*

But this guard was no fool and swung the child between himself and the attacking mother. She tried to dodge around, but he shifted with her, holding the girl out like a shield. One of her original guards, still limping from his groin wound, tackled her from behind and forced her to the ground. Kneeling on her back and smiling in cruel victory, he pulled her head up by her hair and tensed to ram her face into the dirt.

Ora almost yelled out despite herself, but a tall, thin woman, just entering the courtyard, beat her to it.

"No, Alben!" she ordered. "I need her whole."

Alben glanced toward the woman as if contemplating defiance, but he quickly lost his smirk when he saw who it was. He scrambled to his feet and came to attention. "Yes, Lady Trista."

She waved him off in impatience. "Well, don't just stand there, let me see them!"

The three guards scrambled to comply and presented the prisoners to her. Even the girl had sense not to struggle.

Lady Trista started with the mother and examined her closely.

"You have no right to hold us!" the young woman spat. "We have done nothing wrong. Release us now, or my guard-sisters will take this place apart stone by stone."

Ora held her breath, praying for the prisoner's sake, that the mistress was in a good mood. Trista was extremely intolerant—even for a sorceress.

But Lady Trista simply regarded her in bored amusement. "A guardswoman. I thought you had the stench." She turned toward the girl and gently lifted the child's chin. With lips trembling, the young one gazed up at her in defiance. She made a quick move and the mistress jerked her hand back just in time to keep from being bitten. Trista laughed. "Spirited, like her mother, and so beautiful." She glanced toward the young woman. "She also has the gift. You should be proud. Either one of you would suit my needs."

The warrior lunged toward Lady Trista, but her captors held her back. "I said, let us go or when my sisters—"

With inhuman speed, Trista grabbed the young woman around the throat, choking off the warrior's air and lifting her a hand's breath off the ground. The warrior could only make choking sounds. "You are exactly right," Trista continued. "So we must take measures to make sure that your sisters don't find out—at least not right now." She eased off and let the mother have a gasp of air, but she did not let go.

Ora bit her lip, dreading what came next. She shook her head. No matter what Trista threatened—she wasn't going to do it this time. *I will not sew the pattern!*

"Now I do not think you understand the severity of your crime. On my lands, trespassing is punishable by death."

The warrior tried to shake her head no, but Trista held firm. "But I am fair—I will let one of you go." She smiled cruelly. "But the other will stay. You see, this body, while it may appear young, is close to exhausting its life-essence. One of you will resupply it for me."

She released the mother, who, gasping for breath, glared at her in horror.

Ora felt something sticky in her hand. She glanced down and saw she had clenched her hand so tightly, the needle had pierced her skin.

"So which one will it be? You or your daughter? You have until tomorrow to decide." Trista looked toward her men. "Take them to the tower."

Ora's heart's leaped up into her throat when Trista turned to glare directly up into the tower window. The lady's eyes seemed to bore into her skull—Ora was filled with loathing. "Hello, Ora," she called. "I hope you enjoyed the view."

Ora couldn't make her lips do anything other than quiver. *I won't do it this time! Be brave!*

Trista grinned evilly. "As you can guess, I will need the Robe of Life. I want you to resew the magic pattern by tomorrow evening! I am anxious to replenish this body and the speed of your needle is the only thing keeping me from it. Now get busy."

Ora opened her mouth, but no words came out. She swallowed and tried not to think of the shattered leg her first refusal had cost her. *I won't do it!*

"Ora! Did you hear me!"

The woman bowed her head. "Yes, my lady."

Ora stopped before the guarded door and took a deep breath. The guard cut his eyes in her direction, but otherwise ignored her and stared straight ahead. Stalling the inevitable, she inspected the gray wood grains in the rough hewn door and noticed that the hinges were rusty. She hated this part—even worse than the actual transference. *I could run away this time!*

She nearly chuckled at the thought. Run where? She was too old to get very far, and even if she did, Trista would just get someone else to do her dirty work.

Besides, after all this time it seems a little late to be having a change of heart. She had sealed her own doom years ago when *she* had been on the other side of that door.

Ora steeled herself and smoothed down the front of her dress. She nodded to the guard. He quickly lifted the bar holding the door and stood to one side with his sword held ready. Ora gently pushed on the door and gingerly stepped into the room. The door slammed shut behind her.

The prisoner was standing in the center of the room with her hands still tied behind her back. She stood proudly and glared at the newcomer—her mussed hair, coming loose from her braid, nearly covered one eye. Ora was struck with the impulse to push it out of her face. The elder woman looked away.

"You can probably guess why I am here," Ora refused to meet her eye. "Lady Trista is anxious for your answer."

"Then she can wait till the sun goes cold."

Ora shook her head. "You do not understand. About every seven winters, Lady Trista has to replenish the life-essence in her body. Because she is a sorceress, she uses it up very quickly. So take seriously what she said. *She would rather use your daughter because it will last her slightly longer.* But that is not how she plays the game. She likes to be surprised. And surprises don't come easily to someone who was ancient when I first met her as a young woman like you." Ora's voice broke as she remembered the circumstance of that first meeting—and of the decision she had made. She pushed the thought aside and pulled herself back to the present. "And what she said about letting one of you go is true. She only needs one of you, and she will release the other. She keeps her word even if she is evil."

"And you're not."

Ora closed her eyes and fought to keep them from

watering. "Yes, I am evil." She took a deep breath. "It is I who takes the several strands of hair from the victim. And it is I who sews them into the magic pattern of the Robe of Life. But the difference between Trista and myself is that *I know* I am evil. And I loathe it. But my wrongs started with a single act of cowardice which has no comparison. And since then, every other evil deed has been just a minor evil. I'm sure the Goddess Mother wishes she had never let such a vile thing onto the earth."

The warrior tensed and took a step forward. "So if I kill you, then the witch will not be able to do her magic?"

Ora laughed. "It is not that simple. Anyone with half a brain can sew the magic pattern. There is nothing special about me—nor is the pattern very difficult. Trista just has me do it because she knows I hate it. No, it is the lady who holds the magic, and she will not release it until she is wearing the robe. The pattern merely shapes it to her will." Ora sighed deeply. "So what is your decision, warrior? Will you or your daughter be Trista's next victim?"

"I refuse to answer!"

"Very well, I will let you think it over a few moments more." Ora turned and knocked at the door. It slowly creaked open in reply. She paused before going through. "I am going to see your daughter now. Is there anything you would like me to tell her?"

Despite the warrior's stern face, the corner of her mouth twitched. "Tell her that I won't let anything happen to her."

Ora nodded once. "I will tell her." But her thoughts were ahead of her. *She has already made her decision—all mothers would gladly lay down their lives for their children. All except one.*

All except me.

* * *

The guard at the girl's door seemed more troubled, as though he had tasted something bitter. Ora didn't even have to speak to him—he opened the door as she approached.

Inside she found the girl sitting on a straw mat, her knees pulled up to her chin—clumps of straw clung to her hair and her eyes were red. Ora assumed it was from crying. She looked up when the door opened, but sank back down when she saw it was Ora.

"Hello, child," said Ora brightly. "How are you faring?"

But the girl made no reply and just stared at her with large, wet eyes.

Ora took a tentative step toward her. "My name is Ora, and I have a message from your mother."

The child immediately went up on her knees, her smile brightening her whole face. "A message? Is she all right? What did she say?"

Ora's heart went out to her. She was such a beautiful child. Just like Elita. For a moment the painful memories flooded back—the child offering her mother a simple wildflower.

"It's pretty, isn't it, Mother?" she had said.

A younger Ora had chuckled and placed it in her hair. "It's lovely, just like you. . . ."

The girl was shaking her arm. "Please tell me what Mother said."

Ora blinked and tried to shake off the memories. She forced a smile. "Yes, child, I will. She said not to worry, she was not going to let anything happen to you."

The child seemed to mull this over for a moment, and then she smiled. "Mother would say that."

"And she is doing fine. In fact, she is being held prisoner just like you in a room not far from here."

"Can I see her?"

Ora shook her head. "I'm sorry, but Lady Trista won't allow that right now. But I guarantee you will see her tomorrow. Maybe by then this mess will be worked out." *Actually, Lady Trista will suck the essence from your mother's body and you will go free.*

The child mulled this over for a moment and then nodded.

Ora stepped closer and painfully knelt before her. "Your hair is a mess child. Will you let me fix it? I have a comb."

She nodded slowly, a little unsure. Ora sat on the mat and drew the child onto her lap. Memories of her own child flooded back—it seemed like only yesterday that she had done the same with Elita. Ora swallowed hard and took out the comb. She began to run it through the girl's nearly white hair, picking out clumps of straw as she went.

"You have such beautiful hair, child. It's nearly as white as my own. Surely you're not anywhere near an old woman's age?"

The girl giggled. "I am nine summers old. Mother says I'm small for my age."

"Well, I think you're just right. My daughter was small for her age, too."

The girl giggled and scooted farther back into her lap. Despite the laughter, she was very afraid and starved for attention. Once she started talking, the words poured out. "My mother is a guardswoman and they are very strong and brave. Some say she is on her way to be a great warrior. I have been trying to think up a ballad for her, but I haven't been able to think of a good one. Do you know any warriors?"

"I used to." Ora pulled a small knife from her pocket. Without the child even being aware, she reached close to the scalp and cut off a small lock of hair, deftly putting it inside her cloak.

"Yes, but Mother's a *woman* warrior. She says that it takes a very special woman to be one."

Ora resumed combing the child's hair. "Your mother is right—very few make it."

"Who was this warrior you knew?"

Ora sighed. "This warrior thought herself very brave. She fought in the battle to repel the invaders from Percillis, and even won honors from her commander. She wasn't a guardswoman, like your mother, but a mercenary who . . . was attached to Lord Jarack. You wouldn't have heard of him. He died long before you were born."

"What happened to her? Did she become a commander?"

Ora shook her head sadly. "No, this warrior ran into some trouble. She failed a test of her honor and bravery. Failed it miserably. She wasn't worth much after that."

"You sound so sad about it. You must have known her very well."

"Yes, I did." *As well as one can know oneself. After all these years, I still can't believe I did it. Poor Elita— dead as if I killed her myself.*

Ora blinked back the tears and gently scooted the child from her lap. "I have to go now. Is there anything you want me to tell your mother?"

"Tell her I miss her."

Ora nodded, the tears nearly overwhelming her. "That I shall."

Ora sat on her stool in the tower, contemplating the finger-thick strand of hair she held in her gnarled hands. She casually noted the light in the room was growing dimmer as the sun sank behind the horizon. Trista had better hurry with the Robe of Life if she wanted her to finish it before the morrow.

She ran the strand of hair through her fingers feeling its smoothness and noting the strength of each fiber. The strand was dark—the mother's hair. When Ora had shown her the white lock of her daughter's, the mother's resolve had broken. She hadn't even struggled as Ora took the length she needed in exchange for the white one. It always went that way.

Most mothers were afraid for themselves, but they feared for their children more than anything. Mothers were a brave lot—much braver than any warrior. But each had their traitors.

Ora sighed and looked toward the window. Why had she failed? She could remember the time of year, the day, the hour that she had agonized with her decision. But with so much at risk and being so terribly afraid . . . she had become paralyzed by indecision. And by default had chosen to live. When the magic in the Robe of Life had been activated, Elita's life had been sucked out.

Ora wiped a tear from her cheek. She hadn't really believed that such was possible. But she had seen it. She had heard the child's confused wail as she died and the cruel blush of youth touching Trista's cheeks. Ora still heard that final scream in her dreams.

After that, the sorceress had kept her word and escorted her out of the fortress. In shock and anger, Ora had worked her way home fully intending to use her husband's army to burn Trista's fortress to the ground. But the tale of her daughter's death preceded her, only it had been warped in its telling: that Elita had spoiled a meeting with her mother's lover, and in a fit of anger, Ora had strangled the girl.

This was just the perfect lie for her husband Lord Jarack to believe—their relationship had always been strained, and the child its only binding. So when he had heard the tale, he flew into a rage of grief and offered a bounty to anyone who brought him her head. After three failed attempts on her life and a pack of hunters dogging her, Ora was forced to return to the only place Jarack couldn't reach: Trista's fortress.

Ora smiled cruelly. Fitting irony that the one who took her daughter's life should become her protector. And such it had been. Only Trista had no need of her as a warrior, but instead had trained her in needlecraft. And when the time again came for Trista to take a life to supplement her own, it was Ora who sewed the magic pattern. Much later, Ora finally figured out that it was Trista herself who had arranged the false tale and for her return. But by then it was too late, because Trista, by slow degrees, had completed the process of breaking her spirit, until all that remained was a tired old woman with a needle and no place to go.

Ora wiped her damp cheeks on the sleeve of her blouse. She had traded her sword of iron for a needle of bone, but both killed just as surely. The only difference was the sword protected hearth and home, while the needle pierced the souls of mothers and children.

On impulse, Ora stood and carefully laid the strand of hair on her stool. She went to an old chest along the wall and carefully opened it. Inside, wrapped in linen like a corpse, lay her faithful sword. She carefully took it out and unwrapped it. The blade was rusty and dull, and when she hefted it, it felt heavy—too heavy to even hold. Forcing her weak muscles and her creaking joints into a stance, she tried to hold it still, but it quivered and shook, finally collapsing to the floor. At one time, the blade had seemed like a feather.

She hugged the sword to her chest. If only she could run away. Not only from here, but from time itself. Back to a certain decision, to undo it, and make the sacrifice. Surely death was better than living this way.

Ora started as the chamber door slammed open. Light flooded the room as the guards with Trista entered and lit the torches around the walls from the ones they carried. Ora slowly turned, still hugging the sword.

Trista stood in the portal with the Robe of Life draped over one arm. Her eyes fell to the tired, old weapon. "I told you to never take that out."

Ora didn't answer her.

Trista threw the robe to her. "I need this completed by the morn. Have you gotten all you need? Did you get the hair?"

"Yes, mistress. Things have gone as they always do."

She gave a curt nod. "Good. Remember, finished by morning."

Ora cocked her jaw to one side, a sudden anger boiling within her. "I'm . . . not going . . . to do it," she whispered.

Trista wheeled at her. "What did you say?" she demanded.

Ora straightened and pulled back her shoulders. "I won't do it." She threw the robe down and lifted her sword in defiance. "I'm going to treat you as I should have ages ago." She clumsily ran toward her, sword outstretched.

Trista sidestepped and caught Ora around the throat. Ora found herself choking as her tiptoes sought purchase on the floor. The sword clattered away.

Trista grinned. "Isn't it a little late to let your conscience start bothering you? How many mothers have you sewn into me now—six . . . seven . . . ?" She snorted. "You're too much of a coward to defy me. Now sew that pattern."

The sorceress released her, and Ora collapsed to the floor gasping for breath. Trista stepped out of the room without looking back. Her guards followed in her wake.

Ora crawled to her stool and pulled herself up. Slowly getting her bearings, she sat down with the strand of hair, the robe, and her needle. Trista was right. She was a coward. Tears flooded her eyes. There had been a time when she would never have allowed herself to be treated this way. There was a time, when she would have stared into the eyes of a demon like Trista and not flinched. But those days were gone. She was a coward.

She picked at the strands of hair, selecting what she needed. Only there was a white one in the bunch, intertwined with the others: just like a daughter's fate intertwined with her mother's. The two are inseparable, and to pull them apart would not hurt just one, but both. *Mother or daughter?*—it was not a fair choice. It hadn't been fair for her and Elita, nor would it be fair for this mother and daughter.

Ora looked up at the darkening sky through the window. Why was she hesitating this time? Why was this time different? Perhaps it just took a while before you finally made the right decision.

The next morning, at the appointed time, a guard came for Ora. She had hardly slept during the night, diligently working on the pattern for the Robe of Life. Thanks to Trista's magic glowstick, she had been able to see well enough to complete the task.

Carrying the carefully folded Robe of Life draped over her right arm, Ora went with the guard to the mother's chamber. The child was already there, attached to her mother's side. When Ora entered the chamber, both the child and the mother looked up in surprise. Ora simply smiled and gave a slight bow to them both.

Trista entered the room and paused just inside the portal. She scrutinized everyone in the room, not stopping until her gaze came to rest on the Robe of Life and the new pattern sewn into it. She smiled, her quick eyes taking in the stitching and the white color of the sewn hair. She stepped forward and carefully touched it. "I can see from the pattern that we might be in for a surprise on this one."

Ora swallowed and nodded respectfully. "Yes, my lady. It is possible."

The mother suddenly noticed the pattern and looked up in alarm. Her eyes narrowed on Ora and she lunged—but the guards were ready and held her back.

Smirking, Trista looked back to Ora. "Good. I like surprises."

Ora smiled nervously. *No, you don't,* she thought.

You have lived so long you do everything the same, and you don't even realize it.

Trista turned toward the mother. She clasped her hands and smiled. "I want to thank each of you for helping me. I take no joy in knowing that this was a difficult decision. I give honor to you both."

The mother struggled, but the guards held firm.

Trista stepped to Ora and turned to face the mother and child with her back to the elder. "Ora, I think it is time." She reached over her shoulder. "The robe."

"Yes, my lady."

Ora whipped the robe off her right arm and brandished her rusty sword. She reared back to sink it home. . . .

But Trista sensed the coming stroke. She whirled and sidestepped, catching Ora's arm in mid-lunge. In one quick movement, she brought Ora's arm down and snapped it across her knee. Ora heard the bones in her arm crunch as her fingers went limp. The sorceress caught the sword as it fell.

"You're still a coward, old woman. Tried to stab me in the back. I don't know what possessed you, but now I can no longer trust you."

And with that, she jerked the Robe of Life from the elder's good hand and thrust the sword into Ora's chest.

Pain exploded though Ora's being. Grasping her chest, she staggered backward until she hit the wall and then slid to a sitting position. Her hands and feet were ice and the vision of Trista before her seemed distant. She could feel her life slipping away. *Please, Goddess Mother, favor me this one last time. I beg you!*

Through her dim vision, she could see Trista laugh and drape the robe over her shoulders. She traced the pattern of the symbol and spoke the words of power. "I call upon the dark ones. Listen to me. Deslead! Leciton! Tropmie!"

At each word, the presence of magic in the room

grew—a tension one could feel caressing one's skin and pulling on one's hair. As if from a long tunnel, Ora could see Trista working her magic. *This is it,* she thought. *I'm dying.*

Grinning, Trista continued. "Oh, great demoness. Do exactly as I say. Through the mingled essences of the pattern on this robe, transfer the essence of life from the one with plenty to the one in need!"

Like an approaching storm, magic gradually built up in the room. Ora could hear the child crying. A chill wind plucked at hair and clothes. Finally, as the strength of the spell grew, a blinding light filled the chamber. Ora hardly had the strength to think—the room was so very far away. . . .

Suddenly Ora felt a tingling in her scalp, quickly followed by a scream of the dammed. *"YOU TRICKED ME . . . !"*

At last, everything settled and a ghostly quiet filled the room. For a moment, Ora wondered if she was dead. But a heartbeat later the mother swam into view, and to her relief, the child was right beside her. And behind the two of them, there was no mistaking a pile of ashes with the Robe of Life lying in a heap beside it.

Ora tried to sit up. "Both of you are all right?"

The mother nodded. "How about you? You were . . . *dead.* How did you heal yourself and yet kill the witch?"

Ora was feeling better than she had felt in years. And her wound. . . . She looked down. Her blouse had a hole in it where the sword had pierced, and there was still wet blood around it, but she was whole. She looked back up at them in amazement. "I wanted to stop Trista, and I fully planned on killing her. But just in case I didn't, I wanted to try and spare you. So, I sewed my own hair into the pattern. That way she would take my life and not yours." Ora looked down at herself. "I guess that when Trista stabbed me, my life-essence was draining away and there wasn't any more to suck out. It instead sucked out what she had and gave it to me. Like water flowing downhill."

The mother—Ora couldn't remember when she'd gotten untied—helped her to stand. "The guards fled when the magic started. We might be able to slip out."

Ora nodded. "But first, I want to make sure that no one else uses the robe." She went to one of the torches in the wall, took it down, and stuck it in the magic robe. It caught easily.

As Ora watched it burn, the mother came up to stand beside her. "I thank you for helping me and my daughter. I'm sorry I called you evil."

Ora shook her head. "Don't be. You were right. Evil decisions make one evil. But we can always choose to be different, no matter how many evil decisions we've made. It's never too late."

As the last of the robe turned to ashes, Ora stomped out the remaining flames. She looked up with a smile on her face. "It just took me a little longer than most to figure that out."

SMALL CONSIDERATIONS
by Judith Fielder Leggett

Judith Fielder Leggett says she is a horticulturist with an interest in growing plants in space (That's another strange occupation to collect). "When not writing articles and doing research with my husband on Controlled Environment Life Support Systems, I'm trying to break into the fiction market and the photography market." (Suggestion: concentrate on one or the other; either demands a single-minded approach. One of the major pitfalls of trying to build a career in any art is trying to do everything. We even have some people who want to illustrate their own stories—which is an absolute no-no except in the children's stories market, where for some reason it seems to be standard. But not here; in this market it's simply a sign of not being professional—and we like dealing with professionals.)

She grows orchids—lots of orchids (makes me think of Nero Wolfe), bicycles with her husband, shoots a target recurve bow—whatever the deuce that is—and spends a lot of time writing lots of novels and stories that sit in the closet. Oh, no!—they won't do anyone any good in there—get them out and try submitting them somewhere! Novels on the closet shelf very rarely make the best seller list!

"Small Considerations" is about the way our children's lives mimic our own.

"Tansy, Peppermint, Goldenseal. . . ." Mara stopped her litany briefly and heard the small echo

behind her. She smiled wryly as she glanced at her
youngest daughter. The tiny fingers pinching the herbs
in child portions . . . oh, so careful to do it properly.
Since this one began walking, nothing would do but to
copy everything her mother did throughout the day.
Today was no exception. She carried her small-girl
basket that Jacen the basketweaver had woven for her
small-girl arm. It was made the same way as Mara's, of
the same stuff. Mara would have protested the cost, but
her daughter had presented Jacen with payment as if
she were wisewoman indeed at age five. Jacen had not
laughed at the neat little packets of dried herbs. Mara
would have explained their uses except that her daughter had given the litany to the basketweaver. The face
had remained gravely courteous throughout the dis-
course. Only when Jacen had raised his eyes to Mara
had the humor broken out into the clear blue eyes. The
head had moved slightly, and Mara had seen Jacen's
twin girls busy making baskets. They were only four
years of age, but the conversation between them was
Jacen to the word.

"What you do, they do. What you say, they say. It
serves to curb your actions and words unless you wish
them spread throughout the village on the morrow."
The eyes had twinkled merrily, referring to a scene earlier that week that had earned Jacen the frosty silence
of at least two overly pretentious women of the village.

Mara looked again at the curly blonde hair of her
youngest daughter. It would fade with time and age,
this interest in the doings of her mother . . . surely?
Mara went back to her gathering. Today was the day
for walking the village bounds and strengthening the
wards. This she did, trailing behind her a tiny shadow
whose every action mimicked her own: small-girl portions, small-girl moves. . . .

The wards of Firemount Village had been woven by
Mara for the last ten years. Firemount fronted the only

pass that led from the agrarian land of Herlan to the forbidding rocky land of Westridge. There had been peace between the two lands for centuries and then war for the last twelve years. The hunters had become raiders and the raiders had come over the border to burn and destroy. Rumors spoke of wild magic. Rumor was often wrong, but Herlan Council had been unwilling to take the risk. So Mara was here. Her task was to ward the village against magic even as Macsen Strongarm's men warded the pass against raiders. Macsen and she had matched and trysted and three children were the result . . . three girls . . . Macsen had broken the bonds when it was announced that the third child was a girlchild. Mara could not see blaming the child for the shortcomings of her father. To Macsen, Mara had only been a simple healer. Since he had never asked, she had never spoken of what she did besides the simple healings. With his leaving, Mara had had to care for the three children on her own. Her older girls were named and now attended schooling, but for the last two years now Mara had been shadowed by a tiny extension of herself, the gravity of an elder in the body of a child. Mara would have preferred the pranks, laughter, mischief, and games of a child. But it was for her daughter to choose. Weekly they had walked the wards together for more than a year. Mara counted the weeks silently. Fifty-six weeks as of today.

There was a noise that evening in the town square. Macsen's men came thundering into the village with news of battle. Macsen was not with them. There was confusion—and hurts to be tended. The men told Mara wild stories as she worked her healing: stories about red lightning, loud noises, and smoke that turned solid to crush fighting men. Macsen had fallen. Mara heard the tale with quiet. Her hands stayed still and did not tremble. She had not wished him ill and his death grieved her. But only as it was the father of her

children. The years had seen the feelings she had had
for him dim and grow vague. As she could not understand a father turning from his children, so had her
feelings for him grown thin. Her attention was yanked
back to the speaker, though, with his very next words.

"He called to you, Mara, as he fell."

He had called to her? Used her name? A cold hand of
dread closed over Mara. Her wards, her work of the
last ten years . . . in the hands of one who knew her
name they would be as nothing, less than nothing!

"How close are they?" she whispered hopelessly.

"We are safe, Mara. The council said that they had
warded the village."

"How close?!"

Glances were exchanged. No one had ever seen
Mara upset before, not like this.

"They were two hours behind us."

Two hours? Mara felt the dread squeeze throughout
her body. No time to do anything, no time to prepare
even for certain doom. She rose to her feet and turned
slowly to face the direction of the pass. The confident
defenders from Macsen's guard did not comfort her. A
force was approaching, filing in behind a tall figure. A
cloak flashed in the night, lit by strange lights. Beautiful that cloak was, but the face above the cloak was
cold and hard, contemptuous and . . . triumphant.
Macsen had been targeted for this—the waving and
gesticulating was for show. Mara swayed as if she had
been struck, as her work of ten years unraveled with
the calling of her name. The man stalked forward with
that cold triumph in his eyes. His first foot touched the
ward lines and the second one crossed it before he
screamed. The cloak wrapped around him burst into a
fierce fire, and burned, and he burned with it.

Fifty-six weeks, Mara thought dazedly, a number of
power, seven sevens and seven more and built with a
little girl's concentration: gentle, soft stands of magic,
warding the village to child height. Mara saw that

height and could not believe it. If the precaution of undersight had been taken, the invader could have simply stepped over the barrier, the village would have fallen.

IF YOU CAN'T STAND THE HEAT . . .

by P.E. Cunningham

Pat Cunningham says she is female and uses her initials when she writes because "Patricia Elizabeth Cunningham" tends to run off the page—one of the few sane reasons for using a pen name. She lives in Lancaster County, PA, the home of the Amish and the movie *Witness* (I've seen both), and used to hold down a job as editor of an advertising flyer. An unexpected layoff left her with nothing to do but write. That's what it takes sometimes.

Pat dedicates this story to Sue Ann Nivens, "patron goddess of Happy Homemakers everywhere."

When word reached the castle that King Glorim was returning, victorious at last, Mellia dashed to the walls with the rest of the castle staff, but half her mind remained in the kitchen. Three years of war in a foreign land, forced to live on strange fare and camp cooking. He would be starved for decent food. As the King's cook, it was her duty as well as her pleasure and pride to welcome him home properly.

By the time the approaching army had grown from distant specks to dusty individuals, Mellia had dinner preparations plotted out in her mind. Mutton stew, beets, and steamed greens for the soldiers; fresh beef and garden vegetables for the officers. For the King's table, a suckling pig with honey sauce, garnished with glazed carrots and apples. Her staff could handle the rest of it, but she herself would prepare King Glorim's meal. For fifteen years no hands but hers had created the King's repasts, from raw ingredients to that final triumphal walk to the high table with tray in hand. Feeding nobles and castle ladies just didn't hold quite the same taste. Finally, life in the kitchen could get back on its natural track.

She shouldered herself a clear spot on the parapets and peered down at the army. Her heart did a leap of pure joy. Captain Anders rode at the head of the column, just behind the King. She waved madly. His face turned upward, and he offered a jaunty salute. Mellia leaned back, beaming. She had a most specific dish in mind for Anders, one she would serve him in his quarters after the feast was done.

With Anders proven safe and well, she turned her attention to the King. Glorim pranced his horse at the head of the army and waved to his cheering subjects. He looked healthy and, to her disappointment, well-fed. No, wait, his robes did seem to hang a bit more loosely on him. She would soon rectify that. The army marched into the courtyard, and Mellia raced for the kitchen.

That evening the entire castle celebrated King Glorim's victory over Lazan. Nobles and soldiers alike crowded into the hall, jesting and slapping backs like guests at a wedding. Mellia and her staff had worked like fiends all afternoon. The result was a marvel of meat, greens, and pastries she could rightfully say she was proud of. The feasters cheered the appearance of each dish. Even though half the meal would wind up on the floor and their shirt fronts, she still enjoyed their appreciation.

Captain Anders was seated at the high table tonight, three seats down from the King. Mellia brushed his arm as she presented the soup, and he pressed her fingers in return. "I'm looking forward to a bite of your pastries, my darling," he murmured.

"Me, too," she whispered back. "My larder's been empty all this time. I hope you've brought something to fill it. Now let go of my sleeve. I've got to see to the King."

As she spoke, she glanced to the head of the table. The glance became a stare. Caught up in the presentation of dinner, she only now discovered the stranger standing behind King Glorim's seat. He had the look of a Lazani: olive skinned, lean and stiff as a celery stalk, dark of hair and eye. A thin mustache rode beneath his long, pinched nose. He eyed the hall, the King, the nobles, even her food with disdain.

Her food. The King's meal should be close to done. She hurried back to the kitchen.

The suckling pig came off the spit precisely on time and done to perfection. The carrots and apples, already prepared, waited on the warming stones. Mellia arranged it all just so, and added a dish of strawberries. Twin kitchen boys bore the tray, with Mellia preceding them. She personally served the King. She carved a generous slice of the white, tender meat, ladled sauce over it and vegetables beside it, then stood back and waited.

Glorim took a hearty bite, chewed, and savored its slide down his throat. "Excellent as always, Mellia. By God, how I've missed this!" Then, to her naked astonishment, he turned to the Lazani. "What do you think, Sampani?"

The narrow man cut himself a thin slice, sniffed it carefully, then risked a wary nibble. He chewed ten times. She counted. At last he swallowed. His nose wrinkled. "A bit too sweet," he pronounced, "but acceptable. Are those apples with it? How clichéd. I would have chosen another fruit—plums, perhaps, something unexpected. The carrots are adequate, as is the presentation. Overall, I would call it a flawed but not disastrous dish."

Mellia was stunned. How dare he? How dare this scrawny stick of a Lazani speak so about her cooking? Because the King was present, she kept her peace and held tight to her smile, but the air around her boiled like soup in a kettle.

Nor was that the end of it. The Lazani sampled every dish and offered his sniping comments until Mellia seethed with fury. How she would love to carve that superior smirk from his lips, with an unwhetted knife.

The meal, now grown interminable, finally came to an end. The King and his court withdrew. Servants cleared the plates away. Mellia contrived to pass near Captain Anders. "That pig!" she steamed, for his ears alone. "In manners as well as taste. Who is he? Some captive noble? The Lazani prince himself?"

"Worse," Anders growled. His expression was as dark as hers. "He's a chef."

The bad news came at sunrise. King Glorim summoned Mellia to his private chambers, something he had done only four times in all her fifteen years. She noticed first the breakfast tray, with its hot oat cakes and chilled fruit. *She* hadn't made that breakfast. Oblivious to his own blatant betrayal, the king greeted her warmly. "Dear Mellia. Have a seat. Would you like a muffin? No? Well, I've got some jolly news for you. From now on you'll have help in preparing your wonderful meals—"

Her mind seemed to congeal after that. She stared at the tray while the words rolled over her. Gradually their import seeped in, like slime in a stagnant well. While conquering the Lazani, King Glorim had developed a taste for their cuisine. The captive with the horrendous manners was Sampani, chief cook to that land's former King. Glorim had brought him home to instruct Mellia in how to prepare his native dishes.

"But, Sire," she nearly choked. "Surely this isn't necessary. You've always been pleased with my creations."

"And I still am. Did I say I wasn't? That pig last night was superb. But even perfection gets tiresome. You'll love Lazani cooking. They do things with guinea fowl—"

"I don't doubt that," she said nastily.

"Then it's settled. Take him under your wing. Show him the whys and wherefores. Watch him prepare a few meals, and let him work with you. We've brought some stores from Lazan, spices and such. See that they're stocked in the larder."

"Sire, are you sure this is wise? The man's an enemy national. He may try to poison you, or—"

"Oh, yes. Anders went on about that, too. I doubt if he'll risk it, but keep an eye on him if you're that concerned. You'll be working together, after all. Oh, and tell him I'd like that rice dish for lunch. The one with the yellow spices."

Mellia curtsied. What else could she do? "As my King commands."

Mellia had a distinct advantage when it came to culinary skills. She was the daughter and granddaughter of witches, and counted at least one powerful sorcerer in her ancestry. Her gift of magic manifested in the foods she prepared. Egg and flour, yeast and butter, herb and sauce were the tools with which she wove her spells. Men had applauded and even wept upon sampling her finest creations.

And, like every witch, wizard, and cook before her, Mellia was fiercely territorial.

She glowered fit to fry a man's skin at the Lazani, strutting around *her* kitchen and offering his suggestions for improvement. One well-placed blow with a cleaver—but, no. The King had given her an order, and she was constrained to obey. So she held her tongue and observed him as he prepared simple Lazani dishes. She told herself she could live with his condescending tone and the simplistic instructions he gave her. When he criticized her preparation of her own special spice cake, however, her temper finally boiled over. "Listen here," she blasted him. "You're only here to teach Lazani cooking. This castle's kitchen is mine, and I don't take orders from Lazani slaves."

He drew himself up, stiff as an icicle and clearly affronted. "Madam," he frosted, "I am neither slave nor captive. I left my land at your King's request, and by my own free will."

Mellia blinked at him. "Whatever for?"

"What for? Why, for this." He took in the boards, the spits, the ovens with a grand sweep of his arm. "So that I may do what I was born to do. Lazan had fallen. Was I to ply a peasant's trade in some slop-grease inn, or perhaps push a cart full of rancid candies through muddy village streets? Pah! I am Sampani, chef to kings!" He thumped his chest, causing a cloud of fine white powder to puff out from his floury fist. "When it comes to my art, I bow to no one. Especially not to a—"

Mellia shoved a tart into his mouth. "Don't say it. Don't say anything. Just listen. You may have been lord of the ovens back in Lazan, but we're in my kingdom now. I've fed my King for fifteen years, and he's never had cause to complain. And he never will. Understand?"

Sampani glowered down at her. He sampled the tart before he removed it. He smacked his lips, then pursed them. "Needs more honey."

In her mind Mellia repeated Anders' favorite curses. Aloud, she said, "Now we're going to make Brenmanor custard. We'll need some cinnamon. . . ."

* * *

The morning deteriorated swiftly after that. Insults and daggered looks flew faster than plucked feathers. But one would never know it by the exquisite meal that greeted King Glorim at lunch. Mellia and Sampani stood by, smiles fixed to their faces, and subtly jostled each other while they awaited the judgment of the king.

King Glorim lustily delved into each delightful dish, his smile growing wider as he crunched and sipped. "Excellent! Truly excellent!" he said when he was done. "I knew you two would work well together."

"My King is generous with his praise." Sampani bowed deeply from the waist. Not to be outdone, Mellia added a graceful curtsy. "His Highness has my gratitude for allowing me to serve. It has been a most stimulating experience."

"And you, Mellia? How go the cooking lessons?"

"They are . . . enlightening, my King."

"Good. Now here's what I want for dinner." He listed a dozen Lazani dishes. Mellia's face fell farther and Sampani's expression brightened with each concoction named. "Be sure to make enough for twelve. I've got guests coming over tonight." He clapped Sampani on the shoulder. "I want my favorite lords and their ladies to meet my newest chef."

Sampani practically danced back to the kitchen. Mellia stalked behind. "You hear? You hear? 'My chef.' I knew this King was a man of exceptional taste."

"Don't go rearranging the condiment shelf just yet. This is only a phase. I know. He's done this before. In time he'll get tired of foreign food, and then you won't be needed. There's room for only one King's cook in this castle."

Sampani stopped dancing and turned to her. His smile was as acid as sour vinegar. "So there is, m'lady. Perhaps it's time for fresh fixings in the larder, *verlait?*"

"Is that a challenge, Lazani?" She met his smile with a cold slash of her own. "You're on."

And so the war began, fought with salad and entree, soup and hors d'oeuvres and dessert. The ovens and boards became battle-scarred, the hapless staff battle-fatigued. The finest of the weapons created were dispatched to Glorim's table. The conflict raged for days on end without a clear winner or loser ... except perhaps for the King and his court, who began to put on weight.

It did not take Mellia long to realize she and Sampani were too evenly matched for either to claim a clear victory. Unfortunately, as she soon discovered, Sampani had realized this before she did. While she plotted her next maneuver, he launched a flank attack.

The opening volley came with an unexpected summons from the King. Sampani was arranging a colorful salad of radishes, carrots, and greens when Mellia returned. Her eyes were glazed and her face was white as flour. Sampani inquired sweetly, "Is something amiss, my dear?"

"No. Nothing." She groped for a cheese grater. Her hand knocked it to the floor. Tsking, Sampani bent to retrieve it. "How clumsy! One hopes you'll not be so careless once you have a kitchen of your own."

His words broke the coating of shock on her brain. "I already have a kitchen. I'll thank you to mind your tongue in it."

Sampani only sniffed. "One might also hope you'll not be so shrewish to your husband."

Her hands fumbled once more on the grater. "I've no intention of getting married."

"Not even at the King's command?"

Mellia whirled on him, speechless. How could he know already the content of her talk with the King? He returned her stare with a smirk. "You've served him

well for years. It's long past time you retired and took
your reward. Got yourself a husband and children to
cook for. And quickly; you're hardly a maiden any
more. What are you, thirty? Older?"

"You!" She gripped the grater as if she would fling
it. "You put the idea in his head!"

"A suggestion only." Sampani dispelled all blame
with an airy wave of his hand. His eyes glittered like
mica. "He cares for you a great deal. He wants to see
you happy. What woman can truly be happy without a
hearth and husband? Of course, it will mean your
leaving the castle. Don't fret, I'll do my best to ease the
change."

"There won't be any 'change.' I'll—"

"What? Defy the will of your King?" His smile
spread across his face like oil. "We both know our
Glorim. Once he gets a notion in his head, it's hard to
dislodge it. Oh, but I'm sure he'll do right by you. Perhaps he'll wed you to that scruffy soldier-fellow you're
always making eyes at. Or he may choose to gift you to
one of his nobles. One who lives a good distance
away."

Mellia went cold all over. She squeezed the grater
between her palms, as if it were a melon, or a skull.
"This is not finished," she snarled at Sampani.

The Lazani merely laughed and turned his back.
Mellia glared at that rigid line. So that was how he
chose to play the game, eh? Then so be it.

Later that day she conferred with Anders. He agreed,
with some misgivings, to her plan. "You're certain the
King will not come to harm?" he asked worriedly.

"Of course he won't. You know I'd never hurt him.
But he hasn't left us many options. We have to act
quickly, before—" She refused to finish the thought.
"Don't worry, my love. I learned more at Granny's
knee than how to roast a chicken. No harm will come
to anyone, except our Lazani chef."

Much later, after moonset when it became safe, she unlocked the spell book that had been her grandmother's, and took the ingredients she hoarded against emergencies from a bolted trunk.

The next morning Mellia came late to the kitchen, bearing a basket of eggs. She took butter and milk from the larder, then began to measure out flour. Her movements were slow and lacked her usual surety. Sampani's narrowed eyes followed her stumblings, but she did not seem aware of his presence.

Whatever dish she had in mind, it did not go well. She spilled the flour. She overmeasured butter and sugar and had to start again. When she nearly tipped the entire basket of eggs Sampani could stand it no longer. He snatched the basket from her hands. "Clumsy cow! Has the thought of marriage already addled you?"

Mellia drew herself up, and yawned. Her eyes were red, and smudged underneath. "Give me that. I was up all night devising this recipe. I'm going to make Glorim a—"

"No. Don't insult an innocent dish by speaking its name. What do you mean, inflicting yourself upon food in your condition? Do women never think?" He confiscated her ingredients, then shooed her away. "Go, go, get out. You're not fit to be in a kitchen."

Mellia retreated, but she didn't leave. She sulkily set herself up in a corner and proceed to hack away at a bunch of helpless carrots. A pile of orange shavings gathered at her feet.

Sampani paid her no heed. To her eggs and milk and flour and sugar he added cups of tangy berries, and at length produced a lovely pie. The staff applauded when he drew it from the oven. From her corner Mellia stuck out her tongue. "This cannot wait for dinner," Sampani decided. "We will serve it at lunch. Bring me a tray!"

Lunchtime arrived, and with it King Glorim, hungry from a long morning ride. Captain Anders was with him, and the usual retainers, and five lords from a neighboring kingdom. They had been invited to establish trade with Glorim, as well as to meet his famous chef.

Sampani arrived, as always, in a flourish of excellent timing. He snapped his fingers, and serving men and maids arranged the various dishes on the table. Mellia hovered at the back of the line, silent, unnoticed.

Glorim tasted the bouillon. Brilliant. The salad and sandwiches. Superb. The bean and scallion casserole. Better than scrumptious. Then, for dessert, the berry pie. Sampani himself cut the first slice and presented it to the King.

The King fell upon it greedily. King Glorim's sweet tooth was legend. "You've outdone yourself, Sampani," he praised the preening chef. "Sweet as a honeycomb, and tasty as a—*gakkk!*"

Florid as a beet, the King fell choking to the floor. Anders leaped to his feet. "Sire! What is it?"

"My gut," Glorim croaked. "Like it's turned to stone. Ahhh, it hurts!"

Sampani blanched and sputtered. The nervous nobles glanced at one another, then quietly pushed their plates away.

"You!" Anders roared. He drew his dagger and pointed it at Sampani. "Traitor! Viper! You've poisoned the King!"

Sampani shook like a tattered dishcloth. "No, I never! I swear—"

"Oh? Did any hands other than yours touch the food? Did not all of it pass your personal inspection before it was brought to the table?" He shot a glare at the quaking servers, who bobbed their heads in frantic affirmation. Anders' scowl grew darker. "Oh, but you're a clever one. Make yourself useful, win the

King's trust, and then claim your foul revenge. Guards! Seize him!"

"And send for the doctor." When Glorim fell, Mellia had darted out of the shadows. She snatched up a cup of water from the table and knelt on the floor beside the king. Into the cup she sprinkled a pinch of white powder. The water bubbled and fizzed. "Here, Sire, drink. It's an old remedy of my granny's. It may help."

The King sipped gingerly. At length he relaxed, and his complexion lightened from maroon to pink. "That's better," he panted. Then he turned steely eyes to Sampani. "As for that villain. . . ."

Secured in the grip of two burly guards, Sampani alternately sobbed and shouted his innocence. A third guard sampled a bite of the pie, then flung it aside, coughing and choking. A boy scurried forward to remove the vile dish. The servers swore up and down only Sampani had touched the pie, from ingredients to finished confection. The Lazani cursed them all. At a curt nod from the king he was borne away to the dungeons.

"There, Sire," Mellia said, and pressed another sip of tonic on him. "I doubt he meant any real mischief. I'm sure it was all a mistake."

"Tender-hearted Mellia. I'll deal with that spider as he deserves." Glorim patted his stomach, and winced. "Ooph! Still hard as a rock."

"The doctor will tend it, my King. And tonight I'll bring you some of Granny's vegetable broth. That should melt the rock straightaway."

Glorim smiled weakly. "Ah, Mellia, you're so good to me. What would I do without you?"

Sampani was brooding in his cell when furtive footsteps whispered down the corridor. He snarled when Mellia's face appeared at the door. Anders stood behind her. "What, witch? Have you come to gloat?"

"Hardly. I've come to free you." Mellia held up a

keyring. "I don't believe you tried to poison the King. Perhaps something tainted the berries." She shrugged. "Accidents do happen, even in the best of kitchens."

Sampani stood. "And the King?"

"A case of indigestion," Anders said. "He'll be fine by sunrise . . . just in time for your execution. *He* still thinks he was poisoned. Your only hope is escape."

"I see." He thinned his eyes at Mellia. "And the price for my 'escape'?"

"Your recipes."

"Witch! Thief!" the Lazani shrieked. "Hand you my secrets? Never! I'll die first!"

"Yes, you will," Anders agreed cheerfully. "At dawn, by command of the King."

"And your secrets will die with you," Mellia added. "Never again will anyone taste the fine art of Sampani."

The man stood quivering, furious, while pride and ego warred upon his face. In the end his ego won, as Mellia suspected it would. "There's a box at the foot of my wardrobe," he grated. "But they'll do you no good. They're in Lazani."

"I read Lazani," Anders said. He fitted a key to the lock, and the door swung open. "I assure you, they'll be put to excellent use. Now come. I'll escort you to the gate."

By morning King Glorim was feeling much better. Captain Anders reported the treacherous Lazani had been found dead in his cell. The King was disappointed. He was also quite put off Lazani cuisine for a while. Mellia planned a simple beef and carrot ensemble for the evening meal.

That evening she sat alone in her quarters, flipping through a sheaf of translated recipes. A close call, that one. Men grew bored so easily; the occasional surprise was required to keep their attention, lest they stray.

Perhaps she ought to experiment with other foreign foods, keep herself from growing too complacent.

She set the recipes aside with a sigh. Sampani was not the first rival she'd vanquished, but she hoped he'd be the last. Basilisk eggs were getting hard to come by.

SILVER BANDS
by Syne Mitchell

Syne Mitchell reminds me that she has sold four stories to this series and has lived in a different state at the time of each sale. At present she is living in Seattle, Washington, and says that this story idea came when she was sitting in front of her word processor (she's lucky; my best ideas have the bad habit of coming when I am on a transcontinental flight, marooned away from my computer!) having trouble getting started and was playing with her eight-band puzzle ring. She slipped it off, flirting with disaster because she'd never been able to solve this one before. It fell apart—her heart stopped. While trying to put it together again, she worked out the plot for this story. Happily, she finished the puzzle ring and the story the next day.

All I know about metal puzzles is that my younger son was addicted to them when he was about thirteen. I bought him a set of a dozen which I thought would take him all summer to solve, and he solved them all in one morning and wept because he had nothing else to do. I could never have solved even the simplest of them; I am entirely without such skills.

In the previous story, the heroine was completely at home in the kitchen. By contrast, in one part of this deftly woven story, a cook's inexperience leads to an embarrassing "accident," seemingly made worse by the presence of witnesses.

"**Y**ou must help me," the woman in the doorway said, holding out her wedding ring, a hopeless snarl of sixteen thin silver bands.

Quiocet glanced past the woman, scanning the streets. Only when she was sure they were empty did she look down. As intended, the puzzle ring had fallen apart when removed from the young woman's finger. "If you could not be faithful to him, why did you marry the man?"

The young woman looked over her shoulder as if words alone could summon her husband back from the holy wars. "The usual reasons. My father—"

"You could have refused." Quiocet, priestess of the secretly worshiped Clever Goddess, interrupted her excuses. "Our order has fought hard for the right of choice. Why did you not use it?"

The woman straightened, smoothing the all-enveloping white widow-in-waiting robes of mourning that she would wear until her husband returned safely. "I had a duty, my family was very poor—"

"And your new husband is very rich?"

"Yes, yes," she continued, "but I did not know then what a cruel man he would be. The horrors I could tell you!" She blushed. "Can I be blamed, then, for taking solace while he is away?" The young woman brushed a strand of hair from her smooth oval face, a faint smile touching her lips. "After all, it is not as if I am stealing from my husband. What he takes from me is not diminished by my sharing it in his absence."

"What of the sons your husband means to be his own?"

"That is not a concern. Of his four wives, none has borne any living children. He shall not burden me with a child."

Quiocet rolled her eyes. So many supplicants to the temple of the Clever Goddess, so few of them worthy. Those who were suited to be devotees of Menomy rarely had need of her boon. The priestess sighed. It did not make raising funds for the temple an easy task. Perhaps it was the goddess' design that her servants must continually sharpen their wits, conniving for every rupee.

Her charge weighed heavily on her now. It had been years since the temple's last victory. Through careful manipulation, the Sultan had agreed to a match between his daughter and a noble house of goat herders. Unable to revoke his royal words, Sultan Iswara had been forced to proclaim that any woman should have the right to refuse an unsuitable husband. A scribe friendly to the temple had been there and, at much risk to himself, had asked the Sultan to sign his words. In indignation, the Sultan had. It became law.

The unfaithful wife shook the disheveled ring so that it chimed like a dancer's bells. "Will you help me?"

Waving a hand dismissively, Quiocet said, "Ask a jeweler to help you."

"They are not discreet!"

Meaning, Quiocet supposed, that the jeweler's guild realized that a double profit could be had by selling service to the wife, and information to the husband.

"You have the tribute?" Quiocet asked.

The young woman nodded, reached deep into her robes, and brought forth a purse.

The coins disappeared soundlessly into Quiocet's right sleeve. Then, her fingers moving with dexterity garnered from years of embroidery and weaving, Quiocet knit the puzzle ring together. First she plucked the mother and father bands and nestled them together in a tight embrace. Crossed, the two straight pieces formed the figure of infinity and marital union. Then she wove the chevron-shaped child bands between the parents. Each child band crossed its sibling. In seconds it was done.

"That didn't look hard at all . . ." the woman said.

It was the stupidest thing Quiocet had heard all night.

The woman slipped her reconstituted wedding ring back onto a slim golden finger. Her life saved, she did not seem very grateful. Likely she was worrying how she would cover the loss of the money she had given the preistess.

The young woman disappeared into the city shadows from which she had emerged. Quiocet sighed. *Is this what we have come to?* Quiocet wondered as she stood in the doorway and waited for the next erring wife.

The young woman's arrival the next night aroused Quiocet's suspicion. Usually after facing the specter of a husband's wrath, wives thought better of their indescretions, or learned to slip the ring carefully onto a finger-sized stick.

Quiocet scanned the shadows for signs of city guards. If it was learned that the Order was helping indiscreet wives . . . the Sultan had never forgiven their manipulations. While he could not admit that he had been outmaneuvered by a group of clever women, he held emnity for all of Menomy's servants, and would relish their downfall.

She held out the again-separated ring. Her eyes downcast, she said, "It looked so easy when you repaired it that I . . ."

Menomy preserve us from arrogant fools, Quiocet thought in disgust.

"You must—"

"I'll do nothing of the sort." Quiocet scanned the empty street again and saw only a rat, skittering under a building. "Try the temple of Fools. You honor their god by your actions."

The woman's perfect oval face crumpled. Tears leaked out of her dark almond eyes. Quiocet was annoyed to note that her face did not get red and blotchy. Even crying she was beautiful.

The priestess pushed her. "Don't cry here. Go away."

The young woman sniffled and, as quickly as they had come, the tears disappeared. "You must help me. If my husband finds that I have been unfaithful, he will kill me. You have helped me before." Her eyes brightened with sudden insight. "And if I must die, I will not die alone."

What was the goddess doing to give such a creature inspiration? Quiocet cursed. A motion up the street distracted her.

The young woman stamped her foot. "Will you fix the ring, or do I scream and call the guards?"

Damn her, she probably would. All her attention focused on the foolish girl, Quiocet snapped, "Very well. Give me the ring." Quicker this time, for she knew this ring's pattern, she assembled it. "The tribute?"

"Oh, there shall be payment for your actions," The young woman smiled, her face stretching into cruelty. "It is you who shall pay." She whistled high and loud.

Guards poured from the shadows on the street, climbing out of the sewers and dropping from the rooftops where they had hidden.

Quiocet swore, but did not run. She was a clever woman, not a fast one. There was no hope that her middle-aged bones would be able to outrun half a dozen swordsmen.

Rough hands grabbed her arms. Four black-swathed soldiers burst past her, eager to seize whatever other women they could find. The closet-sized stone room where Quiocet awaited her customers was empty, as usual. She heard the crash of pottery and snap of her desk and chair breaking.

"Where are the others?" a guard demanded.

"True to the goddess' mandate," Quiocet said ruefully. "They were smart enough not to be here."

She glanced back. The young woman had shucked

off her silken abayah and stood wearing the black-and-brown mottled robes of a Deceiver. Quiocet cursed the devotee of the Lying God. Delighting in confusion and misdirection, they served their god by entrapping and betraying too-trusting people. They hired out to those who paid well. Few dared employ those who swore fealty to betrayal, but Quiocet sensed the Sultan's hand in this. Those were his soldiers destroying her workroom.

The young woman leaned against the wall. Knowing the Deceivers, that slender figure might not even be female. It was small consolation, knowing that irritating and stupid woman did not exist.

The Deceiver rubbed forefinger and thumb together, more smug than mere employment could account for. The Lying God, who had many names, was the natural nemesis of the Clever Goddess. Fooling those who prided themselves on their perception was a special accomplishment. Quiocet sighed. *The immortals play out their petty jealousies with our fragile flesh,* she thought. *Menomy, aid your servant now.*

But the goddess, if she was listening, gave no sign.

The guards completed their search. A stolen glance showed Quiocet the ruin of years of hard work. The shelves of herbs and simples were pulled from the wall. Each jar was shattered. Quiocet did not know what they had been searching for until, with a smug chuckle, the Deceiver said, "Clever women? They aren't even literate."

So they'd been searching for scrolls of lore, or a membership list. Quiocet smiled inwardly. She and her sisters could read as well as any scholar. But in a land where women were forbidden to learn the written word, a clever woman remembered all she must know.

Quiocet was escorted to the prison beneath the palace's high walls. Into the dank stone tunnel she walked, descending past groping hands that reached out toward the feeble light of the lantern that her jailer carried. The prison smelled of urine and sweat. At last, they came to the lowest level of the prison. The jailer locked her into the last cell. Then he left, leaving her in absolute darkness. She was alone. The only sounds she heard were the dripping of water from the ceiling and the skittering of rats.

With no way to use her wits, and worry her only company, Quiocet slept.

The booming of the prison door woke her. A cultured voice filtered down the stairs. Its clear tones carried easily to her cell.

"—whether you will it or no, I will see this prisoner. I am the Sulteena. If you do not wish to incur my wrath, stand aside."

Interesting. The Daughter of Heaven must have an urgent mission to descend into this pit. With a silent prayer to her goddess, Quiocet arranged her sari to meet her noble guest.

The Sulteena was young, younger even than the supposed woman who had entrapped Quiocet. Her profile was lit by the jailer's lantern. The Sulteena's face was angular, the sharply pointed chin appealing and strong. Braided, her black hair fell to her knees. Gold pins held the hair on top of her head in a twist. Her eyes were as dark as her hair, and sharply attentive. Her skin, sheltered from the sun since birth, was as smooth and light as the clearest honey.

"Leave us," she commanded.

Bowing deeply, the jailer hung the lantern from a hook and left.

Quiocet bowed deeply. "Most honored lady, chosen of—"

"Enough formalities. We do not have much time. My father plans your torture and execution as tomorrow morning's entertainment. I wanted to speak to this clever woman he captured, while you are still lucid."

Quiocet froze at the Sulteena's words. What had she done to deserve Menomy's abandonment? For surely, she had not had a single clever thought since her capture.

"I have not forgotten that it was your sect that tricked my father into proposing my marriage to that goat herder. You knew that once the Sultan had spoken, his words could not be reclaimed."

Quiocet bowed her head. "That is true. However, we knew his love for you would not let him allow the marriage."

"His love for propriety, you mean. He would not have his only child married to such, no matter how noble a house. Nor would he have a clan of goat herders rule after him."

"A suitable replacement was found. You are happily married, and the women of this country have gained the right of refusal. You have not been harmed."

The Sulteena's eyes narrowed. "Why risk so much to better the lot of women you will never know?"

Inspiration filled Quiocet. Perhaps this young and highly placed woman could be turned to a useful purpose. The priestess knew her own life was already forfeit, but perhaps she could plant a seed in the young ruler's mind that other clever women could harvest.

"Why hold out a stick to a drowning man?" Quiocet asked. "Because if you do not, he will die. The women in this city are drowning, Sulteena. Since your mother's death, you have been the ruler of women in this city. Surely you have heard their suffering, their petitions for justice. Do you not wish to help them? Was it so wrong for us to risk an unsuitable husband for you, to free thousands of women from a similar fate?"

At that the Sulteena gave Quiocet a very strange look. "You gambled much on my father's love for me."

"It has long been known that his affection for you is his greatest weakness."

A small smile crossed the Sulteena's lips. Her slender fingers twisted the interwoven set of golden bands on her right hand. "Tell me, wise one, what would my father do if my wedding ring were to collapse into a snarling mess?"

They were dangerous words. Not knowing if the Sulteena was friend or foe, Quiocet chose her next statement carefully. "If that impossible occurrence should come to be, I see three choices for your father: he could hire someone to fix the ring and ensure his eternal silence by the sword, or he could proclaim that puzzle rings are not sufficient proof of adultery. Of these, I believe he would be more compelled to the former, thereby avoiding any smirch to the reputation of his family."

The third option, that the Sultan could turn his erring daughter over to her vengeful husband need not be spoken aloud. The heir-prince would have no cure for the smirch on his honor but to execute his faithless wife.

"I see," the Sulteena twisted the ring on her finger. She held out her hand in front of Quiocet. "Could you untangle a ring this complex?"

Made of gold, the ring was as large as a fig. The top was an intricate weave of bands, tangling in the largest of the sacred knots. Quiocet turned the Sulteena's hand over and counted the thread-thin gold bands that made up the ring: thirty-four.

It was a more complex ring than she had seen in her life; the Sulteena's virtue weighed much higher than that of a common wife. Still, some of the patterns were familiar. After a moment, Quiocet said, "I would try."

"Tell me, priestess, would you risk death to better the cause of women in this country?"

For answer, Quiocet gestured at the stone walls around her.

The Sulteena nodded. "Be ready to obey," she said. With those last enigmatic words she rose, gathered her sari into a pleasing drape over her shoulder and left.

In the darkness of the cell, Quiocet silently recited the multiplication tables. The sacred meditation did not ease her concern. Abandoned by her goddess, in the heart of her enemy's stronghold, it would take a very clever plan indeed to save her.

The guards came for her several hours after dawn. On either side, an armored man gripped her arm. Two others followed behind. A little much, Quiocet thought.

She was brought to the audience room. Twenty courtiers of varying station sat on satin cushions. Eating dried figs and pomegranates, they awaited the morning's entertainment.

The Deceiver chortled when he saw her. Rising from his seat at the Sultan's feet, he strode theatrically across the room. "She is not so clever as she imagines. Not so perceptive to have been fooled by my ruse." He laughed again. "Has your false goddess deserted you, wretched woman?"

Quiocet's reply was drowned out. The brass-studded mahogany door flew open and a lithe figure burst into the room.

"Oh, Father!" the Sulteena cried, her sari, red and gold, flying behind her. Four servants, of varying station, trailed behind her. All eyes turned to watch this new spectacle. The guards holding Quiocet upright relaxed their grip.

The Sulteena knelt beside her father and whispered into his ear. His face darkened, and he stared accusingly at Quiocet. The Sulteena whispered some more.

The ruler nodded curtly. "Bring the woman," he told the guards holding Quiocet.

The Sulteena waved her slaves into the Sultan's private conference hall. The Deceiver stood to follow, but with a swift gesture, the Sulteena forbade it. High color tinged the Deceiver's cheeks. He glared at Quiocet, as if somehow she had maneuvered all this.

The Sultan's private council chamber was spartan in comparison to the audience hall. Cotton pillows piled around an olivewood war table, on which a map of the country was carved in relief. The Sultan sat to one side of the table, the Sulteena kneeling before him.

The Sulteena's face was streaked with tears of worry and panic. "Oh, Father! I was touring the kitchen with Hsfrala," she indicated the highly ranked handmaiden with a flip of her hand, "and I thought what fun it would be to learn to make those sweet-cakes that you like so well—"

"A Sulteena has no business—"

"I know, Father," she wailed, beating her chest. "But with the thought of pleasing you with sweet breads from my own hand, daughterly devotion overcame my good sense. So I had Fatima and Yolanda," she indicated the set of kitchen slaves, "show me how." She glared at her hands in memory. "While I kneaded the sticky dough it—it got under my ring. Then I twisted the ring, just enough to be able to pick the dough free," the Sulteena sobbed, her own body heaving with the effort. "My hands were slippery from the butter, when I twisted the ring—oh, Father—it flew across the room, and collapsed into—this!"

She dropped a pile of bands before the Sultan and fell to the ground, sobbing.

The Sultan's eyes widened. A disheveled ring was classic proof of adultery. "Daughter," he growled, "is this truly how it happened?"

The priest of Aman, who had waited among the servants, stepped forward. A highly ranked old man, he bowed deeply and said, "All was as your daughter said.

I was in the kitchen, seeking refreshments after my morning meditation. The ring flew off, into the dough."

Like bands falling into place, the Sulteena's plan came together. The priest was too old to be suspected a lover. His robes marked him as a devotee of Aman, the Father God, God of Truth and Clarity; his word was beyond question. The kitchen slaves, even the highly ranked handmaiden could be disposed of. A missing priest of Aman, however could spark a holy war and riots in the city.

The Sultan's face darkened like the sky before a sand storm. His mouth worked in anger. The kitchen slaves all but crawled under the stones, prostrating themselves in fear. The handmaiden shifted uncomfortably, and the Sulteena wailed. The priest faced the Sultan calmly, no doubt secure that no harm would come to him.

"You. Woman," the Sultan called to Quiocet. "Fix this and earn your freedom." He tossed the snarl of bands to her.

Quiocet caught the mess. Hope flared in her chest. He had said the words, the priest had witnessed; by custom, they were now law. If she could fix the ring, he would have to set her free.

Her hands plucked the strands into separate piles. She found the father and mother strands. The two large bands that overlaid all, holding the structure together. Of the thirty-two other bands, there were four other sets of mother and father bands. While difficult, the pattern was really only five puzzle rings that nested together. At once, the secret revealed itself; she would be able to reassemble the ring.

Her fingers began to twist the individual rings together. A soft cough made the priestess look up. She met the Sulteena's gaze. The young woman shook her head imperceptibly. The Sultana wanted her to fail? That was insane. It risked both their lives. Then the

Sulteena's words came back to her: "Be ready to obey." And the meaning of those words, like the puzzle of the ring, suddenly revealed itself to the priestess.

Concentrating, she twisted a single band. Carefully, deliberately, she bent it so that it was the twin of the band it should mate with. The ring would never fit together now. Yet, so subtle was her sabotage, only the master jeweler who had crafted the ring would be able to discern the change—and by tradition, he had been killed upon the ring's completion, that no man alive should know its secret.

With a final flourish the ring collapsed back into chaos. Destroyed, along with her chance of pardon. Head bowed with grief and sorrow that was quite real, she said, "Sultan, this ring is beyond my poor skill."

The Sultan snarled, "Fetch the royal jeweler." To another guard he said, "Dismiss the court, there will be no feast on this inauspicious day, and ensure that no one enters or leaves this room." He shook his fist at the Sulteena. "Daughter, you will be the death of me."

The Sulteena had composed herself; she sat cross-legged on the stone, the handmaiden combing her hair. The Sulteena rubbed the empty finger where her wedding ring had nestled.

The jeweler's eyes widened when he saw the disheveled ring. Clearly, he saw his death in both success and failure. No amount of coin could be trusted to silence rumor about the Daughter of Heaven. He threw himself at the Sultan's feet.

"Radhi's work I cannot repair, Sultan. That highest craftsman, gods rest his soul, was as high above me as you are above the lowliest servant."

"You will try," the Sultan snarled and gestured.

One of the Sultan's heavy-set guards moved to stand behind the jeweler, sword ready if he should fail.

Trembling, he tried to repair the bands. Quiocet pitied him. His fear was so great that he could not join the five sets of mother and father bands, the first step to solving the ring. He got three sets together, then lost the whole in a trembling mess. Even without her sabotage, he was a doomed man.

The Sultan scowled at the fumbling jeweler. "Daughter, I fear your folly had been your destruction at last. It may be that this situation is beyond my repair."

"There is another way," Quiocet said in a quiet voice, pitched to carry to every corner of the room.

"What? Speak, woman!"

"Your daughter's mishap illustrates what has long been whispered in the marketplace, that the wedding rings are no sure test of fidelity. A faithless woman, with the sole intervention of a finger-sized stick, can foil them. While a faultless and honorable woman, such as your daughter, can unjustly be executed.

As the words flowed from Quiocet, she felt Menomy's presence settle on her shoulders. What game was the goddess playing with her poor flesh?

The Sultan cocked his head. "A stick, you say?"

Quiocet nodded and gestured how a puzzle ring could be slipped from finger to a stick, never falling into disarray. "It is no secret among the adulteresses of this city. I in my cubicle served only those unfortunates, those who either by accident, or by another's evil design, had their rings disarranged."

The Sultan looked at his daughter, now beautiful and composed. "Father, I am blameless. Do not let me die for the crime of wanting to please you." Her hands outstretched as she implored him.

Quiocet thought it a bit overdone, but the look on the Sultan's face indicated that the Sulteena had hit her mark.

"Tell me what I must do," he said.

"Declare publicly that the rings are not conclusive proof of infidelity. In this manner, you will save your daughter's life, as well as other unlucky but honest women. You will be known as Iswara the Just. Warn husbands of the tricks of adulteresses, and become known as the Iswara the Wise. Let it be known that the execution of a wife cannot be decided by an inanimate object but must be ruled on by a judge, after fair hearing."

The Sultan glared, not liking the law placed before him. "The rings represent a thousand years of tradition."

"A thousand years of foolishness. As Sultan, it is your duty to lead your people into enlightenment, is it not?"

His daughter looked at him, her liquid brown eyes begging for respite. Quiocet was surprised at the girl's facility. She barely recognized the proud young woman she had met the previous evening.

"Very well, then," the Sultan growled. "Let no woman be judged by a thing. The ring is not proof of wrongdoing." His lower lip pulled into a scowl as he considered the uproar this proclamation would provoke. Not least of all in his own house, when his son-in-law heard the reason.

The priest, smiling placidly, removed a tablet from his robes.

The Sultan glared at Quiocet, and suddenly the last part of the Sulteena's plan snapped into place. It was lost on none in the room that Bhikkhu, the priest of Aman, was also that Order's highest scribe.

The Sulteena grinned and hugged her father's knee. "And since Quiocet's actions are no longer a crime, she may go free." She clasped her arms around his neck. "Oh, when did a daughter ever have a father as blessed with wisdom as I?"

Her father was not distracted by her cheerful histrionics. His eyes darkened and he glared at Quiocet, "I see the truth of it now." He pushed the Sulteena from his lap. "You have subverted my daughter."

The priest finished his scribing and held the scroll recording the Sultan's words in front of the King.

When signed, it would be placed in the vault of Aman, with other sacred truths.

Quiocet smiled; she dared not laugh outright. "No, my Sultan. This is not my doing. Your daughter, like her mother before her, was always a clever woman."

THE HAND OF A LADY

by Anne Cutrell

Entirely too often, in the old field of Sword & Sorcery fiction, the females were regarded as bad-conduct prizes for the men, which is the main reason I started the *Sword & Sorceress* anthologies. Here, in a clever variation on that plot, a princess is resourceful about accepting the "usual" outcome.

Anne Cutrell says she was born in Argentina in 1974. She is now 22, and an American citizen. From third grade to twelfth, she spent all her time reading, although she learned in sixth grade that it was better to do her homework. (I wish someone had taught me that; I never had to study till I got into college and so never learned how. It was quite a shock to find out I couldn't do everything automatically ... and that I had to teach myself how to study.) She says she studied graphic design in a private college but transferred to the University of Maryland to study architecture. She says that architecture classes take up all her time, but she took a semester off to work in Argentina in an architectural firm and got to know the maternal side of her family. It's all grist to the mill, though she says that she has learned that "you don't need to be a truck-stop waitress to experience life." There are easier ways to get to know life; the trouble is you need to know it while you're experiencing it.

As I rode my donkey into the cluster of multicolored tents, I looked about me with my usual uncontrollable curiosity. It was a perfect day for a tournament.

The air was crisp and clean—not too hot for the knights imprisoned in their heavy armor. The sun shone, pleasing the noble ladies, who had dressed in their jewel-bright best.

Troubadours strolled about, trying to amuse their patrons and still manage to enjoy themselves. The air was filled with idle chatter, music, the clank of armored men, and impatient mutterings from the horses.

I left my donkey with the horse-boy and he waved aside my proffered coin after a glance at my simple brown cassock. I blessed him and went off in search of the main tent.

As usual, this was a tournament for the hand of a young lady. This time it was for Lord Brier's only daughter. It was to begin in a short time, but contestants were still arriving. Lord Brier greeted them, then ushered them into the main tent to pay their respects to the lady . . . the prize. I liked watching the young hopefuls arrive, to choose my favorite early.

This time I already knew my favorite though I did not have a chance to see him. He had arrived so early that he had missed being greeted by Lord Brier. His name was Mark Barden of Tor Aspen, and I had known him from a babe in arms, as I had stayed at Tor Aspen for several years before moving to the monastery. Not only was he skilled in the arts of battle, he was also the only one of four brothers to escape the cruelty-to-animals stage of boyhood, thereby earning my approval. I thought about going to his tent to visit him, but I knew how most knights hated to be disturbed before a tournament.

The appointed hour came. The host, Lord Brier, left to begin the tournament. Both the armsmaster and I assumed that no more contestants would arrive and had turned away, when one last straggler came in. He was dressed in very plain serviceable armor, his shield a blank brown. He was already wearing his helm, and the faceguard obscured his features.

Of course, the armsmaster did not let him pass unchecked. With all the feuding going on those days, you could not be too careful. He ordered the young knight to remove his helm.

The youngster complied, though reluctantly. His short brown hair framed a foxy, thin face. Indeed, with those wide brown eyes and that slight build, he might almost be taken for . . . no, I shrugged the thought off as absurd.

I wondered who he was, but after an initial grunt of surprise, the armsmaster waved the knight into the tent. He emerged shortly after, the helm once again shielding his face.

The tournament commenced with the customary parade of the contestants upon their tall, carefully bred steeds. At the end of the file the strange youngster looked a bit out of place, dressed in plain brown and riding a horse of clearly inferior breeding. Apparently he had given his name to the herald, for he was announced as "Elwen Trumen." That did not clear up the mystery. No one knew who he was or who his family was. The youth had certainly added a measure of excitement to the proceedings.

Also a bit uncommon was the fact that the lady in question did not make an appearance. I gathered from the gossip around me that she was quite egalitarian in her beliefs, and did not approve of being fought over like a dog's bone. It was not surprising she felt that way, for she had been raised with one brother, and had often ended up as his only playmate.

The tournament continued in the usual fashion, in the form of a melee. It was a sort of mock battle, which usually broke down into a series of single combats. First, the knights were divided into two groups, which set off at each other, lances couched. When most of the knights had been unhorsed, hand-to-hand combat ensued. The knights were equipped with everything from heavy swords to halberds to maces to nets. It was not uncommon or unsporting for several knights to set upon one, especially if he was well known. Defeated knights were sent off to be tended. Ransoms to the victor would be settled later, privately, and in a gentlemanly fashion.

A few of the knights were remarkably good. I spotted Mark right away by his blue-and-silver trappings and his coat of arms, per fess Argent and Azure Boar courant proper, surmounted by the charge of a second son, a crescent sable. He was extremely powerful and seemed tireless. Though I had no wager on him, I was glad he was doing so well.

Gossip circulated about the mystery knight. The speculations ranged from a rich prince in disguise to a young knight of semi-noble origins who had fallen in love with the lady in question and had gathered the courage to fight for her. He did surprisingly well. He lacked brute strength, but he made up for it in speed and intelligence. The more experienced knights battled each other, ignoring the young knight. He allowed them to eliminate each other, while he conserved his strength fighting less skilled knights. Such use of strategy was unusual in a youth and, paired with his excellent sword skills, made him a serious adversary.

The day waned, slowly but surely, and gradually knights were eliminated, until it came down to the final battle—between Mark and the strange "Elwen Trumen." Of course, I wanted Mark to win, but I wondered how he would handle the quick youth.

The battle began and seemed an even match. Both knights rained blows upon each other, and neither would give way. Mark bore a massive two-handed sword, and his opponent a lighter, shorter sword and a long knife. They circled and struck, retreated and advanced. Eventually, the youth faltered, and faltered again. The length of the tournament was beginning to tell upon him. Mark's strength was holding.

At last, the youth lay on the ground, shieldless and

weaponless. Mark stood over him, victorious. He cut
the knight's leather helmet strap with the tip of his
sword. The helm fell back to reveal long blonde braids
and a lady's face!

Lord Brier shouted in astonishment from his box,
"Elyta! How on earth! Why?"

The lady's blue eyes stared at the victor. Her strong
features were smeared by dust, blood, and sweat, and
she panted heavily.

She answered the second question. "I deserve the
right to my own destiny, Father, so I decided to win it
for myself."

The victor removed his helmet and revealed not the
black curls of Mark Barden, but the blond locks and
blue eyes of another Brier!

"I told you I'd win this match, sister," he said as he
tucked his helm and its borrowed colors under his arm
and offered a hand to the lady.

"Well, I had to be sure one of us did, Gawain," the
lady said, without a hint of irritation in her voice, "and
you have to admit I organized this magnificently." She
smiled, took his hand and pulled herself up.

The father simply stared, unable to take it all in. The
slight youngster with the wide brown eyes emerged
from the lady's tent clad in plain armour identical to
Elyta's. I did not doubt young Mark would appear soon
to learn the outcome of his friends' efforts.

Gawain turned to the assembled crowd and said, "I
have won the hand of Lady Brier, in fair combat
according to the laws of our king. But since she is my
sister, I cannot marry her. Therefore, I give her hand
back to her, to do with what she wishes . . . whether it
be to sew, to cook, or to fight."

He touched his hilt to his forelock in salute, and the
lady accepted with a curtsy of imaginary skirts.

TO HAVE AND TO HOLD

by K.D. Barnes

When I was very young—ten or so—there was a romance novel by this name. When my secretary Elisabeth was in college, there was a line of romance books by that name. Editors have all kinds of theories about titles, picking them up from everywhere. This one seems to be from the marriage service, and it at least refers to something in the story.

I've often said that names tell us nothing but the father's ancestry and the mother's taste in fiction. I've seen the fashions in names come and go often; there was a time in the sixties when every third girl-child or so was named either Debra or Carol; now it seems to be Tiffany or Amanda. The name Marion seems to have gone out of fashion now but was so popular when I was a teenager that there were four Marions when I was in seventh grade: McDermott, Harrington, Young, and me. But it's been years since I met a Marion under sixty, and that one was an infant named after me by a fan. This child may grow up hating me and my work because of an unfashionable name.

My daughter says I should have called her Stephanie or something; her name was so thoroughly out of fashion that her teachers could neither spell nor pronounce it (it's Moira, and the first syllable rhymes with Joy). The alternative is to give a child a name which will ensure thirteen or fourteen Davids, Patricks, or Kims in their kindergarten—as with my sons and foster daughter. What price originality? I went to school with a roomful of

Lizzies; then in turn came the Bettys, the Lisas, the Beths, the Libbys, and one can tell the age of an Elizabeth from her nickname. Our household currently has two: Lisa and Beth (or Elisabeth and Elizabeth—I'm glad they have separate phone lines!).

Karen is a name which seems to be ageless; Karen Barnes says, "being allergic to cats, she has substituted two and a half Shelties"—how in the heck does one count half a dog—"and a Rottweiler mix, in addition to her husband and two children." She adds that, like her heroine, she is still at the "utterly besotted" stage of her marriage. Long may it flourish; I remember it well.

Karen Barnes was born on February 29th, 1956, and has recently celebrated her tenth birthday. I was very confused when I read this, having forgotten what happens to people born on Leap Day. (Is this why some of them have half dogs?)

As in an earlier story, a woman's ring is significant for the plot of "To Have and To Hold."

"**I**n token and pledge of enduring love and faithfulness, with this ring, I thee wed." The words of the wedding service echoed in Karis' mind as she rode along the ridge route back to her village. She had traveled to Riversbend for the christening of her niece, Karista. Her younger sister, Hallee, had named the child in her honor. Hallee had begged her to stay the night after the christening ceremony was done.

"The roads aren't safe!" Hallee exclaimed. "There have been strange happenings lately. The herders have come upon lifeless sheep, drained of blood. Why, just a fortnight ago in Shadygrove, there was a man attacked one night as he was going home from the inn. It just isn't safe to travel so late."

"It's only half a day's ride through the foothills," Karis responded. "Why, I'll be home by dusk, sitting in my rocking chair in front of the fire, thinking of you," Karis teased.

"I know you're anxious to return to Mikel," Hallee replied, "but I wish you'd reconsider. It really is not safe to be out after dark."

Now she was on the road home. *Oh, to be home again!* Karis thought. *To see Mikel.* This was the first time they had been separated since their wedding over a month ago.

Karis twisted the wedding ring on her left hand. She still had not grown accustomed to the feel of the slender silver band. Mikel had fashioned it himself from a lump of ore he had found in the hills as a youth. Working evenings at Master Tobard's forge, he fashioned the ungainly lump of ore into fine strands of silver wire. The wire he then cunningly twisted so that each individual strand would interlock with its neighbor to form an intricate puzzle. Karis had been delighted with the gift—especially when Mikel showed her the secret of interlocking the rings. Now she wore the puzzle ring on her left hand as a symbol of their union.

A flock of birds rose from the trees ahead, startled by something. Karis pulled Mist to a halt to look ahead to see if there was anything amiss. She patted the mare's shoulder encouragingly.

"We'll be home in time for dinner," she promised the mountain pony. Satisfied that there was no danger, Karis urged Mist forward and resumed daydreaming of her wedding.

The new spring leaves reminded Karis of her wedding gown. Well, it was really a festival gown, but what better festival than a marriage? Hallee had embroidered meadowsweet and tenzrac flowers around the hem and sleeves of the loose, flowing gown. Karis had worn her chestnut-colored hair loose as becoming a maiden, although truth to tell, she was the oldest bride the villagers could remember. Why, her own sister, Hallee, who was seven years younger than

Karis, was married with two children and another on the way by the time Karis was wed.

Still, it was a beautiful ceremony. Father MacKellar, the village priest, officiated. He was the very same priest who had baptized both Karis and Mikel when they were children. Dame Eldritch, the village midwife and healer to whom Karis was apprenticed, gave the bride away as her parents were no longer living.

Drowsing in the afternoon heat and lulled into a half sleep by Mist's footsteps, Karis relived the wedding once again. She remembered the moment when Mikel handed the silver ring to Father MacKellar for the blessing.

"I, Karis, take you, Mikel, to be my lawfully wedded husband—to have and to hold, to love, honor and obey, in sickness and in health, for richer or for poorer, till death do us part." Karis sighed with contentment as she repeated her vows for the second time that day. So lost in memories was she, that she fell off Mist's back as the pony shied abruptly after nearly stepping on a ridge rattler.

Karis tumbled down the loose shale slope and hoped that the horse would not crush her as she slipped down also.

Finally, they came to a halt on a narrow ledge some fifteen feet below the trail. Beyond the ledge the slope dropped off abruptly until it finally leveled out into the river gorge far below. Karis was scratched and bruised from the fall, but Mist was another matter. The little mare was shaking badly and wouldn't put any weight on her left rear foot. Karis gingerly stood and hobbled over to the pony. Although still trembling from the shock of the fall, her healer's training soon took over. She could almost hear Dame Eldritch's voice echoing in her mind. "First you must calm yourself, then see to the patient."

"There, there, Mist," she soothed, "just let me take a look."

"Oh, no!" Karis exclaimed in dismay as she picked up the pony's left rear hoof and saw the stone firmly lodged in the foot. She tried prying it loose with her fingers but to no avail. It was wedged in too tightly. She needed something to use as a hoof pick—something strong enough to dislodge the stone without causing any more injury to the area. She thought about using her belt knife but discarded the idea as too risky. If she slipped, she would surely injure herself or the pony.

They must make it to shelter before nightfall. She recalled the traveler's hut they had passed about a half mile back. If she could get the stone out, maybe they could make it to the shelter before dark. Unfortunately, she would have to get the stone out first, as the slope was steep and the pony would need full use of her leg to pull herself up the hill.

"One . . . two . . . three . . ." Karis exhaled slowly, deliberately to calm her racing nerves. As she contemplated their predicament, a thought occurred. "Maybe I can use the carved horn spoon in my healer's pack to lever out the stone."

Quickly she rifled through the saddlebags until she felt her healer's kit. Withdrawing it, she rummaged around inside until she held the spoon and a dried bundle of herbs with golden flowers.

"Meadowsweet for mind's ease." she muttered, repeating the words Dame Eldritch so often used. Karis offered the fragrant bundle to Mist. Tentatively the pony whuffled the scent and then, to Karis' relief, started eating.

"Good girl!" Karis praised. "That should ease some of the pain."

Facing the pony's tail, she moved to the left rear leg and lifted the injured foot. Bracing the hoof between her knees to stabilize it, she tried inserting the spoon along the edge between the hoof wall and the

stone. The stone didn't budge. Fortunately for Karis,
Mist was accustomed to having her feet handled and
did not try to jerk her foot back or lean her weight on
Karis as some horses would. Karis tried working the
bowl of the spoon down along the back of the hoof.
Slowly she was making progress. All she had to do was
ease the spoon in far enough to get some leverage on
the stone.

Success—finally. The stone popped out in Karis'
hand. It was exactly the size of the pony's foot, rounded
on the bottom and sharply pointed on the top. As she
probed the foot for injury, Mist flinched, jerking her
foot out of Karis' hands. Karis noticed that the wound
was starting to bleed. Although the greatest danger was
from infection, the bleeding would have to be stopped
before they could move on.

Their first priority was to find shelter before nightfall. Karis pulled her canteen from the pack and
sluiced some water over the wound to rinse away
the blood. Then she packed the hoof with absorbent
moss and covered the entire foot with several layers of
sacking. She removed the crucifix from the cord
around her neck and placed it in her skirt pocket, then
used the cord to secure the sacking around the injured
foot. "It's not the prettiest bandage I've ever done,
but it should work," she thought. "Now to get us to
shelter."

She led Mist up the steep incline. As she had suspected, the snake had long since slithered away. There
was not a trace of it as they reached the trail. Slowly
Karis set off, leading Mist back down the way they had
come—hoping they would reach the safety of the traveler's hut before dark. Already the sun was low on the
horizon and the air had a decided chill to it.

As they plodded on, Karis' mind raced ahead to all
that still needed to be done. "I'll need tenzrac for
fever," she thought, "and water and wood for a fire."

They had passed a narrow creek on the way up, not too far from the shelter. That should be fine for getting water. Common courtesy dictated that each guest of the traveler's hut replenish supplies such as wood and kindling before leaving, so there probably would be plenty of wood for one night. That just left the tenzrac. Karis remembered the sycamore grove she had passed. Tenzrac usually could be found in the deep shade of the older trees. Now was that grove before she had passed the hut or after?

To her relief, the sycamore grove came into view as she rounded the bend. Nearing the grove, she led Mist to a mossy area with a rivulet for water and plenty of grass for grazing. She tied the end of the lead rope loosely to a hanging branch, so as to leave the little mare enough room to move about, but not enough to stray. Karis set off quickly to the larger trees at the center of the grove. There she picked several bunches of tenzrac flowers for brewing fever tea and pulled one plant up roots and all, for the more potent concentrations found in the root nodules. As she started back to the mare, she passed a patch of savory and wild onions. She picked some of each to put in the evening pot.

Securing the bundles in the saddlebags, she loosened the lead rope and resumed leading her patient down the hill. As she walked, she observed Mist. The pony was still limping badly, but would probably suffer no permanent injury if she could treat the foot properly, come nightfall.

Twilight was deepening by the time they made their way to the traveler's hut. Karis had refilled her canteen with water at the creek, so she should not have to venture forth for more water until morning. Leading the mare inside the rude hut, she removed the saddlebags and set them down on one of the two benches in the room. The hut was the typical dirt-floored travel shelter with four walls, a door and a stone fire-place at one end. Karis went outside to gather several armfuls of the meadow grass which grew around the clearing.

"What Mist doesn't eat, I can use for bedding," Karis thought. She filled her travel kettle with water and set about starting a fire. As soon as the fire was lit, she put the kettle on to boil. She remembered Hallee's warning as she bolted the door shut against the night's nameless denizens.

Karis untied the cord and removed the layers of sacking from the injured pony's foot. Carefully she unpacked the moss which was now dark with blood. She once again rinsed the wound and noticed with satisfaction that the bleeding appeared to have halted. Removing several pouches from her kit, she selected one, a dark mahogany-stained leather, and sprinkled the whitish powder into a shallow bowl. She then added water, powdered alyssum root, and a pinch of pennyroyal. Using the horn spoon, she stirred the ingredients, adding water occasionally until the mixture had the consistency of a medium gruel.

Now for the tenzrac. Karis opened the saddlebag and extracted the plants. *The flowers I'll use for brewing tea, but for the wound, I'll need the root nodules. The root extract is stronger.* She reviewed the procedure and then began to wash the roots gingerly, taking care not to bruise the nodules and risk losing some of the precious medicine. Tenzrac tea would keep for days once brewed, but the medicine from the nodules must be used at once for full potency. She laid the nodules on the bench, kneeling in the dirt in front of it with her belt knife in hand. Carefully, she laid the knife blade alongside the largest nodule in preparation for the first cut. Outside the hut, the wind blew fitfully, scraping the overhanging branches against the sides of the hut, almost as if someone were scratching at the door.

Ever so slowly, she cut diagonally into the root nodule and then held it dripping over the bowl with the other ingredients. She repeated this process with three more nodules when she was interrupted by the unmistakable rumble of thunder. In the lull that followed, she once again heard the sounds of scratching at the door. Karis stopped her work and listened intently for a repetition of the sound. Nothing. Shaking her head, she resumed the process of extracting the precious fluid.

Scratch, scratch, scratch . . . the sound grew more insistent. Karis hesitated a moment, reluctant to interrupt her labors, but the scratching continued. She stepped to the door and called out, "Who is there?" Straining her ears to her the muffled reply, she cautiously lifted the bar and opened the door a crack to look outside. The light from the fire inside the hut cast fitful shadows into the night. As her eyes adjusted to the dark, she saw a hooded figure standing in the shadows, well back from the door. The figure spoke in an oddly accented voice. "Can I come in?" he inquired.

She saw that he appeared alone and unarmed. "Yes," she assented. He followed her into the hut and watched as she bolted the door.

"I am called Rushak," he said as he threw back his hood and removed his cloak. Karis was struck by the feeling that she knew this man, yet she knew that was impossible. Few foreigners came into the meadowlands. Still . . . there was something about him.

She noticed his eyes on the herbs laid out on the bench. "You are a healer?" he asked in a soft voice.

"Apprentice," Karis replied, remembering the tenzrac, "and I have to get back to work before the tenzrac looses potency."

"Certainly," Rushak responded, sitting on the other bench.

Karis emptied four more nodules into the bowl and then stirred gently to combine all ingredients.

Satisfied that the poultice was properly prepared, she spooned the mixture directly into the wound. Then she packed the hoof with clean gauze bandages and once again secured the bandage to the foot with the sacking. She slipped her finger between the cord and the mare's leg to make sure it wasn't tied too tightly.

"There now," Karis breathed, "that should help." As she was cleaning up, she couldn't help but wonder about the stranger. He appeared young, no more than twenty or so, and was slightly built. Nonetheless, he exuded an air of quiet confidence.

She was slicing the savory and onions to put in the pot when she glanced at Rushak. He was sitting on the other bench, well away from the fire, *and he had no shadow.* Karis started, and then examined him more closely. He did *not* have a shadow. As her mind raced to the conclusion of who or what had been marauding in the hills lately, he stood and faced her.

Slowly, Rushak walked toward her, and just as slowly, Karis backed away. She had no illusions that she could overpower him if it came to that. With her right hand she gripped the belt knife, hidden now between the folds of her skirt. With her left, she frantically felt in her pocket for her mother's crucifix. It was gone! In its place was a small hole. It must have fallen out. By now, it could be anywhere.

Karis glanced at Rushak. At this distance he appeared older than before, now closer to thirty. His eyes caught hers and held her wordless in his compelling gaze. She stared into his deep, blue eyes as he moved without haste, steadily closer. She tried to break eye contact and finally succeeded in closing her eyes. He stopped in front of her and took her chin in his hand.

"Look at me!" he commanded, and Karis felt her eyes open of their own accord. He stood directly in front of her. His dark, shoulder-length hair curled slightly around his temples and was bound back in a queue. His piercing blue eyes were framed by dark, arched brows. She had the impression of standing on the edge of a deep, still pond and knew that at any instant she would be plunged into the icy water. Karis trembled as he lightly ran his fingertips along her jaw from her chin back to just under her ear. Slowly he smoothed her thick chestnut hair back away from her face. The belt knife dropped to the floor as her fingers relaxed. Her breath was coming in ragged gasps now, as she fought to be free of his influence.

Mist whickered, and the sound reminded Karis of home—of all she held dear. She thought of the first time she met Mikel. She remembered how strong his hands were as he lifted her down from the cart. She remembered how gentle he was with Mist, soothing her with hands and voice. Other images crowded in— Mikel curing a horseshoe in the water barrel, silhouetted against the rosy glow of the forge; Mikel with his head bowed in prayer at Sunday Mass. As she reflexively twisted the silver band on her finger, she had it! Her mother's crucifix was not the only holy relic she possessed. Her wedding ring had been blessed by Father MacKellar just a fortnight ago. She remembered him taking the ring from Mikel and placing it in the Holy Bible as he began to pray for God's blessing on their union.

Karis broke eye contact with Rushak as she lifted her left hand upward toward him. "Leave me!" she commanded. Rushak glanced at the ring and paled. Karis moved the ring up to eye level. Rushak stepped back. Karis followed as step by step they retraced their way across the room. Karis stopped at the door and lifted the crossbar. Rushak fled into the darkness. Shakily, Karis bolted the door and sank to her knees with relief.

The next morning, as she was sweeping the floor of

the hut, Karis spied a glint of shiny metal. As she
stooped to pick it up, she recognized her mother's crucifix. This time she packed it in her healer's kit for
safekeeping. Twisting the puzzle ring on her finger for
luck, Karis and Mist started down the road for home.

A KNIGHT ON TOWER HILL

by Kathrina Bood

Kathrina Bood says she is 23 years old, which seems to be a median age for first sales. She writes, "I enjoy reading, writing, horses, archery, or anything that will get me into a forest," and recently joined the SCA. She is working on the mandatory novel, and trying to fight an unhealthy addiction to British sitcoms. Question: why unhealthy? British sitcoms are supported by the special TV tax; judging by results we should have one here. She says she wishes to dedicate a "A Knight on Tower Hill" to Marjorie Wilcox to fulfill an old promise. She has been published in high school and college, but this is her first professional sale.

In "A Knight on Tower Hill," a search of a castle yields a treasure.

This story was inspired by the song "One Tin Soldier, the Legend of Billy Jack," written by Dennis Lambert and Brian Potter.

Kellin lay in darkness, shivering in the wet cold, and watched the fading embers of the fire moldering in the tinder of damp leaves. Flame licked up the remains of the last dry branches of wood on the crumbling stone hearth. The precious supply of wood had run out long ago, and now, only halfway through the sleeting night, the knight knew that he was slowly freezing to death.

Kellin's hazel eyes stared over the top of his blanket

and wandered about the contents of the tower room. Ruins of furniture, shards of pottery, and shreds of moldy curtains and tapestries lay scattered about the remains of what must once have been a bedchamber. Rubbish, rotting leaves, bird feathers, and droppings littered the stone floor. In the corner lay evidence that a large predator had used it as a den. The wood of the furniture, now cracked and splintered with age and neglect, had been turned into delicate carvings with intricate designs. Kellin had thought briefly about burning the artifacts, but something about the place made that thought impossible to act on. He knew that he should raise himself and move about to get the blood pumping through his veins. Yet he could not; his leaden limbs did not have the strength, and his weary mind did not care. Along with his warmth, the cold had sapped away his resolve.

Kellin closed his eyes, letting his mind wander in a frozen void. *Sleep,* he thought, and with sleep would come death. That thought forced his eyes back open, and with all the strength that remained within him, he shoved himself to his feet. He teetered there for a moment, his head spinning from the sudden rush of blood to his brain. The knight busied himself with removing his armor and then draped his cloak and blanket about his shoulders.

He moved slowly about the room, first rummaging through the scattered artifacts with his eyes and then with his hands. It almost felt as if he were prying. Still, it was something for him to do. Something to occupy his mind and keep his body moving.

The knight inspected odd pieces, turning them over in his hands. His fingers took over when his eyes failed in the dying light, feeling the deep patterns carved in wood or the knotted nap of decaying fabric. A blast of wind blew through the cracks of the sagging oak door, rocking it on its one remaining bronze hinge. Leaves ran before the gust, parting the sea of debris in its wake. Kellin followed it with his eyes. In the farthest corner of the room, hidden in a pile of disturbed leaves, there was a glint of metal.

Kellin froze as something sounded barely within the range of his hearing. He stilled his breathing, senses reaching to capture the sound again. On the edge of the howling of the bitter wind, the jingle of harness reached his ears. Years of training took over and instinct locked out the misery of his body and mind. The smooth, stacked leather hilt of his sword was soon in his hands, and Kellin rested his back against the wall aside the door. Long moments passed, the sounds growing nearer, only to be whipped away by the wind, and come again closer, until the movements seemed just outside the door. Another breath of silence and the oaken portal shuttered and groaned as it was forced inward. A dark form leaned against the door, shoulder braced against the warped wood, and shoved.

Kellin held back his attack, waiting. A voice spoke to him then, a gentle whisper in the back of his mind. It told him that he had nothing to fear from this stranger, and so he held his sword.

The failing firelight was not bright enough to make out the stranger's features, only the silhouette of dark on dark. The faint outline of form said that it wore a cloak, hood drawn to conceal all features within its depths. The intruder stopped when the door was opened and withdrew back out into the sleeting storm. Soon after, the figure reappeared, leading the large, dark mass of a horse through the door. No sooner had the animal entered, than the stranger dropped the rein and turned to reseal the portal. The intruder froze as the realization of Kellin's presence took place; his hand flew to his waist where the silver of a sword blade flashed.

"Who is there?" The smooth voice of a woman spoke the question. The tone was soft and lilting, stressing the ends of the words. An accent that was unfamiliar to the knight.

Kellin withdrew from the shadows and took care in the show of sheathing his sword. The voice spoke to him with the still, calmness of a mountain stream. Danger did not walk with this woman, only a quiet growing pain.

"Kellin, milady. Sir Kellin Whrothwyn. A knight of the castle Shanizar. I mean no harm. I mean only to seek shelter from the storm. If you will, there is plenty of room for you and your steed. I fear I have no food to share." It was custom in the land of Marzipan that when someone offered camp peace, bread was to be broken. Kellin could not even offer travel rations. That chafed at his honor and at his pride. His horse had been killed while fording a river swollen with spring rain, swept away by a wall of rising water. With it had gone all of his supplies. Only by luck and the smile of the gods, had he somehow managed to keep from drowning in the weight of his armor. The woman hesitated at his offer, her hooded head glancing at her horse and then at the storm that wailed outside, at last nodding a curt bow. Only after a quick visual calculation of Kellin and the interior of the tower room did she sheathe her weapon. She was weighing him by his honor. Her life depended on the few words of formality that he had spoken.

"May I ask your name?"

"Moija." The woman said, nothing more. No titles, no lineage or House. Kellin repeated it, tasting the word. It was of the ancient tongue, but not old beyond recognition.

"Will you require assistance with your steed?"

"No," was all she said as she set to work. First she withdrew a bundle from her saddlebags and made for the fire. Kellin could not see what it was, but an instant later the flames were dancing with renewed life, causing long shadows to waltz across the stone walls.

Next she cared for her horse, taking great pains to insure its comfort, before setting up camp for herself.

"It is a magnificent horse." Kellin observed. "From the Condar Valley, isn't it? Daggnar stock?"

Moija stopped searching her gear long enough to glance up at the mare. "Daggnar. Yes." she answered, a note of pride apparent in her voice. The woman produced two circles of flat bread and a small wheel of soft, white cheese and divided it, offering a share to Kellin with a black-gloved hand. The knight accepted the meager, but nourishing meal with heartfelt thanks and devoured it immediately. It was the first real food that he had eaten in two days, unripe berries and raw tubers notwithstanding.

Moija eased herself to the floor, pushing back her hood as she sought a comfortable position. Warm golden light reflected off the fine lines of a sculptured, aquiline face. Long strands of walnut hair escaped from a hastily woven braid and hung along the sides of her face. These she hooked behind her ears as she ate. Dark eyes, Kellin could not make out their color, matched his intense gaze look for look. Moija removed her cloak, spreading it on the ground to dry. The armor that she wore beneath was not the heavy plate mail most common in Marzipan, but a suit of finely interwoven steel rings in a mesh so delicate that it looked more like coarse fabric than chain mail. Her shins and knees were protected by a heavy, double layer of molded leather greaves covered with flat metal studs. Her shoulders and torso were encased in much the same. Silver arm bracers were the only form of plate mail that she wore.

"Why have you come to Tell'Sakera?" she asked quietly, the first voluntary words that she had spoken.

"Tell'Sakera?"

Moija nodded. "This place that you find yourself is Tell'Sakera." She stressed the name as if it were supposed to hold a deeper meaning for him. It did not.

Kellin shook his head. "The name by which I know this place is Tower Hill. I know nothing of Tell'Sakera. For as long as this place has lain in ruins, it has been called Tower Hill."

The woman drew back, a furrow settling over her brow. "Ruins." It was but a whisper. To Kellin it seemed that only then did she realize the state of her surroundings, the crumbling walls, the sagging roof overhead.

"How long has it been?" The words were addressed only to herself and spoken so softly that Kellin was not certain that she had said anything at all. Moija returned her attention to the young knight, her eyes narrowing. "From what city did you say that you are from?"

"Shanizar."

"I have never heard of that place."

Kellin cocked his head to one side. He knew, now, not only was this woman out of place, but out of *time*. It was the only explanation that made any sense. Shanizar was the capital city of Marzipan, all trade and prosperity was ruled from it. Even the Wilders, a race of people who lived out their lives in the deepest forests of Marzipan, would know of Shanizar, if only by name. She looked on the ruins of Tower Hill as if through the veil of a dream, seeing it not as it was but as a memory of how it *had been*. He looked at her saddle where it lay on the edge of the firelight. He had seen saddles like that only in tapestries whose threads were so time faded that they barely held color. Kellin told Moija about Shanizar then, of the workings of the great trade city. Confusion showed openly on her face.

"The ruins that lay below this hill, in the valley, what do you call them?" Moija's mind was like a viper, striking back and forth from question to question, never lingering in one place too long. Her black-gloved hand gripped her sword hilt for it was safe, familiar. She steeled herself for an answer that she did not want to hear, but an answer that had to be heard.

"Whitestone."

"Scareshia." Moija said, as if correcting him. "We knew it as Scareshia. I remember now. I was looking for something. Looking . . ." The woman's voice faded to a whisper. "But now I am too late." With a shake of her head, Moija returned her wandering mind to the present. "Those who dwelt there called it Scareshia. It means 'Valley-home' in the old tongue. By race they were called the Wilders. For many centuries those of us from Tell'Sakera and those from the valley were at peace with one another."

Those of us? No wonder she had been so confused. This place, or what was left of it, had been her home. Kellin sat up straighter as the woman continued.

"Tell'Sakera was blessed with rich amounts of metal ore that we would fashion into weapons and armor."

A candle lit in the knight's mind. Sakerian steel! His Grandsire had always raved about the stuff, of its lightness and strength. Even when others claimed that it was only the prattling of an aged mind. Even Kellin had trouble believing that weapons forged of Sakerian steel would weigh as little as a weapon of only half its size and remain as strong as if it had been forged of normal steel.

"The weapons and armor were taken down to Scareshia and from there taken by caravan to be sold throughout the kingdoms of Marzipan. Tell'Sakera and Scareshia were partners of a sort, but the Wilders were a jealous people, trusting no one from outside their valley. Even the great profit that we brought to them could not earn their trust." Moija's voice had grown distant with memory, her eyes looked, unseeing, into the fire. Many times throughout the story her words faded to silence until she would remember that Kellin was there, and she would take up where she had left off.

"The Wilders grew jealous and distrusting. Where once there had been a peaceful alliance, they now sent armed escorts to the castle to receive the shipments of arms. One day a messenger arrived at Tell'Sakera with a missive from the king of Scareshia. The letter charged our kingdom with betrayal of the trade agreement that promised half of everything Tell'Sakera had to their brothers in the valley. Scareshia claimed that we were hiding a great treasure, buried within the hill. A treasure trove of gold and jewels. The letter demanded that they be given the gold immediately or Scareshia would lay siege to the castle and take it by force." Here her voice halted again, but this time it was to fight back tears.

"My father sent back a reply. If indeed there was a treasure buried beneath Tell'Sakera, we would gladly share it between our two people. The Wilders were outraged. By dawn of the next day the Scareshian army surrounded the walls of Tell'Sakera." Moija stopped speaking, the only sounds that could be heard were the popping of the fire and the wind outside. The kindling on the hearth shifted and a cloud of sparks puffed into the air. Long minutes passed as she paused to stoke the fire.

"For one full cycle of the moon we withstood their attacks, but we were grossly unprepared. War had not touched Tell'Sakera for over a century. We, who forged the tools of war, were unprepared for it." A small smile pulled at the corners of her mouth with the irony of it all. "The gates of Tell'Sakera fell, not from lack of strength, but from lack of will. The Wilders killed everyone that they could find, turning the earth of Tell'Sakera red with blood. They left only one person alive." Moija bit her trembling lips and Kellin ached to reach out. To somehow ease her pain. Nothing could, he knew. So he let the woman face her pain the only way that he knew she could, on her own.

"Only one, to lead them to the treasure. So I did. I led them to the only treasure that I knew of that might have been worth all of my people dying for." She

spoke as if giving directions to a friend who knew the
land well.

"Along the garden path, to the large stone on the lee
side of the great oak tree. I turned the stone and gave
them what was beneath. They laughed when they saw
the book, and then they struck me when I told them
that the book was the treasure that they sought. The
Scareshian captain opened the book, reading it aloud,
and then . . . then they let me go."

Kellin blinked hard. "They let you go? After all of
that?"

Moija nodded and brushed a gloved hand over
her eyes.

"But what was in the book?"

"It . . ." The woman snapped to her feet. "I have to
go. I have to find it."

Kellin jumped up and took hold of her arm,
demanding, "Go where? You cannot just—" The
knight's words were cut short as Moija twisted free of
his grasp and shoved him backward.

"No! There is no more time for stories. The book is
the only thing that matters. If I can find it, perhaps . . ."
She did not finish her sentence, only set to hastily sad-
dling her horse. Kellin did not try to stop her. The
intensity on her face said that if he tried to interfere
again that he might not live to regret it. Only when her
hands strained to open the door did he speak.

"What did the book say?" He asked.

Moija stopped before the open portal, the wind
whipping at her hair and the hem of her cloak. "The
truth," she said, and walked into the storm.

Kellin sat with his back toward the fire, the skin
beneath his tunic burning with the closeness of the
flames. An hour had passed since the woman had left.
Had she been there at all? Patterns in the dust and the
white scrape marks left by the mare's iron-shod hooves

said that she had been. It all seemed like a lingering dream.

The storm had passed, and pale golden light was seeping through the cracks around the warped wooden door. Dawn had finally come. Kellin pushed himself wearily to his feet and walked to the door. Some fresh air would do him good. The reflection of light on metal winked at him from the farthest part of the room and he strode to it. *Déjà vu.* It was exactly what he had been about to do before *she* had come.

The knight went to his knees and brushed away the dead leaves and rubbish. Leather was revealed beneath his hands. The leather and steel binding of a book. The cover bore no writing or ornamentation. Carefully he opened it to the first page. The pages were yellowed with age, the corners crumbling as he touched them. Only a few of the pages remained. Was this the book that she had been looking for? Something inside assured him that it was.

Kellin took the book to read by the light of the fire, careful of the tome's delicacy. The ink was faded, but written in the common tongue. Kellin cleared his throat and read the words aloud.

"So it is written, that peace should be shared among all men, peace being the greatest treasure of all. . . ."

Kellin understood now what Moija had meant by saying that what the book contained was truth. Peace was the treasure for which the Wilders had killed. That must be the reason they lived so deep in the forests, to hide their shame from the rest of the world. Moija would never know. Kellin closed the book softly and began to weep.

THE LONGEST NIGHT

by Lisa S. Silverthorne

Lisa Silverthorne is a microcomputer manager in a Midwestern university library. She struggles with arthritis and carpal tunnel, but figures that even if her hands couldn't write, she'd learn to dictate or find some other way to keep creating stories. She has finished two novels and is working on a third.

Between five cats, some Orandas (a type of fish), and a beadwork hobby, she must be pretty determined if she still finds time to put words on paper (or screen).

Here is a story about what might happen if you use threats to gain power.

Darina clutched the marble rosary in her scraped and burned hands, fearing that Lord Cedric would strike her again. She glanced back at the distant stone Circle and slid away from the campfire. Already, her swollen cheek throbbed.

"Get up," Cedric growled and raised his hand to hit her again.

She recoiled from him, one hand covering the rosary and the other protecting her face.

"I am doing what you asked of me."

When he lowered his hand, Darina returned her attention to the rosary. Her fingers flashed across the slick beads and she felt a magical charge as she began to chant. Every power word she whispered into the night brought the faint gleam of yellow to the beads.

Cedric's worn face pinched with anger, his

impatience growing. He looked more evil now than she had ever seen him. His ruddy hair burned in the crisp night air and the flicker of the campfire exaggerated his harsh features into a demonic mask. Tonight, on the Longest Night of the year, when magic battled magic, he belonged on these desolate plains.

For years, Lord Cedric had challenged the Circle's power, but never had he been strong enough to tap into its energies. In his desperation, he had forced Darina to help him by threatening to destroy her village. He had heard the rumors of her magical gifts from nearby towns. Through her magic, he would wage a war against the Circle's power and conquer it for his own use.

"Why are we so far from the Circle?" He thrust his hands to his hips and glared at her. "Do you think I'm some simple shepherd you can trick?"

"Much magic travels these plains tonight, m'lord. The cover of your camp will protect us."

Darina reached the final bead and slid the rosary back through her fingers to begin the chant again. The pale yellow aura deepened. The beads had to be dark gold before the magic was ready.

"More lies!"

Cedric ripped her up from the ground and shoved her toward the Circle. Darina fell, the rosary slipping from her hands.

"You will not take this moment from me. I will stand beside the Circle when it gives up its power to me."

On hands and knees, Darina clawed desperately at the tall grasses for the rosary. Her life depended on it. Finally, to her left, she saw the faint glimmer of deep yellow in the grass. She reached for it. The rosary was cool against her fingers as she began the chant again.

Arcs of magic rose in flashes of indigo and red across the plains. Her hair bristled at the forces at work around her. She knew she must finish her own task quickly. On this night, the most dangerous place she could be was near the Great Circle.

Cedric glanced unsteadily around him.

"This place grows dangerous," he said, his voice softer. "Finish or I will kill you right here."

"And wait another year for the Longest Night?" Darina asked, the beads glowing a deep gold now.

Once more and the magic would be strong enough.

She gazed at the stone Circle with its heavy stones set deep in the ground. Rising to her feet, she reached out for the nearest stone. It warmed immediately to her touch and began to glow the same deep gold as the rosary beads in her other hand. One last time, she worked the beads through her fingers until she reached the end.

It was done.

Cedric would at last have all the power of the Great Circle at his fingertips.

"The Circle is yours," she said and moved away. She extended the glowing rosary to him.

Cedric snatched the beads from her hand. When his fingers touched the rosary, his form wavered. Instantly, he was transported inside the Circle. A thick sheen of gold light enveloped the stones. Delirious, Cedric drank in the power until his whole body pulsated with gold light. When he was sated, he pointed a finger at her and smiled.

"You will be the first to feel my newfound power. You were a fool, Darina."

Darina laughed and gazed into his dark eyes without fear.

"No, you were the fool, Cedric. I gave you exactly what you wanted. All the power of the Great Circle is at your fingertips, but none of it can ever leave the Circle. And neither can you."

His face contorted with rage, and he tried to cast magic at her. Ignoring his tantrum, she turned on her heel and walked away. His scream echoed across the plains, the anger turning shrill with fear. For the first night in many months, she and her village would sleep well.

BLOOD MOON
by Cynthia Ward

Cynthia Ward was born in Oklahoma and has lived in Maine, Spain, Germany, and the San Francisco Bay Area. She now lives in the suburbs of Seattle and has sold stories to three volumes of *Sword and Sorceress* (VIII, IX, and XI), *The Ultimate Dragon,* and a great number of anthologies and magazines. I cherish a vague memory of having met her at one of our local conventions, but my memory is somewhat uncertain.

"Blood Moon" is about the bond between two friends, a bond strong enough to survive when one becomes outcast.

As the Sunlord drew near the end of his journey across the sky, the witch Winter arose from her labors in the garden. She brushed her hands on her linen tunic and pushed back a lock of hair, white as swansdown, though she was twenty-two. Like her father, she'd had white hair from birth, and her eyes were a pale, translucent blue: signs of the Moontouch.

Winter raised her rowanwood staff from among the kale shoots and started across the clearing, limping slightly. She almost fell when her pet wildcat appeared underfoot. Her familiar twined round her ankles and chirped, telling her clear as words that he hadn't eaten in months. Wanderboy was, like any cat, a great liar. He disappeared for days at a time, but not months.

This time Wanderboy had been gone a week, so Winter was relieved to see him. She'd found him under a fallen tree, the only surviving cub of a she-cat that had died killing a fox; and the forest held bears and wolves as well. More than once in the last few years Winter had glimpsed a wolf in the shadows at forest's edge. It made her nervous, though wolves rarely bothered humans and she always carried her staff. She was glad that in these parts the Moontouch, the witch-talent, did not take a wolf's form, as it did in the distant west, where mountains scraped the sky and towns were governed by "kings," men born to rule as witches were born to protect.

Winter reached down. Her cat darted behind her. She turned and forgot him. A fat black column of smoke bisected the red cloud-streaks of sunset. Winter could not see mile-distant Tjalve for the pines, but she knew the village was burning.

Bandits!

Winter's family had always protected Tjalve. Winter's father had died saving the village from bandits. She had let them come.

Someone emerged from the forest. Winter raised her staff. Then she realized that the figure walking up the grass-grown wagon-track was alone, and small. A child.

Winter ran. She was fast, despite the old leg wound, and unhindered by long skirts; she wore a ragged knee-length tunic, girt by a knife-belt and stained by garden work. Tangled curls brushed her shoulders. An unmarried woman wore her hair long and unbound, but Winter, living in isolation, did not worry overmuch about her appearance. She had chopped off her hair after her exile.

She stumbled and almost fell as Wanderboy ran between her legs. He bounded ahead, determined to accompany her but not to follow, though he had no idea where she was going. When he stopped glancing back, Winter knew he'd spotted the approaching figure. Had he ever seen a child before? Surely not.

The year-old cat spent little time in her cabin. And for the last seven years the villagers had come to Winter only when desperate.

Five feet from the child, Wanderboy stopped. Then, with a deep growl, he flattened his ears, arched his back, and swelled his tail to twice normal size.

The child froze.

Winter increased her speed, though she'd been running her fastest. Wanderboy was friendly to her, and ignored most other humans, but he was still a wildcat.

He crouched, but did not spring. Hissing, he flattened against the ground, his tail curved tight against his body. Winter realized her fearless wildcat was cowering.

Wanderboy fled.

The child's face was hidden in shadow, but Winter could see the hair was black. Winter's dread increased. Only one villager had black hair—rather, only one villager had had black hair seven years ago. This child must be Raven's daughter.

Winter extended a reassuring hand, then recollected herself. "Sparrow, are you hurt?"

"No! I was getting firewood when the bandits came! I hid in the woods. They didn't see me." Sparrow sobbed. And Winter could not offer comfort, for the child feared her. All the children of Tjalve were taught to fear her. "They killed Papa!" Sparrow cried. "They took Mama!"

Fear struck Winter to ice, fissured, near to shattering. The bandits had abducted Raven.

Sparrow said, "Mama told me if something ever happened to her, I must go to the witch."

"She did?" Winter's surprise swiftly dissolved in anger. She hadn't seen Raven in seven years. Raven had made one decision and Winter had made another, and Winter had been banished from Tjalve.

Winter almost fell as Raven's daughter suddenly flung herself into Winter's arms. The witch dropped her staff to catch her balance, then closed her arms around the weeping child.

One child did not fear her.

Winter murmured soothingly, and closed a hand on her staff. The child sagged against her, slack and silent as a bag of flour.

Winter had spelled the child to sleep.

She gathered the small form in her arms and hurried into the tiny cabin. A gesture of her staff lit the few candles, and Winter received her first clear look at Raven's six-year-old daughter. Her heart contracted; for a second it was as if she looked upon Raven in childhood.

Winter laid the child upon her pallet. She spread a blanket over Sparrow and smoothed her soft black hair. "I swear by Moonlady Szethra," Winter murmured, "I will do everything in my power to bring your mother here to wake you."

The scrying bowl was pure silver, gleaming in the illumination of three beeswax candles. The water reflected the village in flames. People wandered blank-eyed among burning buildings, tended the wounded, wept over the dead. Winter rubbed her face with her hands; her nails drew blood.

Winter felt a painful rush of relief to see her mother's sister Thistle binding wounds. Only her aunt had visited her willingly after her banishment from Tjalve. Thistle and her late husband had had no children; she had lost no kin today. But Sparrow had truly lost her father; Deerstalker lay motionless in red mud, arrows in his chest and throat.

Among the dead Winter also saw Mayor Wheelwright. She had thought she would rejoice when he died, but she felt neither joy nor sorrow. Vengeful pleasure was not possible in the face of such devastation. And she and the mayor were as responsible as the bandits for the destruction of Tjalve.

Raven was not in the village. Winter saw few

young women, alive or dead. Where had the bandits taken them?

Winter chanted. In the scrying bowl, the image blurred as if Winter were looking through the eyes of a hawk rising impossibly fast into the sky. When she fell silent, the burning village was a coal, the other villages invisible in the green-black vastness of forest. Near the edge of the bowl, a tiny spark glinted where no village stood.

Winter spoke a few words, and the spark grew to a bonfire surrounded by some fifty ruffians dressed in gaudy rags and bristling with weapons: swords, knives, bows. The bandits feasted, spilling beer into matted beards and tearing meat from greasy joints. At the edge of the firelight stood the bandits' hobbled horses and, penned in a circle of laden carts, the villagers' cattle. The carts, Winter knew, contained the wealth of Tjalve: cauldrons, tools, bolts of homespun, and, most valuable of all in spring, the last of the fall harvest.

Threescore or more young women lay on the firelit ground. Their wrists and ankles were bound, their garments torn and bloodied, but no bandits were near them. They were to serve, Winter realized, as the last course of the bandits' feast.

Winter set the scrying spell moving from woman to woman; she saw grief, pain, terror, despair. She remembered the women's expressions of fear and hatred when she was driven out of Tjalve. Since that day she'd seen none of them save when they had dire need of her healing powers. But seven years of loneliness and anger had not hardened Winter's heart enough to ignore their plight, or her failure in her duty to protect them.

Where was Raven? Had her heart failed? An old fear: Raven had always been excruciatingly shy. Only with Winter had she ever seemed to relax; Winter had even persuaded her to join in youthful pranks upon the other villagers. Few had taken their jests seriously, but

Mayor Wheelwright was humorless and unforgiving. And he had disliked Winter's father. So Winter and Raven targeted him mercilessly until, in their twelfth year, they piled cow manure on his doorstep and covered the stuff with tinder and dried leaves, which they set afire. They knocked on the door and ran away, to peer around the corner of another cottage as the bony, ungainly mayor stomped on the burning leaves and sank ankle-deep in dung. He did not see them, but of course he knew who was responsible.

Then Raven said she'd had enough of pranks, and became even more withdrawn; she was guarded even when alone with Winter.

Winter lost interest in trickery when the bandits attacked. When they were dead or fled, Winter crawled, arrows in her limbs and shoulder, her leg sliced bone-deep, to her father's side. He lay unconscious with a grievous, evil-smelling slash in his gut; a slow-killing wound. Winter cast the healing spell with great care, but she hadn't enough strength, and the spell drained his last traces of energy. She killed her father.

Winter had neither strength nor desire to heal herself. But she recovered, after many months. When she was walking again, her mother, who had never recovered from her grief, passed away.

Winter was old enough at thirteen to take care of herself. She lived alone in her ancestors' cottage, and like her father and ancestors, she treated the ill and injured of Tjalve. The time she had to herself she spent mostly with Raven.

One morning two years after her mother's death, Winter forgot her staff when she went to the cottage of Raven's parents. When she and Raven stepped outside, they found a crowd of grim-faced men and women gathered before Raven's home. Winter looked for her aunt, but did not see Thistle. At the forefront of the crowd stood Mayor Wheelwright, wearing a strange smile. Wheelwright rarely smiled.

Winter said, "Is this a town meeting? We are of age now. Why were we not told?"

Wheelwright gestured. Winter found herself trapped in powerful arms. She twisted, fighting to free herself; she saw Raven in the grip of two of the mayor's five sons, and knew two others held her. Raven stood motionless in her captors' arms, her face bright red. She had always hated to be the center of attention. Winter thought she would swoon.

"What is this?" Winter demanded. "Let us go!"

Mayor Wheelwright did not answer. He turned to the gathered villagers. "There is evil in our midst. It must be rooted out. This is painful, but it is necessary."

Nothing made sense. Not the mayor's words, not the mayor's actions, not the assembly. Had the old fool finally gone senile?

"What are you talking about?" Winter shouted.

Wheelwright faced them. "Winter. Raven. You are fifteen years old, grown women, yet you run around like wild animals. You still spend all your time together, when you should be married and starting families." He focused a stern gaze on Raven. Terror struck her, palpable as a blow; half-fainting, she was kept upright by her captors. "Raven, your father betrothed you long ago to the blacksmith's youngest son." He turned to Winter. "But Winter's father made no arrangements, though a responsible father provides for his children's future when they are young. Especially when he is the last of his line."

"How *dare* you insult my father!"

"I would never insult your father, who died to save us," the mayor said piously. "I am only saying that you were unsupervised when you should have been learning the rules of adulthood." He shook his head. "The failure is mine. I should have become your guardian and had my wife teach you a woman's duties.

You should already be married and bearing heirs to your father's legacy! This cannot continue. I shall betroth you to my youngest son."

Winter burst into laughter. "I'd sooner marry an ox than your dullard spawn!"

Wheelwright's eyes narrowed. Several villagers laughed. They fell silent at the mayor's glance.

"Winter, you will do your duty as woman and healer. You will obey your mayor."

Winter spat in his face.

He wiped away the spittle and addressed the crowd. "It is as I suspected. The witch is unnatural. She looks at other women as a man would."

Someone gasped. Someone else said, "You called assembly to tell us *this?*"

"I called assembly because she disobeys the gods! She ignores the Moonlady's command to her family and lets her father's bloodline die. And I fear she practices evil magic!"

Voices rose in disbelief, but also in fear.

"Liar!" Winter shouted. Wheelwright gestured. "I *never*—" A hand closed over her mouth. She fought with all her strength, but could not break free; she sank her teeth deep into callused palm, but the hand remained in place.

Mayor Wheelwright turned to Raven. The red had faded from Raven's face, leaving it snow-pale under her black hair.

"Raven," the mayor said, "I do not think Winter's evil is in you. I think you are ready to assume a woman's responsibilities. Am I right?"

Raven stared at him fearfully. Winter wanted to strike him dead. But she had left her staff in her cottage—and thereby provided an opportunity which, she realized, the mayor had been awaiting ever since her father's death.

"Raven, you must answer me," Mayor Wheelwright said gently. "Are you ready to marry?"

Raven nodded.

Winter struggled to break free. She tried to speak. But the hands that held her were as inflexible as the mayor's soul.

"Winter," said Wheelwright, "unless you renounce the evil in your heart and assume a woman's duty, you will be banished from Tjalve." He gestured to her captors. "Let her speak."

"Wheelwright!" Her aunt Thistle's voice, angry, coming from a distance. "What are you *doing?*"

The hand left Winter's mouth, closing painfully on her upper arm. "You bastard!" she shouted at Wheelwright. "There is less evil in my heart than a hair of your head!" She could hardly speak for the rage swelling her throat. "If I am banished from Tjalve, Tjalve should expect no protection from me."

She saw horror spread over faces that had previously been stunned or curious or disbelieving. She'd fallen into a trap. By withdrawing her protection from the village, she went against the Moonlady's command to her family, to all witchkind, and thereby seemed to prove Wheelwright's accusation that she was an evil witch. But she was too proud to bend to the vengeful mayor. She would not retract her words.

"Winter, you are banished from Tjalve," Mayor Wheelwright declared. "You may not return, on pain of death. No one may speak to you or aid you, on pain of exile." He looked past Winter, at his sons. "Get her out of here!"

They dragged her out of the village. She watched Raven until Raven was out of sight. Raven didn't look at her.

The mayor's sons tossed her into the forest. She lay where she had fallen, and did not move though day became night, and morning. Then a raw storm struck, and she made her way to the cabin that had been built for Wolfhound, Chief Hunter of Tjalve until a falling branch struck his head. Magic could heal broken skulls, but not broken minds; Wolfhound woke a different man, who did not recognize even his beloved wife, and feared the village. So his brothers cleared a patch of forest and built him a cabin, and brought him food. He'd disappeared a couple of years ago; the villagers supposed he had been slain by wolves or bear.

Taking shelter in the rude cabin, Winter found not dust and cobwebs, but food fresh from the harvest, her clothes and pallet, her grimoires, scrying-bowl, and staff. Before the villagers could gather the courage to ransack her ancestral home, her aunt had borne away her belongings, and had known where she must go.

If Winter were an evil witch, she would immediately have returned with her staff and destroyed the village. She did no such thing, but, save for Thistle, those who disobeyed the mayor's command came to her only to bring the desperately ill or injured, and they watched her fearfully, as if sure she would strike them down where they stood.

How stupid it all had been! Why had she and Raven persisted in annoying the mayor with their pranks? They had been children, but that was little excuse. And what excuse was there for an old man—a leader—to hold a childish grudge?

As the years passed, Winter realized that Wheelwright had wanted control more than revenge. Wheelwright had hated her father for having an authority that did not answer to the mayor; Wheelwright couldn't tolerate this power in a girl. So he had banished her from the village.

Had it never occurred to Wheelwright that sooner or later more bandits would come to Tjalve?

Wheelwright was a bitter old fool. And she was a proud young fool. Between them they had destroyed their village.

Winter's hands tightened on her staff. Among the bandits' captives she'd found a woman whose face was hidden by hair so black it gleamed in the firelight. So black Winter used to tease Raven by saying her father must have been a passing stranger.

The captive raised her head and shook the long loose hair out of her eyes. Her tear-stained face showed not fear, as Winter expected, but anger. She glared at the sky as if raging against the gods.

Winter fought her own rage; she must stay calm lest she disrupt the scrying spell. She didn't know where the bandits were. She widened the spell's focus. The bandits were in a grassy meadow beside a broad river, which would be the Yarszyks, the only river near Tjalve—but *where* on the river?

Winter saw a tall rock with a bandit standing watch upon its peak. The boulder leaned over the river like a huge and crooked fang, and she recognized its distinctive shape. She'd been in that meadow once, seeking a rare flower for a fertility potion. The meadow was a three-hour walk south of Tjalve.

Somewhere in her books of magic was a spell that could take her instantly to the meadow. She had never learned the spell; she feared it. She had three fat grimoires, one in a western dialect; where among the hundreds of handwritten pages was the spell she needed? She had experienced it only once, a decade ago, when she and her father, gathering herbs in the forest, had heard faint screams from the direction of Tjalve. Her father had magicked them back to Tjalve to join the villagers in battling the bandits, and the spell had drained him, slowing his reactions badly; but he'd had no time to waste. Neither did she.

Winter found the spell quickly, and counted herself blessed. She laid the open grimoire before the scrying bowl, and turned away.

She drew on a dark cloak, hiding her white skin and hair, and tied a satchel of bandages and potions to her knife-belt. When she hurried back to the scrying bowl, it responded to her greatest concern and showed Raven. Beside Raven crouched a bald, yellow-bearded bandit, rubbing a lock of her black hair between his fingers.

Winter almost spelled herself to Raven's side. But if she appeared in the midst of the bandits, all her sorcery could not keep her from being immediately killed or taken captive.

With a painful effort she restored the image of the boulder. Then, raising her staff, she read from the grimoire.

Winter found herself beside the boulder. She sagged against rough granite, dizzied by the abrupt transition and drained by the spell. Thank Moonlady Szethra her inexperience had not caused her to appear inside the boulder; she would have died and the boulder would have burst, turning a hundred acres of forest to splinters and annihilating both bandits and captives.

Winter looked up, muttering a quick spell and pointing her staff. The watchman fell off the boulder with no sound save a splash when he struck the river. Had his comrades heard? Winter turned. A score of bandits sat feasting; the rest moved among the captives. Screams rose over the roar of the fire.

Winter could not spell the bandits to sleep; that enchantment, like the healing spell, worked only at the witch's touch. She knew a death-spell that would kill all the bandits—and all the captives. Slaughter-spells didn't discriminate.

Winter would have to kill the bandits one by one.

Fixing her attention on the bandits sitting before the fire, Winter murmured a spell and swung her staff like a sword. Though the staff gave off no jets of light or streams of color, it made a bloodier mess than an ax. Twenty headless bodies slumped to the ground.

Limping heavily in her weariness, Winter ran toward the fire, and almost stumbled over a man upon a woman. The woman screamed and writhed beneath him, helpless, her hands bound. Winter smashed her staff into the bandit's throat and pulled him off the captive, murmuring a quick spell. She released the bandit. He sank down and did not rise. His neck was intact, but windpipe and spine had been severed.

The captive, Miller's wife Aster, fell silent and stared up at Winter. Winter drew her knife. Aster's eyes widened. Winter turned her over and cut the rope around her wrists.

Winter pulled the dagger from the dead man's belt and laid it beside Aster. "When I kill a bandit, cut the woman free."

Aster said fiercely, "I will kill bandits, too!"

Winter studied her expression, and nodded.

Then Winter was almost deafened by a scream so loud and close it drowned all other sounds. She threw herself forward, knocking Aster flat so they were indistinguishable from the other paired shadows around the fire. But the horrific shriek did not attract the bandits' attention. What was one more scream?

Winter ran toward the sound. A bald bandit rose in her path. She leaped back, remembering that the bandit she'd seen crouching beside Raven was bald. She raised her staff and her bad leg gave beneath her. She fell.

The bandit fell beside her. Above his pale beard, his face was red meat and white bone. How could a bound woman do *that?*

Not a woman. A wolf.

The beast leaped to its feet, blood-wet muzzle open in a snarl. Winter raised her staff, though she couldn't finish a spell fast enough to save herself, with the wolf so near.

A wolf roaming among the captives! Was it so maddened by hunger that it didn't care about the dozens of armed men?

The great black beast closed its jaws and stood motionless on ragged cloth and loops of rope, watching Winter with eerily blue eyes. Watching Winter like the wolf she sometimes glimpsed at the edge of her clearing.

Winter glanced at the sliver of full moon peering above the treetops. Her scrying bowl had shown Raven raising an angry face to the moonless sky. Winter remembered the form the Moontouch took in the west. She remembered her jests that black-haired Raven's father must have been a foreigner. She remembered her wildcat's reaction to Raven's daughter.

The wolf crouched. Winter raised herself on her staff. Sweat trickled down her temples. Her hands shook.

"Eleriasza," she whispered, praying the wolf would understand. "Eleriasza, do you know me? Do you know Meliada?" She was speaking Raven's True Name, and her own, which she had never told anyone save Raven. Names were power. Winter prayed Raven would recognize her True Name despite her wolf form.

The wolf stood motionless, watching with pale blue eyes.

"Eleriasza," Winter whispered, "help me."

The wolf bounded silently to a bandit crouching over a bound woman and tore out his throat. Winter went in the other direction. To preserve her remaining strength, she killed with her knife. Some of the women she freed lay screaming or weeping or immobile, but others took up the dead men's knives and joined her in killing bandits. She hoped the uncertain light and the bandits' preoccupation would keep the free women from discovery.

A sharp hiss rose above the fire's roar, and ended in screams of pain. Winter looked about wildly. Ten men stood in a ragged line, nocking arrows. Even as Winter began a spell, the bowmen released their second flight. Her chant ended and her staff slashed. The bowmen's bodies collapsed like puppets whose strings have been cut. The arrows completed their arcs. Winter heard screams and a howl.

"Goddess!" Winter turned toward the wolf-cry.

"Healer!" A hand seized Winter's arm. "My sister is hurt!"

Winter almost swung her staff like a club before she registered the words. She pulled her arm free.

"Other bandits may still live!" she called. "Some of you must find and slay them. Others must help me with the wounded." She saw women nodding. She opened her satchel of potions and bandages. "Clean and bind the wounds that do not demand immediate spell-healing."

The hand returned, closing suddenly on Winter's wrist, pulling her to her knees. "My sister's dying!"

Before Winter lay the blacksmith's new wife, Lily, a feathered shaft in her neck and blood pouring out. Winter had heard no sound from the wolf since that agonized howl. Raven might be superficially wounded, or already dead; Lily had only seconds to live. Chanting, Winter laid her staff on Lily's arm and pulled the arrow out of Lily's neck.

Winter heard gasps as the wound closed. With a shaking hand she touched Lily's smooth neck; the pulse was faint, but steady. Swaying with exhaustion, Winter closed her eyes. She had not used too much of Lily's strength in the spell. She had not killed Lily.

A scream brought Winter to her feet. "Gods, a *wolf!*"

"The witch's familiar. It killed many bandits!"

Winter stumbled toward the voices, leaning on her staff.

"It looks like the bandits killed her wolf."

Raven lay motionless, eyes closed, an arrow jutting from her black-furred side. Air sucked through the wound with a frightful wet sound. The arrow had pierced Raven's lung. She was dying, and Winter, drained by the spell that had brought her here, had spent the remnants of her energy killing bandits and healing Lily. She had been this exhausted when she had attempted to heal her father and killed him. She would not kill Raven!

If she did nothing, she would kill Raven.

Winter placed a deep sleep-spell on Raven, hoping to gain a few precious seconds. Then she began the healing spell. She chanted with terrifying slowness, seeking to ensure that all energy needed for healing would be drawn from her own body. That she might be drained fatally did not matter. She must not kill Raven.

Winter chanted the last word and yanked out the arrow.

Blackness flooded in, drowning Winter.

Motion, jolting; rough board beneath her face. Had she been captured? Did Raven live?

Winter sat up. Her hands were free. Torchlight showed the wolf lying motionless beside her in an otherwise empty wagon-bed. She laid a shaking hand on Raven's side. So still—

No! The wolf's side rose and fell. Raven lived.

Where were they? Who drove them? Winter twisted around. As if sensing Winter's regard, the driver looked back. Her gray hair gleamed dully as iron in the light of torches affixed to the seat-posts. Her teeth flashed.

"Welcome back, niece!"

" 'Welcome back'?" Winter repeated. "I'm in Tjalve?"

"We've left Tjalve," Thistle said.

"Of course."

"No," her aunt said. "We've left because my home and your old cottage were burned down. Winter, you are welcome again in Tjalve. You have everyone's gratitude for killing the bandits and rescuing the women."

Winter bowed her head. "I wasn't even guarding the village! By the time I noticed Tjalve was burning, the bandits were so far away I had to magick myself to their camp with a spell that could have taken me to Tjalve when the bandits appeared! And then I passed out before I could heal more than two women—"

"Winter! Did you and your father save everyone's life the last time bandits raided Tjalve?"

"No, but—"

"This time you fought alone, and single-handedly slew over fifty bandits."

"Not single-handedly! Many of the women helped me—"

"Winter. *You* killed most of the bandits. *You* saved the village. Rejoice in what you have done." Thistle grinned. "Rejoice that Wheelwright is dead."

"I cannot rejoice in that."

"I can," Thistle said. "He was a stupid fool, and he was mayor for years! Why the villagers kept approving him, I'll never know. It's a relief to have him gone."

"I must go back to Tjalve!" Winter cried. "The wounded—"

"—are safe in the care of their families," Thistle interrupted. "They'll survive a little longer without you. You've not regained enough strength for healing spells, niece, you're whiter than the moon." She pointed at the wolf. "I assumed you would want Raven at your cabin so you can claim you found her wandering wound-fevered in the woods."

"How do you know this is Raven?"

Thistle smiled faintly. "A couple of years ago, I was returning late from a friend's home when I saw a wolf jump out the window of Raven's cottage. She and Deerstalker didn't have dogs, and I knew what I saw was not a dog. I knew I must be seeing some spell of yours. So I kept my mouth shut."

. "This is no spell of mine," said Winter.

Now Thistle was astonished. "How is this possible?"

"Aunt, do you know if Raven has foreign blood?"

"Her grandfather was a Westerner who left a caravan

to woo a Tjalve girl. He had hair black as Raven's."
Thistle laughed. "Winter, are you saying outlanders are
beasts?"

Winter was startled into a laugh. "No!" she said.
"But in the West the Moontouched turn into wolves
under the full moon."

"Well, Raven's always been a woman in the
morning." Thistle looked up. Winter saw faded stars as
the wagon rolled into a clearing. Her cabin was near.
"Sunrise is a while off yet," Thistle said. She faced forward. "My niece is alive. I must be the luckiest woman
in Tjalve, for I lost no kin to the bandits."

Winter placed Raven on a quilt in the far corner of
the cabin; she did not want the little girl waking to find
the wolf beside her. Thistle threw a coverlet over the
wolf-body.

"You must stay here, aunt," Winter said. "I'll not
have you living in the mud until your cottage is
rebuilt."

"Not all the cottages burned," Thistle said. "I'm
staying with a friend. Anyway, you haven't room for
another guest!"

Winter walked Thistle out to the wagon, and was
startled by her aunt's embrace. "Get some sleep, niece,
you look ready to collapse! I'll be back this afternoon."

Winter helped her aunt up into the seat, and watched
the wagon until it disappeared into the forest.

Raven's daughter slept peacefully. Winter felt her
exhaustion, a crushing weight. She stretched out on the
floor beside the pallet. She slept restlessly, reliving her
killings. When she woke, her muscles ached; with the
aid of her staff, she stood and limped across the room.

She saw Raven as she had not in seven years.

The wolf-form was gone. Raven slept, her long black
hair spread on the coverlet. Her face was peaceful, but
too thin and pale. She looked older. She looked like an
adult.

She was breathing steadily, but Winter rested her fingertips on Raven's throat to feel her pulse.

Raven opened her eyes. They filled with fear. Winter jerked back her hand.

"Sparrow! Oh, Winter, do you know if my daughter lives?"

"She is well." Winter turned away. She did not exist for Raven. "She sleeps on the pallet."

She heard Raven run across the room with the ease of perfect health.

Winter walked out of the cabin. The morning air chilled her bare arms. She sat on a flat stone near her garden. At her call, her wildcat emerged from the forest. He started toward her, then abruptly turned and fled.

Hands closed on her shoulders. Winter waited, motionless. She sat on the boulder, but she felt as if she were suddenly in midair, falling she knew not where.

"Sparrow sleeps again," Raven said. "How ungrateful I have been, Winter. I did not thank you for rescuing me, or even for saving my daughter."

Winter looked over her shoulder, into Raven's thin, intent face. "I did not save Sparrow," Winter said. "She saved herself."

"She is strong, like her father," Raven said. "I have never been strong." She took her hands from Winter's shoulders. "He loved me, Winter."

"I know." In her scrying bowl Winter had seen it many times, as clear as sunlight on Deerstalker's face, his love of his wife and daughter.

Raven whispered, "How you must have hated me, for my weakness."

"I did not hate you," Winter said. It was not hate that made betrayal sting even after seven years. "But I do not know what can be between us after so many years of silence."

"You mean, you do not know what can be between human and beast," Raven said, voice suddenly harsh.

"Every day I pray my blood has not tainted Sparrow! I should have fled Tjalve before I could conceive. But I was too weak. I told Deerstalker that once a month I got so sick I had to sleep apart from him. And he believed me, and died defending me, thinking his wife a woman. Oh, I should have stayed in the forest the first time I changed! I'm a monster!"

"No!" Winter turned to face her. She was Winter's height, but so thin that the kirtle borrowed from Winter's chest hung on her like a sack. "Raven, you are Moontouched! In the West, the Moontouch takes the form of a wolf. You have Western blood. As the goddess blessed my father's family, so has she blessed you."

"Blessed?" Raven cried. "Cursed! Oh, gods, what I did to that bandit! What I did to so many!"

"You've killed other people?"

"Other bandits! Aren't they *enough?*" Raven closed her eyes, color suffusing her face. "Goddess help me— I loved it."

"Do you love it now?"

"No," Raven whispered. "I hate it."

"That is how I feel. But I don't regret what I did."

Raven's eyes blazed. "You didn't tear their throats open with your teeth and thirst for more blood!"

"A wolf cannot hold a knife. You did what you had to do. We do what we must to survive. You have not killed people at any other time. It is not something you'll keep doing."

"I don't want to risk it! Can no spell break this curse?" Raven's voice rang with despair. "Can no spell save my daughter from this fate?"

Winter remembered her wildcat fleeing the little girl. "You both are Moontouched, and that cannot be changed." Raven closed her eyes as if in pain. "But your Moontouch can be controlled, Raven. Tell me, would you truly want to lose this ability?"

Raven did not respond.

"Wouldn't you like to know how to turn into a wolf at will?"

Raven opened her eyes. "Yes!'

"I have a grimoire that speaks of the Goddess-gift you have inherited. Stay as long as you need, to learn how to change at will." Raven was silent. "You won't become outcast by staying here, Raven. I am welcome again in Tjalve." Raven flushed. "You started turning into a wolf when you started the woman-change, didn't you?" Winter said. "Finally I know why you suddenly became so distant."

Raven looked away. "I didn't want anyone to know. How I prayed no one would find out! All for nothing."

"Those who saw you last night thought you were my familiar. I didn't tell them otherwise. You needn't worry." Winter considered. "Nor need you confine yourself to learning the control-spell."

"I don't understand," said Raven.

"I need an heir," Winter said. "Sparrow has magic in her." Winter smiled. "And so do you."

Raven's eyes widened. "I used to envy you," she said. "How I wanted to cast spells like you did!"

"Stay, Raven," Winter said. "Learn to use your magic. And we will teach your daughter to be a healer."

"I will stay," Raven whispered, and touched Winter's hand to seal her pledge.

BY THE SKIN OF HER TEETH

by Heather Rose Jones

An old English name for "changeling" or "werewolf" is "skinturner," but I always believed that the teeth were exempt. Heather Rose Jones works in our office here while pursuing a Ph.D. in Linguistics at the University of California at Berkeley. She also writes excellent songs, although she says that activity has largely been put on hold until she's done with school. Almost as I write this, she tells me that she has sold her first novel—a historical romance. This story follows the same character from Heather's last two *Sword and Sorceress* stories and contains a serious discussion of the ethics of the skinturner, and matters of loyalty. I like it anyway, though usually I feel that serious philosophical discussions don't belong in fiction.

"Have I told you of how I learned I was to be a skin-singer?"

I saw the corners of Ashóli's mouth twitch, and I could almost hear her thinking, *Ah, no! Not more old stories!* But she spread her cat-skin cloak on the ground beside the fire and sat, listening, as the flames threw sparks up into the growing twilight. I saw her thoughts wandering as I recounted the tale. For three years she had eagerly drunk in my teaching; now she was growing restless.

When she suddenly came alert, I wondered what I had said to recapture her attention. Then I, too, heard what she had cocked her head to listen for. Somewhere up the mountainside, someone was racing a horse through the near-darkness, a horse that was spent and staggering.

We had set our small shelter in a clearing on the road running up toward the pass. It was near enough to Ashóli's village that they could bring us food and news easily, but far enough that we would not be constantly interrupted. (Far enough that when her cousin Goalnen came courting me, it was a pleasant break and not a constant nuisance.) Several times in each year, traders would come across and down, bringing tools and fine cloth and other things it was not worth our trouble to make ourselves. And more often than that, some of Ashóli's people would travel up and over taking furs and carvings and fine needlework and other things they had made to sell.

But this was no trader with slow, surefooted mules. I wondered that the rider had made it along the steep mountain track at that pace without a mortal fall. The hoofbeats came closer and more erratically, and Ashóli and I rose as one and cast our skin-cloaks about our shoulders, ready for what might befall.

She stumbled into the circle of firelight and fell, more than dismounted, from the lathered gray mare beneath her. I was surprised at how young she was—younger than Ashóli, perhaps. She had a different look from the others that traveled that same path, smaller and darker. She looked wildly from the one of us to the other and cried something in a language that was strange to me. Seeing our incomprehension, she tried again in the language that the traders use.

"Please, you must help me! He's coming . . . he will kill me. I didn't do it. It wasn't my fault, but he won't believe me."

I don't know what I would have tried to ask first, but at that moment the mare gave a strange cry and fell heavily to the ground. The woman echoed her cry and ran to take the horse's head in her lap, but the deep brown eyes had already glazed over in death. She began weeping then, in harsh, tearing sobs. I stood stupidly, at a loss for what to do, but Ashóli crouched beside her to stroke the mare's head and softly croon the death-song, the one we sing to release those whose skins we take. I don't know whether she had any thought at he time of cloak-making, I think it was simply the only way she knew to share the woman's sorrow at the death. Later . . . well, but that was later.

By the time Ashóli finished her song, the woman had finished her weeping and began her tale with the horse.

"I raised her from a foal," she began softly, as if talking to herself. "She was always my darling, my swift one, my Sunna. I took her as part of my dowry when they wed me to Gorliv. And whatever happened after that, I could be a girl again on her back—a maiden racing over the hills of home. I never wanted to marry a stranger, but it was a good alliance, and I did what they expected of me. I never wanted to have a child—it terrified me—but Gorliv must have sons, and I did what he expected of me. And then the boy died . . . before he was even named. It happens sometimes," she pleaded, looking up at us as if we were accusers. "Sometimes a babe is sickly and it just dies. There's no need for blame. But he said I had witched it, to strike at him. And they believed him—I had no one to speak for me. So I ran."

She looked back up the trail as if expecting pursuit to follow at any moment. "He won't give up. He will track me down and kill me. He swore it."

I spoke for the first time since she had arrived. "And so you will lead him here and make trouble for us."

Ashóli leaped up and faced me angrily. "Laaki! How can you say such a thing?"

I answered in the *Kaltaoven* tongue so that the stranger would not understand. "Can't you see? Her husband will come here hunting witches, and he will find them. The peddlers who come here . . . they know how to keep a tongue behind the teeth. But I have seen what happens when strangers find us out. Do you want your kinfolk killed or driven off to live as beasts? I have *seen* it."

Ashóli was frightened for a moment, not knowing whether I spoke of past memories or foreseeing. "And what if he doesn't come?" she protested. "What if she lost him on the trail? You can't be sure she's brought danger down on us."

"He'd be a fool if he's on that track tonight," I said. "But I mean to see for myself."

I strode up the trail, out of the firelight and out of sight, before pulling my owl-feathers closely around me. I whispered the skin-song that drew their essence into me. *Él-taov alyev, mél-daegh alyev, Time to wear the feathers, time to fly the night.* And then I spread my wings and soared silently over the tree-covered slopes and up to where the mountain track rose along the rocky heights. Nothing stirred there that did not belong. If he was coming, it was not tonight.

When I flew back home, there was no sign of the stranger-woman in the yard around the dying fire, but I shed my feathers out of sight to be safe. Ashóli met me in the door to our hut with a finger on her lips.

"I've sung her to sleep. Morning will be soon enough to sort things out."

"And send her on her way," I said. "What more have you learned?"

She gave me a troubled glance. "Her name is Eysla. I told her she could stay as long as she needed to."

"What?" I was startled by how angry I felt.

"Laaki, what's wrong with you? She needs help."

"Help is for our kind, for *Kaltaoven*." I spoke to her as if she were a child, and perhaps that was a mistake. "We don't owe anything to strangers."

"I was a stranger to you," she answered quietly. "I

wasn't your clan; you didn't owe me anything. But when my own kin would have cast me out, you took my part. Why?"

I was too angry to answer. It wasn't the same at all and I thought she was baiting me. I cast my feathers around me again and went off to hunt the night.

When I returned in the morning, tired but purged of my anger, I found Ashóli and the stranger flaying the mare's carcass. "When you've finished," I said to Ashóli, "go fetch some help from the village to finish the butchering. No need for waste."

She shook her head.

The stranger looked at her curiously. "I don't mind—it's only meat now, the rest of her is in my heart."

"No," Ashóli said. "It's forbidden to us."

"Because she died and was not properly killed? But surely you have dogs to feed. . . ."

"No, because—"

"Do you plan to make a skin-cloak, then?" I interrupted, shifting back into our own tongue. "From a beast of burden?" It was the only reason I could think of to declare the flesh taboo.

Ashóli shrugged and quoted an old proverb. " 'Who can know what skin will fit?' She was a noble beast, and it will be a new test for me."

The stranger was watching us with no comprehension, waiting to be told—or not—as we saw fit. Her complacency irritated me anew. I wondered that she had had the courage to run at all. When she saw me frowning at her, she stood and came to kneel before me, which did nothing to change my mood.

"Get up, stranger," I said roughly.

"She has a name," Ashóli protested.

I searched my memory. "Get up, Eysla."

She rose to her feet. "Ashóli tells me that I must have your permission to stay here. I will be no burden,

I promise you. I can cook and sew and fetch water, and run errands to the village for you. Ashóli tells me that you are often too busy with her training."

" 'Ashóli tells me,' " I mimicked. "What else does Ashóli tell you?"

Eysla stared at me blankly.

I turned to Ashóli. "Well? What else?" I changed to the *Kaltaoven* tongue again. "Have you told her what we are? Have you told her what she will see down in the village?"

"No, Laaki, I swear! I've been careful."

I turned back to Eysla. "This is as much Ashóli's home as it is mine. If she calls you a guest, that is her choice, but do not expect me to make you welcome. Now I am tired and will thank you to leave me in peace for a while."

When I woke late in the afternoon, I found the two of them laughing softly over some task as if they had been sisters. Of a sudden, I understood Ashóli's rebellion better. She had always been the outcast—lowest and forgotten by her clan—before I saw that she could be a skin-singer. Now here was the first person she had ever known who not only treated her as an equal, but looked up to her. Understanding it did not lessen the danger.

They had managed to dispose of the horse's carcass and Ashóli had cut the skin into a rough cloak-shape and pegged it out to dry. I saw Eysla glance at it curiously from time to time, but I didn't ask what explanation Ashóli had given her.

It was easier than I thought to get used to Eysla's presence. She was quiet and never underfoot. We were fed better cooking in the next three days than we had been in the three years before. And when it was time for Ashóli's lessons and I made a pretense of sending Eysla to the creek for water, she took the jug and asked bluntly when she should return. But I knew it could never last.

And one morning, as we sat eating our breakfast, there came a skittering of paws running up the path toward us and a lean, brindled hound burst into our yard. Before I could move to stop him, Ashóli's young cousin stood and shed his hound-skin before us.

Eysla screamed and jumped to her feet. The boy gaped in dismay, realizing his mistake. Ashóli went for the one and I the other. I couldn't hear what Ashóli was saying, but I scolded the boy so sharply I could almost see his ears droop and the tail creep between his legs. And after all that, his news was of little enough moment to make him so careless.

When I had sent him scampering back home, I turned anxiously to see what had happened with Eysla. I expected her to have run, to have gone mad with fear. Oh, she was frightened, that was clear enough. But Ashóli had drawn her away and was speaking softly and rapidly in her ear. I saw Eysla reach out to touch the spotted fur of Ashóli's cloak, then snatch her hand back as if burned. I let them be—though I doubted how much good mere words would do—and set about the day's chores. It was a long time before the other two joined me again.

There was a long, heavy silence between us as we worked, but after a time Eysla said, "I have wondered what it would be like."

I glanced at her questioningly.

"I used to dream of *being* Sunna sometimes, of running four-footed over the hills and being free of what everyone demanded of me."

I gave a short barking laugh. "Is that all the freedom you can dream of? To be bound with saddle and bridle and bear some man upon your back? That seems to me little different from the life you led."

She looked away then, but Ashóli was staring at her with that far-off look in her eyes. If I had known what she was thinking, I would have sent Eysla packing at once, no matter what the danger.

* * *

But I didn't suspect what Ashóli had in mind until several days later. I had gone down to the village on some excuse, but mostly because it had been too long since I had seen Goalnen. There was an understanding between us, but it didn't pay to depend on understandings. When I returned the next afternoon, the mare-skin was gone from its place and neither Ashóli nor Eysla were to be found. I was filled with dread then, hoping that I was wrong.

I ran to the meadow where we had been doing Ashóli's lessons and found her sitting on a stone, watching a gray mare running in the clearing below.

"What have you done?" I demanded. "She isn't *Kaltaoven*—you will drive her mad trapping her in a skin like that." And then, at the far end of the meadow, I saw the horse shift to a woman, who waved back at us. It was too far to hear the words, but I saw her pull the skin-cloak tighter about her and turn again to horse. "You made a song for her," I said, with horror in my voice.

Ashóli had turned to me with excitement shining in her eyes. "But don't you see? It's the song that has the power, not the singer, or even the tongue it's in. *Anyone* can wear a skin."

I took her by the shoulders and shook her like a naughty child. "Did you think this was something new? Did you think no one else had ever tried such a thing before? Of course outsiders can learn our songs—I've seen it before. And it always means death and disaster for us. They have no sense, no traditions, no clan. They go crazy with it, and we get blamed. What were you thinking of?"

"I was thinking that she wanted it," Ashóli answered, subdued but still stubborn. "She begged for it—to know what it was like. And I wanted to see if I could do it. She can learn what she needs."

"From whom?" I asked. "Your clan will never take

her in. And her own people will call her a sorceress, a monster, as they do us."

"She can learn from me," she said defiantly.

I let go of her shoulders and tried one more time. "And what of your duty to your clan? What of the songs you owe them?"

"Do I?" she asked. "That was *your* bargain—to give them a skin-singer. Mine was to give you the last three years. I've given them nine skin-songs in the past year—plus the two still unclaimed—so any debt is paid. You will marry Goalnen and join them; what need do they have of me?"

In her voice, I could hear a decision made long since that had nothing to do with Eysla. "So what will you do?" I asked.

Her eyes took on their faraway look. "I want to travel—like you have. I want to *see* things, to dream things."

It struck me to the heart. "Child, do you think that I've been wandering by my own choice? Every home I have ever had was destroyed by the greed and fear of outsiders. You should not envy me." It was no use, I could see that.

Hooves thudded behind us, then changed to a tentative footstep. "Ashóli. . . ."

I turned on Eysla and said harshly, "You're a fool."

She flinched from me, but no longer in fear. Wearing the skin-cloak had made that change in her.

"Perhaps you knew no better," I said more mildly, "but Ashóli should have."

She slipped the mare-skin from her shoulders and clutched it tightly to her breast. "You will not take Sunna away from me." She looked to Ashóli for support.

I sighed. It was too late for going back. We would have to play the game out to its end.

It had been long enough that I had begun to hope there would be no pursuit. But the next morning, a trick of the cool, still air brought the faint baying of hounds, drifting down the mountainside. I could not fly out to see during the daylight, so Ashóli took the cloak of raven feathers that had not yet gone to a wearer from where it hung by the also-unclaimed fox-cloak. There was hardly a need for her sharp eyes to confirm what we had heard. Three riders—with twice as many dogs—were picking their way down from the pass. There was nothing else they could be hunting. I sent Ashóli flying down to warn the village. When she had gone, I made my way back to our camp, hardening myself for what must be done.

Eysla was kneeling beside the outside hearth, kneading dough in a trough. I don't know why it bothered me to see her doing such homely things—as if she thought she could make everything right by being a better, more dutiful wife for someone.

"They have come hunting you," I said with no attempt to soften the news. "They came through the pass this morning with dogs and horses. I've sent Ashóli down to warn her kin."

She stared at me dumbly for a moment, then rocked back on her heels and stood, brushing the flour from her hands.

I was angry at her seeming unconcern. "You brought this down on us—on Ashóli. If they find us out, we cannot let them leave. But more will come, and more, and in the end we will be driven from our homes just the same."

She winced at that, but still said nothing. When she disappeared into the hut I started after her, but she reappeared at once, clasping the gray mare's skin about her shoulders.

"What are you doing?" I demanded, though I could guess easily enough.

"What I always do," she answered with a strange smile on her lips. "What you expect me to do; always what others expect me to do."

"And how long do you think you can keep running?" I asked.

She shook her head. "You misunderstand: not what you fear, but what you expect. I shouldn't have to run very long." She closed her eyes and drew the skin around her tightly as she chanted the song Ashóli had made for her. It made me sick to hear a skin-song in a foreign tongue. It was wrong, desperately wrong. Hooves thudded on the hardened earth of our yard as she found her feet and ran.

Even as I heard her hoofbeats fading over the crest of the ridge, the faint baying of the hounds came drifting nearer. They were making no secret of their presence, hoping, no doubt, to flush her out. And so she would satisfy them. It was far from the best solution. If they spread tales of skin-changers in this valley—But there was no reason they should know there were others here at all. They had come chasing a witch and now they would find her.

Ashóli returned with a fluttering of wings and had to pause to catch her breath before making her report. "They will be ready if the hunt comes down to the village. Where is Eysla?"

She looked around and her eyes fell on the kneading trough by the fire, with the dough crusting over in the heat, and then she saw the hooftracks leading out of the yard. "Where is she?" she repeated. "What have you done?"

"I've done nothing," I said. "She chose her own course."

Ashóli faced me, her face white with rage and sorrow. "How could she choose when you offered her nothing else? You drove her back to him because you haven't the courage to find another way."

"It isn't a matter of courage," I answered hotly, "but of wisdom. I can't make the whole world right, and if I must choose, I'll choose to protect my clan."

"*My* clan is large enough to include her, just as yours was once large enough to include me." She took on the raven-skin again, though she looked too exhausted to fly much farther, and set off in the direction of the sounds of the hunt.

What could I do? I followed her. Since my feathers were useless in daylight and I would not take Ashóli's cat-skin without permission, I chose the waiting fox-cloak—good for swift running and sharp ears and nose. But she was flying over the broken ridges and deep gullies of the mountainside, and I must take the longer ways.

It seemed like hours that I ran through brush and bramble, but finally the scent of blood drew me away from the sounds of the hunt and down into a sheltered hollow. Eysla sat there with her back against a stone, a bloody arrow at her side and her thigh wrapped with what had once been Ashóli's tunic.

"Where is she?" I demanded.

Her eyes fluttered open and she gritted her teeth as she turned toward me. "I tried to stop her," she said tightly. "They would have found me soon enough and it would have been over. I showed myself to them, then changed and taunted Gorliv, then changed again and ran. I might have led them back over the pass before they ran me down but for *that*." She gestured toward the feathered shaft. "I tried to stop her, but she would not hear. And when she had bound my leg, she put on the mare's skin and took the other in her mouth and led them on past."

I could hear the sounds of the hunt far off in the distance—too far for fox-legs to catch up with now. Eysla struggled to her feet and reached to me for support. I helped her climb up out of the hollow and onto the ridge where we could see.

The hunt had gone up beyond the trees along the rocky paths leading toward the pass. The gray horse scudded along the road like a patch of fog—they must have wondered at her renewed speed. Surely they had seen the blood. Behind her ran the dogs, and behind them, the three horsemen. They climbed along the scree, the mare in wild unconcern, the hunters more slowly, following a track, traced across the mountainside, that we could barely see. The path disappeared behind a bend just ahead of where the gray horse ran, and where it disappeared, the mountainside fell steeply, nearly straight down, for a very long way.

I held my breath as she neared the bend, guessing what would come next. The mare never slackened her pace, and where the track turned back out of sight, she gathered her legs under her and leaped out into the void.

Beside me, Eysla screamed. I grabbed at her and forced her gaze back toward the distant mountainside. "Look! There!"

The gray shape had fallen so slowly, as if in a dream. And now it seemed to collapse in on itself and a shadow slipped from under it just before it hit the rocks below. Eysla took a deep, ragged breath. "How could she . . . ?"

"She still had the raven-skin, you said. But even so, I doubt I would have dared it." I looked back to the trackway far above. The riders had dismounted and were peering over the edge. Too long a fall to survive; too deep a chasm to be worth climbing down to check. Ashóli knew these tracks like the back of her hand. I had no doubt she had planned that leap carefully. Retrieving the mare-skin would be quite a task.

After a while, the hunters moved on—farther up the trail toward the pass and home. And Eysla and I headed home as well, more slowly and with much pain for her. Finally I made her sit and cast the fox-skin around her shoulders. "If you will permit it," I said, "I will be able to carry you the rest of the way."

She was startled, and looked up at me suspiciously.

"I thought you didn't approve of outsiders wearing skins."

I sighed. "I will not pretend to be happy about it, but perhaps the lines are not so clearly drawn. If Ashóli has claimed you as chosen-kin, I will not deny you." It seemed that Ashóli had begun teaching her the *Kaltaoven* tongue, for she started in surprise when I used the in-clan inflection as I whispered, "*Kael-taov adye*. Wear thy skin!"

I gathered the little lame fox up in my arms and headed home, to where Ashóli would be waiting.

FRIENDS IN HIGH PLACES

by Christina Krueger

Christina writes that when she received my letter of acceptance, "I promptly put a head-shaped dent in my mother's kitchen ceiling. Thank you so much for giving me the thrill of a lifetime." May it be only the first of many; an editor is always looking for writers who will not disappear forever—as all too many seem to do after a first sale.

Christina adds, "As for biography, there isn't much to tell; no white rhino hunting in darkest Africa, no industrial espionage. Sorry. I am a 23-year-old single resident of Warren, Michigan, which is a good-sized suburb about ten miles north of Detroit. I have lived in Michigan my entire life and wouldn't be anywhere else in the world when the trees change color in autumn." (New York is pretty spectacular then, too ... or anywhere in New England, especially Vermont.) She also says, "I have no children but I do live with a couple of rambunctious kittens. My interests beyond writing include juggling, animation (watching, not drawing), and, of course, avid reading."

She says that she is not one of those writers with a cache of unsold novels (don't be snide; those who started with caches of unsold novels include such writers as C.J. Cherryh and Tanith Lee), but she does have a lot of short stories lurking in the file cabinet. "*S&S XIV* will be my first time in print (Yippee!)."

In closing she asks if she can dedicate this story "To Sue, Alex, and Paul for their unswerving faith and support." Consider it done. Everybody needs a support system.

(Maybe if she wants excitement, she needs to travel with Raul Reyes' character from "Death-Hunt". Or maybe not.—reh)

"This isn't going to work, Sim."

Sim turned to his companion, a thin, dark-haired girl two years his junior. His lips curled as he said, "I don't remember asking your opinion, *novice.*"

"I don't remember needing your permission to speak, *acolyte,*" Rayla replied, more exasperated than insulted. Sim's condescension had grown very tiresome during their overnight excursion up the mountainside. She decided to try again. "If the *avir* have as good vision as Master Ramonar's Book says—"

"—then one will spy the lure and drop right into my net," Sim snapped. "The Book also says that the *avir* are not very smart. Not that I expect *you* to have read that far, of course."

Rayla had, in fact, read the entire volume, but she prudently held her tongue. She heaved a sigh and shifted to ease the tension in her knees.

Staring into the beautiful autumn sky, Rayla wondered which god she had offended that she was crouched behind a boulder with a boorish idiot instead of happily working leather at her family's tannery. Out of five siblings, why had *she* been born with the mage talent? And to add insult to injury, she was really quite good at her lessons. That proficiency was the reason Master Ramonar had sent *her* with Sim instead of another student of Acolyte rank. Now they lay in wait for an *avir* to stumble into a trap a six-year-old could see blindfolded. Typically, Sim was making *her* do all the magical work while he only had to pull a rope. As a junior student, though, she had to obey Sim's directions, and he was making sure she knew it. She swallowed her ire and silently rehearsed the sleep enchantment she would cast on the *avir,* if they caught one.

Rayla was startled from a light doze by the sound of great wings beating to a halt on the other side of the boulder. Sim rose to a half-crouch, gripping the rope attached to the large net hidden beneath the carpet of leaves in the clearing. Rayla lifted herself to see beyond the rock, and what she saw made her breath catch in her throat.

The winged being examining the enspelled silver lure was certainly *not* the dim-witted, feral creature described in the ancient Book. Instead, Rayla saw a small female form clad in supple, rune-stitched leathers and linens and carrying a light goldwood bow. Her eagle-feathered wings ruffled and batted slightly as her brown eyes scanned the clearing.

Rayla grabbed Sim's earlobe and leaned close to him. "This isn't right!" she whispered urgently. "The Book said *avir* were wild! *Look* at her, Sim! She's as civilized as we are!"

"Shut up and do as we planned!" Sim hissed, jerking his head away from her. Rayla nodded firmly and released the sleep spell.

Sim gave Rayla a look of shock as he slumped senseless to the ground. With a sigh of relief, Rayla stood— and came eye-to-eye with an arrow.

The *avir* stood astride the boulder, wings wide, bow drawn. Rayla lifted her empty hands and tried to look harmless.

The *avir*'s lips twitched slightly. "Just what did you mean to do, girl? she asked in a musically accented voice. "Whatever it was, it was quite clumsy."

Rayla swallowed hard. "The net was Sim's idea," she said, nodding toward her snoring comrade. "Master Ramonar sent us up here to find one of your kind and take one of your feathers to use in a levitation spell."

"I see," said the *avir* evenly, keeping her bow level

with Rayla's brow. "And how would *you* have gotten one of my feathers?"

"I would have caught your attention with the lure and *asked* you for a feather."

"Good answer." The birdwoman grinned and lowered her bow. "When I petitioned Master Ramonar for an apprentice, he said he wasn't sure if he had a suitable student. I'm glad to see he found one, because I like your way of doing things."

Stunned, Rayla stammered, "Me? But . . . you're a mage?"

The *avir* waved a small hand in Sim's direction and murmured a few words. He moaned and opened his eyes. After one look at the bow-wielding birdwoman, he leaped up and ran for his life, abandoning Rayla to her fate.

The *avir* shook her head in disgust, then smiled as she reached behind herself and tugged gently. "Take two feathers. One is for your spell and the other is for *you*." She winked brightly at Rayla. "See you in the summer, youngling."

As the birdwoman launched herself into the sky, Rayla thoughtfully turned the feathers over in her hands.

Perhaps leatherworking could wait.

THE BLADE OF UNMAKING

by Elisabeth Waters

Elisabeth Waters is another of those we regard as "one of ours" since she sold her first story to me. She also lives here on the premises. She has been here at Greenwalls for about sixteen years, starting out with a sleeping bag on our library floor and a share of the tuna fish and rice. And she still likes tuna fish!

She has developed into a fine writer and has written several novels, even though she has been overheard to say she really didn't set out to become a writer. But her work is so much better than most others that I can't help wondering if that's still accurate. People don't write that well by accident.

"The Blade of Unmaking" is about the way a personal trait that might seem to be our greatest liability might in fact be our biggest strength.

(Her first novel is CHANGING FATE, DAW 1994.—reh)

Alyssa was enjoying a rare moment of quiet in the chapel when the housekeeper summoned her. "Lady Alyssa, there is a Royal Envoy in the Great Hall. You must go greet him at once."

"Oh, no!" Alyssa hated having to meet strangers, and being the only member of her family in residence made it worse. She would have to apologize for her parents' absence, which would doubtless displease the noble guests. But she was a dutiful girl, so she went quickly along the stone walkway to the Hall.

There were three strangers there, an elderly man and

a middle-aged woman, both dressed in the dark blue robes favored by wizards, and a younger man, probably about five years Alyssa's senior, dressed in the most elaborate clothing she had ever seen. The steward stood with them, politely discussing the weather, while one page poured wine into the goblets they were holding and another page took their outdoor cloaks.

"Lady Alyssa," the steward told her, "come greet your guests, the Lord High Wizard Logas, the Lady Wizard Sarras, and Lord Robert Fitzroy." At a sign from Logas, the steward bowed and removed the pages and himself from the room.

Alyssa curtsied, wondering what would bring such a company to her parents' out-of-the-way small castle. Her family was only minor nobility, and, even though Alyssa had never paid much attention to anything outside the castle walls, she knew that the Lord High Wizard was Head of the Order of Wizards and Adviser to the King. As for Lord Robert, while she didn't remember hearing anything about him, the surname Fitzroy indicated that he was one of the King's natural children.

"I regret that my parents are not home to receive you, my Lords, my Lady," she said.

"It matters not," Logas said. "Our errand is to you."

"Me!" Alyssa exclaimed in astonishment. "Are you certain?" she added, before her brain could tell her mouth to shut. Indeed, it still hung open.

"Quite certain," Sarras replied. "I have Seen it. You are the new Guardian."

"Guardian of what?" Alyssa asked. She had an uneasy feeling that she wasn't going to like the answer.

"The Blade of Unmaking," the High Wizard said solemnly. He studied her blank face and added, "You *have* heard of it, have you not?"

Alyssa shook her head, not daring to speak. A familiar feeling swept over her: the feeling that she was stupid, ugly, ill-mannered, and utterly useless. She generally felt this way around her mother, who helped the process by telling her how stupid and useless she was. Alyssa had never been forgiven for not being the son her parents wanted and were still trying very hard to get. They were currently on pilgrimage to yet another shrine which had a reputation for making women fruitful. Alyssa's parents did not consider her a satisfactory offspring; as best she could tell, they had been trying to replace her since the year she was born.

Help came from an unexpected source. "The Blade of Unmaking," Fitzroy declaimed, "is a Holy Relic, one of the Gifts of the Elder Gods. I am writing an epic on the subject—as you may know, I am a poet."

Alyssa hadn't known, didn't particularly care, and thought that anything called "Blade of Unmaking" was more likely to qualify as an *unholy* relic.

"I shall accompany you on your quest, so that I may gather material for my epic."

"Quest?" Alyssa squeaked.

"It's not as dramatic as it sounds," Sarras said reassuringly. "We know where the Blade is, and it's not very large; it's a dagger about a foot long, including the hilt. All you have to do is go get it, and you don't have to do it alone. Lord Logas and I will be with you, and we brought three servants to carry supplies. The previous Guardian chose to live in the mountains north of here, but it's only about a day's journey."

"If you know where it is, Lady," Alyssa asked respectfully, "why do you need me?"

"We need you because you are the only one who can handle the Blade," Logas explained.

"But I can't leave here!" Alyssa protested. "It's my duty to keep the estate running smoothly. My parents will be very angry if I go anywhere without their consent."

"I think this will take care of any objection your parents might raise." Lord Logas handed her a scroll, sealed with the King's seal.

Alyssa opened it. It addressed her by name and ordered her to do all in her power to aid the Lord High Wizard Logas and the Lady Wizard Sarras. She scowled at it. "And I suppose you could use your magic to force me to do what you wanted in any case." She knew she was being rude, but she couldn't seem to stop herself.

"No," Sarras said promptly. "While it might be possible to override your will, our vows forbid us to use magic against any person's mind or will without her consent. It's considered to be black magic."

Alyssa bit her lip. "How do we get to this place?" she asked.

"We walk," Sarras said. "As I already mentioned, it isn't far from here."

"I'm not sure I have proper clothing for such a trip," Alyssa said nervously. "I have never left this estate."

Sarras and Logas exchanged a long glance. Alyssa had the impression that an entire conversation took place between them without their uttering a word.

"We'll find something for you to wear," Sarras said, "and we'll take the journey slowly if we must. The snow has melted by now, so it won't be too hard. You can do it, Alyssa; I know it."

"If you say so, Lady," Alyssa said, suddenly realizing that this was the first time anyone in authority had ever told her that she *could* do something—instead of telling her that she couldn't.

"Would you show me around, Lady Alyssa?" Sarras asked. "I'd like to see your castle."

"Certainly, my Lady," Alyssa said. She looked at the men. "I'll send the steward to show you to your rooms, my Lords."

"I shall need a desk, paper, pens, and ink," Fitzroy said self-importantly. "I must work on my epic."

"I'll have it seen to," Alyssa promised. "This way, my Lady."

*   *   *

Sarras showed a flattering interest in the day-to-day management of the castle and seemed impressed with Alyssa's domestic skills. "You run this place very well."

Alyssa shrugged. "Anyone could do it; it's not difficult. And it's all I'm good for. Father says if I ever get into Heaven it will be the most certain proof of God's Mercy, since I don't do anything to earn His favor."

Sarras raised her eyebrows. "Did your parents want a boy, by any chance?"

Alyssa nodded.

"So did mine," Sarras said. "I was lucky that I turned out to have magical talent. If I hadn't gone to the Wizards' College when I was fifteen, I think I might have killed myself." She looked searchingly at Alyssa. "Do you ever think of doing that?"

"Killing myself?" Alyssa shrugged. "Sometimes I want to, but I won't ever do it. It's a sin; and if I were dead, who would look after the estate?"

"So your faith in God and your sense of duty keep you alive?" Sarras seemed to approve of that answer.

"I guess so," Alyssa said. "I never thought much about it; I'm usually too busy."

Sarras smiled. "Well, let me take over organizing supplies for our journey, and you can tell the steward everything that needs to be taken care of for the next few days."

Sarras was very efficient; by suppertime she had found clothing and boots for Alyssa and organized supplies. She even tried to persuade Fitzroy to go to sleep at a reasonable hour instead of keeping everyone up to listen to the portion of his epic he had composed thus far.

But, Alyssa thought, as she sat fighting boredom with a polite smile fixed on her face, keeping Fitzroy from showing off his talent would require an act of God—or maybe one of his "Elder Gods." Even through the numbing verbosity of Fitzroy's epic, they sounded nasty and ruthless. Alyssa was glad that *she* didn't have to worship them.

Fitzroy's poetry—or prose, Alyssa wasn't sure into which category his work fell—was so stylish it was hard to tell what he was talking about, but, assuming that any of it was true, the Blade of Unmaking sounded more dangerous than the wizards had indicated. Fitzroy spoke of an age when the Blade had passed freely from hand to hand, at short intervals with a good deal of bloodshed involved. There was something about the "Unmade"—who were apparently monsters, people turned into monsters, or maybe people just acting like monsters. Then the first Guardian took control of the Blade, and an era of peace was born. The virtues of the first—and dozens of successive—Guardians were extolled at mind-numbing length, but when Fitzroy finally wound down, Alyssa still wasn't clear on what it was that a Guardian *did*. She was, however, much too tired to care and glad to escape to her bed.

Alyssa was up at dawn as usual, but even Sarras's efficiency was not enough to get Fitzroy out of bed early in the morning. It was mid-morning before they left the castle and started along the road that led to the Northern Mountains.

The day had started sunny, if cool, but by midday Alyssa noticed small bits of something wet hitting her in the face. She couldn't tell whether it was mist, light rain, or very thin snow, and her inability to identify it made her feel even more uneasy than usual. She looked around at the rest of the party, but none of them seemed to notice anything out of the ordinary.

The ground sloped upward more steeply now, and Alyssa slogged grimly on, watching where she put her feet. The path was easy enough to see, a ribbon of barren dirt beside hills lightly covered with clumps of grass, rocks, pine trees, pine cones, pine needles, dead leaves, and bare trees. The snow had melted, but it was still too early in the spring for the trees to have leaves on them yet. The land seemed barren.

There was a sudden noise uphill to the right, and a rock the size of her fist came tumbling down at Alyssa's feet. She jumped and screamed, her head snapping to see who had thrown it. Halfway up the hill a squirrel crouched. It looked annoyed with her, but Alyssa told herself firmly that she was being silly—if the animal was annoyed at all, it was probably annoyed with itself for having slipped on the loose rock. It chittered at them for a few seconds, then turned and ran off into the trees, its gray tail upright like a banner behind it.

Fitzroy sighed. "A squirrel," he said in disgust. "Is there anything you are not frightened of? How am I supposed to write a heroic epic with *this* as source material?"

"Just make it all up," Alyssa snarled. "Isn't that what poets do anyway?" She wasn't afraid of Fitzroy; even on short acquaintance it was obvious that he was an idiot, tolerated only for his birth.

"Enough!" Logas said firmly. Alyssa shut her mouth and turned her attention back to the trail. They continued to climb and the mist—Alyssa decided that must be what it was—drifted in white clouds around them. Soon it was so thick it was difficult to see the ground, let alone the rest of the party.

But Logas led on, and Alyssa grimly followed in his footsteps, praying to God to give her the strength to keep up. Her legs burned, her mouth was bone dry, her head ached, and every breath was an effort. She wanted to ask if they could stop and rest, but she was afraid that if she stopped, she would never be able to walk again. So she slogged onward uncomplaining, thinking only of the next step. The sky added rain to the mist, but Alyssa was beyond caring.

It seemed like an eternity later when the now muddy

path gave way to a slate walkway. Alyssa, by now almost sleepwalking, didn't notice until she turned her left ankle on the edge of it. Sarras moved to her side and grasped her elbow. "Be careful here," she murmured; "the stones turn slippery when they are wet."

Alyssa focused carefully on the placement of each step, glad of Sarras' supporting arm. Her ankle hurt each time she stepped on that foot, but so much of her body hurt by now that it didn't seem to matter.

Soon she noticed that the stones were dry underfoot. She glanced up and saw that they were entering something midway between a building and a large cave.

"Here we are," Logas said with satisfaction. "We made better time than I expected. Now all we need is to get the dagger and take it to its new home."

"Tomorrow." Sarras said firmly.

"What?" Logas looked at her in surprise. "We can use our wands for extra light."

"It's raining," Sarras pointed out. "The path is slippery even now and will be a mudslide within the hour. And your Guardian is in no condition to travel more tonight. Just look at her!"

Logas surveyed Alyssa thoroughly from head to toe, frowned, and ran his right hand past her side about a foot away from her body. "Soaked to the skin, chilled, every muscle from the waist down is seizing up, and she's suffering from altitude sickness and dehydration. And she has a sprained ankle." He shook his head in disbelief. "Lady Alyssa, why didn't you say something?"

Alyssa looked blankly at him. "What was I supposed to say, Lord?"

Logas sighed. "You're right, Sarras; our task can wait until morning. There's a wall chamber ahead to the left. Take her there and do what you can for her. The rest of us will sleep in the inner hall."

"Very well." Sarras turned to the servants. "Please

put our bedrolls in the wall chamber—and a full water-skin as well."

"This place is incredible," Fitzroy said excitedly. "Never have I seen anything like unto it. Now which words shall I use to describe it?" He wandered farther into the structure, muttering to himself in iambic pentameter.

"I don't care if he is the King's son—"

"Sarras, would you like me to make some hot soup?" Logas said, cutting off whatever she had been about to say. "I shall be starting a fire in a few minutes in any case."

"Yes, thank you, Lord," Sarras said formally, reminded of the presence of listening servants. She dragged Alyssa off to the wall chamber, seated her on a wooden bench there, and began to pull things out of her pack. A servant laid out the bedrolls and left, and Sarras shoved the waterskin at Alyssa. "Drink some of that, but slowly—don't gulp it, or you'll make yourself ill."

Alyssa did as she was told, barely noticing when a servant came in with a pile of wood and arranged it in the fireplace. Sarras lit it with an absentminded Word as the man left, drawing the leather curtain over the chamber doorway behind him.

Logas came in with two mugs of soup and handed one to Alyssa. "Drink this," he said. "Your body needs food." He set the other mug on the bench beside her, knelt on the floor in front of her, took her left foot, and started unlacing her boot. Alyssa, horrified by the thought of having a man see her ankles, pulled her foot away and shoved her skirts down, nearly spilling the soup in the process. The motion didn't do her ankle any good either; she blinked back tears at the sudden stab of pain.

Logas sat back on his heels and looked her straight in the eyes. Alyssa hastily dropped her gaze to her soup. "Sarras," he said quietly, "please come help me heal Lady Alyssa's ankle. She won't be able to walk on it for several days if we don't heal it, and we didn't bring enough provisions for a week, did we?"

"No, we didn't," Sarras agreed, "and she's suffered quite enough already." She knelt at his side and patted Alyssa lightly on the knee. "You've never had a wizard do a healing on you before, have you?"

"I've never even met a wizard before," Alyssa said. "But it's not proper for a man to see my ankles."

"It's perfectly proper for a wizard to do so," Sarras said firmly. "Healing is a gift from God. Haven't you ever heard of the Laying on of Hands?"

"Yes, but I thought priests did that."

"Logas is a priest."

"He is?" Alyssa was astonished. Her parents' chaplain never wore anything but a plain black robe, and she had thought that all priests dressed like that. As for wizards and magic, they had not been part of her studies.

"Yes, I am," Logas said. "Quite a few wizards are also priests, usually Healer priests. The Order of Saint Luke is full of them."

Sarras took Alyssa's foot and carefully removed the boot. Alyssa looked down at her ankle in dismay. Not only did it hurt, but it was also red and noticeably swollen.

"Don't worry," Logas said. "We can fix it easily enough. You just drink the rest of the soup and let us do our job."

"All right," Alyssa said. She felt nervous and awkward and horribly shy. She sipped the cooling soup and watched as Logas held one hand above her ankle and reached the other hand toward Sarras. She took it with her free hand, the one which was not supporting Alyssa's ankle. It looked to Alyssa as if their skin was turning blue, or maybe green, first where their hands were clasped together and then spreading to their faces and the hands around her ankle. Blue-green light flowed from their hands and covered her ankle, and the swelling diminished visibly as she watched. After a moment the light faded, and her ankle looked perfectly normal.

"Good heavens," Alyssa murmured in surprise. "It worked." She wriggled her foot experimentally and discovered it didn't hurt at all now.

"Finish your soup," Logas told her. "Some of the energy for a healing comes from the injured body, so you need food and rest. But you should be back to normal by tomorrow." He rose smoothly to his feet and left the room.

Sarras reached out and picked up the other mug of soup without moving from the floor. "Lord God, I'm tired," she sighed, "and you must be exhausted." She drank the soup down in one long gulp. "Let's get out of these wet clothes and into bed."

Alyssa finished her soup, tried to stand, and promptly fell over. Sarras hauled her to her feet and stripped her with an efficiency which spoke of previous experience. She then dried the girl's body with a large square of rough linen and tucked her into her bedroll. Alyssa wasn't sure whether she fell asleep or blacked out, but she didn't remember anything more.

She heard voices, but she thought she was dreaming—it was too dark and quiet for it to be morning.

". . . Fitzroy?" a woman's voice asked softly.

"I left him supervising the burial detail," a man's deep voice responded. "It's just as well that we spent the night; no one told me that the Guardian was still here. I thought he had servants, but, if he did, they must have run off when he died."

"What about the Blade?"

"On the altar, where it belongs. It should be safe enough there until the girl wakes and claims it."

Alyssa realized that she was not at home and that she probably was awake. She opened her eyes and saw that she was in the wall chamber where she had collapsed the previous night. The fire was still burning, although it looked low enough to die out within the hour unless it was fed more wood. She was lying on the floor, wrapped in her bedroll. She tried to move, and pain shot through her body. Her ankle was doubtless healed, but all the muscles she had used the previous day *hurt*. She gritted her teeth against a scream and lay still.

"I'll go wake her," Sarras said. "I feel strongly that the Blade should be in her custody as soon as possible."

"Surely you don't think the servants are going to try to touch it."

"Not the servants," Sarras said, "but I wouldn't bet on Fitzroy."

"Come now, Sarras," Logas said patiently, "I know you don't like the boy, but he's not a complete idiot."

"You must see signs of intelligence in him that I have missed, my Lord," Sarras said, her voice dripping with irony. "At least Lady Alyssa doesn't whine, complain, and try to impress people with her exalted social standing."

"If you mean she doesn't have sense enough to tell when she's hurt, you're correct," Logas said. "And I don't think she's realized yet what being the Guardian does to her social standing."

"At least *she* didn't slow us down on the trail."

Alyssa saw the leather curtain start to move and hastily closed her eyes. *No need for them to know I heard them talking.*

Robes rustled next to her ear and a hand pressed gently against her shoulder. "Lady Alyssa, it's time to wake up."

Alyssa blinked up at Sarras. "It's morning?"

"Mid-morning," Sarras said with a smile. "You were very tired, so we let you sleep."

Alyssa sat up slowly, clenching her teeth against the pain, and discovered that she was naked inside the bedroll. She clutched it to her breasts. "I think this is the first time I've slept past daybreak in ten years," she remarked. "In here, you can't see the dawn."

"No, you can't," Sarras agreed. She picked up Alyssa's clothing from a pile next to the fire and tossed the shift over Alyssa's head. "Can you get your arms through this?"

Alyssa managed, although the process was painful. Sarras helped her to stand up and finish dressing. "Walk around a bit, it will loosen up your muscles. I'll get you some soup."

Alyssa paced slowly back and forth next to the fire. To her astonishment, Sarras was correct; the more she moved about, the easier it got. When Sarras returned with the soup, Alyssa was able to sit on the bench and eat it. "Are we going home as soon as we get the Blade?"

"Yes," Sarras replied. "If we're lucky, we'll make it back to your home by tonight. You'll have to go to the College of Wizards for training at some time, but—"

"Fitzroy!" Logas cried out in alarm.

"Oh, no!" Sarras gasped and rushed from the wall chamber. Alyssa set down her soup and followed, wondering what could upset two senior wizards.

Lord Robert Fitzroy stood in the entrance to the cave. He held an iron dagger in his right hand. His clothing was slashed and blood ran down his face and arms. "I'm no good," he said dazedly. "I'm a bad poet. Nobody likes my work. Nobody likes me. I'm nothing."

"Fitzroy!" Logas said sharply. "Put down the blade!"

Fitzroy, unfortunately, did not seem to hear or see anyone. "I shouldn't exist," he continued dully. "I should be dead." He pointed the dagger toward his chest, starting at it as if hypnotized.

"Alyssa," Sarras said urgently, "take the blade away from him!"

Alyssa responded to Sarras's tone of voice without

thinking about it; obeying the orders of her elders was a long-established habit. She ran across the room and tried to wrestle the dagger away from Fitzroy.

Unfortunately, he was older and stronger than she was, and her muscles were still weak from yesterday's ordeal. They fell to the floor together, still struggling over the dagger. By the time Alyssa succeeded in pulling it away from him, both of them were covered with his blood, he had stab wounds in his chest, and blood trickled from his mouth when he tried to breathe.

Logas knelt beside Fitzroy, running his hands through the air just over his body. "Sarras!" he snapped. "Come help me!"

Alyssa scrabbled out of the way as Sarras knelt at Fitzroy's other side. The two wizards linked hands over his body, and the blue-green light emanated from them, pooling in the space between them.

It looks like the mist we went through on the way here, Alyssa thought. But this mist dispersed around Fitzroy's body as if there were a wind blowing it away. After a few minutes, Logas and Sarras released each other's hands and sat back. Logas reached over to close Fitzroy's eyes, and Sarras turned anxiously to Alyssa.

"Are you all right, Lady Alyssa?" she asked.

Alyssa stared down at the dagger in her hands. "This is the Blade of Unmaking." It was not a question. She could feel it, the force bound within the blade, the force which had made Fitzroy kill himself and wanted her to do the same. It was as if a voice, like her mother's voice, spoke in her ear, telling her she was nothing, that she was ugly, stupid, and useless, that she should never have been born, that she should correct this obvious error. . . .

But Alyssa had lived for years with this feeling and knew it for what it was. It was an emotional response, it made her miserable, but she didn't have to act on it. She was stronger than it was. Whether anyone loved her or not—even if everyone in the world hated her—

she was alive because God had willed it so, and she would live as long as He willed, and no chunk of iron, however sharp, was going to make her seek to change that.

This is why Sarras asked me if I ever wanted to kill myself, she realized. *This is why I was chosen to be the Guardian of this Blade. Fitzroy died because he was accustomed to being flattered and praised, and the shock of feeling like this was more than he could handle. I've felt like this many times before, and no doubt I shall again, but I* can *handle this.*

She looked calmly at Sarras and Logas. "I'm fine," she said. "It's nasty, but I'm not going to be stupid about it."

"Set it down on the floor," Sarras said. "I don't think anyone else is going to touch it now." She looked at the servants who were all standing just outside the entrance, staring in horror. "I'll get you some silk to wrap it in."

Alyssa placed the blade on the floor and made a face. "Would you get me some water as well, please," she requested. "I don't want to wrap it while it's covered with blood—it would only stick to the silk."

Sarras nodded and went into the wall chamber, returning with the waterskin and a square of black silk. Alyssa cleaned and wrapped the blade while Logas instructed the servants to assemble a litter for Fitzroy's body, and Sarras packed up the rest of their supplies.

Alyssa stood and looked down at the body. "We had better get him back to my home as quickly as we can," she pointed out. "We don't have the supplies we need to clean and lay out a body with us, but if we take him home, we can use our chapel. I suppose the King would not want us to bury him here."

"Quite right," Logas said. He looked around. "Do we have everything?"

"Almost." Sarras turned and ran to the back of the building, returning a moment later with a black leather sheath with thin leather ties attached to it. She handed it to Alyssa. "Put the blade in this and tie it to your back; you'll want your hands free for the journey home."

"Thank you." Alyssa stuffed the wrapped blade into the sheath and arranged it so the blade was across her upper back. Then she put her cloak over it; after all, she wasn't going to need to draw *this* dagger in any hurry.

The trip home was only slightly less miserable than the previous one had been. At least it didn't rain. But the path was muddy and slippery, and going downhill used a different set of muscles, and having to carry the litter with Fitzroy's body slowed the party down quite a bit. The servants took turns carrying it, and even Logas took a turn. Nobody asked Alyssa to carry anything but the Blade, but that was quite enough. The silk and the leather helped a lot, but still it seemed to whisper to her.

Darkness fell when they were still several miles from home, but the two wizards simply kindled mage lights on the ends of their staffs and the party continued on. None of them wanted to stop and try to make camp. Alyssa felt she could have walked twice the distance as long as she knew that at the end she could get out of her blood-stiffened clothing and sleep in her own bed.

Nevertheless, by the time they reached the castle gate, it was almost midnight and she was ready to drop in her tracks. The guard looked strangely at them, for which Alyssa did not blame him in the slightest. All he said, however, was, "Your parents are back."

Alyssa closed her eyes briefly and sighed. "Thank you for telling me, Jon."

Jon opened the gate, and the party passed quietly into the courtyard. "You go to bed, Alyssa," Sarras told her softly. "I remember where the chapel is, and we can take care of the body."

"But it's my duty—" Alyssa began.

"Your first duty now is to take care of the Blade," Sarras reminded her. "You are the only one who can handle it safely, and you need to stay healthy to do that. Go get some sleep."

"Yes, Lady Alyssa," Logas said firmly. "Go to bed. We'll handle the body. If I had paid more attention to him, this would not have happened. This is my responsibility."

"All right." Alyssa was too tired to argue. She crept up the stairs to the solar, tiptoed past the sleeping bodies of the maids and sewing women in the main room, and slipped through the curtains into her sleeping chamber. She placed the blade, still wrapped in silk, under her pillow, stripped off her clothes and left them in a pile on the floor, sponged the blood off her body using a rag and the pitcher of water next to the wash basin, put on a clean shift, and crawled into bed.

For the second day in a row, Alyssa slept past dawn and was wakened by a woman's voice talking about Lord Robert Fitzroy. This time, however, it was her mother.

"Merciful God, it's true!" Alyssa opened her eyes to see her mother staring at the pile of blood-stained clothes she had left on the floor. "You killed the King's own son! God knows I've been disappointed by your behavior in the past, but this is more than I can bear!"

She whirled, grabbed Alyssa by her shoulder and began shaking her like a rag doll. "Your father and I provided you with a home where any sensible girl would be happy to remain, and what do you do as soon as we turn our backs? You run off with the King's natural son—and then you kill him!"

"I didn't kill him!" Alyssa protested, but she was suddenly assailed by the uncomfortable feeling frequently engendered by he mother's lectures. *At least I*

THE BLADE OF UNMAKING

don't think *I killed him, but it all happened so fast . . .
did I kill him?*

"Don't you talk back to me!" Her mother slapped
Alyssa across the face, knocking her across the bed.
The pillow slipped, and it and the silk-wrapped dagger
fell to the floor.

"What's this?"

Alyssa struggled to a sitting position in time to see
her mother unwrap the Blade of Unmaking and take it
into her bare hand. "Mother, no!" she screamed. "Put it
down! It's dangerous!"

"I told you not to talk back to me!" her mother
shouted at her. "Is this what you used to kill him—and
do you plan to sleep with it for the rest of your life?"
She advanced on Alyssa, pointing the blade at her
daughter's heart. "I should kill you myself, and save
the King the trouble."

Alyssa sat frozen on her bed, starting in shock and
horror at her mother. *She really* does *look ready to kill
me. And she's holding the Blade of Unmaking as if it
were her eating knife; it doesn't have any effect on her.*

Strong hands reached out through the curtains and
grabbed the woman's arms. Lady Sarras came the rest
of the way into the room and said, "I doubt that the
King would appreciate your killing your daughter. He
feels strongly that justice is *his* prerogative."

"But she's only a girl, and he's lost a son!"

Lady Sarras sighed. "Alyssa, take the blade, please."

Alyssa's paralysis wore off with the clear instruc-
tion. She stood up and pried her mother's resisting fingers from the dagger. It fell to the floor, and Alyssa
hastily picked it up and wrapped it in its silk covering.
For good measure she shoved it back into its sheath
and put the whole thing at the far end of her bed.

"Sarras?" a man's voice called from the solar.

"In here, Logas," she replied.

Logas entered, followed by Alyssa's father. Sarras

shoved Alyssa's mother at them; Logas grabbed her. Alyssa grabbed her robe and hastily put it on.

Fortunately her mother had stopped screaming and now seemed dazed. "Take charge of her," Sarras ordered Logas. "I'm taking Alyssa and the Blade to the Wizard's College."

"Today?" Logas asked. "Why?"

Sarras jerked her head disdainfully at Alyssa's mother. "She held the Blade, and tried to kill its Guardian."

"Oh, dear me," Logas sighed. "And usually the wretched thing goes from one Guardian to another with no trouble at all."

"Usually the new Guardian isn't still living with her parents," Sarras said grimly. "Alyssa, I'm sorry; I would not choose to resume our journey so early, but there's no help for it. Pack what you need to take with you; we're leaving for the College as soon as you are ready."

"Lady Sarras?" Alyssa asked, feeling bewildered. "How long will we be gone?"

"You won't be back here while your parents live," Logas said.

"But this is my home!"

"Not anymore," Sarras said, shaking her head. She put an arm around Alyssa's shoulders and hugged her gently. "I'm sorry, child, but you can't stay here. Don't worry; you hold an honorable position, and the people at the College will be nice to you. I expect you will be very happy there."

"You can't just come here and take my daughter!" Alyssa's father protested. "Who's going to run the estate?"

"Someone else," Logas said coldly. "And we most certainly can take her; we have the King's written order."

"But his son just died yesterday—or so the servants

told me." Alyssa's father sounded confused. "How could you get a written order from him so quickly?"

"What does Fitzroy's death have to do with Lady Alyssa?" Logas was starting to sound almost as confused as her father.

"They think I killed him," Alyssa explained.

Logas and Sarras both stared at her. "What?"

"Why?"

"I guess because we showed up in the middle of the night with a body, and I'm the one whose clothes were covered with blood." Alyssa suddenly felt very sad. "That's enough to start the guards gossiping, and then the servants—and my parents have always been ready to think the worst of me."

Logas stared at Alyssa's father. "She did not kill him; she got blood on her clothing trying to save his life. That she failed is no fault of hers." He turned to Sarras. "You are correct again, Lady. Take her to the College as soon as you can. I'll deal with taking Fitzroy's body to the King and explaining the matter to him, then I'll join you there. Safe journey." He left the room, dragging Alyssa's mother. Her father followed without looking back.

Alyssa stared after them. "I'll never see them again, will I?" she said, suddenly feeling hollow inside.

"Not if you're lucky," Sarras said grimly.

"But she wouldn't really have killed me," Alyssa protested. "She's always angry with somebody—usually me—but she never killed anyone before."

"She never held the Blade of Unmaking before either," Sarras said gently. "Yes, she could very well have killed you."

"But the Blade didn't have any effect on her," Alyssa said, still puzzled by that. "Why is she immune to it, and wouldn't that make her a more fitting Guardian for it than I?"

"She's not immune to it," Sarras explained. Nobody

is. Think about it; what do you feel when you touch the Blade?"

Alyssa frowned. "Despair, I guess; the feeling that I should not exist and that I should correct that mistake. That's what happened to Fitzroy, isn't it?"

Sarras nodded. "Yes, it is. Most people feel that when they touch the Blade; it seeks to make them nothing—to unmake them. The Guardian must be someone who can feel that and set aside the feeling." She sat on the edge of the bed, suddenly looking very tired. "But there are a few other people who can handle the Blade without seeking to kill themselves—the people who are already Unmade. These are people for whom other people are not people, but things; people who see themselves as the only true people in the world. If they get the Blade, they still feel its desire for death, but they turn it outward instead of inward. Where a normal person becomes a suicide, one of the Unmade becomes a murderer. That is why the Blade must have a Guardian."

"Are you saying that my mother is one of the 'Unmade' that Fitzroy was talking about?" Alyssa asked incredulously. "I thought he was describing monsters."

"In a way, he was," Sarras said gently. "To lack the capacity to feel another person's pain is to lack an important part of what it is to be human. It's probably no comfort," she added, "but you are not the first Guardian to have a parent who was one of the Unmade. A child who survives to grow up in those circumstances is a very strong person."

So the Guardian has to be strong enough not to kill herself," Alyssa began, "but . . ." her voice trailed off as she searched for the right word.

"But compassionate enough to understand other people's feelings," Sarras finished. "A Guardian must have a balance of strength and compassion, Alyssa, as you do. It is a rare balance, and a special destiny." She stood up and said briskly, "Speaking of balance, can you ride?"

"A horse?" Alyssa asked. "Not very well. Are we riding to the College?"

Sarras nodded ruefully. "We really are broadening your horizons, aren't we?"

"Definitely," Alyssa said. "I'm learning about a lot of muscles I never knew I had. I bet I'll discover a whole new set by the time we get to the College—and who knows what I'll learn there." *Whatever it is, it's bound to be more interesting than running an isolated estate for the rest of my life. And Sarras—and even Logas—seem to like me; if the other wizards are anything like them, I might actually learn to be happy there.*

She smiled at Sarras. "Lady Sarras, being around you is truly an educational experience."

THE STONE-WEAVER'S TALE

by Cynthia McQuillin

Cynthia lives in Berkeley with her partner, Dr. Jane Robinson, and three cats. She and Jane perform around the Bay Area and at sf conventions across the country individually and as the music/comedy duet Mid-Life Crisis. In addition to being a gifted writer of fantasy, Cynthia is a prolific and versatile songwriter. Her work has been featured on more than seventy musical collections, and she has recorded eight solo tapes/CDs, five of which are still in print.

She owns and operates Unlikely Publications, a small recording and publishing company, and, like the heroine of her tale, she also makes beautiful, hand-crafted, one-of-a-kind jewelry, which she sells along with the tapes and songbooks at science fiction and fantasy conventions.

Cynthia tells us there really is a lapis cat like the one described in the story, which she obtained in much the same way as her heroine did. It sits on the shelf next to where she writes, and has—she says—been wanting for years to be included in one of her tales, so now it has been.

"*Rego, rego!*" cried the ragged boy triumphantly as he snatched the necklace of stone, bone and feathers from Shallisa's basket. Holding the woven choker high so his companions could see his prize, he grinned at her with jagged teeth.

The indigo swirls that covered his face marked him

as one of the gypsy-like Regosi who eked out a marginal existence on the plains just beyond the edge of the King's Quarry. A plainswoman herself, Shallisa was Itari from the fertile lowlands which lay under blessing and protection of the Stone Maiden of Itar.

Pursing her lips, though she was actually more inclined to smile at the youngster's antics than to be angry, she muttered a small spell under her breath. The boy gave a startled yelp and dropped the necklace in the dust.

"Come, boy," she demanded. "Return the charm. It wasn't meant for you and will only bring you misfortune."

Eyes wide, he stooped to retrieve it, then came reluctantly forward to drop the choker into the wide basket she held balanced on one hip.

"What's your name?" she demanded, drawing the brightly patterned shawl from her shoulders to cover the basket.

"Dab, Lady," he said, bobbing his head respectfully despite a chorus of jeers from his companions. "No harm done, eh, Lady?"

"Don't you know that it's wrong to steal, Dab?" she asked, eyeing him sternly. But she knew the answer. If you were poor, stealing wasn't a crime, it was a way of life. "Well, never mind. But thieving from a magecrafter, even a lowly stone-weaver, is never wise."

"Yes, Lady." He looked amazingly contrite; then his eyes brightened and he said, "Perhaps the lady would hire me to carry her wares."

"No, you don't, impudent bratling!" she laughed, slapping his hand away as he reached for the basket. "Get back to your brothers, before I haul you off to see one of the King's peace-men." Still chuckling to herself as he scrambled back to the pack, Shallisa shifted the weight of her basket and strode toward the arch that marked the entrance to the Stone Market.

"You shouldn't be so soft with their kind," Kirkan,

the King's toll-taker, chided as she counted out the coppers required for her entry to the market and the silver piece which licensed her to sell her wares for the day.

"Have you no memory of youth, old bureaucrat?" she teased, tugging playfully at his beard. In return, he slapped her generous rump as she swayed past emulating the exaggerated languor of the courtesans who came with their servants to buy gemstones and precious metals, and sometimes, a charmed necklace from a lowly stone-weaver.

She had been coming to the Market all her life. First she had come with her mother, Malia, who had also been a stone-weaver. Then later, after Malia died, Shallisa had come alone, taking her spot in the bazaar.

"Shallisa!" cried Mirga, the dark-eyed daughter of Jallam—the chief cook at the Stone Mansion—as she dodged through the crowded walkway. The Stone Mansion, whose imposing edifice rose above the chaos of the Market, housed all the King's stone-workers from the noblest stone-mage to the lowliest apprentice and all of their staff.

"What has you so excited?" Shallisa demanded as the girl all but ran into her. "You're as high-strung as a Hebit mare in season."

"You *must* see the new treasures Maldor has brought from the stone-crafters hall. There's a keelie-bird carved of Isturan amber with a beetle trapped in its belly."

"That must be Master Maldor's own work," Shallisa laughed. "It sounds like his sense of humor."

"Oh, and there's a platter of rhodochrosite with the most beguiling pattern."

"Does he still have the lapis cat?" Shallisa asked, when Mirga paused to catch a breath.

"That old thing?" It was the other girl's turn to look disdainful. "Gods, he'll never sell it. Who would want a blue cat, anyway?"

"Who indeed?" Shallisa smiled to herself. She had wanted the lapis cat since she was ten years old. But when she had been so foolish as to ask its price, Maldor had laughed at her, saying that such costly things were not for a stone-weaver's daughter, even a pretty cat-eyed girl like her. He had called her cat-eyes ever since, for blue eyes were a rarity among the people of Jadasia, but common among the furred folk.

Her father, a stone-mage from the mysterious east who had dallied a season with her mother as rumor had it, had possessed such eyes.

"Eyes like blue topaz, skin pale as ivory and hair like spun gold," her mother had said, on one of the rare occasions when she spoke of him. Shallisa had inherited her father's complexion as well, but not his hair; hers was thick, and black as a raven's wing. Exotic among the dark-eyed, dark-skinned Itari of the plains, she was even more striking among the golden, brown-haired city-dwellers.

"Ah, no," Maldor sighed as she approached his canvas-tented booth. Being the master mason in charge of fine ornaments, the fat, balding stone-crafter was not obliged to preside over the tables himself, but he often did, claiming that the noise and closeness of the work-rooms affected his delicate nerves and thus his creative flow. "Gods! Not you two again. Why do you come, Cat-eyes? You never buy."

"I would buy, if your prices were not so high," she grinned impudently back.

"Go peddle your witchery and leave honest merchants to their business," he said, making a shooing motion with his broad, fat-fingered hands.

"Mirga tells me you have a carved amber bird too clever for words," she persisted.

"Yes, here it is," the younger girl cried, reaching for it. Maldor plucked the precious piece from her greedy fingers with practiced ease.

"Ahhh," Shallisa murmured, pretending to study the

workmanship, "a fine piece indeed. But surely, Master Maldor, this must be yours. I can think of no one else who would create such an exquisite carving simply to make a crude and obvious joke."

"I should have known better," he muttered, setting the bird back in its place on the table. "Why are you here? As if I didn't know."

"I see that you still have the lapis cat." She managed not to smile as her fingers traced the exquisite curve of the cat's muzzle as though the sculpture were a living thing. Seated elegantly on its haunches, it was the size of a half-grown kitten. The color was not the best—white speckled blue at the top of the head grading to blue speckled white at the feet, but the stone was richly veined with pyrite. This not only raised the value of the lapis, but gave the cat's coat a most unusual, and to Shallisa's eye, beautiful pattern.

"I have lowered the price to one hundred silver," he said. "That's as low as I can go."

Considering that nine years earlier he had asked two hundred and fifty, this was indeed a bargain, but it was still more than she had. Patting the cat regretfully, she breathed a heavy sigh and turned to go.

"All right, for you, seventy five. But I swear you've put a curse on the thing so that no one else will buy it!"

This was untrue, of course, but rather than denying it, she looked at the tiny blue face with hungry eyes and said softly, "I only have fifty, and that will take every coin I have saved."

Tears of longing edged her lashes as she turned to meet the master stone-crafter's gaze. It seemed for a moment that a current opened between the two, for his expression suddenly softened.

"Take it, then," he muttered. "But I'll not hear your words when you curse me as you starve this winter."

"Oh, thank you. Thank you!" Shallisa cried. "Keep it for me until tonight. I'll return with your money before the market closes."

"Are you mad?" Mirga hissed as they stepped from Maldor's tent to push their way through the crowd.

"Perhaps," Shallisa laughed, hardly able to believe the cat would be hers after so long. "Come with me to see Kirkan. He'll have to make the arrangements to get the silvers, and I'm afraid he'll be cross."

Shallisa had gone without dinner that evening, giving everything she had made that day back to Kirkan to put into her now meager account. She would need it to get through the winter. Spending her entire nest egg had been a foolish thing to do, but she didn't care, the lapis cat was worth it. Carefully she drew the small statue from its velvet-lined bag, wondering who had crafted the piece. If Maldor had known the artist, he wouldn't say.

Every detail was perfect from the upright ears to the feathering of the ruff, except for the eyes, she noted with a frown. There was only a slightly curved surface beneath the lids; the artisan had failed to cut the stylized hollows which would give the impression of eyes. Odd that she had never noticed this before. Sitting down at her worktable she examined the cat's face more closely in the soft flicker of the candle—she could hardly afford to waste lamp oil now, unless she was working.

The longer she looked, the more she felt the wrongness of the cat's face. Suddenly dipping her finger in the half-dried indigo dye she used to paint her charm beads, Shallisa dabbed a little in the center of each eye, then playfully marked the insides of each ear and the tip of the nose, finally tracing the line of the lips with the last of the thick blue paste.

"There, my dear," she laughed, "now you have eyes to see, ears to hear, a nose to smell and a mouth to speak!" The transformation was amazing.

"What a handsome fellow you are," she said with a smile; only a male would have such a ruff. In the soft glow of the candle it seemed that the lapis cat smiled back. She blew out the flame and settled onto her pallet.

"Come, stone-weaver's daughter," a voice called softly in the darkness as Shallisa stirred restlessly in her sleep. "Time to rise and to walk with the wind."

"So tired," she murmured, burrowing deeper into the covers. But suddenly, to her surprise and dismay, she was drawn up out of her body, and right through the top of the tent.

Turning every which way as she rose, she saw what seemed to be the entire world stretching around her like a silvery plain. The moon shone overhead as bright as the sun at noon and the breeze, which eddied around her like the waters of a swift running stream, drew her out and away from the campsite where she lived during the spring and autumn trading seasons.

"Come, quickly," the voice urged. It had a decidedly male quality, and stirred a pang within her like a poignant but half-forgotten melody.

Silently she followed where it drew her, gliding ghostlike above the empty streets, until she came to the steps of the Stone Mansion. But it wasn't to the sumptuously appointed residences above that she was drawn, but to the workrooms in the vaulted caverns beneath.

All was still within those halls, but it wasn't dark as she had expected. Instead, a soft light seemed to emanate from the stone walls, allowing her to see what lay about her as she made her way to the innermost chamber. This room was smaller than the others and filled with all manner of strange things. Rows of jars, vials and boxes lined the shelves, and a slab of chalcedony stood in the center of the room. Etched into its surface were many strange symbols and devices, and a small table stood to either side.

In the center of the altar, for surely that must be what

the stone was, sat a small, shrouded figure. Stepping forward, Shallisa drew the golden cloth away to find the lapis cat hidden beneath.

"How did you get here?" she asked aloud. But the cat made no reply, being only stone.

His face was unpainted, as it had been when she first brought it home, but a small pot of dark blue salve sat on the right hand table. Seized by a strange compulsion, she dipped her finger into it, dabbing the color on his eyes as she had before, but this time she spoke as if reciting a spell.

"Eyes open that the spirit might see."

Then, dabbing another fingerful of the sweet-smelling ointment into his ears, she whispered, "Ears open that the spirit might hear." Then she anointed the nose and mouth, saying respectively, "Nostrils open that the spirit might breathe. Lips open that the spirit might speak."

She could hardly believe her eyes when the blue stone cat flicked his ears, blinked once, then said, "Well done. But now, stone-weaver's daughter, you must give me the final gift."

"What gift? I am no maker of great magic."

"Be still!" the cat demanded. "Time grows short! You must breathe life into my body before the tide of the spirit wind turns."

Leaning forward to lay her hands on either side of the cat's body, Shallisa pressed her mouth to his. The stone seemed to grow warmer beneath her touch, taking on a slight vibration. Three times she breathed into the cat's mouth, then she began gently stroking his body, smoothing every inch of him from his proud upright ears to the tip of his elegant tail.

"Ah, what bliss," he rumbled, standing up to stretch. Then, with a gravelly purr, he settled once more into the sitting position he had affected for so many years and, looking at her, he said, "Now you must give me my name."

"Name?" Shallisa echoed, once again at a loss.

"Yes, my name. Everything must have a name. Of course, not every name is known or spoken, but you must speak mine now, or I shall never be free of this prison."

But hard as she tried, Shallisa could think of nothing that sounded right. "It's no use!" she said at last. "How am I supposed to know what to call you?"

"How do you know which stones to weave so that the magic in your necklaces will be right?"

"I listen to the stones with my fingers, and they tell me what I need to know."

"Then perhaps you should listen with your fingers now."

Closing her eyes to clear her thoughts, she placed her hands once more on the cat's body, allowing his essence to flow into her.

"Nizirae!" she gasped, eyes flying open in surprise at how clear the sending had been. "Your name is Nizirae." And that was the last thing she remembered when she woke back in her tent the next morning to discover that the lapis cat had disappeared.

"Where is my cat!" she cried, upon finding Dab near mid-afternoon. She had searched every tent and stick house at the edge of the market to find the Regosi whelp, certain that he or one of his friends had taken it to get even with her.

"Cat, Lady?" he cried in alarm. "How was I to know the beast was yours? I caught it by the garbage dump. We had nothing to eat, you see. . . ."

"No, no," she cut him off with an anxious gesture. "Not a real cat. A stone cat. Look, I understand it was only a prank to get even with me for yesterday, but I must have it back."

"A stone cat!" he replied in the most affronted tone she had ever heard one of his folk use. "The Regosi thieve to live—a coin or two, anything we might sell or trade quickly, and food most certainly—but to take such a thing. . . ." His eyes widened into an expression of injured pride as he made a gesture of denial.

"But who then, if not you?" Panic and despair washed through her as she read the truth in his indigo-patterned face.

"Tell me about this stone cat," he said, concern replacing indignation as Shallisa burst suddenly into tears.

"It's a statue about so big," she sniffled, measuring the cat's dimensions with her hands. "It was carved from speckled blue-and-white stone."

"A magical thing then, this blue cat." His eyes widened.

Of course *he* would think so. Blue was a sacred color to the Regosi. On the other hand. . . .

"By the Stone Maiden, you're right, of course. It *is* a magical thing." she said, recalling her dream. "But to create such a spell would be far beyond the working of even an accomplished stone-crafter. But perhaps not beyond a Master's skill."

Maldor's face flashed through her mind. But why would he sell her the cat, then steal it back? Their wrangling over the years had been friendly enough, and considering how many people knew that Shallisa had bought the statue, he certainly couldn't sell it in the market again.

"A spirit walked the great Stone Mansion last night," Dab softly said, glancing superstitiously over his left shoulder. "Two servants saw it in a hall below, but no one listens. That could be something."

"Could be," she thoughtfully agreed, wondering if it hadn't been her dream-journey that had caused the stir. In any case, it was someplace to start. "I have a friend who lives in the Mansion. Perhaps with her help. . . ."

"I will come, too, to wipe away the stain you set upon my honor," Dab said. "Think on this," he added, meeting her unspoken denial with dark, earnest eyes.

"The Regosi are thieves, quick and silent. You will need such skills."

"All right," she said at last. "But I have no money to pay for your services, Master Thief."

"We shall trade, skill for skill," he grinned, ignoring the scathing tone of the honorific she had bestowed. "You shall make for me a stone-weaving with the charm of my choosing. Agreed?"

"Agreed," she said, taking the grimy hand he offered firmly in her own to seal the bargain.

"Hold the torch higher!" Shallisa hissed as she and Dab crept down the steep, narrow stairs that led to the workrooms below the Stone Mansion. It was the back entrance the servants and apprentices used, Mirga had said when she was instructing them on how to navigate the mazelike lower corridors. She had refused to join them on their quest, but knowing how much trouble her friend would be in if they were caught, Shallisa hadn't pressed her.

"Here's bottom," Dab whispered. Going left into the corridor at the foot of the stairs as Mirga had instructed, he paused long enough for Shallisa to clear the bottom step.

Cocky as he was, the boy proved his worth when they came to the first door, worrying the lock expertly with the thin irregular piece of metal he produced from his belt pouch. It yielded at last with soft click, and opened with a turn of the ring. A warm, rather electric feeling began to gather in Shallisa's hands as they entered the first of the subterranean chambers.

"Yes! This is one of the rooms from my dream," she whispered, excitement replacing apprehension.

Taking the torch and the lead, she swept through the cavernous room and the two beyond as quickly as Dab could open the doors. Never pausing to look at the wonders displayed in various stages of completion on the worktables and shelves they passed, she quickened her pace till Dab had to scramble to keep up.

Her hands were fairly tingling by the time she entered the last of the large outer workrooms. Anticipation sang through her body like the caroling of bells. But when she came to the place where the door should be, there was a wall of stone blocks.

"No!" she cried. She had been so sure the entrance was there. How could it not be?

"What's wrong?' Dab whispered, startled and anxious.

"It was here, I'm sure of it," she said, fingers reaching to touch the roughly-shaped stones. She had half-hoped the wall might be an illusion, but it felt real enough beneath her questing fingers . . . and yet something was not quite right. Before she could identify the wrongness she sensed, her concentration was broken by the sound of a familiar voice and the sudden flare of a lantern.

"Lost your lapis kitty, Cat-eyes?"

"Maldor!" She turned to face the master stone-crafter, anger flaring. "So, it *was* you who took the cat."

"Not so, pretty Cat-eyes, though it was my intention that you should come to this place."

"But why? I don't understand."

"Have you never wondered about your father?" he asked, fixing her with a disquieting gaze.

"Not you—"

"No, not I," he gave a sad little laugh, "though not for want of trying. But Nizirae was the better man, I'm afraid, in many ways. Unfortunately, in the long run this proved more of a detriment than an asset."

Nizirae! Shallisa's eyes grew wide as she recognized the name. Narrowing her gaze, she considered the stone-crafter for a long moment. Seeing this, Dab pulled a short, flat blade from where he kept it hidden in his boot and took a protective stance.

She gestured the boy to lower the blade, asking, "What became of my father, then? Is he dead?"

"No more so than stone," Maldor replied, with a cryptic smile.

"No more so than the lapis cat?" she responded.

"Very good, Cat-eyes," he said, settling his bulk onto one of the benches that were scattered among the worktables.

"And just where *is* the lapis cat, by the way?"

"Where you believe it to be." He gestured to the wall behind her. "The trick is getting inside. If you can do that, then you can take back the cat."

"But I'm only a lowly stone-weaver," she began.

"Are you indeed?" he blandly inquired. "Think you, with your cat's eyes and pale skin, that no trace of your father's blood runs in your veins ... no trace of your father's power?"

"Power?"

"Yes, power. It was your father who should have been first among us here in the Stone Mansion. Never have I seen a stone-crafter more gifted than he, and trained by the stone-mage Archimita herself to the working of it."

"If my father was so powerful, then what became of him?" she demanded. "And why is that no one but you, not even my mother, has ever spoken his name to me?"

"Ficallan, who was then the king, was an ambitious man. He had always craved power, but when his health began to fail with age, he began to crave immortality as well. Knowing that Nizirae had learned the secret of animating stone from his mentor Archimita, the king demanded he create a great idol in the form of a desert cat which he would then imbue with Ficallan's own life-force, just as the Stone Maiden had been imbued with the spirit of the Itaran plains.

"With no choice but to defy the king, for there is no greater sacrilege to a stone-mage than that of creating a false idol, he shaped the lapis cat instead. This he presented to Ficallan when the king demanded to see how the work progressed. So outraged was the king by such blatant defiance that he sentenced Nizirae to a traitor's death by slow torture."

"Then he *is* dead," she said with a sinking feeling.

"I said he was sentenced," Maldor chided with a throaty chuckle. "But that sentence was never carried out. When I came the next morning with the King's guard to offer what comfort I could, the workroom was empty save for the lapis cat, which sat covered in a golden cloth on the stone block he used for magical workings.

"Since there was no way out of the room, I knew that he must have secreted himself in one of the many closets hidden in the walls of the chamber. Suspecting that he had transferred his spirit into the stone body of the cat, I took the statue before the guards could see.

"When Ficallan heard that chamber was empty, he called upon Beharn, another of the stone-mages residing in Jadasia at the time and your father's bitter rival, commanding him to seal the chamber so that Nizirae's spirit would be trapped within. When this was done, Beharn constructed a wall into which he set a binding spell to keep anyone who might wish to help Nizirae from getting in.

"Unable to do anything else, I kept the lapis cat hidden until Ficallan died. Then I set it on my table in the market and waited for you to come of age and prove your blood."

"Such a price for honor!" Shallisa murmured, sorrow for the loss of this father she had never known blooming like a thorn-flower in her heart. Unused to such angry pain, she fought to control it, leaning her back against the rough-hewn stones of Beharn's wall. Pressing her palms hard against that unyielding surface, she struck out with her thoughts, longing to batter the stones into rubble. The wrongness she had earlier sensed surged through her, as if in answer to her psychic assault.

"How were the wall and room spelled?" she demanded. "Do you know?"

"Not the specifics of the spell, but the way that it must work . . . yes, that I know. But I have not the strength or the skill to break it; the gods know, I *have* tried."

"Never mind. There are two of us now, and blood calls to blood, just as the lapis cat has called to me all these years." She turned to the boy then. "Dab, you'll be our sentry. Make sure no one enters until we're finished."

"No one shall pass," he said, with a grim nod, then flitted soundlessly across the vastness of the chamber to take his place outside the door.

Settling onto the floor with her back to the wall, Shallisa gestured Maldor to sit before her and, taking his hands in hers, she said, "I entered the room unhindered last night in my dream-form and saw the lapis cat there. How is this possible?"

"The spell that was set to bind the stones was a physical one only and the seal set upon the chamber was specifically to keep Nizirae's spirit within, so your spirit would find no barrier either coming or going. But if the cat was indeed able to enter the room," he said with a thoughtful look, "then I must believe that you somehow stumbled upon the spell I have sought so long in vain, which would allow Nizirae's spirit to take command of the stone form. Able once more to work his magic in that form, he would have had no trouble entering the hidden chamber, only leaving it once he had."

"I see." Shallisa nodded, remembering how she had playfully dabbed the indigo paste on the cat's eyes, ears, nose and lips. "Very well, Master Maldor, show me what you know of the spell that binds the stone."

Closing her eyes, she took a deep breath and opened

herself to the wall as she had to the lapis cat. Gradually her senses seeped into the stones, tracing the web-work of the spell that held them physically unbreachable. Then she began, with the master stone-crafter's help, to trace the pattern of its making.

It was a weaving—she was heartened to realize—not unlike one of her own necklaces; but the pattern was woven through the stones, rather than the stone being woven into the pattern. For just a second she caught a flash of the design in its entirety. Then it faded, but it was enough!

Patiently, carefully, she began unraveling the magical threads just as she would have picked apart the strands of a carelessly woven necklace. The work was tedious and draining, but at last the web was undone. With a cracking sound, the wall crumbled, showering them with a hail of gravel-sized bits and dust.

When they had dug themselves free and cleared a path to the door, they found it was locked, so Dab had to be called back from his sentry's post. He grinned when the ring turned with a rusty squeal and a muffled click, then he bowed as deeply as any courtier swinging the door wide so that Shallisa could enter.

Surprisingly, the air within held none of the lifelessness usually found in long-sealed places, and as Maldor's lantern and her torch lighted every corner of the small room, she saw that everything was exactly as it had been in her dream—the stone block, the tables at each end and the gold-shrouded figure in the center. It was all perfectly preserved without even a hint of dust or tarnish.

Coming closer, she lifted the cloth with careful fingers, dropping it onto one of the tables. As lifeless and blind as when she had first seen him, the lapis cat sat in the center of the circle of strange devices that had been etched into the top of the chalcedony block. Without hesitation she dipped her finger into the pot of indigo salve and repeated the ritual she had performed the night before in dream-form, and once again the cat stretched and preened and finally spoke.

"At last, to be free again! Thank you, daughter-of-mine." He rubbed his smooth blue muzzle against her hand as she reached unthinkingly to pet him, then he was still.

"Good-bye, Father?" she whispered.

"Say no farewells just yet; I am here," said a voice from behind. She turned in time to see a tall, very fair man step from a hidden closet within the stone wall. He was clad in the golden robes of a stone-mage.

"Ah, you have your mother's hair and face, but my eyes," he said, in a voice surprisingly warm for someone who had been sealed in stone for twenty years. Shallisa came hesitantly into his embrace. After a moment, he released her. "How good it is to be able to speak to you again, old friend," he said, turning to embrace Maldor then. "I must reward you for your years of faithful care."

"Seeing you alive and well is reward enough," Maldor replied, roughly returning the embrace. "But you look just the same. How can this be?"

"I wove a stasis spell into the chamber so that time would not rot my flesh while my spirit resided within the stone of the statue. How else could my body have survived all these years? I knew you would guess what I had done when you saw the cat on the altar, but in my haste, I forgot to leave you a copy of the spell to animate the stone."

"We should go soon," Dab said nervously from the doorway.

"The boy is right," Maldor agreed. "There will be enough to explain with all this mess, and you, old friend, are still proscribed as a traitor under Ficallan's edict and subject to a traitor's death under the law."

"Then I must leave the city at once, but where should I go?"

"We could travel to the eastern lands," Shallisa suggested.

"*We*, is it?" Nizirae smiled, stroking her cheek with gentle fingers. "You shouldn't be so eager to throw your lot in with mine, Shallisa. Even though I am your father, I am also a stranger from an even stranger land. This city and the Itaran plains are the only home you have ever known."

"Then it's about time I saw something more of the world, don't you think?" she stubbornly replied.

"Ah, now, Cat-eyes," Maldor teased, grinning at her. "What would a lovely stone-weaver like you do in the great civilized cities of the east?"

"Study to become a stone-mage," she replied. "I believe I've proved I have the talent." Clenching her jaw, she silently dared them to deny it.

"She is her father's daughter," Maldor said, winking as he caught his friend's eye.

"And her mother's too, I'm afraid," Nizirae said, with a laugh. Then he looked at Shallisa, and said, "Come with me, then, and we shall see."

"I will go, too," Dab piped up, to everyone's surprise. "You will need help on your journey, and many doors have locks."

"He might be of help, at that," Shallisa said as she carefully lifted the lapis cat from the altar, wrapping the statue once again its golden shroud.

"Why not," Nizirae sighed, shaking his head in mock resignation as he gestured her to lead the way out; but there was no mistaking the proud smile he flashed Maldor as she started toward the doorway.

THE HOLLOW DANCER

by Mary Soon Lee

Mary Soon Lee writes an admirably brief and business-like letter, stating that she was born and raised in London, England, but now lives in Pittsburgh, Pennsylvania, where she runs the Pittsburgh Worldwrights, a speculative fiction workshop. "A science fiction story of mine, 'Ebb Tide' (*F&SF* May '95), recently qualified for the preliminary Nebula ballot. My fantasy credits include stories published in *On Spec* and *Pirate Writings*, as well as a forthcoming story in *F&SF*. In my nonwriting life I am thirty years old, married, without children. We have no pets at the present time," but she concludes—probably facetiously—that some day she would like to keep llamas—as I said, I believe this is facetious.

Has she ever smelled a llama up close?

"The Hollow Dancer" reflects on some of the same ideas as Lisa Waters' story, and, like Cynthia McQuillin's "Stone-Weaver's Tale," gives us a look at fatherhood. It also offers a suggestion for a more human way to wage war (but anybody who'd listen to such a rational idea probably wouldn't fight a war at all).

The night before the battle Hellia danced with the enemy. Everything about it was strange to her: walking past the sentries, her face hidden behind the golden death mask, the soldiers stopping their tasks to stare at her, the way the rough black cloth of her shirt scratched at her skin.

For four years, every day since her twelfth birthday,

she had practiced the dances, the formal steps she must make with a partner, the steps she must take on her own. But until this night she had never danced in front of strangers.

Behind the golden mask, her face was clammy, fever-hot, as she paused at the entrance to the enemy commander's tent. She wasn't ready. She wanted to vomit.

The sentry lifted the flap leading inside the tent. "Captain, the Death Dancer." The sentry gestured her forward.

Hellia stepped into the tent. Oil lamps hung from iron poles, yellow light flickering over well-worn furnishings. A much-patched quilt lay over a mattress; two wooden stools rested by a narrow table. At the far end, a young boy sat on the ground, working at a rust-spot on the captain's armor. A stray lock of hair fell across his brow. His eyes darted up to Hellia's mask, darted away when he saw her watching him.

Behind the mask, Hellia bit her lip. The boy was scared of her. She turned away from the boy, nodded at the man standing in the shadows. "Captain." He was shorter than she'd expected, and his cheek bones stood out sharply. The captain said nothing, staring over her shoulder at the sentry as if she were not there. "Captain, are you ready?"

He glanced at her, looked away again. "Let's get it over with."

He strode past her, out into the darkening air. Hellia followed, lengthening her paces until she drew alongside him, her sheathed dagger pressing against her calf as she walked. Around them, the soldiers were forming into a great circle, set within the greater stage of the eastern plain.

Hellia and the captain stopped in the center of the circle. She glanced at him sideways. His thin face had set into hard lines that she couldn't interpret. The night air was cold, but Hellia was too hot. Her shirt and her trousers scratched at her. Inya, her teacher, should be here, not Hellia.

But Inya lay dead in their own camp. Hellia had thought Inya was still asleep, and hadn't ventured inside the tent until noon, reluctant to disturb the older woman; Inya had looked so tired these past weeks. By the time Hellia went in, Inya's body had started to stiffen, her mouth twisted. Hellia wouldn't let anyone else into the tent while Inya looked like that. Inya shouldn't have died alone, without solace, without witness, but at least Hellia could give her back the dignity that was so important to the older woman. For half an hour she had tried to smooth Inya's contorted expression, pushing at the cold flesh. Hellia shuddered, and thrust that memory away.

The circle of soldiers yielded to let four white-robed arbiters step inside, the only other figures within the circle's expanse. The tallest arbiter raised a hand, and the circle of soldiers fell quiet. Nothing stirred except the wind, carrying faintly the sweet scent of heather-berry.

Hellia heard the too-fast sound of her breath, the captain breathing beside her. She looked up at him briefly, his face set in that hard expression that she couldn't read.

The arbiter pointed at the captain. "Do you accept, in the name of your soldiers and of your king, our arbitration in the coming battle?"

"I accept."

The arbiter pointed at Hellia. "Do you take upon yourself, according to the tradition of your order, the duty of carrying out our judgment?"

"Yes," said Hellia, but she did not know if she could take the next step down that path. She was empty inside, void of the goddess' blessing. Inya had said the goddess would come to Hellia in time. But it was past time and Hellia was still alone.

"In pledge of your joint agreement," said the arbiter,

"and to honor the goddess who holds us all in her hands, let the dance begin."

The captain moved in front of Hellia. His bare fingers reached for her left hand. At his touch, a ball of white light flared above them, magicked by the arbiters.

Hellia's eyes watered from the sudden brightness. She laid her right hand on the captain's shoulder. His hand settled on her back, heavier than Inya's touch, alien. Her breath would not come as she took the first step, her body awkward, everyone staring at them. The man smelled of lamp oil and sweat.

They took the next step, and the next. A vast hollow beat echoed each time Hellia's feet touched the ground. She knew the arbiters caused the sound to summon the goddess, but she could not shake the sensation that she was dancing over the skin of some giant animal. She gazed past the captain at the ring of soldiers, and for a second she could not remember the moves of the dance, the steps she had practiced for hour upon hour.

The captain's breath hissed against her cheek. "*Look* at *me*."

Startled, Hellia looked into the hard lines of the captain's face, glossed by the white light, and abruptly she read the hatred there. She stumbled, her foot catching on a stone, and he caught at her harshly.

His hand tightened painfully around her fingers. "Do you think about what you do? Does it keep you from sleeping?"

Hellia came dangerously close to laughing. The captain didn't realize she'd never done this before, never danced with a man, never killed—she looked away from him, up into the dark sky.

"*Look* at me," said the captain. "You've turned war into a tidy game. Not too many deaths, no wounded soldiers limping home. You bitch—"

Hellia yanked the man into a faster movement, watching him struggle to keep up, letting her nails bite

into his flesh. He had it backward. She hadn't forced
him to this point, hadn't ordered him to battle. No, that
was the fault of his king, and it was her duty to mini-
mize the grief that decision would cause. Her duty—
and she remembered how Inya's face used to go still
when she spoke of duty, of responsibility, of how
people's fear made them angry.

Inya had never let herself be a mirror to other
people's anger, and nor would Hellia. Shamed, Hellia
slowed the pace. The man's expression never altered.
She could not watch that face and concentrate. So she
shut her eyes. Through her closed eyelids, the light
reduced to a red-tinged glow. Under her feet the
ground echoed like a hungry beast.

"*Look* at me," said the man.

Hellia shook her head, eyes closed, and focused on
the pattern of the dance. Gradually the noise and the
ring of soldiers receded from her mind, until there was
only the dance, one step leading to the next. Each step
carried her farther away, out to a dark center where
there was nothing but the next move of her foot.

Something tugged at her hand.

She opened her eyes. Sweat beaded the captain's
forehead. His chest heaved. Beyond him, the arbiter
signaled for the dance to end. Hellia stopped dancing,
bowed once to the captain without meeting his eyes,
bowed to the group of arbiters.

Then she walked out of the circle, back to her own
camp, to keep vigil beside Inya for the second night
since her death.

Hellia started awake guiltily at dawn. She had meant
to watch Inya's body all night. Her shoulder ached
from where she had fallen asleep on the mat by the
bed. Outside, she could hear the soldiers moving about.
Quickly she washed her hands in the bowl of cold
water, adjusted her clothes. She picked up the golden

mask, stopped. She set the mask down again and knelt beside Inya.

"Please—" there was no point in continuing. Inya couldn't hear her anymore. She rested her forehead against the other woman's cold cheek. Her eyes stung. She stood up sharply, put on the mask, and walked outside.

The two armies were lining up on the plain. Banners fluttered with the shifting wind. Hellia walked through the nearby line of soldiers, the dawn light catching on their swords. Between the opposing armies stood an earth mound, four times the height of a man. At the summit stood a circle of white-robed arbiters, facing inward.

Hellia clambered up the mound, and the arbiters parted to let her within the circle. The enemy death dancer sat alone in the center wearing a silver mask.

"Sit down, child," said the enemy dancer. "It'll be a long day."

Something in the woman's voice reminded Hellia of Inya, and suddenly she was furious. The woman had no right to talk to her softly, as if they were friends, as if there was anything they would ever have to say to each other. Hellia turned her back on the other woman, and stared rigidly at the soldiers, trying to recognize those she knew. The few women were easiest to spot, their long hair bound up with ribbons.

A lone bugle sounded. As the deep note decayed into silence, the arbiters turned to face outward. Abruptly the soldiers froze, caught like toys in mid-motion, one with a hand raised to scratch his chin.

The arbiter nearest Hellia gestured once, and a soldier subsided to the ground. Another arbiter gestured, and a second man fell. Hellia looked round to the line of enemy soldiers. They stood immobile, caught in time, but then she saw a soldier fall, and then another. Hellia could see no blood, no injury on the soldiers, but the arbiters listened to the goddess and marked those who would have died in a normal battle. Men who might yet die if they were unlucky.

Hellia swallowed down bile, and looked down at the earthen mound, unable to watch any longer. Later the arbiters would release eleven out of every twelve of the fallen soldiers, displaying the mercy of the goddess. Of the remaining casualties, Hellia would kill those of the enemy, and the opposing death dancer would kill those of her side.

She stared at the ground all day long. Once an ant crawled over her leg, intent on some private duty. The sun climbed high and slowly sank. An hour before sunset, a bugle sounded.

Hellia looked up. The soldiers were moving again, all but the figures lying still on the ground.

The arbiters walked down from the mound, their shadows elongated in the fading light. They paced along the soldiers' lines, pausing to touch eleven out of every twelve prostrate figures. Eleven out of every twelve rose to rejoin their own troops. When the arbiters were finished, only two dozen bodies were left behind.

Hellia stood. Beside her, she saw the other death dancer walk down to the battlefield. She did not watch; these steps she must take on her own.

Down she went, down to the field and the first of the enemy. A middle-aged man with a boil above his right eye. She was empty inside, bereft of the goddess' grace as she knelt by the man's side. She laid her hands over his, laid open the gates of her mind, and reached for his thoughts.

Fear slammed into her.

The impact rocked her back onto her heels, blunt and solid and bitter. But she held on tight to the man's hands. At last the fear ebbed, and through the link she wove a picture in the man's mind. He stood in a high place, on a cliff far above a gray ocean. Sunlight burned a track of liquid fire across the water. A seagull glided past, its path marking the wind's curve. The man smiled inwardly, watching the bird.

Hellia let go of him with her right hand, and pulled her dagger from its sheath. She thrust it hard between the man's ribs, blood standing up for a moment in a line, before the red spilled over.

She wiped the blade on the trampled grass. She stood up, her legs shaky. She walked to the next prostrate figure. Dimly she heard shouting. She looked up. The enemy captain was arguing with the arbiters—an irrelevance, unimportant. She knelt beside the prostrate figure, a heavyset lieutenant with broad callused hands.

When she stood up again, her head spun. There was someone to her left, blocking her path to the next soldier. The enemy captain faced her.

"Wait. Please." He sounded hoarse. His hand gestured brokenly. "That's my son. Let me take his place."

Hellia stared down at the figure on the ground. It was the young boy from the captain's tent, the one who had been scared of her. "No, captain. There are no exceptions, no pardons, no trades."

The words were as hollow as she was. She knelt on the ground, and laid her hands over the boy's. Fear sliced into her. From far away she heard the captain: "You think you're giving my son to the goddess, but you're wrong."

She accepted the boy's fear, waited for it to ease, started to form a picture in his mind—a high place, with a gull's call aching on the wind—the captain's voice broke her concentration. "You think I want my son to belong to the goddess, but you're wrong."

Dissonance, the link breaking in blood and fear.

Hellia screamed. Hot liquid splashed her. Her eyes shot open. The captain crouched over his son's body. The hilt of a dagger jutted from the boy's neck. Blood drenched the boy's tunic, pooled on the grass.

Hellia reached for the boy's mind. Gone.

The captain stared at her. "You think the goddess blesses you—"

"No," said Hellia. She lifted her hands from the corpse, and stood up carefully, her limbs unsteady. "I hope she blesses what I am sent to do."

It was hard to walk past the captain, hard to go to the next figure lying on the ground. She knelt down beside him, void of the goddess' blessing, and she did not believe that blessing would ever find her.

LA FAIE SUIATEIH

by Lisa Deason

Lisa Deason is one of "our own" and has just become an active member of SFWA, the society for Science Fiction and Fantasy Writers of America. The title of this story is the only thing I can fault about it. I feel very strongly that every "strange sounding name" in fiction should be absolutely pronounceable—either obvious from spelling or in context. There is a school of thought which feels that if names are too obvious the story will be too simple; my own feeling is that simplicity is best, and I keep urging people to simplify, simplify, simplify.

One of my major precepts is that you should be able to describe the plot of a story in a single sentence; if you can't tell me in a single sentence "what the story's about," it's too complicated. Even a novel the length of *Gone With the Wind* can be summarized in plot in a single sentence. If you find you are explaining your stories at greater length, suspect that you are overcomplicating them. I once had a harsh lesson about this; I was describing the plot of William Hope Hodgson's *The Boats of the Glen Carrig*, and my first husband asked me why I could never describe the plots of my own books so simply. From that moment I made a point of being able to sum up my plots on a 3 x 5 card. That was when I started selling steadily. It's still a good exercise, and when I taught writing classes, I always asked the student to begin by summarizing the plot of her (or his) story as follows:

1) Who is the main character?

2) What does he or she want?
3) What is keeping him (her) from getting it?
4) Will he or she get it or not?

Believe it or not, in the answers to those four questions, lie the whole art of writing as I've learned it in almost sixty years. Lisa learned it, and so can you.

Enya was slumped against the trunk of one of the thousands of oaks in the Forest, her odd-colored eyes of fine marble and dark steel but mere slits in her angular face. The brown, very bloodstained cloak tangled about her was parted just enough to reveal a dull glint of chain mail splattered and crusted with red. One gloved hand was curled in her lap, the other rested slackly upon the ground next to her thigh. Though she was only twenty-eight, the once rich chestnut hair brushing her shoulders was salt-and-pepper and had been for several years.

It was difficult to judge how long she had been there. The thick curtain of leaves obscured the passage of the sun far overhead.

Thudththump, thudththump. Hoofbeats, felt in the earth as much as heard. Her heart leaped, but she didn't raise her gaze, not until after a long, long stalemate.

The body was sleek and sheer white with a luxurious mane and tail and hooves that flashed like flint with each motion. A twisted spiral horn of silver and gold was set above luminous blue eyes.

There was recognition in those eyes, recognition . . . and triumph. The delicate nostrils flared, then came a whicker of pleasure at what the scent carried.

Of the many names for the creature, Enya chose one of the oldest and most obscure. "La faie suiateih," she said and the sculpted head gave a mockery of a polite bow.

The distance between them was crossed in an abrupt, easy stride. Razor-sharp silver and gold rammed square

into the center of the bloodstained breast piece without
mercy or conscience.

She came awake abruptly. Not more than a foot or
two away yet another set of shimmering blue eyes
watched her. But this time they were guileless, framed
by raven-black hair, and set in a human face.

Pain pulsed beneath the mail and her fingers found
the deep dent in the armor; she was going to have quite
a spectacular bruise on her breastbone.

The young man observed her curiously and the budding horn on his smooth forehead rippled in the
dappled light, a very faint gray and pale butter yellow
against the ivory skin. He was nude; doubtlessly la faie
suiateih had broken the human tie of clothing long ago.

"My prince, do you remember your name?" she
asked gently and a crease marred the expanse between
the feathery black brows.

"My name?" the young man whispered as though the
notion were utterly alien yet paradoxically as familiar
as his own skin.

Maybe she would have stirred his memory given
more time, but with the next breath, a squeal of fury
split the air like a thunderbolt thrown down by an
angry storm deity.

"No!" the prince cried as he was knocked harmlessly
back by the charge.

La faie suiateih reared, cleaving the air with sharp
hooves, then landed heavily and tore up great hunks of
the grass and sod near Enya's legs.

"Check your dead more carefully," she said, her
voice and mien steady despite the display of strength.

Abruptly, the horn found the indentation in the
armor again and pushed with increasing force.

"Isn't it bad for your image to kill a defenseless
woman?" she ground out fearlessly though the pressure
made her gasp.

La faie suiateih snorted derisively but . . . was there a hint of real concern?

"Please, don't," the young man interjected and his hands, far too soft, far too inadequate, gripped the twisted hardness and sought to pull it back. "I beg you, don't!"

La faie suiateih bellowed, frustrated, but relented in deference to his tender skin, shouldering him a strict distance away from the woman on the ground.

"You've denied him his rightful place for too long," Enya said. "It's time for him to return home."

The equine mouth gaped in parody of a grin. "And you'll be the one to take him?" The melodious voice, as breathtaking as a thousand angels singing, issued from deep within the barrel chest. "You protected him so well, didn't you? I'm certain you were quite commended on the job you did."

Her mouth thinned into a single tight line, but she held in an angry response, refusing to be baited.

"How many months did the guards comb the Forest?" the exquisite voice sibilantly asked. "How many years did *you* walk the Forest, cursing me with every breath? No one can find me if I don't choose for them to and no one can capture my mate! But I am amused that you decided to drag your dying carcass back one last time to try and redeem yourself. Or . . . did you think perhaps I'd take pity on you? Spare your worthless life and Change you as well? Even *were* you as magic-touched as he—" a thrust of the slender muzzle indicated the prince who was taking in every word and looking increasingly stricken "—you long ago lost the innocence needed to start the Change. Nor are you worthy of the honor."

"What do you know of honor? You ambushed a lone guardswoman and stole a ten-year-old child from his family." And though she didn't want it to, the memory violently erupted in her mind, scalding her with the heat of shame undiminished by time.

The Queen was clearly uncomfortable with the suggestion, but Enya knew she would be able to sway her.

"So close to the castle and with so many guards in hearing range, what could it hurt to let the boy play within the fringe of the Forest?" she said with patient persuasion. What could possibly be lurking in the shadows that she, one of the few guardswomen appointed to the elite Legion of Swords, couldn't handle? There was nothing to fear from a few trees, now was there? The Queen was simply being overprotective.

"On my honor, I'll keep him safe, Majesty," she said firmly and could see in the Queen's eyes that she appreciated the heaviness of what she was swearing. "Nothing will happen to the prince while he is under my care."

The kidnapping was well planned, needing only an overconfident guard to set it in motion, and Enya had fit the need to perfection. Of all the dangers that did inhabit the Forest, she never would have thought to fear a creature always thought of as the embodiment of goodness. Only later did she discover the truth that lurked beneath the bard's songs and children's tales and it was far darker than she would have ever dreamed.

"I've given him a greater destiny than he ever would have had beneath a crown on a human throne," the beast said arrogantly.

"And you also gave him no choice. I've studied you these past six years," Enya said. "I know you steal the memories of your victims, so they know no better than to do your bidding. I know it takes a nick of your horn to start the Change and that it takes a decade for it to complete itself."

"What else do you know, foolish mortal? Tell me of my unmatched speed, of my intelligence and of my beauty. Tell me of how in the long reign of my kind we have learned to seduce humans into loving us even as we prey upon them to replenish our numbers. Tell me all of this, dying one, and perhaps I'll be kind and end your miserable life. I assure you that I'll not make the mistake of leaving you alive a second time."

"Do you hear, my prince? You mean nothing. You're but a means to an end. La faie suiateih wishes a mate, so your life is forfeited."

"Silence!" the beast screamed and the angels within its voice darkened, fell. "You will be silent!"

A fire-spark hoof struck the tree trunk in rapid succession, missing Enya by bare degrees, and sending a wild spray of wood splinters into the air.

The young man suddenly threw himself at the beast, pounding the muscled arch of the pure white neck. "I'll hate you forever if you do this!"

La faie suiateih immediately stopped the attack and turned to him, luminescent blue eyes taking on a glow bright enough to challenge the sun. "You don't mean that," the voice said, and the angels then sang of love and trust. "You mustn't be distracted by what this intruder has said. She's a *mortal*."

He stood straighter. "So am I."

"No, you're confused. She's confused you. Let's be rid of her—" and the head swung back to where Enya was sprawled . . .

. . . where no one was sprawled . . .

It would have never worked if la faie suiateih had been standing a few paces away. Even caught off-guard, no mortal could've crossed any sort of distance before being struck down by horn or hooves. But la faie suiateih, focused on resnaring the prince's slipping faith, had neglected to step back.

Enya came up directly beside the creature's neck, letting the large head turn into her. From beneath the tangle of her cloak, she produced a shortsword, stubby in length but thick and strong enough to cut through a tree limb.

Her left hand closed on the horn, her right brought the weapon about in as hard a chop as she could manage. La faie suiateih reared in panic. Enya came off the ground as she clung desperately to the horn and to her sword, trying to twist out of range of the sharp hooves. As soon as her feet were down again, she gave several hard pulls, utilizing the weight of her body as well as her strength, and bone cracked.

The beast tried to savage her with its teeth, and she nearly took off her own arm while making a second chop.

Suddenly, she had the prize secure in hand and leaped free, prepared to use the trees for makeshift shields and the sword to defend herself. But la faie suiateih, a bloodless, blackening stump in place of its silver-and-gold horn, crashed to the ground, thrashing in agony.

Enya darted out and moved the prince away from the heaving, careening body when he seemed too stunned by the turn of events to get himself out of harm's way.

"How . . . ?" la faie suiateih asked. "You smell of death and of blood . . ."

"This cloak was worn by a brigand who was killed when he attacked me." She flipped back the long sleeve of her tunic, revealing a bandage, freshly stained scarlet, wrapped around her left forearm. "The blood was simply a necessary sacrifice. I had to make you think I was helpless, dying, so that you would be careless."

"Clever . . ."

"I warned you to check your dead more carefully." She stabbed her sword into the ground within easy reach and waited.

The creature's flailings finally stilled and the unearthly eyes dimmed to a flat blue, a sheen of pure white light radiating from within its body outward. "No," it said and there were no angels in its voice anymore.

The horn Enya held disintegrated into a handful of silver and gold powder that the next breath of wind sent scattering, a vanishing shimmer in the uncertain sun-and-shadows.

The prince gasped and his lustrous blue eyes darkened to a clear green. A puff of smoke issued from the budding horn upon his brow; then, like water on a hot grill, it sizzled away into nothingness.

La faie suiateih groaned in soul-deep despair and a blaze of white engulfed its body.

When the light faded, the prince whispered, "I don't understand . . . A woman?"

"Of course. She was Changed just as she tried to Change you." Enya briskly went into motion, removing her cloak and giving it to him, showing him how to wrap it around himself. Then she slipped out of her chain mail and took off her long outer tunic, standing clad in her sleeveless undershirt, trousers and boots.

The blonde, brown-eyed woman stared at her with undisguised hate as Enya held the tunic down to her. "Keep it," she hissed.

"You can't run around the Forest naked," Enya said evenly.

"I want nothing of your humanity!"

"Your choice." She let the shirt drop to a puddle of coarse linen on the grass, then said to the prince, "Sire, if you'll come with me, I'll have you home in a few hours."

He looked from her to the now-human la faie suiateih. "She . . . she can come with us, can't she?"

Enya made a noncommittal sound as she shrugged back into her chain mail, then retrieved her shortsword and thrust it through her belt.

"I won't live in a human world," the blonde said, getting shakily to her feet, her two soft, fleshy feet that had been four hard, fire-spark hooves but moments before. "This Forest is my home. I've been here for more than a century."

The prince paused, then said, "It is my home, too. The only one I know. I don't want to leave it."

"Sire," Enya started but words utterly failed her. All these years, she had known how it was going to be: the Queen's face would be ecstatic as she embraced her son, and she herself would be hailed as a hero for returning the prince safe and sound. "*Enya never gave up,*" they would say. "*She outwitted la faie suiateih and reclaimed her lost honor.*" Then, an outcast no more, she would be welcomed back into Her Majesty's Legion of Swords with loving, open arms.

She could go home again.

But, for it all to happen, the prince had to go back with her.

"Sire," she said. "*You can't mean this.*"

"I do. I don't belong in a human world. Not now, anyway. Perhaps after I've discovered what it means to be mortal again. . . ."

Enya's hands tightened into fists. She'd been prepared to fight to the death, but *this* she couldn't defeat with strength or by sword. It was the only battle she had never once imagined having to wage.

"She'll never allow it. It's a matter of *honor.*" In la faie suiateih's newly human mouth, the word became an obscenity.

There was no question that Enya could take him by force; not even he and the mortal-bound la faie suiateih together could stop her. She could take back what she had lost and let the prince and the Queen and the whole lot of them sort out his life after that. The *afterward* part was none of her concern.

"You're right," she told la faie suiateih, "it's a matter of honor."

She strode to the prince and he stared her full in the eyes, unflinching. "I beg you to reconsider," she said.

"I'm sorry, I cannot."

She sighed slightly. "Then, when you're ready, follow the river north to the Castle E'Mala. That's your home and it will always be waiting for you."

"Will you be there as well?"

"No, I won't," she said softly. "But the people who will be love you dearly and you mustn't ever forget that."

With a respectful bow, she did the hardest thing she'd ever had to do.

She walked away.

La faie suiateih had been defeated and the prince released from his enchantment, all as she had sworn to do, yet still she couldn't go home. In her heart she knew she had her honor back, even if no one else would ever know, and that was enough.

It had **to** be.

VENGEANCE

by Dorothy J. Heydt

Dorothy Heydt is another writer I am happy to claim as "ours" since she has appeared mostly in my anthologies—which indicates to me that other editors are missing something good. Dorothy and her husband Hal have two surprisingly articulate children, both of whom have sold stories to me: one to *Marion Zimmer Bradley's FANTASY Magazine* and the other to *Towers of Darkover*.

This is another of Dorothy's stories of an ancient Greek sorceress. This qualifies as fantasy because if you go back more than about 300 years in the past, you have to make most of it up anyhow, reliable records not being available.

"Captain, the lines are fast."

"Very well. Welcome to Alexandria, my lord. From here, on so high a tide, you'll see her better than from anywhere else but atop the King's roof. All this before us, within those walls, is part of the Palace. And there to the north, the Temple of Isis, shining in the sun. You should visit it while you're here, my lord, you and your companions. The Temple of Isis, my lady.— You there, send out the gangplank."

There were four to disembark at the Royal Harbor: the nephew of the Tyrant of Syracuse, and his companions, and a few slaves. The nobleman's name was Arkhimedes, and he was young, the first wisps of beard still trying to take root on his chin. He shifted his shoulders within his fine tunic, as though he would rather have been swimming naked in the sea. Next behind him was a youth his own age, dressed not quite so finely, and behind him an old man, gaunt and vacant-eyed, whose robe had once been costly but had seen a lot of wear since then.

Last came a tall woman in black, her swollen abdomen bound up in sashes to ease her back. She guided the old man's steps down the gangplank and pulled her stole over her eyes against the hazy autumn sun.

Their baggage had been discreetly searched, their collection of books politely examined for titles unknown to the Library (and none found), and a dockmaster's agent assigned to guide them to the palace of King Ptolemy.

"Well, that seems to have worked," Demetrios murmured, throwing his cloak back over his shoulder. In doing so he caught sight of old Palamedes, humming tunelessly in the warm sun, and Cynthia leading him by the hand. "I trust the King will have physicians in his house," he added, "as well as poets."

"Without a doubt. We'll have your father seen to, and Cynthia, too. If any physic can help her." Arkhimedes shook his head slowly. "What was it came on her while she was away?"

"Friend, do I know? She vanished from the market at high noon; she came back after the war, with that Punic woman and her baby, and having once delivered them into safety, she sat down like a stone and stopped moving. She still eats what's set before her, so I don't suppose she'll die, but I fear she may go mad."

Walking dutifully behind them, trailing Palamedes by the hand, Cynthia listened to them and thought about that undiscovered country, madness. A better place than where she was, perhaps—but no, how could she remember Komi if she lost her wits?

She pulled her stole closer across her eyes, till she could see nothing but Demetrios' feet before her. The air was dry, making her hair crackle like a stroked

cat. It smelled of brick-dust. The steady footfalls of
the King's escort on either side of her, the cries of the
gulls, the voices of the servants and soldiers who clus-
tered before the steps of the palace, all were dulled to
her ears.

Then someone screamed.

It was as though the prickly autumn air had gathered
itself into a lightning bolt and dropped itself at her feet.
Her eyes flew open. She dropped Palamedes' hand and
pushed back her stole. There it was, an overturned cha-
riot with a broken pole, and the fallen driver climbing
to his feet, and the wild-eyed stallion plunging and
rearing while men came running to reach for his bridle.
A cloud of panicky pigeons rising from the ground,
whirling in a dust devil of their own making, their
wings clattering. And a little cluster of anxious men by
the wheel, bending over a graybeard who lay clutching
his leg and moaning.

Cynthia went past the royal escort and moved the old
man's companions aside like so many nervous sheep.
"Let's see your leg, Grandfather. You, boy! Bring the
bag with the red strap!" She tucked up the old man's
robe, exposing a blue swelling larger than her hand,
and the skin over it cut, but not too deeply. The bone
appeared not to be broken. Still, so great a bruise could
cripple the whole leg if left to itself. When the slave
came up with the bag, she took out a strip of linen and
bound it firmly round the bruised place.

The King's men had gotten the frightened horse
under control and led him away. Cynthia sat back on
her heels and looked at her patient's companions: three
young men so like him they must be his sons. All four
had blue eyes like Hellenes. The anxiety was fading
from their faces, and they smiled.

"What's your name, Grandfather, and where do you
live? I want to visit you tomorrow with a poultice for
this."

"I am Ezra ben Yaakov, and I advise the King on matters of commerce. I live in the Weavers' Street, in the Delta." He jerked a thumb eastward. "Right behind the Palace. It's not far."

"Good. Can you men get your father home all right? Then get him to bed, and don't let him set foot to floor. I'll be 'round tomorrow."

The King's escort were around her now, urging her to her feet. "Tomorrow," she said again, and followed the guards through gates and up steps and between walls to a guest house set in a water-garden. Six palm trees made shade overhead, and a white lotus in the pool made the air fragrant. Life, Cynthia mused. It did go on, however much unasked.

"The water for your hands and face, my lady."

"Mmm? Oh. Put it over there."

"And will it please you to bathe in the pool later on? If you are going to the Temple of Isis—"

"Tomorrow, maybe. That's all." *Now that's strange. This is the third, maybe fourth, total stranger with the same invitation. Maybe they're trying to drum up business?*

The slaves sent away and the door shut behind her, Cynthia unwound the sash from around her belly. She caught on her toe, as it slipped floorward, a polished turtle shell and set it on a table. The white papyrus shone through the neck- and leg-holes: the six books of magic that Palamedes no longer had the wit to read from. If the Library's agent had known of them, they would have gone off for copying with no guarantee that it would be the originals that were returned. Cynthia had worn the shell, bound to her in a sweaty false-pregnancy, since they had left Syracuse, and it had just paid off. Now she lined up the six scrolls, peering at the titles inked along the outer edges. Where to begin? Look: this one said "ELEMENTA," and she would bet that it wasn't Euklides' Elements of Geometry. She tucked the other scrolls back into the shell and bound it back into place—the whole compound was full of slaves, their own and Ptolemy's, eyes and ears everywhere. When they got a place of their own, nearer the Library and farther from the Palace, then she could have a convenient "miscarriage."

In the evening Arkhimedes went to dine in the King's hall, but his friends stayed in the guest house and ate simpler fare without ceremony.

"I'm not sure you should be reading that," Demetrios said, as he chewed the leg of a roast duck.

"I see no reason why not," Cynthia said. "Listen, it even says here that I may. 'To make fire. This spell is so simple that even a woman can learn it.' Thank you very much, you old magician, for the confidence you place in me. He's right, though, it's only three words." She spoke them and pointed at the wick of a lamp resting on a table, and it obediently burst into flame. Demetrios jumped, and gulped for his wine to keep from choking.

"Here's another. Two words spoken over your cup or plate renders any poison harmless. We should teach that to Arkhimedes, if he's going to rub shoulders with kings and princes." She tasted the wine in her cup, spoke the words, tasted again. There appeared to be no difference. Just as well.

In the morning she selected dried herbs for a poultice, and saw to it that someone was taking care of Palamedes, and stowed all the scrolls away again in the belly of the tortoise. Arkhimedes had made a late night of it in the King's hall, and was only getting up as she left her room.

"Good morning. Going out? To the Temple of Isis maybe?"

"Oh, you noticed that, too."

"Noticed what?" said Arkhimedes, yawning as he turned toward the breakfast table. Cynthia opened her mouth and shut it again, and threw her stole around head and shoulders. She made her way through the water-garden, between walls and down steps and through gates, out of the Palace.

The outermost gate guard told her how to find the Jewish quarter called the Delta, and the people there told her how to find Ezra's house in the Weavers' Street. Five houses up from the fountain, with a bronze knocker on the door. . . .

It was a pleasant neighborhood, not glittering with wealth but well-kept and clean. Except for those stains on the doorpost, there—and the next, and the next. And here at Ezra's door too, with the bronze knocker that rang sharply under her hand, the doorposts and lintel stained with splashes of dark brown—

Zeus! It was dried blood!

And at that moment the door opened, and one of Ezra's sons led her to his bedside. She poulticed the bruise, which was looking as well as could be expected, and he asked her about her travels, and she asked him about the customs of his people, and they fell to talking like old friends.

". . . it's the blood of the Passover lamb, with which we mark our homes in the spring. (And it hasn't rained much since then, you see.) Long ago, when we were slaves in Egypt, God sent a curse upon the firstborn of every Egyptian household, except for ours where we ate the Passover meal and marked our doors; and so we do to this day."

"And yet here you are back in Egypt."

"Oh, yes—" (an eloquent shrug) "—but this time it's to our advantage."

". . . and the ring of Arethousa shielded me from Tanit's curse, but it struck my husband and drowned him in the sea—"

"Ah, there. No, go ahead and weep; your tears bear witness to his worth. Listen: the souls of the just are in the hand of God; death's torment can no longer touch them. They seemed, indeed, to die—in the eyes of

those who knew no better—and when they left this
world, they seemed to be destroyed. But they are at
peace."

"But does that go for everyone? or only for your own
people?"

"I am convinced," Ezra said, "that God knows all the
just for His own and will not let a single one of them be
lost." A pause. "But I don't know what they would tell
you in Jerusalem. Come, have another honeycake."

It was mid-afternoon before she left Ezra's house,
and long shadows were stretching eastward across the
street. The roof of the Jews' house of prayer was still in
sunlight, its cornice bright with a frieze of flowers
picked out in gold. And just visible to the north, the
much-famed Temple of Isis, its pillars gleaming white
in the sun, wound round with golden vines. She supposed they were vines. Her eyes were good, but not
that good—

"Cynthia! Is it you! Oh, it is!"

Cynthia looked again. The woman clutching her
arms was her own age, maybe, but soft and rounded
with easy living. Subtract half the flesh, take away several years—"Gorgo! By all the gods! Life's been good
to you."

"Off and on. My man Diokleidas is well-off, but a
terrible fool. Yesterday he bought me five fleeces for
seven drachmas, such a bargain, he thought; but it was
all tail-ends and dirt. But what about you? You've
grown so thin. Did you ever marry, or—" she glanced
at Cynthia's abdomen, and glanced away.

"Married and widowed. And I've traveled all 'round
the sea. My father died in Italy."

"Oh, what a shame, without seeing his first grand-
child, and your man, too! But children are a great comfort. You'll see."

"If the gods will it," Cynthia said, clenching a fist
where Gorgo couldn't see it. "I'm glad to have seen
you so well. Now I must—"

"Oh, no, no, you mustn't rush off like that; why, I've only just seen you. I was just going off to see Praxinoe; you remember her, don't you? She lives just along here."

Gorgo had Cynthia's arm firmly tucked into her own, and she had the advantage of weight. Cynthia gave up the struggle. It would do her no great harm to spend an hour in the company of old friends, even if they had gone soft and foolish.

"Gods, what a crowd! They're like ants, there's no counting them. Though Ptolemy's done well by us these days: no more cutpurses creeping up the street. Don't step on us, my good man. I'm lucky I left the children home. Here's the place."

She knocked at the door, and after a few moments a girl with unkempt hair opened it, squinting against the afternoon sunlight. "Hello, Eunoe. Is Praxinoe at home?"

"No," the girl said.

"Gorgo, dear!" The voice was high-pitched, almost shrill. "I *am* at home to *you*. Come in, come in, it's been a long time." Praxinoe bustled them through the heavy door into the women's court. "And Cynthia, by the gods! It's been ages. Sit down. Take this cushion. Eunoe, you lazy girl, bring wine."

Cynthia settled down to endure it. The wine was good, and the two of them could be left to chatter away to each other like sparrows in a grainfield—

"And of course, we both spend a lot of our time attending the service of the Goddess."

"Ah," Cynthia said: as neutral a comment as she could make.

"Have you visited Her temple?"

"No; everyone keeps telling me I should, but just at present I have other things—"

"Do you not believe in the Goddess?" Praxinoe was watching her as a crow watches a fat earthworm.

"If you have seen as many Goddesses as I have, you wouldn't believe in 'em either."

"Seen?" Gorgo's eyes were bulging, and she clutched her breast as if she found it hard to breathe.

"Well—let's see." Cynthia held up a finger. "I had a vision, or a dream, of the Earth-Mother that eats her children. Then, I went under the earth in Phaneraia and saw some nameless old earth-goddess, worn out and forgotten, with only a few dozen souls left in her larder.

"Then I went to Panormos and ran into Tanit in one of her temples, and sorry I am to say it, we did not like each other. So I went away again." *And after she drowned my man, I turned her curse back against her and sank a whole fleetful of her worshipers.* She sipped her wine. What the women didn't know wouldn't hurt them. "So I don't think I want to encounter Isis, or she me, thank you."

"But—but you *have* met Her."

"All the Goddesses are the same Goddess."

"Demeter, and Aphrodite, and Artemis, and Syrian Astarte, they are all the same."

"And to have seen Her in three different guises: you must have been greatly favored."

"You must go to Her at once."

"Madame, there's a litter at the door."

"So soon? Good. Come, Cynthia, we'll attend you on your way." Each of them had a good grip on one of her arms, and if she had dug in her heels, they could have picked her up and carried her. Eunoe held the door as they led her out.

There was not only a litter at the door, gilded and curtained and carried by four massive men: there was a procession at the door, flute players and flower girls and half-a-dozen shaven priests in white linen. They bundled Cynthia into the litter on the near side, and she swept open the curtains on the far side to assess her chances. There was the holy place of the Jews, which had been given the right of sanctuary by the King—but hundreds of people stood between her and it; she would never make it. The priests took stations around the litter; the procession moved forward.

But no order was given, was her next coherent thought. *Praxinoe never said anything but "Bring wine." But someone in the Temple knew I was here.*

"Sing praise to the mother of all life," the priests chanted, "the mistress of the elements, the first-born of time."

It's Isis herself who knew I was here, who set lures for me in every unheeding mouth, who set a trap for me in Praxinoe's house and sent Gorgo after me like a ferret. Maybe it's true that the Goddesses are all one Goddess; and that Goddess has laid an ambush for me.

Well: She has found herself a worthy opponent. And she settled back into the cushions and began furiously to think.

It took perhaps half an hour to get from Praxinoe's house to the Temple: she had spent no longer than that indoors, so the litter must have been sent out at once. Isis was quick on her feet. The bearers set down the litter and Cynthia stepped out, scorning the hand a priest held out to her. "*Don't* you touch me," she said, and had the pleasure of seeing him step back.

"Be of good cheer, daughter," an older priest intoned. "Your child will be born among the initiated."

And Cynthia allowed herself a smile, just a little one. So Isis didn't know everything—or at least, her priests didn't.

They ascended the steps: nine in number, broad and smooth, in shining marble. And here were the great pillars, entwined not with vines as she had thought but with gilded serpents, their long bodies as thick as her thigh, with crystal eyes that glittered. Within the colonnade was a wide pool abloom with lotuses and the feathery crowns of papyrus. A narrow bridge stretched across it, and Cynthia went over it with two priests ahead and four behind. No knowing how deep the water was. She could swim, of course, but better not to let them know that yet.

Beyond the pool was a pair of huge doors. Inside them was a large hall with a great statue of Isis, wearing enough paint for a whole whorehouse, and holding a sistrum in one hand and a boat-shaped dish in the other. Her eyes stared, unseeing, over their heads. The priests paid no attention to her; they hurried Cynthia across the floor to a little side-door the same color as the wall, and thrust her through it.

Inside, the only light was from torches held by two veiled women; the shape of their heads was strange till Cynthia realized they were wearing bulky woolen wigs. A third held a cup made in the shape of a lotus. She stepped toward Cynthia and put the cup into her hands.

The stuff smelled sweet and musty. Cynthia murmured two words.

"What's that?" a priest asked sharply.

"A blessing," Cynthia said, and drank. It tasted like ordinary wine.

There followed a long quarter of an hour while she sat on a bench just inside the door, and the priests and the veiled priestesses stood watching her. In front of her the dark corridor went forward about a spear's cast and turned to the left. Soon, when they thought her properly tamed, they would lead her into a labyrinth as great as Minos', maybe, and she would have her work cut out to find her way out again.

And a map appeared in her mind, a map no pen had ever drawn: her old neighborhood, far to the west of here, where she had run about till she was twelve. Probably all changed now, but still clear in her memory. *Let's see, we entered this place from the east. Say the steps were the houses of those three Corinthians, then the lotus-pond is where the camel market was, and the hall would be the new market plus about two rows*

*of houses, and the door we came through is Philon's
bake-house. Then we're looking down Threadneedle
Street, and it turns left onto Fleshers', and then I'll just
have to see.*

More of the veiled women had come in from somewhere; there must be ten or twelve of them now. Some
carried torches; some carried baskets; one came up to
Cynthia carrying a little box of gilded wood, shaped
like the full moon.

"Sing," she said. " 'I am the Queen of Heaven: I am
the morning star.' "

" 'I am the Queen of Heaven: I am the morning
star,' " Cynthia repeated dutifully. Her voice would
never be her fortune, but she could carry a tune at least.

" 'I am the mother of all living,' " the woman sang,
turning to walk down the dark corridor that mapped to
Threadneedle Street, and Cynthia followed her, repeating each line of the song. " 'I will rise up and go
about the city. You women of Byblos, have you seen
my love?' " Down Fleshers', along the alley behind the
Golden Goose, and a sharp turn right across old
Medea's doorway—

The torchbearers had gathered up ahead, making a
pool of light around something on the floor: a shape
like a hand.

She bent down and picked it up: a hand, the dried
and embalmed hand, smelling strongly of resin and
spices, of some long-dead man who had been torn in
pieces like Osiris and scattered abroad. One of the
basket-bearers took the hand from her, and stowed
it away.

" 'I sought him whom my heart loved; I called for
him, but I could not find him.' " The tears brimmed in
her eyes. The veiled woman took her hand and led her
along.

So the script of the drama was plain enough: she was
to take the part of Isis, singing her songs and traveling
her sorrowful journey, searching for the fourteen scat-

tered members that were the fourteen days of the
waning moon. If she'd taken the drink in the form it'd
been given to her, she might have come to believe
it all.

After the first few turns, it proved easier than she
had expected. They led her here and they led her there,
but it all boiled down to a great double-loop around the
Golden Goose at one end and the house of Xerxes the
rug-merchant at the other; and every time she went
over old Medea's doorstep, she found another body
part. She was even beginning to recognize the wall-
paintings by now: here, a man and women dressed in
fine linen, their hands raised in worship, the woman
holding a sistrum. There, a pool set 'round with date-
palms and fruit trees. The air was reasonably fresh:
they could not be too far underground. No sign of any
window, though, or skylight or smoke-hole through
which an agile and desperate person might escape.

The thirteenth piece was the skull, and the fourteenth
the lower jaw. They had not given her the mummy's
torso to find; perhaps it would be too heavy to carry, or
too large to conceal in a basket till needed. But that
was all that remained, unless—

The priestess was leading her a different way now,
past Medea's into Crocodile Street, and along where
the bridge over the canal should have been. And
there she was, sure enough, opening her golden box
where she thought Cynthia couldn't see, and laying
down some small object on the floor.

Of course. Cynthia came forward and picked it up, a
little thing like a segment of a crumbling dead branch.
*What's-his-name, Typhon, scattered Osiris' members
across the earth, but the phallus he threw into the sea
and the fishes ate it. Like Komi. And she made a substitute of wood.* "I sought my brother, my spouse. I flew
round the earth wailing, I did not alight until I found
him. I made to rise up the helpless members of him

who was at rest. I drew from him his essence, I made for him an heir."

But no one can gather up Komi. That dirty bitch Tanit killed him, and if it's true they're all the same, then that dirty bitch Isis killed him, and now She expects me to put Osiris back together for Her—

Straight down Canal Street now, without a turn, and there was a light at the end, a high-vaulted room with something like an altar in the center. The torchbearers were singing, "The cord is broken, the seal is undone; I am come to bring thee the Heart of Osiris; thy heart is to thee, O Osiris. I have not come to destroy the god on his throne: I have come to set the god on his throne. I have risen up like a falcon: I have gone forth like an eagle: morning star, make way for me."

In the center of the room, on a dais only a few steps high, the mummy of Osiris lay on its bier, naked and neatly reassembled. *And what if I put the last part back where it belongs? Will the dead god sit up and speak?*

At the head and foot of the bier two women stood, dressed in linen, angular shapes on their heads whose ritual meaning was a blank to Cynthia. The one at the head was clearly carven of wood: there was a patch the size of her thumb where the paint had peeled away from her ankle. The other—

The other turned her head and looked at Cynthia. Her eyes were cold and dark. "There you are," she said.

"Here I am," Cynthia said, and spoke three more words. The bit of rotten wood in her hands blazed up, and she threw it quickly atop the mummy.

Someone screamed. Cynthia spoke the words again, at the top of her lungs, and the torches blazed up like fiery trees. The priestesses tore blazing veils from their heads. The stench of singed wool from their black wigs was heavy in the air. Burning resin roared and crackled. Horrible to tell, the burning mummy was moving, raising its arms, trying to slap out its own flames, till the hands fell away from its arms.

The air was getting thick. Cynthia dropped to hands and knees and found her way to the door. She ran back down Canal Street and retraced her path as quickly as she could. There were angry voices behind her. Threadneedle Street. Philon's bake-house; there was the door. She pushed it open and ran across the hall while a pair of acolytes stared, too surprised to follow. There was something to be said for long legs. She slowed down a little for the bridge across the lotus pond, picked up speed between the white columns.

Outside, to her surprise, night had fallen. The full moon was brilliant overhead, the color of new bronze. She had spent more time in that place than she thought. There were people in the streets, rogues and wastrels, but they gave her no trouble; indeed, they fell back at the sight of her and turned and ran. Back toward the Palace. Here was the north gate—but it was locked and barred, and the guard paid no attention to her knocking.

Maybe it didn't matter. The cries of angry pursuers had died away. Perhaps she had lost them, and could make her way round to the harbor gate, or—

Someone was singing: a drunken whore, her veil askew, walking along the moonlit streets scattering fragments of song like petals. She vanished between two darkened houses, where even the moonlight did not penetrate—and Cynthia heard a little gasp, and nothing more.

Out into the moonlight, between the darkened houses, they came like fluid streams of gold: two, four, a steady line of them, the golden snakes that had entwined the marble pillars of Isis's house. Cynthia gathered up her skirts and ran again, scrolls rattling in her tortoise-shell belly. No time now to get them out and search for a counterspell. Without thinking she had turned to the east, toward the Delta: maybe she had hoped the faceless God of the Jews would have little sympathy for an angry Goddess. There was no one in the streets, not even a thief, to distract the effortlessly gliding serpents. Weavers' Street. She ran up two steps and pounded on the door. "Ezra! Ezra! Let me in!"

The door opened: Ezra's eldest son, with a rushlight, and some daughters-in-law peering round his shoulders, and Ezra himself, out of bed against medical advice, leaning on a staff and reaching out to draw her in. "Come, come. What are those things? Never mind, they can't get in. See?"

The golden serpents had gathered in the street; back and forth they went, never daring to come closer. One stretched out its head, leaning toward the door with tongue flickering, and drew back as if it smelled something unpleasant.

"Go away, you old serpents," Ezra said. "Or stay if you like; you can't get in. The Lord of Hosts protects this house. They can't get past the Paschal blood, you see, any more than the last Egyptian curse could. Someone bring more lamps, and food and drink. I expect they'll go away when the sun rises, but we may as well make sure." He sat down on a bench his daughter-in-law had brought him, and made Cynthia sit beside him. "Last time, you know, the high priest Aaron laid down his staff on the ground and it turned into a serpent. And all the Egyptian magicians said, 'That's nothing, we can do that, too,' and they laid down their staves and they turned into serpents. And Aaron's serpent ate up all the Egyptian serpents and turned back into a staff in Aaron's hand. So you really can't expect a son of Aaron's house to be afraid of a lot of silly reptiles like that."

They sat up while the moon westered and set, while Ezra and his family sang to their God whose name must not be spoken, and Cynthia marveled at the power of faith. As the sun rose, the serpents faded like mist and were gone. "Told you so," Ezra said.

"So you did," Cynthia agreed. "I wish I believed in

anything as much as you believe in your God; I could pick up the Temple of Isis and drop it into the sea."

"I wish you could, too," Ezra said. "Now from what you've told me, I think you've made Alexandria too hot to hold you. We'll have to think how to get you out safely. I don't know if the Lord will part the Red Sea for you, but we ought to be able to manage a small boat."

THE MOONGATE TROLL

by Patricia Duffy Novak

Patricia Duffy Novak has been in most of my anthologies since I began editing them; besides fourteen appearances in my anthologies and magazine, she also had a story in the December 1995 issue of *Realms of Fantasy,* and has recently made a sale to *Adventures of Sword and Sorcery.*

She says that "like most writers" she has a novel making the rounds and is working on another novel. She was recently promoted to a full professor of Agricultural Economics at Auburn University. She has also completed a Master's degree in English, a project undertaken for her own pleasure. I envy you, Patricia; I can't write or study when I'm teaching; I get so much of words in class that I can't even read on the side, much less write. This is why I never finished my Master's degree; I was too busy turning out commercial writing—with kids to support.

In "Moongate Troll," two adventurers, without any skill at magic, embark on what appears—at first—to be a classic tale of "rescue the princess from the enchanted castle."

The troll stared at Shale, and she stared back. A moment before, Shale had been alone in front of the moon castle, taking a cautious look around. And then the troll had appeared from nowhere, as if magicked onto the spot.

"Urggg," said the troll, in what Shale hoped was a

conversational tone. Her sword would be useless against the troll's tough hide. Shale took a quick mental inventory of her other belongings. One pair of scuffed boots, leather breeches and vest, brass wristlets—

Hmm. Her gaze flicked to the thick metal bracelets. Trolls were known to favor golden bribes. They were also known to be fairly stupid, and the moonlight was not exactly blinding, even if the moon was nearly full. Shale slipped off one of the wristlets and waggled it invitingly at the troll. "Troll like nice gold? Pretty. See?"

With a swipe of its massive paw, the troll grabbed the proffered bauble. It held the bracelet above its head, examining it for a moment. Then the troll sniffed the air with a decided air of disdain and flung the wristlet down the hill, toward the forest. No mistaking the meaning of that, Shale thought. Not so stupid after all then, at least when it came to brass and gold.

Instinct, more than cunning, directed Shale's next move. She ducked and rolled. The slope of the hill was not great, but it was sufficient for her purposes. At the bottom, she rose and ran, trying to ignore the thundering footsteps in pursuit. Earlier, when she'd scouted the area, she'd found a narrow crevasse which led back into a stony hill, just beyond the end of the high, smooth wall that surrounded the tower. With luck, she'd fit into that hole. Otherwise, she'd probably end up as the troll's midnight snack.

Pumping her legs as fast as she could make them go, Shale raced along the wall. The troll's fetid breath steamed against her bare upper arms, and the massive swings of its huge arms set her short hair aflutter. *Mother of a Bog-Burner, it's going to be a tight fit,* Shale thought, as she jammed herself into the narrow hidey-hole, scraping her arms raw in the process. Good thing she and Karl had been on such tight rations since they left the city of Noria six weeks ago. At her normal weight, she might not have fit.

Squeezing herself sideways into the crevasse, she turned her head to watch the troll. *Maybe it will go home,* Shale hoped. Wherever home might be for the creature. There weren't even supposed to any trolls in this part of Askuria.

Instead, the troll sat on its haunches, nasty yellow eyes glaring at Shale. Dawn wouldn't break for hours. Shale supposed she was in for a long and miserable night.

The troll threw back its head and let out a long and mournful howl. It shuffled a little closer to the hole, so that its stinking breath misted Shale's face. Just then she became acutely aware that her bladder ached. A long night indeed.

Shortly after dawn, Shale pushed open the door of a tavern on the Street of Fools where she and her partner Karl had contracted for meals and sleeping space in exchange for keeping the peace during the busy evening hours. Her muscles throbbed from the long night of crouching in the crevasse, and the deep scratches along her arms burned like strips of fire.

Karl lay sprawled on the floor with a blanket over him. As she neared, he woke with a startled snort and struggled to a sitting position. His long red hair had tangled into his beard and his eyes were shadowed and dark, as if he'd not had much more sleep than she.

"You look worse than that troll," Shale said.

"What troll?" Karl wiped the back of one hand across his eyes.

"The troll that had me pinned in a crack in a mountainside all shreeging night." Shale tossed her scabbarded sword to the floor, where it landed with a dull thunk.

Karl shook his head and then stretched. "There aren't any trolls this far west of the Irondog Mountains."

"Go tell that to the troll. Fram's forehead, Karl! Didn't you notice I never came back?"

"I figured you slept in the woods. The ground would be more comfortable than this floor." He rose creakily. He'd slept in his pants and vest, but his boots were missing. Shale spied them across the room, near one of the tables, leaning drunkenly against their packs.

She snorted. "I spent the night crammed in a crevasse, with a troll waiting to get me if I came out."

"Sorry." He sounded honestly contrite. "I really didn't think you'd be in much danger. You have a way of handling yourself. Better than three men, that's what I think."

"I suppose it's just as well," Shale said, a bit mollified by the praise. "If you had come looking for me, the troll probably would have made short work of you. You're too big to fit in the crevasse that sheltered me, for all that you've dropped at least a dozen pounds since we left Noria."

Karl patted his lean ribs. "If we succeed at this job, we won't ever have to worry about our meals again."

"A big if, Karl." Shale frowned. "The parchment made no mention of a troll on guard."

"No, it didn't," he agreed. "What about the castle wall? Can we get over that?"

She shook her head. "Unscalable. We'll have to go through the gate, and the parchment says the gate only appears by the light of the full moon."

Karl crossed the room, sat on one of the sway-backed wooden benches, and started to pull on his boots. "That'll be tomorrow. Think that troll will still be there?"

"I don't see why it wouldn't be."

"I'd better figure out how to get rid of it, then."

"Good." Karl was not as competent a fighter as she, but he could think well enough when he wanted. Shale was more than happy to leave the puzzle of the troll to him. Too tired to worry about washing the blood from her arms and the dirt from the rest of her body, she stretched herself on the blanket Karl had abandoned, hoping there'd be time for a short nap before the tavern's staff arrived. Or maybe even a long nap. The place didn't open until noon.

A clattering noise woke her. Heart pounding, she sprang to her feet, one arm snaking out to grab her sword.

"Sorry, Miss." The low-pitched voice came from the shadows at the far side of the bar. Although the sun streamed brightly enough through the window near the doorway, the light didn't carry very well into the back of the tavern.

Shale peered into the gloom. The voice, she soon discovered, belonged to Will, the tavern owner's son. A pleasant-mannered young man whom Shale had met for the first time yesterday morning, when she and Karl had arrived in the town of Leapersfalls.

Broom in hand, Will stood beside an upended chair. "I tried to be quiet, so as not to wake you, but the broom handle caught on the back of a chair and pulled it down."

Her heartbeat, by this time, had returned to a nearly normal rhythm. She managed a smile. "It's all right. What time is it, anyway?"

"Eleven hours." Will answered her smile with one of his own. "I didn't expect to find you still sleeping at this hour. Someone should have warned you that the wine in these parts is stout."

"Stout wine was the least of my concerns last night. I was playing tag with a troll."

"There aren't any trolls around here."

"That's what I thought, too."

Will stepped from the shadows, still carrying his broom. He was a tall, fair-haired youth with the long chin and straight, narrow nose of his father, and the dark and heavy-lidded eyes of his mother. He pursed his lips and surveyed Shale, an odd expression in his dark eyes. "There's blood on your arms. Are you hurt?"

"Not badly."

His gaze stayed riveted on her face. "Are you trying to rescue the princess?"

She nodded.

"My Mum thought as much, but my Da said no, that you were just a pair of hire-swords down on your luck, that neither you nor the man looked like a wizard." He squinted at her. "You still don't. But then I suppose wizards don't always wear their robes."

"Neither one of us practices magic," Shale said. "I'm a licensed swordmaster. And Karl is—" She hesitated. Karl had studied magic in his youth, but he didn't have the skill to make a wizard. But he understood magic, even if he couldn't practice it, and he was not unhandy with a sword. "Karl's a good one to have along in a tight spot."

Will looked doubtful. "All the others were wizards."

"All the others failed." She hefted her sword. "Me, I trust in swords."

"Well, I wish you luck, Miss. You'd better keep your business quiet, though. My Mum and Da don't favor heros."

"No?" Shale raised a brow. Usually tavern masters were glad of occasional adventurers, with their wild stories and aura of romance.

"My sister ran off with the last adventurer we sheltered," Will said glumly. "A wizard name of Frolo. Now I have to do twice as many chores."

Shale thought death had been the fate of all those who'd attempted to free the Princess Arminna from the moon castle. "This Frolo lived?"

"Aye," Will said. "My sister may have talked him out of venturing the castle, for all we know. He arrived here one night about a month ago. The next morning he and Belinda were gone. A trader who came this way that afternoon said he saw a man in wizard's robes traveling north with a girl riding pillion behind him. Last we heard of either the wizard or Belinda."

"Sorry," Shale said. It did explain why the tavern had been short of help. Will looked as if he had a wiry strength in his long limbs. She supposed he'd done bouncer duty before he'd been co-opted to wait tables. Shale looked around the tavern and spied a door at the back. "Would you mind if I cleaned myself up in the kitchen?"

"Be my guest," Will said. "There are towels above the stove." He continued to look at her in a speculative manner.

"What is it?"

His eyes took on a rather avid gleam, and his face flushed darkly red. "I don't suppose you'd want to carry me off, would you?"

"What?"

"Carry me off. You know, put me on the back of your horse and take me away from all this." The young man gestured with his broom. "I'm getting awfully tired of double chores."

"Sorry." Shale was not remotely tempted, for all Will's good looks. The lad couldn't be much more than twenty, a good dozen years her junior. "Seducing young men isn't one of my hobbies. Besides, I don't have a horse."

Will let out a sigh. "That fixes it," he said with an air of disgust. "I've never even seen another woman adventurer. Not likely I'll meet another. I guess I'm stuck here. Belinda always did have the luck." With that, he resumed sweeping, apparently resigned to his mundane fate.

Struggling to suppress her mirth, Shale set off for the kitchen. After a few quick cranks, the pump released a thundering flow of water into the metal scrub basin. Shale started to chuckle. Carry off the lad! What a thought! Grinning from ear to ear, she grabbed a bar of harsh, yellow soap and began to lather an arm.

* * *

Shale frowned at the small sack nearly engulfed in Karl's hand. Around them, the first customers of the evening sauntered into the tavern. Quiet so far. It would be a couple of hours, and many tankards of ale, before any trouble threatened. "What's that?"

"Troll bane. A local herb-witch sold it to me."

"How much?"

"Two coppers." He shrugged in response to her skeptical glance. "After we rescue the princess, money won't be a problem. Do you know any better way of dealing with a troll?"

"No," she admitted. She took the bag from him and sniffed. The herb had a strong, pungent odor—unfamiliar to Shale. "How's it work?"

"The witch said it's like catnip for trolls. We sprinkle it on the ground, and the troll will roll and frolic like a kitten."

Now that would be a sight, Shale thought. Oh, well, so long as it kept the troll out of commission while she and Karl rescued the Princess Arminna of Noria from the sorceress who'd captured her. Arminna's father had promised a hefty reward for her return.

None of the other adventurers who had passed through the moongate ever came back. The risks were sobering, but Shale was willing to take her chances. Ten years ago, when she'd entered the sword guild, she'd sworn an oath to fight for justice. The Princess had done nothing to deserve imprisonment, other than to inspire the jealous hatred of the sorceress, who had been called the fairest woman in the land until Arminna came of age. Her gods smiled at good deeds of all types. If Shale got rich in the bargain, so much the better for her.

The night had advanced to well past midnight before Shale and Karl left the tavern. The evening crowd had been loud and quarrelsome; more than one rowdy patron had been set outside before the night's work ended.

The walled castle lay about a mile east of the village, at the foot of a minor mountain chain. Not far off, the falls from which the village got its names tumbled through a rocky passage. A faint murmuring from the falls carried to Shale, who crouched with Karl behind a stout pine, a bowshot from the center of the starkly white wall. A cloud obscured the moon, so that a shroud of darkness covered the woods. So far there was no sign of the troll, but last night the thing had not appeared until Shale had nearly reached the gate.

As the moon emerged from behind the cloud, a glowing gold opening appeared in the fifty-foot-high wall. Through it, Shale spied the long central tower of the enchanted castle. Karl pointed. "The gate."

"Why a moongate, I wonder?" Shale murmured.

"I'd guess the sorceress is a moonwitch," Karl answered. "She has to let power in somehow. Or else the structure—which must be built on illusions— would crumble and fall. And so the gate. Unfortunately for us, her power waxes with the moon as well." He frowned slightly as he studied the gate. "The best weapon against illusion is hard steel. Keep your sword busy, no matter what you think you see, and we'll succeed."

Shale hoped Karl's knowledge of the arcane would be adequate for the task at hand. Her own skills lay entirely in her sword arm. "The troll seemed real enough," Shale said.

"The troll is the puzzling bit. The sorceress must have lured it here somehow." From his belt, Karl unfastened the bag of troll's bane. "Here goes." He darted up the hill, toward the gate.

Before Karl made it to the gate, the troll came shuffling around the western edge of the wall. Karl, meanwhile, frantically dumped the contents of the bag, then backed away.

A few feet from Karl, the troll stopped abruptly, its head raised and its nostrils aquiver. It sat on the spot where Karl had scattered the herb, but rather than frolicking, it put its monstrous head in its paws and let out a series of heartrending howls. Shale stared at the troll, puzzlement overriding her other concerns, until a rock skittering near her feet caught her attention. At the edge of the gate, Karl waved frantically urging her to come on.

Shale unsheathed her sword and scurried up the hill. With a last glance at the sorrowing troll, she followed Karl through the narrow gate, too small by half for the troll to squeeze through. In fact, it was a tight fit for Karl.

Moonlight bathed the cold white tiles of the castle courtyard. Not a single tree, shrub, or other living thing marred the crystalline beauty of the place. Like moonlight captured and turned to stone, Shale thought, exactly as Karl had speculated. From the center of the tiled yard, the spire of the castle rose skyward, equally cold and beautiful. High on the side of the spire, a narrow window gleamed silver. Shale saw no other opening. Other than their own breathing, the silence was absolute. The troll's mournful cries, as well as the murmur of the falls, had apparently been shut out by the wall.

"What happened to the troll?" Shale whispered. "I didn't think that was how the bane was supposed to work."

Karl turned his hands up. "Who cares? We're in."

"What now?" She pointed to the smooth surface of the tower.

He shook his head. "I'd planned to walk in the front door." He stared at the tower. "Only there isn't one. Maybe I can boost you up."

Even standing on Karl's shoulders, Shale could reach only half the desired distance. She cursed softly and jumped down. "We'll have to go back for a rope. I only hope that troll bane of yours lasts long enough."

A noise at the gate caught Shale's attention. She spun, sword in hand, ready to fend off whatever demon had made an appearance. Her eyes widened as she took in the spectacle that met them. Will, the tavern lad, carrying an ax and a rope.

A rope. Her annoyance at the Will's interference was quickly replaced by a mild feeling of gratitude. "How did you know we'd need that?" she said, pointing at the rope.

"Before my sister ran off, I used to come stare at the castle by moonlight. I would've tried to rescue the princess myself, except all those wizards kept failing. Figured I didn't stand a chance."

"What about the troll?" Karl said. "Weren't you afraid of it?"

"I never saw that troll before," Will said. "But it's been some weeks since I've had a chance to come. I watched what you did with that bag of spice, by the way." This last to Karl. "Amazing that it worked. Old Mary sold you a bag of oregano. She was laughing about it all over town."

"Oregano?" Shale puzzled over the strange-sounding word. "What's that?"

Will grinned. "It's one of my Mum's favorite cooking spices. Good for flavoring tomato sauce. Absolutely no magical power in it at all."

"Sister of an Ice Slyvern," Karl hissed. "That disgusting old hag could have gotten us killed."

"Well, as you said, it worked." Shale shrugged. "Let's get on with this rescue. Give me the rope, Will."

She tied her dagger to the end of it. Climbing again on Karl's shoulders, she cast repeatedly into the window, until the dagger caught. Trusting fate and her own tough hide, she pulled herself up and in.

Beyond the circle of moonlight, the room was pitch-dark. Groping, she found the end of the rope, tangled about some sort of stone statue. Reclaiming her dagger, she secured the rope around the statue, then leaned out the window. "Come up, Karl." As the big man clambered up the rope, Shale saw Will, waiting behind him, ready to follow. As soon as Karl made it over the ledge, Shale jerked the trailing end of the rope into the room. "You run home," she admonished Will. "Your mother's already lost one child. That's enough."

Will's mouth dropped open. "That's not fair!"

"Tough!" said Shale, pulling her head back into the darkness of the room.

The moon moved behind a cloud, plunging the room into absolute darkness. "Karl?" she whispered. No answer. She whipped out her sword and shuffled forward in the dark. Her boot connected with the stone base of the statue. She put her hand out, to steady herself, and her fingers touched a stone beard. Now that beard hadn't been there before, she thought, puzzled. With her foot, she poked the base of the statue and encountered no rope. Her fingers ran lightly across the large, stone face, tracing all-too-familiar features. Karl! And something in this room had turned him to stone.

The best weapon against moon sorcery is hard steel. She took a two handed grip on her sword, and closed her eyes, so she would not be tempted to rely on them in this place of absolute darkness. A swordmaster could fight blind, relying on smell and hearing. Her nostrils flared as she inhaled deeply, trying to sort the scents of the room into understandable components— silk, stone, copper, the lingering trace of garlic from Karl's now-stopped breath. There! An unnatural musky scent emanated from her left. She held her breath and strained her ears. A low, irregular breathing noise came from the same direction as the scent.

For all she knew, the creature had night sight. Shale turned, as if heading for the far corner of the room. Air movement behind her alerted her to the creature's rush.

She turned and swung, her blade meeting a fleshy resistance. Something shrieked. Hastily yanking her sword free, she brought it down again, higher this time, where she believed the creature's neck would be. This time the shriek died half-uttered, followed by a thump.

Shale pulled her blade loose from the carcass. "Karl?" she whispered again.

"Huh?" came a murmured reply. "Where are you, Shale? I can't see a thing. Am I blind?"

"No. The room is completely black. Did you bring any flares?"

Almost before she had finished speaking, Shale heard a small sputter. A feeble green light illuminated the room. But after the pitch-darkness, it seemed to Shale like a floodlight. A hideous warty creature sprawled at her feet, its hide a mass of grayish bumps.

"A stone demon," Karl said. "Good work, Shale."

Other than the creature, the room appeared ordinary enough, like a sitting room in a noble's house, except one side was lined with statues. Around the feet of one, the rope remained tied. None of the statues was particularly handsome, and most had rather bizarre expressions on their stone faces. "Odd choice of decorations," Shale murmured.

"Not decorations," Karl said. "The demon's other victims."

"Why didn't they come alive when I killed that thing?"

"The spell can't be reversed after a full day has passed." Karl shifted slightly and sighed. "Too bad. We could use the help."

At the far end of the room, the lines of a door stood out against the dark marble wall. "Through there." Karl drew his sword and pointed with it.

On the other side of the door a stairway reached into the shadows. "Up," Karl said. "The sorceress gets her power from the moon. She'd hide the princess at the castle summit."

Their boots thudded against the uncarpeted stairs. Whatever lurked upstairs would have ample warning of their arrival, Shale thought grimly, if it didn't already know they were coming. Halfway up the long stairway, the flare sputtered out, pitching them into darkness again. No sooner had the light gone out, than Shale heard a rustling in the air above her head. She stabbed and something cried out. Shaking her sword, she dislodged a small heavy object.

"Ow!" That from Karl. "Careful, Shale. They bite."

Karl's warning came too late. Razor sharp teeth nipped at Shale's arm. She grabbed her dagger with her free hand and stabbed. Another one of the creatures down. Both blades moving in a protective dance about her face, she moved forward, following the sound of Karl's steady footsteps and his intermittent curses.

A dull thump, followed by another curse, marked the end of their journey upward. "I found a door," Karl said. And then, "Ow! Stop that!" A swish of blade, a sharp nonhuman cry, and a small thwack. "Hurry up, there are more of these flying things up here."

As soon as she reached his side, the big man shoved against the door. It gave reluctantly, groaning as it swung inward. Karl shut it behind him, thwarting the batlike creatures on the other side, but also blocking their escape, Shale noted. Well, she couldn't blame him. Thanks to her own sword skill, she'd received only one bite. From the number of Karl's curses, he'd received at least a dozen.

Four windows in the roof of the tower room let in enough moonlight for Shale to see the interior reasonably well. Two lamps also burned, one at either end of a long divan. Another sitting room of sorts, although without statues this time. At first, she thought the room empty of other occupants, but then a form moved from the shadows.

"My heroes," came a low, pleasing voice. As the woman stepped into the lamplight, Shale observed her slender beauty. Gold hair fell in long waves over white arms. Wide, thickly lashed eyes met Shale's gaze with candor. A long tunic of some shiny material swirled in soft folds across the gentle upswelling of her breasts and along the smooth curves of her hips. Karl caught his breath sharply, obviously finding the woman pleasing to more than his sense of esthetics. No wonder the young woman had inspired a sorceress' envy.

The beauty glide-stepped toward them, her gaze flickering from Shale to Karl and remaining there. "I've waited so long to be rescued," she said. "Let me reward you with a kiss."

She reached those white, lovely arms toward Karl's neck. Her long, tapered nails glittered red in the lamplight.

Shale watched, her thoughts aswirl with speculations. Incongruously, a phrase of Karl's beat a steady tattoo in her head. *There aren't any trolls this far west of the Irondog Mountains.* Something flashed in the moonlight, just beyond the edge of the reaching hands. Before the long white fingers could close behind Karl's neck, Shale took her dagger and flung it.

Karl screamed before the woman did. "Shale! You murdering fool!" He bent over the crumpled form. "Dead!" He glared at Shale. "By the Gods, woman, you've never been jealous before!"

Shale snorted. "Is that what you think? And you call me a fool. Look at her nails. Go on."

Karl picked up the dead woman's hand and held it toward the light. "Moon-daggers!" He shook his head. "How did you know? Surely you didn't see from that distance. I was closer."

Shale moved forward and looked at the long red nails. As she had suspected, embedded in their tips were a series of wire-thin needles, gleaming an eery moon-gold. Ten in all, although any one would probably have been sufficient for Karl's end.

"I saw something flash in the light," she said. "But

that only confirmed my suspicion." Levelly, she met Karl's puzzled gaze. "Karl, my friend," she said gently. "Do you think a real princess, no matter how grateful, would really want to kiss that garlic-reeking, fur-covered maw of yours?"

"Just because you don't like beards and garlic, you think all women share your squeamish little ways."

Mother of a bog-demon, Shale thought, were all men this shreeging vain? Although Karl was by no means ugly, he was hardly the sort of man a noble lady would desire. Certainly, the red-ringed welts rising on his face and arms did little to enhance his natural attractiveness, such as it was. She bent to retrieve her dagger. "We'll put your appeal to the test. Let's go claim the real princess."

"You know where she is?" Karl raised a coppery brow.

"Of course. You told me yourself."

"What?" The second brow joined the first, making an inverted V on Karl's forehead.

Shale grinned. "Come on. I'll show you."

As Shale slid down the rope into the castle courtyard, she heard Karl, who had preceded her, mutter an oath. "Dragon's dung! Where could that lad have gone! I hope the troll didn't get him."

"I'm sure he's fine," Shale said.

As she ducked through the gate, Shale saw Will's blond head gleaming in the moonlight. In his arms, he clasped a young woman, whose face was shadowed by Will's shoulder. "There's your princess," Shale said to Karl, gesturing at the embracing couple, who seemed oblivious to their presence.

Karl stared. "What the blazes? Where did she come from?"

"You said it yourself," Shale answered with a grin. "There aren't any trolls this far west of the Irondog Mountains. The sorceress must have transformed the princess. I thought the troll was menacing me. She was probably pleading for help."

Karl shook his head. "A moonwitch can't cast a spell like that. Only a powerful blood-wizard can work that kind of magic. The princess must have slipped out the window ahead of us." He started to walk toward Will and the young woman.

Shale followed Karl across the short space. "Well, Will," Karl called gruffly. "I see you've kept the princess safe for me."

Will jerked to attention. Shale saw with surprise that the young woman he'd been embracing had only an ordinary prettiness. Attractive enough, but nothing spectacular. How had the moonwitch conceived a jealous hatred of this poor young thing?

"Princess?" Will repeated, head cocking in surprise. "This is no princess. It's my sister, Belinda."

Shale felt her mouth drop open as she reached Karl's side. Karl laid a heavy hand on her shoulder, as if he needed some support to keep from falling over. To be cheated of a princess not once, but twice, in the space of a night was—Shale figured—more disappointment than most men met.

Shale studied the girl. "How did you get here?"

The girl twisted her hands in the heavy cotton fabric of her skirt. "Frolo brought me. He tricked me into thinking he loved me, that he would take me to Noria and set me up in a fine house. Instead he bound and gagged me and brought me here, hiding me in that little cave where you sheltered the other night, lady. Then he turned me into a troll. Oh, I tried to warn you, but I could not utter a single human word!"

"Where is the princess?" Karl said.

"Gone with Frolo." The girl bobbed a half curtsy at Karl. "He hoodwinked the moonwitch, promising to transform the princess into a monster. The witch paid him handsomely for that. But I was the one transformed." A large tear ran down her cheek. "Oh, it was too cruel."

"Too cruel, indeed," said Shale, as visions of the reward melted away, replaced by the far less pleasant prospect of continued penury. Well, perhaps the castle held something of promise. She turned and looked, but even as she did, the moon slid behind another cloud. Softly, like feathers floating to earth, the castle drifted apart, turning to dust.

"My parents will reward you well," Will said, his own eyes turning toward the ruined castle. "Or as well as they can," he amended. "You could probably have permanent jobs at the tavern if you wanted them."

"Thank you, no," said Shale, biting back a sarcastic reply. She was a swordmaster, not a brawler-for-hire, for all that she'd been forced to hire out that way of late. Karl said not a word; he only stared with darkly weary eyes first at Belinda and then at the fallen castle.

"I haven't thanked you yet," Belinda said. She took Shale's hand in hers, knelt, and kissed it. Then she looked at Karl, a shy smile on her lips. She stood on tiptoe and planted a firm kiss on his cheek, startling him out of his brooding silence.

"Well, that's something for my trouble," he said, winking at Shale. "I told you I had a way with the ladies."

"Good for you," said Shale, with far less enthusiasm than Karl appeared to feel. "Why don't you use your charm to advantage and find some local woman of means who needs a couple of guards? We got nothing from this adventure save some bites, scratches, and lost sleep."

"And my gratitude," Belinda said.

"And mine." Will sidled closer to Shale.

"I'm not carrying you off," she said to him in a low voice. "I have enough problems already."

"Now that my sister's returned, I find I'm not so eager to leave. And I can probably help you find some better work than patrolling taverns, such as that guard duty you mentioned. I have certain, um, contacts among the wealthier ladies of this town. Will that serve as a reward?"

Shale looked from the brother to the sister, who beamed at her with patent gratitude. She'd set out to rescue a princess, and had freed a tavern maid instead. But in Fram's reckoning, the tavern girl's life held as much value as any other. And what would she do with riches, anyway? Grow fat and soft and lose her skills? She felt the muscles in her sword arm twitch. A job as a guard would probably suit her better than a life of indolence. "That will serve nicely," she said. "We'd be glad of your help."

"And in the meantime," Karl said, "do you think your parents would give us proper beds to sleep in?"

Will nodded. "I'm sure they will. And some cash in the bargain."

Shale grinned, her spirits rising. "Come on, then." She grabbed Karl by the arm and set off down the hill. They'd done a good thing, freeing the tavern girl and destroying the moonwitch. And a reward was a reward, after all.

LIFESTONE
by Mary Catelli

Like a great many young writers, Mary Catelli is a computer programmer—today's version of the pick-up job which you can leave at a moment's notice; it's great to have a "career" job, but chances are they won't want you writing on the side. So what you want is a job where you can tell the boss at a moment's notice to "take this job and shove it" if you get a chance at writing your great novel. Mary Catelli also said that for lack of anything else to read she would read cereal boxes. That's fine, but the plots there are a little thin. You need to learn to keep paperbacks in your handbag and never go anywhere without one, properly folded to keep your place. Another tip: On trips, pack your reading material before your clothes. I still remember being stuck on a train with nothing to read except Ayn Rand's *Atlas Shrugged*, which is almost a fate worse than death. In hotels there is usually a Gideon Bible, and at least that's full of action and violence.

(Marion, "FOLDED"?! I'm shocked; since my childhood days as an earnest user of the Monterey Public Library (where I first checked out Dr. Dolittle books and heard the librarian read from Mr. Bass's Planetoid and The Borrowers), I always carry a bookmark, or improvise one.—reh).

Here is another tale of unmagical people hoping to vanquish someone with evil powers, and an attempt to rescue one of his victims by turning his own tools to good.

"The Scarlet Citadel, indeed," Richard said, looking up at the gray rocks looming overhead, stark against the brilliantly blue sky. "Wonder where they got that name."

Jonathan drew a deep breath, stepping up on the rocky shelf beside the other knight. "The Wizard of the Scarlet Citadel is certainly enough to drain life out of any place." He squared his shoulders and looked at the narrow crack they were heading up. The cliff face was as barren as a desert, without even a loose rock. "The wizard's got to be around here somewhere."

Richard glanced at him. "We are drawing near his stronghold. We should be more cautious; he will be strongest here." His voice slowed. "Perhaps we should even go back—tell the rest of the order that we caught him gathering forbidden herbs."

"We already wounded him," Jonathan pointed out and started up the track, "and consumed most of the spell-craft that he had prepared. Anyone who comes after will give him time to prepare again." His voice took up briskly. "Master Frederick would be ashamed of you; the first principle of fighting a wizard is to always remember that it takes him longer to strike a blow than it takes you."

Richard grimaced and followed him. "The chief point to remember in fighting a wizard is that you should fight to win, by whatever means will bring you victory. If we die, no one will know what the wizard was up to."

Jonathan started up the cliff; Richard sighed and came after. "You're going to get us both killed one of these days," he observed casually.

Silence fell as the young knights saved their breath for climbing. A sharp breeze blew up the mountain; Jonathan looked down, and grimaced at the thought of the height. He turned his attention ahead, reminding himself that there was no telling what the wizard of

the Scarlet Citadel was up to; he and Richard had
kept the wizard from getting the deathberry he was
after, but that could have been needed for one specific
spell.

He looked ahead. The citadel was not far ahead, and
it looked as if the cliff face turned into a brief flat area,
just before the walls. He tried to see if the wizard had
any surprises waiting for them there.

"You fools!" The wizard suddenly loomed out of
the rocks ahead of them, his white hair and beard wild,
his eyes fervid, his lips pulled back from his teeth.
Something dark and red glittered in his hand like a
sword.

Jonathan drew his sword and leaped to the attack.
The wizard's crimson robes still carried the stain of
blood, and the wizard himself moved stiffly. Jonathan's
sword swept up to parry the wizard's blow, and a bitter,
unearthly sound echoed. A glance showed Jonathan that
the sword was unharmed, but he resolved not to let that
enchantment touch his flesh.

Richard's sword flashed beside him, and Jonathan
jumped to one side, up to the plain. The wizard snarled
and fell back; his hands flashed, too quickly to be seen,
and something shimmered in the air before him. He put
out his free hand, and found it colliding with a slick
wall of glass.

The wizard laughed, his thin body shaking. "Come
and join me, you knights! Nothing but glass bars your
way!"

Jonathan took a step back; he looked about, but there
were no loose stones here either. Richard stood to
one side, his sword still in hand, but his expression
was resigned. "We've got to go back," he said, his
voice low.

Jonathan started to put up his sword. This would,
indeed, take more knights from their Order.

The wizard went on laughing. "You fools! You fools! To challenge the Wizard of the Scarlet Citadel!"

Something moved against the walls, behind the wizard. Jonathan frowned, realizing the movement was near a small door. The wizard noticed his attention and, breaking off his laughter, looked over his shoulder. A hideous smile broke on his face. Jonathan and Richard looked at each other, and back at the wizard, needing to know what he was up to.

A pale, thin woman cowered against the wall. The wizard's hand flashed out to fasten on her shoulder. "How convenient you are," he purred, and dragged her out into the open. Her brown eyes looked through the glass wall at the knights, but her face showed no further animation. The wizard pulled a sullen red stone out of his pocket and held it up; the gemstone glittered a little in the sunlight. "Watch what you have done, you fools, so proud of having harmed me!" He lowered the gem toward the woman. She shuddered, but did not try to pull away.

The gemstone touched her shoulder. His hand folded over it. "Watch what my Lifestone does for me, you fools!"

Red light began to pulse through his fingers, steady as a heartbeat. Jonathan took an involuntary step toward him. Blood seeped through the woman's thin dress. She shuddered, her eyes closing. The Lifestone continued to glow, and the blood drew back from the cloth, toward the stone.

The knights watched in horror. Richard moved closer to Jonathan and whispered, "We have to warn the Order, get someone up here who can deal with him."

Jonathan could not bring himself to move, or speak, or even look away. Minutes ticked by, and the wizard's robes no longer stuck to a wound; he did not withdraw his hand. His cheeks flushed with rosy color, and exhaustion flowed from his face. The woman started to slump, and the wizard did not hold her up, but he did not take his hand from her shoulder as she fell to her knees. Her eyes opened and looked blankly at the young men. Jonathan found that his breath was harsh and shallow.

He looked at the sunlight glinting off the wall, the only sign of its presence. He drew a deep breath, unable to remember more than one bit of lore: go straight through a broken window, without hesitation, and it would not cut. He backed up.

"What are you doing, Jonathan?" Richard whispered. He looked at the woman. "We've got to get out of here, to get help."

"Trust me," Jonathan said, through stiff lips. He drew a deep breath and broke into a run. A second before he collided with the wall, he shut his eyes.

The wall shattered, an enormous sound, all around him. Slivers cascaded over each other and chimed; they brushed against his face and clothing, but he felt no cuts as he fell forward. He opened his eyes and saw the scraps of glass surrounding him. He hurried to his feet, glad of the armor that would protect him from more than swords.

Richard shouted with glee and came running. The woman, pale as bone, did not even stir, and the wizard stared blankly. Jonathan went for his sword.

The wizard dropped the Lifestone and started gabbling. Jonathan and Richard reached him, their swords flying and cutting through the wizard's robes; blood spurted from his arms, but not before he pronounced the last word.

The door of the citadel creaked open, and an armored statue came out, every joint creaking as it approached them. Jonathan stopped by the woman, knowing Richard was right: they had no idea what wizard's preparations were within his own stronghold, and they did have to warn the rest of the Order. The wizard scrambled back, and Jonathan dived for the Lifestone. Whatever else happened, the wizard would not get that back. His arm went around the woman as he shoved the Lifestone in his pocket.

"Let's go, Richard," he said, glancing down the mountain. The statue took up position before the wizard, protectively, but came no closer.

Richard nodded, put up his sword, and said, "I'll carry her; you guard our backs."

The wizard limped inside the citadel. The woman did not seem even to notice as Richard hefted her to one shoulder and started down the trail. Jonathan shoved the Lifestone deep in his pocket, and followed after, keeping one wary eye on the trail.

Jonathan stood against the whitewashed wall in the infirmary, his eyes flitting nervously about the room; Richard stood next to him, as anxious. The cause of their anxiety, Selina, mistress of the Keep of the Gryphon, sat gravely beside the sickbed, her yellow-and-silver robes bearing the symbols of her rank. The doctor, Althea, ignored Selina and fussed over her lily-pale patient; Jonathan wondered how she managed it.

"You are the woman Pearl whom Richard and Jonathan here rescued from the wizard of the Scarlet Citadel?" Selina asked gravely.

Weakly, Pearl nodded.

Selina inclined her head. "This order is dedicated to the purpose of bringing justice to these lands. I wish you to tell us of the wizard, and what manner of man he is."

"He is very wicked." Pearl stopped. A minute later, she gathered her strength again. "He has a thing, a Lifestone." She gestured vaguely. "It drains life from one person to another; he drains the people of the citadel to death." Her eyes moved to Jonathan, to

Richard. "Even when he is not injured, he uses it, to keep his youth." She fell silent, not taking her eyes from the young man. "I saw you."

Jonathan shifted his weight uncomfortably. Pearl drew up her strength again. "I saw you and knew that someone had to know what he did. So I came out of the citadel. I knew he could not resist the temptation of health, so close to hand."

Jonathan looked at Richard; the other young knight looked as pale and shocked as he felt.

Even Selina looked a little paler. "I thank you," she said formally. "What you did shall not be in vain. We shall drive this evil from our land." She rose to her feet. "I pledge to you that the wizard of the Scarlet Citadel has claimed his last victim."

Pearl nodded. Her eyes closed. Selina glanced at the young men and started from the room; Richard and Jonathan followed.

Althea came as far as the door. "Ah, Mistress Selina?"

The other woman turned, tilting her head to one side.

Althea lowered her voice. "The wizard's last victim may be here. I do not think that Pearl will live."

Jonathan swayed, his hand going out to the wall for support. Selina looked sharply at him and Richard. "We are going to assail the Scarlet Citadel immediately, before you have time to rest. Therefore you will not be one of the force."

Jonathan bobbed his head obediently.

"Eat and rest, then." The woman turned and swept off briskly toward the armory.

Jonathan and Richard looked at each other. "The kitchens?" Jonathan proposed. Richard nodded, and the young knights started off.

Half a dozen knights were still sitting around the table, eating meals that duty had deferred. They nodded to the young men as Jonathan and Richard sat, murmuring something about their work; the rumors must be flying, Jonathan thought. He sliced off a piece of bread and spread butter on it.

A plump and scholarly knight came and sat by them. "I have heard of what you brought back from the Scarlet Citadel," Timothy began. He gestured. "The Lifestone?"

Jonathan thought of Pearl, lying in the infirmary. "Deathstone would be a better name for it," he said. "A piece of diabolerie!"

Timothy looked shocked at this error in his field of knowledge. "It is not diabolerie; it involved no demonic work. Nor it is specifically evil."

Jonathan slammed down the bread on the table. "That's impossible!" he protested. "To what good uses could it be put?"

Timothy looked abashed. "I do not know," he said, carefully, putting the tips of his fingers together. "Yet when I tested it, it did not register as black magic."

"Easy, Jonathan," Richard urged. Jonathan's shoulders slumped, and he nodded. Richard turned to Timothy. "The wizard got the better of us." His mouth twisted. "Mistress Selina may defeat him, but he defeated us. The woman we tried to rescue is dying. The Lifestone killed her."

Timothy nodded, murmuring about what a tragedy such a death was, and how distressing a good knight found his first failure. Jonathan dished himself up some soup and stared moodily into it. Pearl was dying, in spite of everything.

He thought about the Lifestone again. A gemstone that drained life from someone, and gave it to someone else. . . . He turned abruptly to Timothy. "Have you found out much else about the Lifestone?" The other knight looked up from his soup. "Need the stone kill its victim?"

Timothy shook his head. "No, it takes minutes for the gem to do that. It must drain much life to kill."

Jonathan nodded. A minute later, he excused himself and hurried off into the keep. Richard looked curiously after him, but Jonathan did not dare stop for his friend as he hunted in the storeroom where all magical things were kept for the Lifestone.

It shone a sullen crimson again in the torchlight. Jonathan drew a deep breath, picked it up, and hurried out of the room, toward the infirmary. A stone to give life to another—a Lifestone, indeed.

Althea was gone from the room; Pearl slept on, her face still and pale as a lily. Jonathan sat on the bed, and she stirred a little, but did not wake. Jonathan took one of her hands in his, pulled out the Lifestone, and laid it between her hand and his shoulder. It began to glow.

Pain knifed into his shoulder. Jonathan's teeth sank into his lip as he fought against crying out. His free hand reached out to take her other hand. "Even braver than I realized, to endure this." Pearl murmured a little, and he said, soothingly, "It's all right, you're getting better."

The Lifestone pulsed like a heartbeat. The agony spread, dragging itself from every limb. Color began to flush Pearl's cheeks, and she stirred. "What?" she said, bewildered.

"It's all right," Jonathan assured her, though he was beginning to feel faint. Her eyes fluttered open and looked at the scene before her. Comprehension flooded them. With a violent cry, she jerked her hand away from his shoulder, sending the Lifestone flying. "What . . . what did you think you were doing?" she demanded.

Jonathan dropped his free hand to the bed, to hold himself up, but did not release her hand. With the pain gone, the drain did not seem so great, but Pearl's cheeks were still rosy. "I counted on your taking only as much as you needed, refusing to take my life." He smiled. "There was enough for both of us." He yawned, leaned forward, and slid into sleep on the bed beside her.

Pearl looked at him for a long minute, but his color was good, his breathing deep and regular. She yawned herself and fell asleep, her hand still linked with his.

WHITE ELEPHANTS
by Christopher Kempke

Christopher Kempke says of himself, "I am male, 28 years old. I was born in Cleveland, Ohio, raised in Minnesota, and did graduate computer work in Oregon." I suspect computer work has become popular among young writers, because computers seem almost fantastic to those of us who grew up tied down to typewriters and carbon paper. As soon as typewriters reached the point where they were really easy to use, and carbon paper outgrew the smudgy stage, along came the computer and both were obsolete. A few writers make a point of clinging to their old typewriters, proving that the only real word processor is the brain, and everything else, from a number two pencil to a number two thousand computer, is only the tools. About the morality of instant obsolescence, that's something about which (at least for the moment) I'll withhold comment.

Christopher Kempke says he has been reading *Sword and Sorceress* since he found the first volume during high school. Some of his stories have appeared in *Quanta,* an electronic science fiction or fantasy "e-zine"—but this is his first professional sale. He says he has a laptop full of "novel fragments" but prefers writing short stories. He calls himself an avid reader of everything but is especially fond of science fiction and fantasy. So was I, but when I was in high school they used to take magazines (not to mention comic books) away from us and burn them in the furnace. Aren't you

glad you didn't go to school in those days? I suspect
they've grown more tolerant because kids will actually
read science fiction when they can't be coaxed to read
anything else.

The last three miles to the Warlord's fortress were the
hardest of the journey. Every hundred yards a body
was propped up against a tree or nailed to a post. Lia
recognized many of the bodies: friends and allies who
had attempted to break the Warlord's power by stealth,
assault, or incantation. These attempts were largely acts
of desperation; the Warlord's uncountable minions had
conquered all but a few pockets of humanity.

Approaching the fortress itself, Lia's hand itched as
she suppressed an urge to cast defensive magic. She
had spent several hours the night before removing
residual protection spells, some of those spells several
years old. She must not, under any circumstances,
seem a threat to the Warlord's safety.

Two guards waited outside the castle. Between them
stood the fortress' only entrance. The massive stone
arch contained a powerful artifact. Raw power crackled
between the ancient stones, forming an opaque barrier
of swirling magic. Beyond it, no new spells could be
created; beneath it, no lies told. None could pass
through, except at the Warlord's word. This triple de-
fense had proven fatal to Lia's predecessors; she stood
before it now with an uncertainty she dared not show.

One of the guards nodded toward the gate. Lia drew
a spell-bottle from her robes, showed it to the guard,
and stepped into the maelstrom.

Immediately, she felt mired, immobilized as though
trapped in glass. There was no backing out now, and no
going forward unless the Warlord allowed it.

"What is in the bottle?" asked the guard.

"This bottle holds a spell the Warlord greatly
desires. I will freely give it to him."

"You have no other spells or weapons on your person?"

"I do not."

"Will you do the Warlord harm?"

"No." Lia all but held her breath. This was the moment of truth, the closest she had come to a lie. The questions asked at the gate were well known; this one was slightly ambiguous. All her hopes rested on the gate being unable to unravel this slight bending of the truth.

Seconds passed, and suddenly Lia could move her arm and hands, though her feet remained still. The curtain of power faded somewhat, and she found herself looking into a great hall. Ornate designs on the walls and floors drew the eye to the center of the room. There, seated in a throne of simple design, sat the man who had brought a world from decades of peace to slavery and war.

"You bear the ultimate magic?" The Warlord spoke softly, but his voice was greedy.

Lia lifted the bottle. "It is here. Open the bottle, and all your wishes shall be fulfilled, the instant you think of them. Merely imagine something, and it shall become reality. It took me a year to craft this spell, studying ancient manuscripts. It has not been cast in centuries."

The Warlord laughed. "Others of your profession have died rather than make this spell for me. Why do you bring it of your own will?"

Lia spread her hands. "I wish to prevent the further annihilation of my friends and allies. The reluctance of my predecessors has not saved them, or this world, any suffering." Another half-truth, but she was confident now.

This time the Warlord's laugh was deeper. "I presume, then, that I cannot use this spell to finish their destruction?"

Lia shook her head. "The spell will not affect me, nor will it have effects outside this fortress. The magic will last for exactly one day, no less, and no more. At the end of that time, your wishes will stop being fulfilled, and neither this spell nor any other like it will ever have an effect on you again. Other than that, the spell is unrestricted. As fast as you can form your thoughts, they will become reality."

"Enough," the Warlord said. "The gate is quiet. Give the spell to me."

Abruptly, the paralysis ended. Lia covered the several yards between them, and placed the spell bottle in the Warlord's hands. He opened it without hesitation. There was no visible effect, and for a moment the Warlord's eyes narrowed.

Suddenly, a pile of gold appeared in the hall. The Warlord looked at Lia and laughed. He held out his hand; a ruby appeared in it, then grew to several times its original size. A fountain running with wine appeared, then vanished as the Warlord's whim changed. His eyes widened.

"It seems your magic is sound. Though I am still surprised you would grant me such a gift."

"White elephants," Lia said. Instantly, two of the great beasts appeared. There was a trumpeting roar, then the elephants vanished at a scowl from the Warlord.

"I don't understand," the Warlord said simply.

Lia smiled without warmth. "The spell does exactly what I said it does. It grants your every thought, immediately. I mentioned elephants, your mind made them real."

She paused, to let her words sink in. "I told you this spell had not been cast in centuries. That's simply because it's far too dangerous. No one can completely control their own thoughts, mighty Warlord, and the spell lasts for an entire day. A long time to avoid imagining, even for the smallest moment, your own death."

Lia turned away. "Perhaps you're even thinking about it now."

TRAVELER'S AIDE

by Kathi Thompson

Kathi Thompson says she makes her living as the controller for a design firm, "which requires more creativity then most people realize"—probably more than most of them possess, I suspect. She is one of those rare native Californians and has lived in the Los Angeles area most of her life. (It's true that most Californians come here trying to escape the snow and ice—but everybody has to be born somewhere.) She says she spent a few years in Oregon after college.

She says, "I play the guitar (usually a twelve-string), a variety of wind instruments, and like to rewrite song lyrics to amuse my friends (I feel that is a temptation which should be resisted with all your strength, Kathi). I never met a craft I didn't like and have a few rubber stamps . . . more than 1200." Maybe this is why so many young writers disappear after one sale; having found out they can sell, they go back to other crafts; writing demands a single-minded devotion. She submitted this story after being inspired by my introduction to *S&S* XII. She loves to go camping and hiking, has an ever-increasing collection of bunnies in all shapes and sizes. Now that she has a computer, she has discovered the Internet. "But," she concludes, "my favorite place is the one that appears when my four-year-old nephew says 'Let's Pretend.' "

It looks as if there's still hope for you, then.

It was not the thunder echoing wildly through the surrounding hills nor the howling wind whipping the

rain against the stone walls of the keep that roused her.
It was the steady and insistent pounding at the heavy
wooden door of the hall that invaded her dreaming and
finally snapped the thread.

"Bright Lady, why do they always come in the
middle of the night?" she muttered, trying to recall
the vision, but it was no use. She was left with only the
vague idea that it had been promising and the regret
that she could not use it for her art. Ah, well, perhaps
tomorrow night would be fruitful. As she fumbled at
the bedside to light the lamp, the pounding continued.
Rising, she grabbed her robe from the chair, pulling it
on as she crossed the chamber. At the door she stopped
and turned back toward the bed.

"Coming?" she inquired of the gray lump curled
motionless at the foot of the bed. The only movement
was the opening of one large golden eye. The cat
regarded her solemnly for a moment and the eye closed
again.

"Well, have it your way. You usually do," she said,
but she smiled as she opened the door and hurried
down the hallway.

She held no fear of whoever stood outside her door
this night, knowing that the keep could only be found
by those with clear intent on Traveling. Anyone with
other thoughts would merely wander in the hills until
their resolve weakened or the hills claimed them. The
keep door was heavy and always stubborn in damp
weather. When it finally yielded to her efforts, she
stood facing a large bearded man.

She spoke no greeting, but simply regarded him,
waiting. For all his impatient pounding on her door, he
suddenly seemed unsure.

"Is this the Keep of the Traveler's Aide?" he inquired cautiously.

"So it is," she replied as she had countless times
before. "Enter and be welcome." She stepped back and
narrowly missed being drenched as he strode past her

and swept off his sodden cloak before she could even shut the door. She shook her head; they were always in such a hurry.

"Leave your pack by the door and hang your cloak by the fireplace. I keep no servants," she told him, "So if you would be good enough to tend the fire, we will both be more comfortable. I will see to some refreshment."

He nodded, hung up his cloak, and set to work as she left the room. When she returned with her tray a few minutes later, a cheery blaze brightened the hall and he made himself comfortable in one of the carved chairs beside it. She offered him spiced wine, bread, and cheese and then settled herself into the other chair.

Finally, she broke the awkward silence by saying, "Tell me why you wish to Travel." She didn't really need to know, but the years had shown her that the Travelers needed to tell. She nodded occasionally, only half listening as he told a familiar tale about injustice and treachery and the need to regain what was right-fully his. Then she realized that he had fallen silent. The time had come.

"You have the Price?" she asked softly. He nodded, crossed the room to his pack, and returned to place a parcel in her hands. Carefully, she unwrapped the four layers of oiled skins that protected the precious contents. She smiled for the first time as the last layer came away and revealed a sheaf of paper, white and pure as newly fallen snow. She touched the top sheet thoughtfully, reaching into it with her senses. Good quality, few impurities, no magic residue. It would suit her purposes well. Inks were easy for her to make with the bounty of the surrounding forest, but paper was beyond her skill and hard to come by, so the Travelers filled her need.

"Accepted," she said, and rose from her place by the fire to go to a small wooden cupboard on the other side of the room. She opened it and gently placed the paper on a shelf. On the shelf below were a thick book and an hourglass.

The book was covered in dark blue leather, worn in places from the touch of many hands. Some of the pages were yellowed with age, while others were the color of ivory, still others white and pale. They bore no words, but on each was an illustration, executed with great care for detail and clarity. On the cover in an ornate gilt script were the words "A Traveler's Guide to Other Worlds."

Carefully she picked up the book and the glass and carried them to a table, motioning him to join her and sit. She placed the book in front of him and moved to the other side, to sit facing him with the hourglass at her left hand. He reached to open the book, but she caught his arm.

"Not yet. There are certain things that must be dealt with first, according to custom. What do you know of the book?" she asked.

"That the pages are gates to other worlds where Travelers may go to find what they seek."

"So they are, but there conditions to be met. Once the book has been opened, I shall turn the hourglass and you may examine the contents for no longer than it takes the sands to run their course. At any page, you may ask two and only two questions of me, that I may only answer yes or no, but which, as Traveler's Aide, I am bound to answer truthfully. When you make your final choice, you may ask one additional question before using the gate. But you must ask your question and be through the gate before the last grain of sand falls, or the price is forfeit and you must depart as you came. Agreed?"

He hesitated for a split second, but firmly answered, "I agree."

"Then by my will, you may begin," and with that she turned the hourglass and the sands began to run.

He quickly opened the book in the middle and turned

several pages, passing pictures of seemingly barren wastes and heavy seas. He stopped at one of purple moors and asked, "Can I hire mercenaries here?" "Yes," she replied. He glanced up at her briefly, but her face gave away nothing. "Will they remain loyal in our world?"

"No."

He moved on and at a page showing a clear mountain stream, started to speak again, then hesitated. He smiled thoughtfully and asked "Can I hire mercenaries here that will remain loyal to me in our world?"

"Yes," she replied, and though her face gave away nothing, inside she laughed. Ah, he caught on quickly! Perhaps this time. . . .

The minutes passed quickly as the pages turned and the questions became more detailed and concise. She glanced at the hourglass and as she opened her mouth to warn him that his time was nearly gone, he spoke.

"I have chosen," he said finally, turning to a page he had questioned her about only minutes earlier.

"Good. Do you have a final question for me?"

He looked up, meeting her eyes for a long moment. "Will I succeed?"

She laughed softly. How often she had heard this question. "I am not a seer to predict the future, I can only give information to aid the Traveler on his way. Since I can give you no true answer, you may ask another. But quickly, the sand is almost gone."

He thought for a moment, the shook his head and said, "No, I am ready."

"As you wish." She rose to gather his things and after giving them to him stood just behind him. "Look carefully at the picture and then close your eyes. Recreate it in your mind, then place your hand on the picture and imagine yourself there." As the last words left her lips, he vanished, along with the page.

She stood motionless for a moment, then slowly reached down and closed the book. She'd had such hopes. Wearily, she picked up the book and the hour-glass and returned them to the cupboard. Then she crossed to the fire, banked the embers and slowly climbed the stairs to her chamber.

"Well, Cat," she said, settling gratefully into bed. "Another one sent on his way." The cat opened one golden eye again, and gave a small inquiring meow.

"No," she sighed softly, as she extinguished the lamp. "But maybe the next one will be wise enough to ask the final question."

"How do I get back?"

THE LAST WORD

by Rachel E. Holmen

I'm excited to be working with Marion Zimmer Bradley on this prestigious anthology series, seeing stories from old friends such as Diana Paxson and Adrienne Martine-Barnes, and discovering writers new to me: Lee Martindale, Mary Soon Lee, Kathi Thompson, and others. Marion had all the stories chosen before we realized that my help on this project would be useful; next year I'll start at the beginning, reading all the submissions as soon as she has finished with them.

Did you notice that we managed to uphold several established fantasy traditions? We had at least one vampire story and one werewolf story—but I doubt you spotted either one early in their respective tales, so we have avoided cliché.

The themes of these stories are varied: what it means to be a mother, daughter, sister, friend; the importance of self-respect; the meaning of power; the depth of love between a father and his child (perhaps surprising in stories written by women); issues of aging, jealousy, betrayal, loyalty, responsibility, redemption. Several express powerful anti-war sentiments. A whole subgroup is about nurturing the next generation, or those younger than ourselves. Many of the stories are about winning competitions and passing tests, daring to be ambitious. I don't think there's a single conventional love story in the lot. Fantasy has a reputation as the inconsequential literature of elves—but I hope you found these stories anything *but* trivial. Still, a fantasy anthology is supposed to be escape literature, and you didn't pick this up intending to read A Serious Book. So I hope we entertained you as well, and that this was one of those books that you read on the bus, read during lunch, read at the laundromat, and plan to lend to a friend as soon as you've reread each story at least once.

While I've been working to finish this anthology and deliver it to DAW for publication, several people have asked if we planned to compare *S&S* to the new *Xena: Warrior Princess* series on television. I had never even watched the show—but now I'm hooked! Marion thinks the show's concept is a bit on the flippant side, but I think it's delightful, and it probably fulfills the same need among TV viewers that led Marion to begin this anthology series: so the heroines can have adventures and starring roles. I love Xena's delighted grin when she turns to an adversary, ready to hack anyone to bits who dares to threaten the defenseless, her cry of Ai-ai-ai-AI!!! as she goes into battle. (But I wasn't surprised when the actress who plays the part complained in a magazine interview that the costume was *cold* when she had to ride horseback in the wind. Well, at least her leather tunic's not white.)

So who am I, anyway? Why do *I* get to work with Marion on this terrific project? Well, first, I'm over fifty and I've been reading fantasy since childhood and science fiction since the golden age of eleven (or was I nine when I checked out *Between Planets* and those Lucky Starr books?). And in my real life, I've had my share of joy, grief, and adventures—for instance, last year I took some lessons on the high trapeze, and learned what the world looks like when they push you off a plank sixty feet in the air! My B.A. is in psychology, and never in my life did I expect to work as a professional editor or art director in science fiction— but when I grew tired of a lengthy commute, a friend told me about an opening at *Locus*, the science fiction newsletter, and I worked there for five years. Since then, I read slush for a time under the late Terry Carr ("Conan the Grammarian") and worked for another five years as publisher for *Marion Zimmer Bradley's FANTASY Magazine*. The last three years, I've also been training as an acquisitions editor ("person who buys stories") under her supervision. I enjoy working with authors to improve their stories—perhaps it's no accident that one of my other skills is pruning rose-bushes. And if I have any spare time, I play backup viola, work in my garden, and sew quilts.

When I became publisher for *Marion Zimmer Bradley's Fantasy Magazine,* Elsie Wollheim of DAW Books, who had known me since my *Locus* days, paid me a high compliment: "When I heard you had taken over the magazine, I knew it was in good hands," she said.

As other writers have been dedicating their stories to friends and supporters, I'd like to dedicate my contribution to the memory of Elsie Wollheim, who died in the spring of 1996.

Thanks for reading these stories. Marion and I both hope you have enjoyed them. If you have comments, or want subscription information for *Marion Zimmer Bradley's FANTASY Magazine,* please write to us at PO Box 249, Berkeley CA 94701-0249, or check our Web page: http://www.well.com/user/mzbfm. (Marion is NOT online, however. Write to her the old-fashioned way, with paper and an envelope.)

MARION ZIMMER BRADLEY

THE DARKOVER NOVELS

Mercedes Lackey

The Novels of Valdemar

Jennifer Roberson

THE NOVELS OF TIGER AND DEL

CHRONICLES OF THE CHEYSULI

OTHER

Edited by Jennifer Roberson.
A tribute anthology to author Marion Zimmer Bradley, with contributions by Jennifer Roberson, Melanie Rawn, Charles De-Lint, Andre Norton, C.J. Cherryh, and others.

Melanie Rawn

EXILES

- ☐ **THE RUINS OF AMBRAI: Book 1**   UE2668—$5.99
- ☐ **THE RUINS OF AMBRAI: Book 1** (hardcover)   UE2619—$20.95
- ☐ **THE MAGEBORN TRAITOR: Book 2** (hardcover)   UE2730—$23.95

Three Mageborn sisters bound together by ties of their ancient Blood Line are forced to take their stands on opposing sides of a conflict between two powerful schools of magic. Together, the sisters will fight their own private war, and the victors will determine whether or not the Wild Magic and the Wraithen-beasts are once again loosed to wreak havoc upon their world.

THE DRAGON PRINCE NOVELS

- ☐ **DRAGON PRINCE : Book 1**   UE2450—$5.99
- ☐ **THE STAR SCROLL: Book 2**   UE2349—$5.99
- ☐ **SUNRUNNER'S FIRE: Book 3**   UE2403—$5.99

THE DRAGON STAR NOVELS

- ☐ **STRONGHOLD: Book 1**   UE2482—$5.99
- ☐ **STRONGHOLD: Book 1** (hardcover)   UE2440—$21.95
- ☐ **THE DRAGON TOKEN: Book 2**   UE2542—$5.99
- ☐ **SKYBOWL: Book 3**   UE2595—$5.99
- ☐ **SKYBOWL: Book 3** (hardcover)   UE2541—$22.00
